# REVOLUTION AND RELIGION IN
# THE MUSIC OF LISZT

Plate 1. Liszt in 1883 (photograph by Nadar)

# REVOLUTION AND RELIGION
## IN THE
# MUSIC OF LISZT

### PAUL MERRICK

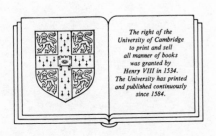

The right of the
University of Cambridge
to print and sell
all manner of books
was granted by
Henry VIII in 1534.
The University has printed
and published continuously
since 1584.

## CAMBRIDGE UNIVERSITY PRESS

*Cambridge*
*London   New York   New Rochelle*
*Melbourne   Sydney*

Published by the Press Syndicate of the University of Cambridge
The Pitt Building, Trumpington Street, Cambridge CB2 1RP
32 East 57th Street, New York, NY 10022, USA
10 Stamford Road, Oakleigh, Melbourne 3166, Australia

First published 1987

Printed in Great Britain at
the University Press, Cambridge

*British Library cataloguing in publication data*
Merrick, Paul
Revolution and religion in the music of Liszt.
1. Liszt, Franz – Criticism, interpretation etc.
I. Title
780'.92'4   ML410.L7

*Library of Congress cataloguing in publication data*
Merrick, Paul.
Revolution and religion in the music of Liszt.
Originally presented as the author's thesis
(doctoral – Sheffield University).
Bibliography.
Includes index.
1. Liszt, Franz, 1811–1886 – Criticism and
interpretation. 2. Liszt, Franz, 1811–1886 – Religion.
3. Liszt, Franz, 1811–1886 – Views on revolutions.
4. Revolutions – Europe. I. Title.
ML410.L7M4   1987   780'.92'4   86–17551

ISBN 0 521 32627 3

*For Marion*

Proudhon's pamphlet *The Philosophy of Progress* . . . has given me such a strong impression of the truth of my belief 'L'Homme–Dieu'. Liszt in 1855

I stopped with him for nearly two hours and never enjoyed myself more. We talked of all kinds of things, music, religion, Germany, England, the people we mutually knew, etc., and it pleased me, as you will understand, to find him quite simple and good-hearted, a thorough accomplished man of the world, without spite or conceit, no forcing forward of his own music, or abuse of other musicians, etc.

He was not tall, but in that limited space was concentrated the pluck of thirty battalions. He was in an Abbé's dress, long black coat and knee breeches, with buckles in his shoes; which became him well. His hair is grey, his face very refined and *luminous*, and his hands the perfection of delicacy.

Sir George Grove, writing from Rome in 1868

# CONTENTS

ix

# ILLUSTRATIONS

# PREFACE

Of the many misconceptions surrounding Liszt, the greatest is the belief that his Masses, oratorios and church works do not form an integral part of his output, and that their music is weak, yet to hear *Christus* or the *Gran Mass* is to recognize instantly the composer of the Piano Sonata or the *Faust Symphony*. The neglect of this side of Liszt's output calls for explanation in the hope that this may lead to reparation.

The outline of Liszt's career is familiar, and is generally agreed to move in a straight line – until Rome. The move from Weimar to Rome has been seen to follow a hiatus, and has been explained variously as the unfortunate result of a cancelled wedding or of Liszt's failure to realize his ambitions at Weimar, or as a relapse into religion as consolation for years of weary endeavour. Biographers treat his entry into the Church much as novelists used to treat the tragic heroine's entering a nunnery. It is seen as a farewell, a renunciation of the past, an escape from the world, a sad ending. But Liszt was a composer, and if his actions have any deeper meaning, then this must be sought in his music. There we are presented with a quite different picture; the path to *Christus* starts with Liszt's youth in Paris, his friendship with the Abbé Lamennais, and his enthusiasm for movements of social reform. This path begins, both biographically and musically, with the 1830 revolution and Liszt's sketched *Revolutionary Symphony*.

The first part of this book traces Liszt's relationships and his attitudes to the twin themes of revolution and religion. His ideas about the reform of church music, the influence of Lamennais and Liszt's standpoint regarding the Church before 1848, his reactions to the revolutions of that year as they are reflected in his music, his religious views and those of Wagner as expressed in their correspondence during the Weimar period, and the long process of the divorce of Princess Wittgenstein, her attempts to marry Liszt, and his eventual transfer to Rome, are presented in detail. The second part covers Liszt's plans to reform church music and some of his works composed for the Church, as well as giving an account of the Masses, psalms and oratorios. The third part investigates Liszt's programmatic use of fugue and the implications of

# Preface

this in the light of the composer's widespread use of a Cross motif, for a programmatic interpretation of the B minor Piano Sonata. It ends with a summary of Liszt's development as a serious composer, showing that, with its emphasis on a particular approach to programme music, this process was not confined to one type of music, but applies to both sacred and secular works, the overlap resulting from the transference of common ideas, in particular the theme of redemption. The chronological table of Liszt's years at Weimar in the Appendix shows how the composer's transfer to Rome, though not on the surface an obvious step, can be seen to be the consequence of a mental and spiritual development taking place behind the scenes and in his compositions.

Of the many people to whom I am indebted, first mention must be made of Miklós Forrai, whose recording of *Christus* formed the spur to my endeavours. A grant from the Leverhulme Trust enabled me to engage in full-time research for two years. The late Humphrey Searle recommended Hungary as the place for this, and it is to Hungary and Hungarian musicologists that all acknowledgement must go: to Imre Sulyok for information on the *Chorales*; to Dr János Kárpáti, librarian of the Liszt Academy, for allowing me to study Liszt's books then under process of being catalogued, among which are volumes containing plainchant and a biography of Palestrina with Liszt's markings; to Dr Dezsö Legány, whose work as a historian of Liszt's activities in Hungary must be the model and inspiration for all Liszt scholars; and to Professor József Ujfalussy, who published much of chapter 5 in *Studia musicologica academiae scientiarum Hungaricae* 21 (1979) under the title 'Liszt's Transfer from Weimar to Rome: a Thwarted Marriage'.

Acknowledgements are due to Dr Vernon Harrison, Chairman of the British Liszt Society, for permission to reproduce part of a letter containing information given to him by Mme Blandine Ollivier de Prévaux, Liszt's great-great-granddaughter; to Eunice Mistarz, Secretary of the Society, for obtaining copies of scores of Liszt's choral works; to Erika Smith for translations from German; to Eva Salam for tracing the Stargardt Catalogue in Wolfenbüttel Library; to Penny Souster and Ian Rumbold at Cambridge University Press for knocking the whole book into shape; and to Professor Edward Garden at Sheffield University under whose guidance the material was originally presented as a doctoral thesis.

*Budapest 1986*

# ABBREVIATIONS

| | |
|---|---|
| *Br.* | *Franz Liszt's Briefe*, ed. La Mara [M. Lipsius], 8 vols. (Leipzig, 1893–1902) |
| *BruS* | *Franz Liszt: Briefe aus ungarischen Sammlungen 1835–1886*, ed. M. Prahács (Kassel, 1969) |
| *BrZ* | *Briefe hervorragender Zeitgenossen an Franz Liszt*, ed. La Mara (Leipzig, 1895–1904) |
| *Cpr* | *Franz Liszt, pages romantiques*, with an Introduction and Notes by Jean Chantavoine (Paris and Leipzig, 1912) |
| *CWD* | *Cosima Wagner's Diaries*, ed. Martin Gregor-Dellin and Dietrich Mack, trans. Geoffrey Skelton (London, 1978) |
| *GRJ* | *The Roman Journals of Ferdinand Gregorovius 1852–1874*, trans. from the second German edition by Mrs Gustavus W. Hamilton (London, 1907) |
| *HFL* | Emile Haraszti: *Franz Liszt* (Paris, 1967) |
| *Hsd* | Marcel Herwegh: *Au soir des dieux* (Paris, 1933) |
| *L* | *Letters of Franz Liszt*, trans. Constance Bache, 2 vols. (London, 1894) |
| *LAA* | *Liszt Ferenc levelei báró Augusz Antalhoz* [Liszt's letters to the Baron Augusz], ed. V. Csapó (Budapest, 1911) |
| *Lacg* | *Lamennais: correspondance générale* (Paris, 1977) |
| *LCA* | *Briefwechsel zwischen Franz Liszt und Carl Alexander, Grossherzog von Sachsen*, ed. La Mara (Leipzig, 1909) |
| *LMA* | *Correspondance de Liszt et de la Comtesse d'Agoult*, ed. D. Ollivier (Paris, 1933–4) |
| *LMW* | *The Letters of Franz Liszt to Marie zu Sayn-Wittgenstein*, trans. Howard E. Hugo (Harvard, 1953) |
| *LOM* | *The Letters of Franz Liszt to Olga von Meyendorff 1871–1886*, trans. William R. Tyler (Harvard, 1979) |
| *LZB* | F. Lewald: *Zwölf Bildern nach dem Leben* (Berlin, 1888) |
| *PL* | Eleanor Perényi: *Liszt* (London, 1974) |
| *RAM* | Lina Ramann, trans. E. Cowdery: *Franz Liszt, Artist and Man, 1811–1840* (London, 1882) |

# Abbreviations

*RLL/RLS*  Peter Raabe: *Liszts Leben* and *Liszts Schaffen* (Stuttgart, 1931: reissued with additions by Felix Raabe, Tutzing, 1968)

*SFL*  Adelheid von Schorn: *Franz Liszt et la P'cesse de Sayn Wittgenstein* (Paris, 1905)

*SML*  Humphrey Searle: *The Music of Liszt* (New York, 1966)

*WL*  *Briefwechsel zwischen Wagner und Liszt*, ed. F. Hueffer (Leipzig, 1887; Eng. trans., 1888)

*WRC*  Janka Wohl: *Francois* [*sic*] *Liszt. Recollections of a Compatriot*, trans. from the French by B. Peyton Ward (London, 1887)


## Note

Numbers in brackets after musical titles, e.g. *Inno a Maria Vergine* (S39), refer to the catalogue of Liszt's works by Humphrey Searle in *The New Grove Dictionary of Music and Musicians*, ed. S. Sadie (London, 1980), XI, pp. 51–71.

# PART I

Music must recognize God and the people as its living source . . . the creation of a new music is indispensable . . . the Marseillaise and the beautiful songs of liberty are the fruitful and splendid forerunners of this music.

Liszt's article 'On Future Church Music', 1834

# 1

# 1830: A REVOLUTIONARY SYMPHONY

Already in 1830, M. de Lamennais had taken as his motto for *L'Avenir*: 'God and Liberty'. I immediately adopted this motto very seriously myself . . . for God is love, and liberty lies in work.
                                                                    Liszt in 1848

The Paris revolution of 1830 inspired the 18-year-old Liszt to compose a *Revolutionary Symphony* (S690), of which only a sketched fragment survives (see *RLL*, Appendix). The importance of this fragment is considerable, however, for what it tells us about Liszt's attitude to revolution at the time. The sketch is headed 'Symphonie' and is dated '27, 28, 29 Juillet – Paris'. At the side of the music, in which the *Marseillaise* is clearly identifiable, Liszt sketched a 'programme': 'indignation, vengeance, terreur, liberté! désordre, cris confus (vague, bizarrerie), fureur . . . refus, marche de la garde royale, doute, incertitude, parties croisantes . . . 8 parties différentes, attaque, bataille . . . marche de la garde nationale, enthousiasme, enthousiasme, enthousiasme! . . . fragment de Vive Henri IV dispersé. Combiner "Allons enfants de la patrie".' It is clear from this that Liszt sympathized with the revolutionaries. As for the musical content of the work, differing accounts exist of Liszt's plan. Ramann (*RAM*, 230) says Liszt 'founded his symphony on three melodies' which she identifies as a Hussite song of the fifteenth century (later arranged for the piano (S234) in 1840), *Ein' feste Burg ist unser Gott* and the *Marseillaise*. However, in his sketched programme Liszt mentions *Vive Henri IV* (also later arranged for the piano (S239), *c.* 1870–80), which makes a fourth tune to Ramann's three. Searle repeats Ramann's information, suggesting that 'this choice of revolutionary songs from the Slavonic, Teutonic, and Latin worlds no doubt symbolized the universal brotherhood of revolution against oppression' (*SML*, 6). This is surely not the correct interpretation of Liszt's mind on the matter. At the age of 18 Liszt's view of revolution was exclusively centred on 1789, and was more French than European. Furthermore two of the melodies intended for the work have a religious character. The Hussites were an early movement of religious reform in Bohemia, while *Ein' feste Burg* was the Lutheran battle-song of the Reformation; Meyerbeer, for example, used the theme to represent the religious revolutionaries in *Les Huguenots* in 1836. If Liszt intended to use these tunes, it was surely not for their nationality. Throughout his life, where revolution was concerned, he referred musically to the *Marseillaise* or the Hungarian *Rákóczy March*.

In the context of Liszt's sketched programme, the significance of his choice of melodies is probably thus: *Vive Henry IV* represents the Royalists, the *Marseillaise* the people, *Ein' feste Burg* and the Hussite song, God. The Royalists are scattered, and he sets out to depict this with a 'fragment de Vive Henri IV dispersé'. The people triumph, and their tune is, of course, the *Marseillaise*. But Liszt says 'Combiner "Allons enfants de la patrie".' What did he have in mind as a melody to 'combine' with the *Marseillaise*? The answer must be one of the remaining tunes, both of which are religious. In other words, Liszt wanted his symphony to celebrate the triumph of liberty in the name of God and the people. Here we have the clue as to why the work remained unfinished; for, as it was sketched 'on the spot', while the actual fighting was going on, it represents what the 18-year-old Liszt hoped would be the outcome. When the real outcome was different, he regarded the revolution as a failure, and definitely not something to write a symphony about. Liszt referred in later life to 'mon scepticisme de 1830'.

Another important feature of the work is the character of the programme. Six months before Liszt met Berlioz (which he did in December 1830) and heard the *Fantastique*, he had planned the work, and the programme, far from being pure fancy, was a serious matter, involving Liszt's beliefs and involvement with the real world. This was to remain a characteristic feature of Liszt's approach to programme music. From the start Liszt's programmatic composition, of which this is the first manifestation, had a religious ingredient. Between it and the next work of a similar seriousness, composed in 1833, Liszt turned his attention to the movements of religious and social reform alive in Paris in the 1830s. The *Revolutionary Symphony* lay dormant until 1848, when the revolutions of that year made him take it up again, but in a revised form.

The Paris revolution of 1830 brought to an end the reign of Charles X and the Restoration. Another Bourbon, the Duc d'Orléans, took the throne of France, calling himself King of the French rather than of France. Taking the name Louis Philippe, he represented bourgeois values, courted popularity, and was known as the Citizen King. On 14 August he accepted the Constitutional Charter, which allowed for the initiation of legislation to end Catholicism as the state religion of France. He also dissolved the royal corps of musicians, thereby curtailing the music for Catholic worship. That the religious element figured strongly in Liszt's disappointment is clear from what he wrote in the *Gazette Musicale* in 1835:

# 1830: a revolutionary symphony

The temporal power, always more or less in a state of open hostility towards the Church, broke definitively with it in July 1830 . . . The law being atheist in France, His Majesty Louis-Philippe, who hardly if ever goes to Mass, justifiably thought musicians ('une chapelle') superfluous, their jobs having become sinecures. Thus from the first days of his succession to the throne, he hastened to dismiss *chaplains* and *artists* whilst intimating to his family that henceforth the plainsong at Saint Roch was sufficient music for them.

Certainly just this one disgrace out of the thousand and one that make up the *order of things* is sufficient in itself to arouse our indignation.                    (*Cpr*, 63)

In October 1830 Liszt started attending Saint-Simonist meetings in Paris. Claude Henri de Rouvroy (1760–1825), Comte de Saint-Simon, was the founder of Christian Socialism. He announced a new epoch marked by industrialism and the power of scientific and technical knowledge, and called for a new aristocracy to replace the defunct orders of Church and nobility. Liszt was probably introduced to the circle by Émile Barrault, one of its members, whose writings gave to artists a significant rôle in the new order: 'Only the artist . . . by the power of that sympathy that embraces God and society, is fit to direct humanity' (*PL*, 101). Many of the ideas put forward by the Christian Socialists remained with Liszt all his life. In 1863 he wrote:

At the risk of still seeming very naïve to you, I will confess that I think more highly of the utility of certain ideas formerly preached by the disciples of Saint-Simon than it is expedient to say in the drawing rooms of *statesmen* . . . 'the moral, intellectual and physical amelioration of the poorest and most numerous class', 'the pacific exploitation of the globe', 'science associated with industry', 'art joined to worship', and the famous assessment 'each according to his capacity' do not seem to me fantasies empty of sense.                    (*Br.* III, 169)

Liszt wrote this in Rome, where he was engaged upon the composition of *Christus*. In his copy of Volume I of Lina Ramann's biography *Franz Liszt als Künstler und Mensch*, Liszt wrote similar quotations from Saint-Simon in the margin. In 1833, when the Comtesse d'Agoult returned a book containing Saint-Simonian doctrines to Liszt, she wrote: 'I am struck by the clarity, justice and force of a great number of the ideas contained in the Saint-Simonian book you lent me. Indeed, I am often amazed that you did not join the brotherhood' (*LMA*, I, 54). In 1853 Liszt wrote:

I have never had the honour of belonging to the association, or, to put it better, to the religious and political family of *St Simonisme*. Notwithstanding my personal sympathy with this or that member of it, my zeal has been but little beyond that which Heine, Borne, and twenty others . . . showed at the same period, and they limited themselves to following pretty often the eloquent preachings of the *Salle Taitbout*.                    (*L*, I, 162)

By 1830 the ideas of Saint-Simon were being expounded by his suc-

5

cessor, Pierre Enfantin, who in comparison was a charlatan. He proclaimed himself the new Christ, and founded what would nowadays be called a commune. Liszt later in life wrote disapprovingly of Enfantin and of Heine's admiration for him: 'I remember how, during the time I lived outside the Church, I was outraged by Heine's dedication of his book on *Germany* – in which he asked permission from P. Enfantin to commune with him across eternity. There is nothing more pernicious to the soul than this masquerading with things sacred' (*Br.* VI, 177). This remained Liszt's viewpoint throughout his life, later maintained within the framework of his support for strict canonical Catholicism. The Emperor Louis Napoleon, for example, whom Liszt greatly admired, was one of the later followers of Saint-Simon, and wrote a book on *The Extinction of Poverty*. As Liszt expressed it: 'An artist can have abstract ideas, but he cannot serve opinions without making his vocation impossible; for art, the solution of all opinions lies in the feeling of humanity' (*RAM*, 406).

In 1831–2 this 'feeling of humanity' led Liszt to explore beyond his usual social milieu. 'He visits hospitals, gambling casinos, asylums for the insane', wrote one of his pupils. 'He goes down into the dungeons, and he has even seen those condemned to die. He is a young man who thinks a great deal.'[1] The only composition from these years is the *Grande fantaisie sur la clochette de Paganini*, Liszt having attended the violinist's Paris concert given on 9 March 1831.

# 2

## 1834: LAMENNAIS AND
## *WORDS OF A BELIEVER*

I have only once in my life felt (for the Abbé de Lamennais) anything resembling a tremendously deep liking ('la folle et profonde sympathie').

Liszt to George Sand

Three months after the July revolution there appeared a new paper entitled *L'Avenir*, founded by the Abbé Félicité de Lamennais and including among its editorial staff Henri Dominique Lacordaire and Charles Montalembert. The motto of the paper was 'Dieu et la liberté', and its message the rejection of the divine right of kings and its replacement by the doctrine of the sovereignty of the people.

Lamennais was a visionary of genius, one of those men whose unseen intellectual influence has served to inspire Catholicism up to the present day. He was undoubtedly the greatest single non-musical influence on the mind of the young Liszt. One of Lamennais' ideas, that the papacy should abandon its dependence upon the temporal power, and trusting only to its spiritual authority should lead the world into a new order based on constitutional liberty and moral regeneration, partly came to pass: in July 1870 the dogma of Papal Infallibility was promulgated, followed in September by the entry of Italian troops into Rome, thus bringing to an end the temporal power. Lamennais never lived to see this realization of one part of his prediction, and the second part proved to be no more than a romantically apocalyptic dream. However it was exactly this which inspired Liszt, and made him see in the ideas of Lamennais a reflection of his own visionary ideal.

Born at St Malo in 1782, Robert Félicité de Lamennais became a priest in 1816, was offered the cardinal's hat by Pope Leo XII in 1824, which he refused, and died an apostate in 1854. His book *Paroles d'un croyant*, which appeared in 1834, brought upon his head the anathema of the Roman Catholic Church, as its revolutionary ideas were eagerly read by both the youth of the time and more mature intellects. Liszt's friendship with Lamennais started in April 1834 and continued throughout his years as a travelling pianist in the form of occasional letters and a choral work (*Le Forgeron*) written to his words in 1845. From the beginning Liszt was an ardent admirer not only of Lamennais' writings, but of the man himself, who evidently possessed great personal qualities and was an inspirational force among the younger generation of artists. Even George Sand came under his spell, writing in 1835: 'If I had met the Abbé de la Mennais in a stage-coach, disguised as a commercial traveller, I would still have recognized him for a great man' (*Lacg*, VI, 961).

The ideas of Lamennais mingled philosophy, religion and politics, and his strength as an inspirational force derived from a visionary attempt to weld into a unity the separate forces unleashed by the revolution. As a contemporary put it to him in a letter: 'France and Europe are awaiting the great moment you are erecting in your retreat; you are working, sir, at the great mission of the century; to unite religion and philosophy, science and faith, and to propound the unity of truth. There indeed lies true glory, sir, and the papacy of genius' (*Lacg*, VI, 752).

From the start, Lamennais concerned himself with the nature of power and the rôle religion should play in this. In 1808, in *Réflexions sur l'État de l'Église*, he waged war against religious indifference and the philosophical materialism of the previous century, though politically he supported the monarchy at the time. In 1812 he argued, in *Tradition de l'Église sur l'Institution des Évêques*, that the election of bishops, contrary to French practice, should be confirmed by pontifical sanction. In 1817 appeared the first volume of the *Essai sur l'Indifférence*, whose impact was perhaps more widespread even than that of Chateaubriand's *Génie du Christianisme*, and which, whilst attempting likewise to rekindle faith in the hearts of unbelievers, did so intellectually with a vast polemic refuting the arguments of infidelity. At the same time he published articles defending the alliance of the Throne and the Altar. Thus, inevitably, Lamennais was driven into the political arena. During the reign of Charles X, however, he changed his political creed, became a republican, and argued the supremacy of the Pope in the spiritual order. When the July revolution of 1830 broke out he hailed it as the dawn of a universal republic of which he was already dreaming, but with the *Avenir* in September Liberal Catholicism was born. The new paper urged the papacy: 'You have reigned over kings; those kings have enslaved you. Separate yourselves from kings, offer the hand of fellowship to nations; they will sustain you with their robust arms, and what is better, with their love.'[1] In the autumn of 1831 money for the paper ran out, and Lamennais travelled to Rome to appeal to the Pope. Gregory XVI, however, did not approve of revolutions; he even reproved the Catholic Belgians in 1830 for rising against Protestant Holland. In August 1832 he condemned the whole Liberal Catholic programme in the encyclical 'Mirari vos' and on 10 September the editors of *L'Avenir* announced submission. But Lamennais was still smouldering.

This was the situation when Liszt came within his orbit. He is first mentioned in a letter to Lamennais from Montalembert in March 1833: 'I can't remember ever having met a more sincere enthusiasm; this enthusiasm he has lately concentrated entirely on our religious and political doctrines; they have brought him to a real and practical faith' (*Lacg*, V, 702). Liszt's interest in their 'religious and political doctrines' at this time found musical expression, starting with the religious. The piano piece *Harmonies poétiques et religieuses* (S154), to a collection of poems by Lamartine, was written the same year. The date given in the catalogues is 1834, but this must be wrong. In a letter to the Comtesse d'Agoult dated 30 October 1833, Liszt refers to 'ma petite harmonie lamartinienne sans ton ni mesure' (*LMA*, I, 48).

In the same letter he asks Comtesse d'Agoult to send him the piece, adding: 'I set great store by these few pages. They vividly recall a time of suffering and delight.' As Liszt had been staying at Croissy, the home of Comtesse d'Agoult, during the summer of 1833, it would appear that he had left the manuscript behind. Furthermore, if the piece was composed as a result of 'a time of suffering and delight', the inference is clearly that Comtesse d'Agoult was involved. The previous May she had written to Liszt: 'If it were not so long, I would copy out for you the harmony entitled *Bénédiction de Dieu dans la solitude*. No one will ever describe so completely what I am experiencing ... you have awakened in my soul universal benevolence [la charité universelle], the love of everything, that was stifled in me by my personal sufferings' (*LMA*, I, 111). The poem *Bénédiction de Dieu dans la solitude* is from Lamartine's collection *Harmonies poétiques et religieuses*, upon which Liszt based his 1833 piano piece. In 1834 Liszt wrote: 'Our harmony will be dedicated to Lamartine; I shall first publish it alone, and later I shall write half a dozen.' So from the start Liszt intended to compose a series of pieces. Ten years were to elapse before this intention was put into effect, and the first piece to be completed was *Bénédiction de Dieu dans la solitude* (S173, 3) in 1845. Was it mere coincidence that the rupture between Liszt and Comtesse d'Agoult had occurred in the previous year?

In May 1833, when she wrote to Liszt about the poem, Montalembert had already written to Lamennais about Liszt's religious enthusiasm. By October the piece entitled *Harmonies poétiques et religieuses* was written, and for the first time Liszt had given musical expression to his religious feelings. More remarkable, however, is the revolutionary character of the music; from the standpoint of form, key, harmony and rhythm, it is startlingly different from the music he had so far composed, and the piece must be counted as Liszt's first really original composition. Indeed, considering its date, it is arguably the most original piano piece of the century. It combines a religious subject and a revolutionary

9

approach, at a time when Liszt had become a disciple of Lamennais. His next works to show real originality were all to be associated with Lamennais, and it is perhaps not just coincidence that his plan to compose a set of pieces to Lamartine's *Harmonies poétiques et religieuses* was carried out only after he had met the Princess Wittgenstein. The Princess, as her literary work entitled *Causes intérieures de la faiblesse extérieure de l'Église en 1870* shows, was a disciple of Lamennais.

The other aspect of Lamennais' ideas, the political, found musical expression in 1834. On 9 April, after attempts by the government to suppress trade union activities, the silk-weavers of Lyons rose in a revolt lasting four days. Fear of insurrection was so great that on 12 April 150 republicans were arrested in Paris, and a rising on 14 April was crushed by the army. Liszt made his sympathies clear: he composed the march-like piano piece *Lyon* (S156, 1), dedicated to Lamennais and bearing the inscription: 'Vivre en travaillant ou mourir en combattant' ('To live in work or die fighting'). Again it is to be remarked that Lamennais is associated with the composition of one of Liszt's finest early works.

Liszt met Lamennais in April 1834, shortly after the turbulent days of the Lyons uprising. 'I have made the acquaintance of Liszt,' wrote Lamennais on 18 April from La Chênaie, his home in Brittany, 'whom I liked very much. That young man is full of spirit [plein d'âme]; he will come this summer with d'Ortigues [*sic*] to spend some time here' (*Lacg*, VI, 66). Joseph-Louis d'Ortigue (1802–66) was a writer on church music who later, in 1857, founded *La Maîtrise*, a periodical devoted to church music, and published works on plainchant. It is probable that he introduced Liszt to Lamennais. On 22 April 1834 Lamennais wrote to d'Ortigue a letter which deserves extensive quotation, as it contains sentiments echoed by Liszt in later life.

The words which Liszt and yourself have written to me, my dear friend, were so welcome that I am immediately writing to thank you. Nothing in this world is worth so much as the warmth of kind and sincere feelings. We are brought together by our minds, but it is only in the heart that we become united, and unity is life, the life beyond words which expands endlessly in the eternal origins of every living being, as in love itself. I am eagerly looking forward to the moments we shall spend here together. I hope that the health of our dear Liszt, so weakened at the moment, will be improved by this sojourn among fields, fresh air, the scent of flowers, and above all the peace which reigns in this solitude. If it were not for the absence of my friends, I would ask nothing more of Providence in this life save these quiet hours of study and thought, in the bosom of nature, far from the tumult of the city and the vain clamour of human passions. However, I am also well aware that duty calls me to other work. The time for rest has not yet come. There is too much unhappiness on earth, too many evils and disorders, for it to be other than cowardly to flee the combat. I shall therefore struggle on as long as I have the strength, and it shall not be said that I remained silent and

inactive while mankind lay gasping on the ground beneath the feet of its
oppressors. *(Lacg,* VI, 68)

Much of this could have been taken from the programmes of orchestral
works by Liszt such as *Ce qu'on entend* or *Les Préludes.* The visit to
Lamennais at La Chênaie for the summer of 1834 was planned by Liszt,
Sainte-Beuve and d'Ortigue. In the event Liszt went alone.

On 30 April Lamennais' book *Paroles d'un croyant* was published. Its
effect on the 22-year-old Liszt was enormous. Carried away by his
fervour, he wrote in May to the author:

Dear Father,
   Although it is almost *impudent,* and even *ridiculous* of me to pay you *admiring*
compliments, I cannot resist the urge to tell you (quite *poorly* and *feebly,* it is true)
how your latest pages have transported me, overpowered me, torn me to pieces
with sadness and hope! . . . My God, they are sublime! . . . Sublime, prophetic,
divine! . . . What genius, what generosity of heart! . . . From this day onwards, it
is obvious, not only to the chosen few who have loved you and followed you for a
long time, but to the whole world it is obvious, from this latest evidence, that
*Christianity in the nineteenth century,* that is to say, the whole religious and political
future of mankind, lies in you! . . . Your vocation is quite stupendously glorious
. . . Oh! you will not fail, will you, whatever may be the anguish and terror in your
heart, you will not fail! . . .
   Do I need to tell you that not a day passes in this populous desert where I am
consumed by boredom and vexation, but the memory of you does not come into
my heart, like a reviving balm, a powerful solace? . . . Perhaps you do not yet
realize that I love you from my very bowels, and that very often – I do know why
or how – the wish to devote myself more entirely to you, to be something to you,
no matter what, troubles and torments me a lot? . . . It is really childish and stupid
of me, I know, but, as I have been told, *sometimes I have to be given too much of a pardon*
– so I shall ask your pardon at La Chesnaye [*sic*]. *(Lacg,* VI, 603)

*Paroles d'un croyant* remained one of Liszt's favourite books. In July 1854,
20 years after its publication, he was able to quote a substantial passage
from it in a letter to Marie Wittgenstein, the daughter of the Princess. He
had seen a painting by Tassaert of a mother and daughter, based on an
episode from the book. Significantly, Lamennais had died in February
the same year.

In *Paroles d'un croyant* and later writings, Lamennais expressed a lyrical
if vague awareness of a 'tremendous revolution going on at the heart of
human society', a revolution which was the march of 'the peoples' and
would produce a 'new world'. He denounced 'wage slavery' and casti-
gated the rulers of society for neglecting their responsibilities to society.
'If you reject peaceful reform you will have reform by violence.'[2] The
book is cast in 42 short sections, which are couched in the devotional
language associated with writers like Thomas à Kempis. An English
translation appeared in 1848. The author's preface, headed 'To the
People', begins:

11

# Revolution and religion

This book has been principally made for you; it is to you that I offer it. May it, in the midst of so many woes which are your lot, of so many afflictions which crush you down almost unremittingly, help, in some measure, to cheer and to console you.

Its message may be gleaned from the following extract:

You live in evil times; but evil though they be, they will pass away . . . Hope and love. Hope brightens all, and love renders all things possible . . .

Now it is men who judge and punish; soon it will be God who will judge . . .

When those who abuse their power shall have passed before you, like the mud of the brooks in a day of storms, then you will comprehend that the good alone is durable, and you will shrink from polluting the air which the breath of heaven has purified.

Prepare your souls for that time, for it is not far off: it approaches.

The Christ crucified for you has promised to deliver you.

A few quotations from some of the 42 sections will show how Lamennais succeeded in preaching revolution within the framework of Christianity:

## I

Eighteen hundred years ago, the World scattered abroad the divine seed, and the Holy Spirit fertilized it. Men have seen it flourish . . . At present earth has grown dark and cold again.

Children of the night, where the sun has set there is blackness, but the east begins to brighten.

## II

I see the nations rising in tumult, and kings growing pale under their diadem. War is between them, a war to the death.

And I was carried into ancient times, and the earth was beautiful, and rich, and fertile; and its inhabitants lived happily because they lived as brothers.

And I saw the serpent creeping in the midst of them . . .

And after having heard the word of the serpent, they arose and said, We are Kings . . . and . . . took a sword . . . from cottage to cottage.

Men, terrified, cried out: Murder has again appeared in the world.

## IV

Love one another, and you will fear neither the mighty, nor princes, nor kings.

## V

When you see a man conducted to prison . . . do not immediately say, That's a wicked man . . . perhaps he is a good man who has wished to serve men . . .

Eighteen centuries since . . . the pontiffs and the kings of that time nailed upon the cross . . . one whom they called a rebel . . .

## VII

God has made neither small nor great, neither masters nor slaves, neither kings nor subjects; he has made all men equal.

## VIII

Now there was formerly a wicked man . . . and he hated labour . . . He went by night and seized some of his brethren, whilst they slept . . .

For, said he, I shall force them with rods . . . to work for me, and I shall eat the fruit of their labour.

... and others did likewise, and there were no more brethren; there were only masters and slaves.

## IX

Poverty is the daughter of sin, and the germ of sin is in every man. Poverty is the daughter of servitude, and the germ of servitude is in every society.

## XI

And all the human race appeared to me as a single man.

And that man had done much evil, little good ...

And then that which had previously seemed to me only one man, appeared to me as a multitude of peoples and nations.

And their intelligence opened, and they perceived that the sons of God, the brothers of Christ, had not been condemned by their father to slavery, and this slavery was the source of all their woes.

... and, love stirring within them, they said to each other: We have all the same thought – why should we not all have the same heart? Let us work at our salvation, or die together.

... and I heard their chains snap, and they combated six days against those who had shackled them ...

And there were neither poor nor rich, but all had in abundance the things they needed, because all loved and aided each other as brethren.

## XIX

It is sin which has made princes, because, instead of loving ... each other ... men have commenced by injuring each other.

And the power of these usurpers ... is the power of Satan ...

And, therefore ... every one may, and sometimes must ... resist them.

## XX

... for the name of Liberty is holy.

Liberty shall shine upon you, when, by force of courage and perseverance, you shall have emancipated yourselves ...

## XXII

And the violence which will put you in possession of liberty is not the ferocious violence of thieves and robbers ... but a will, strong, inflexible – a courage, calm and generous.

## XXXVI

Young soldier, whither goest thou?

I go to combat for God, and for the altars of my native land.

I go to combat for justice ...

I go to ... deliver my brethren from oppression, to break their chains ...

I go ... that all may not be the prey of a few ...

I go ... that each one may eat in peace the fruit of his labour ...

I go to combat for the poor, that he may no longer be robbed of his share in the common heritage.

I go ... to overthrow the barriers which separate nations ...

I go to combat that all may have in heaven a God, and on earth a country.

May thy arms be blessed ... young soldier!

## XXXVIII

Liberty is the bread which nations must gain by the sweat of their brow.

## XLII

And the fatherland was shown to me.

I was conveyed far above the region of shadows, and I saw Time carry them away . . .

And what I heard, what I saw was so living, my soul seized it with such force, that it seemed to me that all which I formerly believed to have seen and heard was only a vague dream of the night.

And I felt what is the true fatherland, and I was intoxicated with light . . .

And then I saw the Christ at the right hand of his Father, radiant with immortal glory.

. . . and all creatures in nature palpitated with a new life, and all raised their voice, and that voice said: –

Holy, holy, holy is He who has destroyed and conquered death.

Shortly after the appearance of *Paroles d'un croyant*, Liszt wrote to the Comtesse d'Agoult, who did not approve of the book or its author:

You maliciously object to me that the *Paroles d'un croyant* are not evangelical, so allow me to answer you with the Gospel. 'The Kingdom of Heaven suffereth violence, and the violent take it by force.' The Son of Man did not come to bring peace, but the sword. It's an odd sort of Christianity which certain people profess, whose avowed moderation is in reality no more than a cover for their cowardice. Christianity is in a state of dumb servility, completely occupied in getting cheap means of subsistence and a few pennies from charity, stupidly stammering a few decrepit formulas, lying stretched out on the ground, gutless, impotent and foolish in face of the countless evils and terrible iniquities of society. Oh! if the Son of Man were to come now, where do you think he would find faith . . . ?

I appreciate all the criticisms and clever remarks that can be made about this magnificent book. But in all conscience, is it for you, or me, or both of us, to throw stones at the great priest who with his fiery words and winged pen has consecrated Liberty and Equality, the two great dogmas of Humanity?    (*LMA*, I, 78)

In another letter, Liszt continues:

Still Lamennais and the republican arguments? I don't know why you are angry . . . I have had the good fortune to follow for quite a time, day by day, the development of your *lofty intelligence* . . . so that I can no longer be mistaken about your political and religious opinions.

Allow me to say also that I am quite convinced that in this matter there can be no disagreement or real antagonism between us. To speak frankly . . . Lamennais' oeuvre does not seem to me of a definitive or dogmatic character; it is merely an outpouring of feelings; words of thunderous indignation against the great and the powerful of this world – words such as a priest who feels in his heart all the misery and anguish of the people *must* utter aloud. But it is only from God that I await deliverance, and the time has not yet come.    (*LMA*, I, 85)

And again in another letter:

Once again a few words of argument . . . (I had better quote them to you as you remember nothing): 'It is obvious that Christ only preached war against ourselves and our passions, the violence done to our corrupt nature, etc. . . . ' Don't you think that this indifference, this sacrilegious neglect of the fate of our unfortunate brothers which has withered our hearts may not also be a consequence of our corrupt nature to which violence must be done? ... Don't you see the devouring, all-powerful flames of charity ceaselessly turning round and round within a circle of selfishness, 'Oh, if you knew what it is to love'? Are you perhaps of the same opinion as our dear Baron who said to me one evening in all seriousness: 'The Gospel was addressed only to individuals and not to the masses ... Nevertheless, let it be known, *we only do not want to fight out of despair for the cause.* We do not want to either today or tomorrow, for the hour has not yet sounded. The *Paroles d'un croyant* are merely simple advice to the brutal governments who humiliate and crush us. Before resorting to arms, we shall exhaust all peaceful and progressive means. But, finally, if the day comes when it is plain to all that it is *absolutely impossible* to reconcile the privileges of the few with the well-being of the majority – then if we must fight, we will; if we must die, we shall not fail ... ' This is, you realize, (for me at least) only an extreme possibility, extreme and terrible ... but perhaps necessary. (*LMA*, I, 91)

However, Comtesse d'Agoult stood firm, and Liszt finally lost his patience, quoting from her latest letter:

With regard to one small quotation ... 'Although I am not very ultramontane, yet I would no more be a follower of Lamennais than I would have been a disciple of Luther or of Calvin.' Would it be very impertinent to ask, Madame, what your opinions actually are and how you consider yourself in this matter? Deist like Rousseau, no; Pantheist like Goethe and Schelling, still less ... ; Nihilist then, again no. Bayle said very truly: 'You know I am Protestant, that is I protest against everything anyone says or does.' (*LMA*, I, 95)

In spite of Liszt's passionate championship of Lamennais, and his own pronouncements against the contemporary situation in which the Church found itself, he still harboured hopes for a renascent Rome. 'And yet something still tells us,' he wrote to Mlle Valérie Boissier in the spring of 1834, 'that Rome is not dead, she is merely sleeping, and the day is not far off, perhaps, when she will revive once more in her angelic splendour and she will then be more than ever powerful, and will dominate the world with benevolence and knowledge' (*HFL*, 32). Even so, to follow Lamennais was, in practical terms, to leave the Church of Rome. Writing to the Comtesse d'Agoult, Liszt confirmed this: 'Lamennais has just been suspended by his bishop; the fulmination of Rome will not be long in coming. Will he have the courage to take it? I hope so, although I can't believe it. Surely he is able to say: "Rome is no more in Rome, she is wherever I am." ' (*LMA*, I, 101).

The 'fulmination of Rome' was delivered by Pope Gregory XVI on 7 July 1834 and reached Lamennais on 15 July. In the form of an encyclical entitled 'Singulari nos', it specifically condemned *Paroles d'un croyant*, describing it as 'small in size, but immense in its perversity'. The encyclical expresses horror at Lamennais' ideas:

In a succession of assertions as unjust as they are unprecedented, he argues, by a prodigious calumny, that the power of princes is contrary to divine law, is moreover the result of sin, is even the power of Satan himself; he castigates in the same infamous manner those who preside over holy matters as well as heads of state, by virtue of an alliance of crimes and conspiracies which he imagines to have been concluded between them against the rights of the people . . . We censure, condemn and wish for ever to be held censured and condemned, the book we have been speaking of . . . in which by an impious abuse of the Word of God, the people are criminally urged to break the confines of public order, to overturn different authorities, to incite, support, spread and strengthen sedition in the dominions, disorder and rebellion.                              (*Lacg*, VI, 182)

Henceforth Lamennais was an apostate. He was, however, 'never formally excommunicated, and there is no definite date on which one can say he ceased to be a member of the Church'.[3] In the same summer as the encyclical was issued, Liszt set out to visit him at La Chênaie. Before he left, a letter arrived from Lamennais: 'Please, arrange to prolong as long as possible the favour that I owe you. Think how I shall miss you when we are separated again. Come quickly, dear child, so that I can press you to my bosom and feel in that moment the throb of new life' (*Lacg*, VI, 281). Liszt's biographer Eleanor Perényi says: 'At La Chênaie he received his vocation . . . and it did not materially alter in his own mind for the rest of his life' (*PL*, 107).

Liszt arrived at La Chênaie probably on 8 September 1834 and stayed until 6 October. A long letter to Comtesse d'Agoult describes the Abbé Lamennais, his household, his books, his daily habits, and adds: 'Luckily, I have kept for you a little notebook of our conversations which we will go through together' (*LMA*, I, 120).[4] This notebook has not survived, unfortunately. Its contents would have been interesting, because after his visit Liszt wrote his first article, 'On Future Church Music', published in the *Revue et Gazette Musicale* in 1835. This contains ideas similar to those of Lamennais, and was obviously written under the influence of his stay at La Chênaie. Its importance lies in the fact that for 20 years these ideas lay dormant, and only after Lamennais died in 1854 did Liszt start to produce large-scale religious choral works whose character clearly derives from the visionary aspirations of his youth. Indeed the visionary quality in Liszt's music became more pronounced, rather than less so, in his old age. As the pieces grew generally shorter, and their texture more sparse, so the 'message' was all the more startling. A work like *Ossa arida* of 1879 parallels closely in musical terms the religious–revolutionary vision exhibited in the pages of *Paroles d'un croyant*.

Some writers, among them Haraszti, seem completely confused over the position of Lamennais, and hence of Liszt, with regard to the Church at this time, but Lamennais makes his position, as he himself saw it, quite clear:

## 1834: Lamennais and *Words of a Believer*

I have written to Lerminier to . . . put him right . . . over my position with regard to the Church. I am a Catholic, and I wish to remain so, without this obliging me to adopt the politics followed by the hierarchy or their opinions in general which do not touch upon faith. As for the matter of the future, to me it seems extremely dark; I see plainly that great changes are needed, but I do not see anything like so clearly where they will stop or what will succeed the present state of affairs, which cannot last. Several times I have tried to determine the point where the dead wood meets the living; *L'Avenir* was nothing more than one of these attempts; it failed: God, who knows what we do not, is digging ever deeper to cut off the wood lower down . . . A distinguished man wrote to me recently: I realize that to be a Catholic as the Pope wants us to be I must renounce not only my beliefs as a citizen, but also my beliefs as a man . . . When we have reached such a state, it is clear that ominous events are in store for the world, for it is impossible that one should have to choose between being a man and being a Christian.

(*LMA*, I, 304)

These sentiments are echoed by Liszt in his article 'De la musique religieuse', published in 1835.

This Church which is only concerned with muttering old formulas and living comfortably for as long as possible in its dilapidated state, this Church which can only make use of excommunication and anathema upon those whom it should exalt and bestow blessing upon, which has no sympathy for the deep need for love felt by young men and women, which has no capacity or means to assuage the hunger and devouring thirst of the human soul for a spirit of fairness, liberty and love, this Church as she presents herself before us in antechambers and public places where peoples and princes attack it simultaneously from both sides, this Church, let us declare unhesitatingly, has completely ceased to win the love and respect of our age. Forsaken by the people, by life and art, it seems that its destiny remains none other than to perish, exhausted and abandoned. (*Cpr*, 62)

During the period of Liszt's stay at La Chênaie, Lamennais was working on his magnum opus, *Esquisse d'une Philosophie* in three volumes, which appeared in 1840. The third volume deals largely with art, and just as his ideas on religion and the Church were echoed by Liszt, so it seems were his ideas on art, as Liszt's views correspond closely with those of Lamennais. Furthermore, these views recur much later in Liszt's life, particularly in letters to the Princess Wittgenstein. But as Lamennais appears to have been something of an amateur musician, and collected Breton folksongs, perhaps the process was reversed. Did Liszt have ideas which he gave to Lamennais? Although only 22 years old, he had read widely in the field of philosophy and aesthetics, and Lamennais was very impressed, writing to Baroness de Vaux in October: 'I wish to speak to you about M. Litz [*sic*], whose prodigious talent as a pianist is known to you. He will come and see you on my behalf, and you will find in him, in every respect, much more than just an artist' (*Lacg*, VI, 310). At the end of Liszt's stay at La Chênaie, Lamennais, in a letter to Sainte-Beuve expressing his approval of the latter's return to writing poetry, let fall a remark that immediately recalls Liszt:

> If I were a poet, I should simply sing out, but I should also like to be a musician so that my songs, combining the resources of harmony, could affect simultaneously all the forces of man. The ancients, in the springtime of the world, when everything flourished, did not separate the two, and they were right. Nowadays everyone upholds the economists' maxim concerning the division of labour; words from one person, music from another. This makes two arts instead of one. Therein obviously lies some profit. (*Lacg*, VI, 302)

The letter was given to Liszt to take with him to Paris. 20 years later, in his article on Berlioz's *Harold in Italy* written in 1855, part of Liszt's defence of programme music invoked the epic poetry of the Greeks, because it was sung, and represented a union of words and music. This idea must have already been in his mind for some time, perhaps even as far back as December 1830 when he met Berlioz and heard the *Symphonie fantastique*. Whatever their origin, these and other ideas were shared by Lamennais and Liszt. The following are quotations from *Esquisse d'une Philosophie*:

> The notion of art originally includes that of creation; for creation is the outward manifestation of a pre-existing idea, a bringing to expression in a sensible form. God, whom Plato . . . calls the *Eternal Geometrician*, is also the highest artist: His work is the world.
>
> Since, then, God Himself is the prototype which He produces outwardly in creating it, the Divine artist expresses Himself in His own work . . . and reveals Himself through it. His work, therefore . . . expresses the infinitely beautiful, but . . . broken . . . by the opaque medium of the world of appearances . . .
>
> Each . . . corporeal form represents its ideal type, and each ideal type, as it belongs to . . . the Divine form, is a partial reflection of it. If, then, all the types now existing in God were realized, the world would be the perfect expression of the . . . infinite . . . But as the infinite is in opposition to the essence of the world, it follows that the *infinite* is the *ideal aim* which it approaches . . . without ever reaching it, and therefore the work of God is *eternally progressive; and Divine art, through the ever-increasing variety of infinite forms harmoniously united, strives incessantly to reproduce the unity of infinite form, or the absolutely beautiful – primordial beauty.*
>
> The world is, therefore . . . truly the *Temple of God* . . .
>
> All art, then, is comprehended in the building up of the temple to the . . . finite image of the infinite prototype of continuous creation, namely God.
>
> No art originates in itself, and none subsists by itself, so to speak, alone for itself. *Art for the sake of art* is therefore a platitude. *Its aim is the perfectioning of beings*, whose progress it expresses.
>
> Music, a sister of poetry, effects the union of the arts, which appeal directly to the senses, with those which belong to the spirit; their object is . . . to second the efforts of humanity, that it may fulfil its destiny of raising them from the earth, and therefore by inciting to a continual upward striving.
>
> Art then . . . in binding the laws of organism with those of love . . . leads them to *aim at the perfection of all that is loftiest in human nature.*
>
> *Therefrom it appears that art, like science, is infinitely progressive, that it is trivial to suppose that an eternal, impassable final boundary exists for it.*

Art therefore is an expression of God; her works are an infinite manifold reflection of Him.                                                                  (*RAM*, 375–9)

It was against this background that Liszt wrote his article on church music. It combines many of the ideas so far discussed: contempt for the Church as it then stood; a republican outlook combined with the concept of the people as a religious entity; the belief that religious music should reach the masses, if necessary outside the Church; an ardent belief in the dawn of a new age for humanity. It was published in the *Revue et Gazette Musicale* on 30 August 1835, where it forms the last part of a longer article entitled 'De la musique religieuse'. This itself belongs to the series of articles 'De la situation des artistes et de leur condition dans la société'. Lina Ramann, whose German translation appears in volume 2 of *Franz Liszt's Gesammelte Schriften*, gave it the title 'Über zukünftige Kirchenmusik. Ein Fragment (1834)'. Liszt gave it no title, just marking it off from the preceding text, and adding the footnote: 'The following lines are taken from a long article written in 1834, with the aim of demonstrating that there is a need to launch a competition for poets and composers to write tunes, canticles, songs and hymns that are national, moral, political and religious, to be taught in schools.'

### On Future Church Music

*The gods are no more, kings are no more; but God remains for ever*, and the nations arise: doubt we therefore not for art.

According to a law voted by the Chamber of Deputies, music, at least, will shortly be taught in the schools. We congratulate ourselves on this step, and regard it as a pledge of greater things to come to influence the masses: we mean the ennobling of *church music*.

Although by this word the music executed during the sacred ceremonial only is generally understood, I use it here in its most comprehensive signification.

When the sacred service still sometimes expressed and satisfied the confessions, the necessities, the sympathies of the people, when man and woman still found an altar in the church before which they could sink on their knees, a pulpit whence they could fetch spiritual food; when, at the same time, it was a spectacle, which refreshed their senses, and raised their hearts to holy rapture, then only church music could fully withdraw into its own mysterious circle, and was content to serve the splendour of the Catholic liturgies as an attendant.

In the present day, when the altar trembles and totters, when pulpit and religious ceremonies serve as subjects for the mocker and the doubter, art must leave the sanctuary of the temple, and, coming abroad into the outer world, seek a stage for its magnificent manifestations.

As formerly, nay, more so, music must recognize God and the people as its living source; must hasten from one to the other, to ennoble, to comfort, to purify man, to bless and praise God.

To attain this the creation of a new music is indispensable. This, which for the want of another designation we would baptize *humanitary*, must be *inspired, strong, and effective, uniting, in colossal proportions, theatre and church; at the same time dramatic and*

19

# Revolution and religion

*holy, splendid and simple, solemn and serious, fiery and unbridled, stormy and calm, clear and fervid.*

The Marseillaise, which has shown us the power of music more than all the mythical relations of the Hindoos, Chinese and Greek – the Marseillaise and the beautiful songs of liberty are the fruitful and splendid forerunners of this music.

Yes, banish every doubt, soon shall we hear in fields, in forests, villages, and suburbs, in the working-halls and in the towns, national, moral, political, and religious songs, tunes, and hymns, which will be composed *for* the people, taught *to* the people, and sung *by* the people; yes, sung by workmen, day-labourers, handicraftsmen, by boys and girls, by men and women of the people.

All great artists, poets, and musicians will contribute to this popular and ever-renewed treasure of harmony. The State will appoint public rewards to such as, like ourselves, have been three times at the general assemblies, and *all classes* will at last melt into one religious, magnificent, and lofty unity of feeling.

This will be the *fiat lux* of art.

Come, then, thou glorious time, when art will unfold and complete itself in all its forms, soaring up to the highest perfection, and, like a bond of fraternity, unite humanity to enchanting wonders. Appear, O time, when revelation shall no longer be to the artist that bitter and fleeting water which he can scarcely find in the unfruitful sand into which he digs. Come, O time, when it will flow like an inexhaustible, lifegiving fountain. Come, O hour of deliverance, when poets and musicians, forgetting the 'public', will only know one motto, 'The People and God!' *(RAM, 383–5)*

The verbal description of the music Liszt imagined fits many pages of his Masses and oratorios. But the extraordinary feature of the article is the mention of the *Marseillaise* as the 'forerunner of this music'. So far, Liszt's only use of the tune had been in the sketch for a *Revolutionary Symphony*.

The musical result of Liszt's stay at La Chênaie was a remarkable work which still remains unpublished and unperformed. Writing to the Abbé Lamennais in January 1835, Liszt informed him:

I shall have the honour of sending you a little work, to which I have had the audacity to tack a great name – yours. – It is an instrumental *De Profundis*. The plain-song that you like so much is preserved in it with the *Faburden*. Perhaps this may give you a little pleasure; at any rate, I have done it in remembrance of some hours passed (I should say *lived*) at La Chênaie. *(L, I, 7)*

The work in question, *De profundis: psaume instrumental* (S691), is for piano and orchestra, and is dedicated to Lamennais. It begins with a long, wild and stormy introduction for piano and orchestra; the piano part is brilliant, but the orchestration, which is in Liszt's own hand, is only sketched in the most bare and simple manner. After a series of repeated held chords, the piano announces the main psalm theme, the words of Psalm 130 being written against it in the score; it was this theme and these words which Liszt later inserted into *Pensée des morts*. A good deal of the work consists of a 'kind of struggle between the psalm theme and the stormy motives of the introduction' and it 'ends with a section in the style of a march, containing a new version of the psalm theme' *(SML, 12)*.

20

Although it has no programme, it is clear from this description that it represents a musical counterpart to the ideas expressed in Liszt's article 'On Future Church Music', themselves partly inspired by *Paroles d'un croyant*. Furthermore, both Liszt's piano concertos end with 'a section in the style of a march, containing a new version' of earlier material.

*De profundis* thus appears to contain Liszt's earliest 'thematic transformation' used to express triumph, a common feature of his later works, where slow music is transformed into fast music using the same thematic material. In this respect it is interesting that the other two 'Lamennais' pieces, *Harmonies poétiques et religieuses* and *Lyon*, both contain vestiges of the 'transformation' idea. *Harmonies* was originally planned for piano and orchestra. Furthermore, the piece *Pensée des morts*, no. 4 of the collection *Harmonies poétiques et religieuses* published in 1853, is in fact a conflation of the 1833 piece (rewritten) and the psalm theme from *De profundis*. The two pieces were thus clearly associated with each other in Liszt's mind. The reason may be that they were both prayers, but composed for the piano. Here we have the beginning of what was to become Liszt's characteristic mode of musical expression. The fact that it originated as piano music indicates the autobiographical element, and also links the idea of prayer to Liszt's use of programme music. For 'De profundis' was the text not only of Liszt's first setting of a psalm, but also of his last (in 1881). The words of Psalm 129 (= 130) describe the path to redemption, beginning 'Out of the depths have I called to thee, O Lord' and ending 'For in the Lord is love unfailing, and great is his power to set men free' ('et copiosa apud eum redemptio'). This emotional scheme was inseparable in Liszt from the inspiration he gained from Lamennais. The use of thematic transformation signifies the redemption process, and this use remained constant throughout Liszt's life. Later manifestations of this scheme, which was essentially a binary-form concept, incorporated as a transitional stage a personification of love (e.g. Gretchen in the *Faust Symphony*), leading ultimately to Christ, the mediator of mankind. At this point the need for thematic transformation disappeared – it is not used in *Christus*. Taken as a group, *Harmonies poétiques et religieuses*, *Lyon* and *De profundis* represent Liszt's first emergence as an original composer and may be said to contain the seeds of the greatness that was to emerge during the Weimar period.

In the letter of January 1835 quoted above, Liszt wrote to Lamennais: 'Unless something very unforeseen occurs, I shall come again and beg you to receive me for a few days towards the middle of July.' However 'something very unforeseen' did occur: in May 1835 Comtesse d'Agoult informed Liszt that she was pregnant, and by July they were both in Switzerland. Liszt did not see Lamennais for a whole year, from May 1835 to May 1836. Presumably this change in his life accounts for the fact that *De profundis* remained unfinished; there appears to be no other reason why the work should not have been completed, orchestrated and performed. (In the same year, 1834, Liszt did, however, complete his *Grande fantaisie symphonique* on themes from Berlioz's *Lélio* (S120), for piano and orchestra, which was performed in Paris the following year, though it remains unpublished.) According to Searle, *De profundis* is so nearly complete ('there is something written in every bar') that 'with a little ingenuity it might be possible to complete the score' (*SML*, 13). If it had been performed, Liszt's reputation as a serious composer might have been established sooner; as it was, his fame rested for more than a decade on transcriptions and virtuoso pieces which tended to eclipse his more serious output, with the result that later he had to fight all the harder to win recognition as a serious composer. One of his first completed serious choral works, *Le Forgeron* (S81), to words by Lamennais, appeared in 1845, though it remained unpublished until 1962. Lamennais was obviously important for the serious-minded side of Liszt. What was his influence on Liszt between 1835 and 1845?

These of course were the years of Liszt's liaison with Comtesse d'Agoult, which came to an end in 1844. It would be untrue to say that the period which produced the Swiss and Italian pieces of the *Années de pèlerinage* (S160–1) and saw Liszt's beginnings as a song-writer was unproductive of serious works. But during this period he commenced his career as a travelling pianist, partly to earn money for his children. The fact that it escalated into a career of unprecedented proportions was largely unforeseen, and due to circumstances beyond his control. Apart from his talent and personality, he was historically opportune, for he articulated in music the revolutionary fervour of the years leading up to 1848. Such universal enthusiasm must have seemed to him like a dream come true, and the disciple of Lamennais perhaps wondered whether it had not been given to him to usher in the new age prophesied in *Paroles d'un croyant*. For surely in Liszt's case self-glorification and pecuniary greed are not sufficient motives to account for his extraordinary career during the virtuoso period. As recently as 1974 a biographer has written that 'Liszt could never have achieved his colossal celebrity if he hadn't believed . . . that something larger than himself was involved' (*PL*, 159). Certainly it was during this time that Liszt began to feel most acutely the gulf that existed between his ideal vision and the reality. In simple terms, this showed itself in the kind of music that roused the masses.

Often, seeing the inane silence that has followed performances of the finest works of Beethoven, Mozart and Schubert, while the most wretched trifle produced transports of enthusiasm, I have sighed with despair. Very often . . . I have been led to reflect whether, in the end, art is, as I had thought, the universal communion of truth and beauty, or merely a spicy dish eagerly sought after by the wealthy and the privileged . . . and I was seized by bitterness and doubt.

(*Cpr*, 79)

These were his most worldly years; Haraszti (*HFL*, 199) even goes so far as to say that Liszt 'devait perdre la foi' at this time. But Liszt's letters to Comtesse d'Agoult do not support such a claim. Instead we receive the impression that to some extent he continued his concert tours against his will, as if borne along by an irresistible force. Comtesse d'Agoult on the other hand came to disapprove of his concert-giving just as earlier she had disapproved of his friendship with Lamennais. Yet one source of strength for Liszt must have been the knowledge that in the ideas of Lamennais lay the possibility of resolving the contradictions emanating from his artistic position. According to Lamennais, the gulf between these distant extremes, between the masses and the privileged, between the ignorant and the educated, between vulgarity and taste, between Man and God, could somehow be breached. All that was needed was faith and a willing heart. Certainly, during his liaison with Comtesse d'Agoult, Liszt made every effort to maintain his friendship with Lamennais.

In the spring of 1836, Liszt returned to Paris via Lyon, where he gave concerts. There he received a letter from Lamennais, to which he replied: 'Your letter, dear Father, only reached me the other day, a little before my departure from Lyon . . . I bless you a hundred times over . . . Though I had flattered myself that I perhaps deserved some evidence of affection, I nevertheless didn't dare hope for it' (*PL*, 139). A week later, he wrote from Paris: 'I shall expect you. Whatever sorrow there is in the depth of my soul, it will be sweet and consoling to see you again' (*L*, I, 9). After he had seen Lamennais, Liszt wrote to Comtesse d'Agoult: 'The Abbé Lamennais has arrived, we have seen each other and understand one another. Thanks be to God my task here is at last finished. *Everything is alright now*' (*LMA*, I, 174).

After returning to Geneva, he and Comtesse d'Agoult were joined in the summer by George Sand for a trip to Chamonix. Then in October, Liszt and Comtesse d'Agoult returned to Paris, where they were joined again by George Sand, this time to promulgate 'humanitarian art' through *Le Monde*, a newspaper edited by Lamennais. For two and a half months, Liszt, Comtesse d'Agoult and George Sand lived at the Hôtel de France, rue Neuve-Lafitte. Together with Lamennais, they wrote articles advocating many of the ideas probably discussed during the summer of 1834. The circle also included Pixis (a pianist), Adolphe Nourrit (the tenor who sang the rôle of Don Sanche in Liszt's youthful opera of that name and later sang Raoul in the first performance of *Les Huguenots*) and

# Revolution and religion

Chopin, and all of them were present at a dinner party given by Chopin on 13 December 1836. Heine, Berlioz and Meyerbeer may also be added. 'Vox populi vox dei' was virtually the motto of *Le Monde*.

From May until July 1837 Liszt and Comtesse d'Agoult stayed at Nohant with George Sand, returning to Switzerland in the summer, and travelling to Italy in September. There Liszt gave concerts in Milan, and wrote in December to Lamennais:

I am still not very advanced in my Italian journey. The beauty of these parts . . . and some altogether unexpected successes, have kept me in Milan and the neighbourhood . . . much longer than I had foreseen . . . I am hoping and longing ardently for your next book [*Le Livre du peuple*, Paris, 1837], which I shall read with my whole heart and soul, as I have read all that you have written for four years. I shall owe you just so many more good and noble emotions. Will they remain for ever sterile? Will my life be for ever tainted with this idle uselessness which weighs upon me? Will the hour of devotion and of *manly* action never come? Am I condemned without respite to this trade of a Merry Andrew and to amuse in drawing-rooms? (L, I, 20)

The hour of action did come in April 1838, when Liszt went to give concerts for the benefit of the victims of the Danube flood. In the words of Liszt, it was these concerts whose success 'determined me on a virtuoso career'.[5]

From the start, the successes occasioned by his concerts were ambivalent in their effect. Almost immediately Liszt gave vent to sentiments that haunted him for nearly a decade: 'All the time I am asking myself why I have come here, what I am supposed to be doing, what good the acclamations of the crowd are doing me, and this empty, noisy, puerile celebrity' (*LMA*, I, 227). In October 1839 Comtesse d'Agoult departed for Paris from Florence, leaving Liszt to make his way to Vienna, and on to Hungary. At this time Spontini had returned to Italy, and had proposed a reform of church music, an idea reported with approval by Liszt in the *Gazette Musicale*, 28 March 1839:

Spontini . . . horrified by the decadent state into which church music had fallen, realized that an attempt at reform was needed, because it depended, in effect, on the efforts of a single individual.

Shocked and scandalized, like all whose religious feelings are joined to the artistic, to hear during church services and the celebration of the holy mysteries nothing but ridiculously inappropriate reminiscences of the theatre . . . he conceived the noble idea of relieving the Church of this scandal by reinstating serious and austere music, as written by composers like Palestrina, Marcello and Allegri. He ended by suggesting the most efficient means of ending the abuses, and of founding a new school of sacred music.

That Liszt's attitude to the Church matched what he thought of its music shows in the concluding lines:

24

All of which will probably not prevent the reform plan, which in addition Spontini intends to publicize widely in France and Germany, from slumbering in some forgotten box in the pontifical chancellery. (*Cpr*, 287)

We do not know what Lamennais, who lived until 1854, thought of the phenomenon of Liszt's concert successes. In the middle of this 'noisy, puerile celebrity' Liszt wrote a letter from Seville in 1844 describing his reactions to the cathedral:

One cannot use any set phrases about such a monument. The best thing to do would be to kneel there with the faith of the charcoalburner . . . or to soar in thought the length of these arches and vaulted roofs, for which it seems that there is even now *'no longer time'*! – As for me . . . I am constrained to stand with my nose in the air and mouth open. Nevertheless my prayer sometimes climbs up like useless ivy lovingly embracing those knotted shafts which defy all the storms of the genius of Christianity. (*L*, II, 494)

This view of art and architecture was part of Liszt's Catholicism, and formed the kernel of his dislike of Protestantism. In 1835 he had written:

By what bizarre circumstances did the reformer, whilst proscribing painting and sculpture in their temples, manage to retain music and oratory, 'first among the arts'? How was it that their particular concerns and prejudices led them to forget that beauty is but the splendour of truth – art but the radiance of thought? . . . How in the end did they not perceive that to try to spiritualize religion to the point where it subsists devoid of all external manifestation is tantamount to claiming a reform of the work of God, the great and sublime artist who, in creating the universe and mankind, revealed himself as the omnipotent, eternal and infinite poet, architect, musician and sculptor. (*Cpr*, 90)

In 1844 Liszt and Comtesse d'Agoult terminated their liaison. Early the following year, at the request of Lamennais, Liszt wrote him a long letter outlining the arrangements that had been agreed upon regarding the children, their education, and Liszt's contribution to their upkeep (*Br*. VIII, 40). Comtesse d'Agoult's family had accepted her return to Paris on the condition that the children went to live with Liszt's mother, Anna. This episode in his life now over, Liszt began once more to turn to serious composition, for which he also felt there was 'no longer time'.

# 3

## 1848: REVOLUTIONS AND A MASS

Has Belloni sent you my Mass for 4 voices . . . ? How much I yearn to continue
my work in this vein of feeling, which is that of my youth, and belongs to the
deepest regions of my heart!                                              Liszt in 1850

On 12 February 1845 in Lisbon, Liszt finished the composition of *Le
Forgeron* to a text by Lamennais. On 28 April, he wrote to Lamennais:

Permit me, illustrious and venerable friend, to recall myself to your remembrance through M. Ciabatta, who has already had the honour of being introduced
to you last year at my house. He has just been making a tour in Spain and
Portugal with me, and can give you all particulars about it. I should have been
glad also to get him to take back to you the score, now completed, of the chorus
which you were so good as to entrust to me ('the iron is hard, let us strike!'), but
unfortunately it is not with music as with painting and poetry: body and soul
alone are not enough to make it comprehensible; it has to be performed, and very
well performed too, to be understood and felt. Now the performance of a chorus
of the size of that is not an easy matter in Paris, and I would not even risk it without myself conducting the rehearsals. While waiting till a favourable opportunity
offers, allow me to tell you that I have been happy to do this work, and that I trust
I have not altogether failed in it . . . At the beginning of winter I shall resume my
duties at the Court of Weimar, to which I attach more and more a serious
importance.                                                              (*L*, I, 68)

*Le Forgeron* represents a major step in the development of Liszt as a
serious composer. Content to leave the revolutionary element to the text,
which, using the metaphor of a blacksmith and his forge, urges the
people to 'strike the iron', Liszt concentrates on constructing a large-
scale piece for piano and choir of men's voices. Although not a religious
work as such, *Le Forgeron*, like *Paroles d'un croyant*, combines its revolutionary message with the conviction that God is on its side, as the closing
words indicate:

> Let all who are men fight. Heaven looks down
> At us! It will be our faithful companion
> In our battle. Today there is but pain,
> But the Day already awaits us,
> When dawn will beckon!
> Hard is the iron! But hit it, strike it!
> God looks down from on high.

26

# 1848: revolutions and a Mass

During the 1840s Liszt had gained experience as a conductor. In 1840 he conducted a concert in Pest, and after his appointment as Grand Ducal Director of Music Extraordinary to the Court of Weimar in November 1842, he conducted there each year. With regard to choral music, Hallé tells us in his autobiography that round about 1840 Liszt formed and conducted a choral society of amateurs in Paris.

On 1 June 1845 Liszt wrote again to Lamennais: 'M. de Lamartine, with whom I have been spending two or three days at Montceau, told me that you had read to him *Le Forgeron* so I played him the music' (*L*, I, 73). Lamartine's poetry provided Liszt with the inspiration for what was undoubtedly his greatest composition for the piano to date, *Bénédiction de Dieu dans la solitude*, which was sketched in 1845. The quality of the music he produced indicates Liszt's development towards a more personal expression. The religious context was not new, only the increased mastery as a composer.

Another poem by Lamartine, *Hymne de l'enfant à son réveil*, also from the collection *Harmonies poétiques et religieuses*, again inspired Liszt in 1845. This time he produced a choral work for women's chorus, harmonium and harp (S19). We may regard this significant step as a turning-point, because before this time Liszt's choral works had been to secular words, and his religious music had been instrumental, inspired by religious poetry. By setting a religious poem to music intended to be sung, he had made the transition towards writing liturgical sacred music, the first examples of which appeared in 1846.

These two pieces show Liszt's instinctive path of development outside a specifically church context. In 1845 he was still a disciple of Lamennais and nothing had happened to alter his critical opinions of the 1830s. He put his feelings into music before attaching them to Rome.

Liszt was now increasingly beset by the need to devote time to composition. In April 1846 he wrote to Comtesse d'Agoult (with whom he corresponded regularly until 1848, when the Princess Wittgenstein came to Weimar): 'My manuscripts have too long been in abeyance, and I feel terribly a longing to write, but unfortunately the things I want to compose would not bring in any money' (*LMA*, II, 355). The following month he wrote of his forthcoming visit to Hungary: 'At the time when I am stepping boldly into the career of a composer, I cannot resist returning to where I started as a pianist' (*Br.* VIII, 45). During Liszt's visit to Hungary, there occurred a historic change in the outlook of the Roman Catholic Church. On 15 June 1846 Cardinal Mastai-Ferretti was elected Pope Pius IX. 'In most ways,' according to a modern commentator,

the new pontiff differed from his predecessors. He was much younger, being only fifty-four, and had travelled extensively, even to South America where he had served on the staff of the Delegate to Chile. He had enjoyed a distinguished career as a diplomat and as an administrative prelate . . . later had come a vocation and the cassock. He . . . was a man of imposing and handsome presence who was not alarmed at the new order and as a sovereign was willing to negotiate and indeed quite anxious to make concessions to liberalism. Only thirty days after his installation he was given the salutes and plaudits of a popular ruler . . . A general amnesty was proclaimed for all political exiles and prisoners of whom there were about two thousand from the previous reign. It was announced that railroads, noisy symbols of progress, would be permitted within the papal territories and that henceforth there would be few or no restrictions to prevent the publication of newspapers.[1]

At last Rome seemed to be adapting to the modern world. From this time dates Liszt's return to the Church, and his composition of church music. Also, whether by coincidence or otherwise, there was henceforth no further correspondence between Liszt and Lamennais.

In October Liszt met the future Primate of Hungary, Bishop János Scitovsky, who invited him to stay at his summer residence at Nádasd[2] from 25 to 27 October. 'I had the honour of knowing the Cardinal,' Liszt wrote to the Princess on 25 April 1865, 'when he was Bishop of Fünfkirchen [Pécs], in 1846. It was because of a promise I made him at that time that he commissioned from me the *Gran [Esztergom] Mass*, performed ten years later' (*Br.* VI, 73). He may also have visited Father Albach, the priest he had known as a boy in Eisenstadt. The *Ave Maria* (S20) and *Pater noster* (S21), which constitute his first church works, were published that year. Many of Liszt's church works were composed for Hungary, or received their first performance there.

On 6 October Liszt wrote to Carl Alexander at Weimar: 'The moment is approaching (*Nel mezzo del camin di nostra vita*) – (35 years old!) when I shall break the chrysalis of my virtuosity and let my thought flow freely' (*LCA*, 8). It is significant that when Liszt abandoned his virtuoso career, the first large-scale work he composed was the *Male-Voice Mass* (S8).

At the beginning of 1848 Liszt returned to Weimar from Russia, where he had spent the last months of 1847 with the Princess Wittgenstein. Thus, when the revolutions of that year broke out, he was already installed as Grand Ducal Director of Music, and had given the official last concert of his virtuoso career. Henceforth he intended to devote himself to composition and conducting. Attempts have been made to determine Liszt's attitude to the revolutions of 1848 and to explain the apparent inconsistency in his behaviour in not taking part, as for example Wagner did in Dresden in 1849. Because Liszt was known to have republican sympathies, and had appeared as the incarnation of revolutionary fervour during the virtuoso years, even causing the Austrian Minister of Police to produce a dossier on him in 1838, he had aroused special expectations. In the event, however, he did not join the barricades, confining his activities to a visit to them in Vienna at the

# 1848: revolutions and a Mass

beginning of the summer, as described by his companion János Dunkl:

In the stormy days of 1848 I visited the barricades with Liszt, which were being commanded by Karl Formes, the well-known bass singer. Liszt presented cigars and money to the workers on guard. Instead of all his medals, Liszt wore a cockade of the Hungarian colours in the button-hole of his jacket.[3]

The 'stormy days' in Vienna occurred in March and May. As Liszt was in Weimar in March, he presumably visited Vienna in May 1848. The question immediately arises as to what Liszt was doing in Vienna at this time. The answer is to be found in a letter of 15 June 1885 addressed to the composer J. P. von Király in Eisenstadt: 'In 1848 I visited the dear affectionate Father Albach at the Franciscan monastery of Eisenstadt, and dedicated to him my Mass for men's voices' (L, II, 471). If this be allowed as evidence that Liszt had already composed the Mass by the summer of 1848, then it is of some importance because various writers, among them Haraszti, have suggested that Liszt fled from the revolution into the Church, thereby betraying his earlier revolutionary ideals.

The difficulty lies in the lack of any precise information about the composition of the work. Liszt, in a letter to the Princess dated 10 June 1885 refers to 'ma Messe pour voix d'hommes, écrite à Weymar en 48' (Br. VII, 424). If 'écrite' does not mean 'composed', but simply 'written down', an earlier date for its actual composition is possible. Evidence for this is to be found in Liszt's letter to Breitkopf und Härtel written in 1852:

With regard to the publication of the Pater Noster and of the Ave Maria, please do it entirely to your own mind . . . but whether you publish these two pieces with the Mass, or whether they appear separately . . . will suit me equally well. For more convenience I have had them bound in one, as having been written at the same time and as belonging to the same style. (L, I, 143)

The Pater noster (S21) and the Ave Maria (S20), both already published in 1846, were republished by Breitkopf und Härtel in 1853 at the same time as the Mass, all three bearing a dedication to Father Albach, who had died that same year. The version of the Mass known today is the later, reworked version of 1869.

The first version is a substantial work and must have taken some time to compose. Before the summer of 1848, Liszt was in Weimar only during February and March. He then left to wait for the Princess at Krzyzanowitz. On her arrival from Russia they travelled together until June, when they returned to Weimar. Liszt may well have taken the Princess with him to visit Father Albach; in his Testament dated 14 September 1860 he mentions two watches, 'one with a portrait of Pius IX which Carolyne gave to me in Vienna in 1848'. Knowing the religious enthusiasm of the Princess Wittgenstein, it would seem probable that during Liszt's stay with her from October 1847 until January 1848 he may have worked on the Mass. Certainly the fact that Bishop

# Revolution and religion

Scitovsky had commissioned him to write a Mass in 1846 suggests that Liszt had divulged his wish to compose such a work. Why else should the Bishop have asked Liszt, when until that time he had published no church music?

Thus we cannot be sure exactly when Liszt composed the '1848' Mass. There is no reference to the work dating from that year at all. However, there are other works by Liszt that certainly did spring from the revolutions of 1848, and it is these we should examine to discover his reactions to the events of that year. The works in question are the *Hungaria Cantata* (S83), the *Arbeiterchor* (Workers' Chorus) (S82), the piano piece *Funérailles* (S173, 7) and the symphonic poem *Héroïde funèbre* (S102).

The events of 1848 which one would expect to have affected Liszt most deeply are the following:

*22–24 February* Demonstrations in Paris, leading to abdication of Louis-Philippe; installation of Provisional Government under Lamartine.

*11–15 March* Disturbances in Prague, Vienna, Budapest; Metternich forced to flee; Hapsburg Emperor promises constitution; Hungary given virtual independence.

*29 April* Pope announces neutrality in national war against Austria; papal troops withdrawn from Italian forces.

*23–26 June* Bloody street fighting in Paris after the dissolution of the National Workshops. Thousands of workers killed. Severe reaction follows.

*16–25 November* Popular insurrection in Rome forces Pope Pius IX to flee city.

*10 December* Prince Louis Napoleon Bonaparte elected President of the French Republic.

Liszt's reaction to the events of February in France was enthusiastic: 'Just now,' he wrote to the Princess on 28 February, 'the most incredible news has been despatched by telegraph from Strasbourg about the latest events in Paris. The import of these events will be enormous, but we must await confirmation.' Later the same day he wrote: 'The news from France is confirmed. Provisional Government. Lamartine Minister of Foreign Affairs. What did I tell you? The king in flight . . . in fact France not only in revolution, but a republic' (*Br.* IV, 26). On 1 March he wrote to Dingelstedt: 'Belloni [Liszt's secretary] is more fortunate than I. As a lieutenant of the National Guard, he dated his last letter from the Paris Town Hall. But I am forgetting that I hate politics, and indeed during the last 15 years, this is the first enthusiasm which has gripped me' (*Br.* VIII, 55). Later the same month he wrote to Comtesse d'Agoult: 'Lamartine's manifesto which so eloquently advocates the fight for peace is one of the things in my life I have gained most satisfaction from . . . God save France! And Christ will deliver the World through love and liberty!' (*LMA*, II, 393).

# 1848: revolutions and a Mass

Two statements about these events made by historians may illuminate Liszt's enthusiasm. L. B. Namier has pointed out that the February revolution was initially 'not anti-clerical, still less anti-religious', and F. Fejtö wrote that the 'romantic and unrealistic character of the February revolution is of course explained by the fact that the working class had asserted itself for the first time.'[4] The text of Liszt's *Arbeiterchor* ends with these words:

> Glory may be given to God by all creations,
> He who has faith in him has done right.
> He who has given steel for swords and tools,
> Now looks down at us with blessings.
>
> Therefore rally to the great brotherhood,
> Heart to heart, lips to lips,
> The Father sees us from Heaven,
> We must all brethren be.

The author of the text is unknown, as is the exact date of the composition of the work, which may not have been 1848. If not, however, it could only have been earlier, as Liszt refers to the work in a letter of June 1848. As is evident from the above extract, the ideas and sentiments belong to the world of *Le Forgeron* and its text by Lamennais. Regarding publication, Liszt wrote to Haslinger: 'Dear Karl, as the present situation provides a quite abnormal commentary on the workers question, perhaps you should put aside the publication of this Arbeiterchor, so that it can appear at a more suitable time. I leave the decision to you.'[5] In the event Haslinger did not publish the work.

On 24 March Liszt wrote to the Princess: 'My compatriots have just taken a step which is so decisive, so unanimously Hungarian, that it is impossible to withhold a tribute of legitimate sympathy' (*Br.* IV, 29). By the middle of April, he was in the midst of composing music to a text by Franz von Schober, Councillor of the Austrian Legation at Weimar, addressed to the Hungarian people. Liszt wrote to the author from Castle Grätz, where he had met the Princess on her arrival from Russia: 'Your dear letter brought me still nearer to you in the crisis of the *estro poetico*, which the "Hungaria" brought forth in me; and, thanks to this good influence, I hope you will not be dissatisfied with the composition' (*L*, I, 87). The work ends with the chorus singing 'Éljen' (literally 'Viva', but with strong nationalist overtones, meaning something like 'Long live the Hungarians') to music of a *Fidelio*-like character. Once again, as with the *Arbeiterchor*, publication for this revolutionary work was not forthcoming, and it remained in manuscript form until 1961. This may have been due to the course of the Hungarian struggle for freedom from Austrian rule, which ended in August 1849 with Russian troops assisting the Austrians in defeating Hungary. Francis Joseph, who had acceded as Austrian Emperor in December 1848, was not crowned King of Hungary, however, until 1867, and during the intervening years there was fierce repression by the Austrians. In such circumstances no Viennese publisher would have risked bringing out a work expressing Hungarian nationalist revolutionary enthusiasm.

These two works gave voice to Liszt's sympathy for the socialist and nationalist causes, the former in a French context, the latter in that of the country of his birth. However, the revolutionary fervour of the 1830s was not rekindled in Liszt for long in 1848, and he quickly became disillusioned. For example, the Hungarian piece which was published, *Funérailles*, is not an ardent hymn to liberty; dated 'October 1849', it is a monument to those who died in the failed revolution. 13 generals were hanged on 6 October alone.

The symphonic poem *Héroïde funèbre* was to have been part of a reconstituted version of the sketched *Revolutionary Symphony* of 1830. The new version was never completed, but its character would have been quite different from that of the early work, with its youthful championship of revolutionary ideals. The later work was to be cast

in the form of a five-movement symphony. The first was to be Héroïde Funèbre, the second a setting of 'Tristis est anima mea', the third was to be based on the Rákóczy and Dombrowski marches (symbolizing Hungary and Poland), the fourth on the Marseillaise, and the last movement was to be a setting of Psalm 2, 'Quare fremuerunt gentes' ('Why this tumult among nations, among peoples this useless murmuring?').                                            (*SML*, 6)

Liszt's preface to *Héroïde funèbre* is a denial of martial values:

De Maistre remarks that over thousands of years it is hard to find any during which, by rare exception, peace reigned on earth – which otherwise resembles an arena where peoples fight each other as did the gladiators in former times, and where the most valiant salute Destiny as their master and Providence their judge, before entering the lists. In these wars and carnages that succeed one another like sinister games, whatever the colours of the flags which rise courageous and proud against each other, over both camps they flutter soaked in heroic blood and inexhaustible tears.

In 1848 Liszt told Fanny Lewald in Weimar:

I would be the first to answer the call to arms, to give my blood and not tremble before the guillotine, if it were the guillotine that could give the world peace and mankind happiness. But who believes that? We are concerned with bringing peace to the world in which the individual is justly treated by society.

(*LZB*, 341)

In France it was in June 1848 that the revolution turned sour. The labourers in the National Workshops, employed on useless earthworks, fomented discontent. The Government closed the workshops, and a fierce battle between workers and the army took place, lasting four days. It is possible that these events, and not the February revolution, gave rise to Liszt's *Arbeiterchor*, presuming the work to have been written in 1848. By this time, Liszt had already dedicated his Mass to Father Albach. The musical result of any change of heart concerning revolutions was not the 1848 Mass, but the planned recast version of the *Revolutionary Symphony*.

In November 1848 a Republican Constitution was promulgated in France, and in December Louis Napoleon was elected President. The 1848 Mass received its first performance on 15 August 1852 at Weimar, to celebrate the birthday of the President of the Republic. A connection between the work and Liszt's admiration for Louis Napoleon may be deduced from this, and his reasons for associating the two are not hard to find. When Napoleon died in 1873, Liszt wrote to the Princess Wittgenstein:

I honestly believed at the time, and do so still, that Napoleon's reign was the one most in keeping with the requirements and advances of our era. He has set noble examples, and accomplished or undertaken great deeds . . . the protection of the Church in Rome and in other countries . . . the earnest attention paid to the lot and to the interests of the country people and of the working classes; the generosity and encouragement to scholars and artists, – all these things are historical facts.                                                                                    (*L*, II, 222)

In 1848 Louis Napoleon was one of the few leaders in favour of disarmament. When in November of that year Pius IX fled to Gaeta, leaving Rome in the hands of Italian nationalists, he was rescued by Louis Napoleon; in July 1849 the Roman Republic fell to French troops, who restored the Pope in April 1850, and remained to protect him until 1870, when they were recalled to France on the eve of the Franco-Prussian war. Whatever their motives, such actions on the part of the President of the French Republic could only win the admiration of Liszt. Had not Lamennais argued for a European Republic governed by the Pope? Catholicism and republicanism were the ideals that inflamed Liszt.

From now onwards Liszt's sympathies, sympathies which harmonized with his loyalty to France and the ideals he had acquired there in his youth, lay entirely with Rome. For Liszt, as for most artists of the time, 1848 proved a bitter disappointment, but in Liszt's case the failure of the revolutionary outbreaks to bring any nearer the kind of world he envisaged drove him towards the Church. Gone was the possibility he had envisaged in 1834 of the day dawning when '*all classes* will at last melt into one religious, magnificent and lofty unity of feeling'. In September 1848, after the murder in mysterious circumstances by the mob of his friend Prince Felix Lichnowsky, Liszt wrote: 'What a sign of the times! As for myself, I return more than ever, and without cowardice or childishness in my opinion, to my point of departure, that is, Christianity' (*LMA*, II, 399).

On 11 November 1851 the military historian Theodor von Bernhardi wrote in his journal an account of a conversation he had heard at the Altenburg:

Liszt joins in. He undertakes the apology for strict canonical Catholicism, which forbids any individual opinion or conviction . . . He was formerly a freethinker allied with Lamennais and others; but latterly he has seen that this negative point of view must lead to the extremest revolutionary action – that *la guillotine serait introduite partout comme un instrument permanent de l'orchestre politique*; and therefore he has decided to *se rejetter fortement dans le système catholique* . . . He assured us that many people in France thought as he does.[6]

The quotations in French are doubtless the words of Liszt. This renewed devotion to the Catholic Church and a Christian social vision did not necessarily imply, however, any loss of revolutionary zeal; he referred, for example, in 1849 to 'economics, the deep study of which must begin' (*LZB*, 341). Just as before 1848 revolution and religion were twin facets of a single ideal for Liszt, so they remained afterwards.

During the Weimar period this twin-faceted ideal was transferred from life to art. One of his most successful works during this time was the *Gran Mass*, performed at Esztergom and then in Pest in 1856. When the work was performed in Paris in 1866, a critic wrote: 'So much passion, so much fire, so much anger in a religious piece. Indeed the author of the Revolutionary Symphony is not dead in Liszt' (*HFL*, 226). If the critic had known the intentions behind the sketched *Revolutionary Symphony* of 1830, he need not have been surprised at the appearance of similar traits in Liszt's religious music. The difference was that whereas the 18-year-old had put religion into a revolutionary work, the 44-year-old put revolution into a religious work. The church music was thus not a reaction to 1848. Before starting the *Gran Mass*, Liszt wrote to Augusz:

For a long time I have been strongly attracted to the idea of composing church music. Before I had the honour of your acquaintance [i.e. before 1846] I made a deep study in Rome [i.e. in 1838–9] of the masters of the 16th century, in particular *Palestrina* and *Orlando di Lasso*. Unfortunately until now few opportunities have presented themselves whereby I could take advantage of these studies and give rein to my personal inspiration, for it must be said that religious compositions meet with small chances of promotion at the moment, and their authors can barely earn the price of a cup of water. In spite of this I published a few years ago (through Breitkopf und Härtel in Leipzig), as an experiment, a Mass for male voices with organ accompaniment, a Pater noster and an Ave Maria, to satisfy a heartfelt need more important to me than certain external advantages. These works were only a step I had to undertake before preparing myself to accomplish others to follow, more fully worked out.                                                            (*LAA*, 51)

The revolution of 1830 inspired a symphony which was not carried out, but whose sketches contain the *Marseillaise*. During the 1830s Liszt's dream of a new 'religious' music derived from the inspiration of the *Marseillaise*, as he declared in the article 'On Future Church Music'. Before 1848 he had composed music for the Church, now apparently responsive to the modern world after the election of Pius IX. The failure of 1848 caused Liszt to return to the *Revolutionary Symphony*, but the part of it he actually completed, *Héroïde funèbre*, quotes from the *Marseillaise* as a memorial to the fallen. This does not represent a 'change of heart'. Quite the contrary; the failures of history served merely to strengthen Liszt's visionary idealism.

# 4

# WEIMAR: LISZT, THE CHURCH AND WAGNER

My role of privy-councillor at Wahnfried forbids me to vex Wagner, all the more so since I share his opinion in almost every respect – theology excepted.

Liszt from Bayreuth in 1879

## Pius IX

On 14 March 1848 a new Constitution was promulgated by Pius IX. On 16 November there was a popular insurrection in Rome, and four days later Pius had to flee the city. This experience shattered any dream the Pope may have held of an Italian federation under his rule. His religious position and the position of the more extreme Italian liberals like Mazzini and Garibaldi were irreconcilable. To appreciate the feelings of the Pope and of many Roman Catholics in the nineteenth century, it is important to remember that at that time they regarded the temporal power as vitally necessary to the proper functioning of the papacy as a spiritual authority. Pius IX called the papal states 'the robe of Jesus Christ' and was prepared to be a martyr over their liquidation. Thus it was that between 1846 and 1848 Pius had been the idol of the Italian nationalists, but after 1848, when the Church was on the defensive, he appeared in the guise of a blind opponent of all reforms.

The true position was rather more complicated. Naturally the Pope's attitude to the *risorgimento* tended to reinforce any ideas he harboured favouring ultramontanism in the Church (the absolute authority of the Pope in matters of faith and discipline), but within the Church itself there were differing schools of thought. The movement of European liberalism generated by the French revolution had had its repercussions among the clergy, some of whom supported the idea of religious toleration and the separation of Church and State. (Cavour and Montalambert spoke of 'a free Church in a free State'.) The opposite pole was represented by de Maistre and his disciples, who argued that libertarian ideas were subversive of law and order, would lead to anarchy, and were the outcome of rejecting the Christian doctrine of authority in Church and State. They were thus anti-liberal, and wanted to restore the firm alliance of Church and State. The opposing factions polarized thus: Christians versus Liberals, and clericalism versus anti-clericalism. At this point it should be remembered that Lamennais, who is regarded as the founder of Liberal Catholicism, shared one characteristic of the anti-Liberals: although politically a republican, he argued the supremacy of the Pope not only in the Church, but by implication in society as well. Lamennais, who won Liszt's youthful admiration, did not envisage a free Church in a free society; he envisaged a free society led by the Church. Thus he made no proviso for the real predicament produced by the course of history: what rôle to play in a society hostile to the Church.

Pius IX treated the Liberal Catholics as traitors. In France there was persistent conflict between these and the ultramontane Catholics, whereas in Germany the arguments were more intellectual than political. At Munich Dr Döllinger (1799–1890) was at the centre of a school of Catholic theologians and historians who sought to apply the same critical standards as were used by the Protestants; they saw the need for a new presentation of Catholic faith in the light of philosophical and scientific thought, and for a more critical reckoning with the facts of history. He was regarded with suspicion at Rome.

Liszt's position, as will be made clear, fell between these opposing camps. He may be described as ultramontane inasmuch as he fervently supported Pius IX and believed in the need for authority. Yet he was to the end of his days a Liberal who expressed tolerance and open-mindedness. Liszt's argument was simply that with faith there was no need to fear for the future, although he acknowledged the weakness of the Church and the threat to its position. He thus supported all the measures taken by Pius IX to strengthen it.

After his restoration in 1849, the Pope revoked the Constitution in April 1850. Henceforth he actively opposed many aspects of modernism, and set the course broadly taken by the Roman Catholic Church ever since. Liszt, by the end of the following year, was already arguing the case for strict canonical Catholicism. In 1859 most of the papal states were overrun by the army of Victor Emmanuel II, King of Sardinia. On 26 September 1860, Garibaldi met Victor Emmanuel and proclaimed him King of Italy. The Pope's temporal power was doomed.

In the following month, on 27 October 1860, Liszt wrote to the Princess:

'Il mondo da sè' ('the world goes its own way'), said Machiavelli; 'l'Italia farà da sè' ('Italy will go her own way') people have said since – but Antonelli has had the brilliant idea that the Holy See can subsist 'da sè', which seems to me an idea of genius. It is at the feet of the Holy See that the world should kneel. Without being unjust to the courageous and honourable men who have taken up arms in its defence, I am nevertheless inclined to think that its best troops, and the most invincible, are – the guardian angels! (*Br.* V, 84)

In December 1864 the encyclical 'Quanta cura' and the 'Syllabus errorum' were promulgated. In the 'Syllabus', Pius IX condemned all the Liberal Catholic groups and tendencies. It contained an overall condemnation of rationalism, indifferentism, socialism, communism, naturalism, freemasonry, the separation of Church and State, the liberty of the press and the liberty of religion, and denied that 'the Roman pontiff can and ought to reconcile himself and reach agreement with progress, liberalism and modern civilization'. Most Catholics were disconcerted, and diplomatic protests poured into Rome. But Liszt wrote of 'the *Syllabus* – to which I submit and give my support as Catholics are duty-bound to do' (*HFL*, 278). In 1864 Liszt was in Rome, preparing to receive minor orders. Gregorovius reports seeing Liszt play in a concert 'for Peter's Pence in the new barracks on the Praetorian camp . . . Liszt played, the papal choir sang . . . Tremendous applause . . . Liszt shows himself fanatically catholic' (*GRJ*, 202).

Soon after the promulgation of the 'Syllabus', Pius announced that he was contemplating the summoning of a General Council. This pleased the Liberal Catholics, who assumed the bishops would check the advance of ultramontanism, and show that the Pope was not the only authority. At the beginning of 1869 a quasi-official organ of the Holy See announced that the Council would be short, and would be concerned with the proclamation of the dogmatic infallibility of the sovereign pontiff. This immediately produced a storm of controversy. The Council met in December, with the task of preparing a comprehensive statement of Roman Catholic teaching. Because of the political situation there was not time for lengthy debate, and the question of Papal Infallibility was brought forward to be settled in the remaining time. There were three main parties within the Church: the ultramontanes who wanted an extreme definition; those, like Döllinger, who opposed the doctrine on historical and theological grounds; and the 'inopportunists' who, although they did not deny the doctrine, felt that it was inopportune to define it under existing conditions.

Pius IX was well suited to promote loyalty to the papacy as the centre of the Church. Cardinal Newman said of him:

His personal presence was of a kind that no one could withstand . . . The main cause of his popularity was the magic of his presence . . . His uncompromising faith, his courage, the graceful mingling in him of the human and the divine, the humour, the wit, the playfulness with which he tempered his severity, his naturalness, and then his true eloquence.[1]

Pius took up the position that Christendom had apostatized, and therefore the appropriate action of Catholics was intense loyalty to the central power, uniting among themselves, and separation from the outside world. Gregorovius wrote in March 1870: 'The Pope is firm as a rock in the conviction that he is predestined by God to place the dogma as a crown on the structure of the hierarchy. He holds himself a divine instrument in the shattered system of the world, as the mouthpiece of the Holy Ghost' (*GRJ*, 357).

During this period Liszt composed a work, not published until 1936, entitled *Inno a Maria Vergine* (S39). The last lines of the text, by an unknown author, read:

> Vedi, vedi, fra quanti perigli
> si dibatte la nave di Pier!
>
> Ah! dall'ira di crude tempeste
> per te regga sicuro il gran Pio
> Su la terra, ministro di Dio,
> pieghi l'alme suo giusto voler!
>
> (See through how many perils
> struggles the ship of St Peter!
>
> Ah! through you the great Pius securely
> withstands the anger of cruel storms
> on earth, minister of God,
> all souls bending to his just will!)

Voting was due to take place on 18 July 1870. Beforehand about 60 of the 'inopportunists' left Rome, refusing to vote. In the event, 553 voted for the decree, 2 against, and the Vatican Council declared the dogma of Papal Infallibility in matters of faith and morals. Liszt supported the dogma, for reasons he later told to Adelheid von Schorn: 'Our Church is not strong, and she must exact total obedience. We must obey, even if we hang for it . . . and that is why all the princes of the Church will adhere to it: not one of them can remain outside' (*SFL*, 227). Liszt was correct in his prediction; all the abstaining bishops later announced their submission to the new dogma.

The day after the voting took place, war was declared between France and Prussia. In August the French troops were withdrawn from Rome, and in September Italian armies invaded the Pope's territory. Rome capitulated, the Kingdom of Italy was established and the temporal power of the papacy was finished. The Vatican Council adjourned 'sine die', and the Pope and his entourage became virtually prisoners in the Vatican. Liszt wrote from Hungary to Princess Marie Hohenlohe: 'The huge events that startle the world also bear on my little existence. I had planned to return to Rome during the first days of October; but considering the actual state of things . . . it wasn't much of a task for them to persuade me to prolong my stay in Hungary' (*LMW*, 144).

Thus came to an end the Rome Liszt had lived in for nearly ten years, and where he had composed *Christus*. The fact that history took this step between the completion of the work in 1868 and its first performance in 1873 may account for the strange fate it has suffered; like a survivor from a lost world, it has made occasional appearances in the concert hall, but has so far been denied general acceptance and a place in the repertoire, even though its musical stature is acknowledged.

Gregorovius returned to Rome in October 1870, having been absent since July. The shocked state of mind occasioned by what he found there is discernible from his *Journals*:

> The violent transformation of the city seems to me like the metamorphosis of jugglery. Italians have relieved the papal troops . . . The Pope has announced himself a prisoner, has issued protests, and has suspended the Council by a Bull. Rome will forfeit the cosmopolitan, republican atmosphere which I have breathed here for 18 years. She will sink into becoming the capital of the Italians . . . The Middle Ages have, as it were, been blown away by a tramontana, with all the historic spirit of the past; yes, Rome has completely lost its charm.
>
> (*GRJ*, 388)

In October 1873 Liszt spoke with the Pope:

> I had asked to be admitted to an audience of the Holy Father. He was so gracious as to receive me alone on Monday morning and to converse with me for more than a quarter of an hour. The persuasive charm of his words touched me deeply. There is something prodigious about his health, and his spirits do not flag. While telling me about the present trials of the Church he developed admirably a text of St Paul, the gist of which is that one can easily imprison, inflict suffering on, and even kill the body, but one cannot touch the free and immortal soul. Moreover, those who suffer with Christ shall share His Glory . . .
>
> At the Vatican, I saw again Cardinal Antonelli, Monseigneur de Mérode, Monseigneur Pana. The Cardinal is in very good health and perfectly imperturbable in spirit. Neither he nor Pana has been outside the Vatican since September '70.
>
> (*LOM*, 99)

Pius IX died in February 1878. Liszt wrote to the Princess:

> Pius IX was a Saint! Never has anyone inspired so many countless panegyrics in all corners of the world as he has. In his lifetime, he was practically submerged beneath universal eulogy – and this will continue to grow, if that is possible, after his death. The whole of Catholicism is united in almost adoring worship of the Pope who proclaimed the dogma of the Immaculate Conception of the Virgin Mary, and that of the dogmatic Infallibility of the Supreme Pontiff, Vicar of Jesus Christ, and the legitimate successor to St Peter. For a long time, schismatics, heretics, and even the majority of unbelievers have been full of respectful devotion and praise for the person of Pius IX, including those who contributed to 'discharging' him of his temporal royalty.
>
> (*Br.* VII, 209)

# Weimar: Liszt, the Church and Wagner

The pontificate of Pius IX was the longest in the history of the papacy (31 years and 7 months). His successor, Leo XIII, tried to restore the prestige of the papacy and the influence of the Church by pursuing a policy of conciliation with modern society. He was the friend of democracy and sound learning, and opened the Vatican archives for research. Liszt dedicated two choral works to Leo in 1881: *Dominus conservet eum* and *Tu es Petrus* (S59, 1–2). His pontificate lasted until 1903.

## WAGNER

In March 1846 Wagner sent Liszt the scores of *Rienzi* and *Tannhäuser*, writing in a letter: 'As I perceive more and more that I and my works . . . are not likely to prosper very much . . . I proceed with perfect openness to rouse *you* up in my favour' (*WL*, I, 4). In 1849, after his involvement in the revolution at Dresden, Wagner fled to Liszt at Weimar, who secured his escape to Switzerland. From Zurich he wrote to a friend: 'My deep-rooted friendship for Liszt supplies me with strength from within and without to perform [my] task; it is to be our *common* work' (*WL*, I, 21). He remained an exile from Germany until 1860, during which time he relied heavily on Liszt for encouragement. This took the form of Liszt's active championship of his operas, financial aid, the publication of articles in support of Wagner, and a lengthy correspondence between the two men. During the Weimar years Liszt became increasingly desirous of composing religious works. When in 1855 he was commissioned to compose a Mass for the reconsecration of the cathedral at Esztergom, the floodgates opened, releasing the stream of religious works that were to pour from Liszt's pen.

A study of their correspondence reveals the difference in attitude of the two men towards religion and the Christian Church. This was a strong contributory factor towards the rift which gradually drove them apart, as Wagner's virulent hostility evidently wore away Liszt's patience. At the same time, Liszt grew weary of the burdens of conducting. In 1853 he wrote to Wagner: 'You may assume that my passion for your tone- and word-poems is the only reason why I do not give up my activity as a conductor' (*WL*, I, 335). The same year, Liszt determined on the idea of composing *Christus*. At the time of his departure for Rome, both Wagner and Cosima attributed his devotion to church music as an unfortunate result of the influence of the Princess Wittgenstein. Only after the appearance of the score of *Christus* in 1872 did Liszt make any moves to restore their friendship, and Wagner and Cosima attended the première at Weimar in 1873. The following year Liszt composed *Die Glocken des Strassburger Münsters*, which Wagner eagerly studied, and from which he took the opening theme for *Parsifal*.

# Revolution and religion

From the beginning, Wagner revealed his attitude towards religion. In August 1849 he sent Liszt a copy of his article 'Art and Revolution'. 'Whether you ought to show the Princess my manuscript,' he commented, 'I am not quite certain; in it I am so much of a *Greek* that I have not been able quite to convert myself to Christianity' (*WL*, I, 42). The following year Liszt gave the first performance of *Lohengrin*. In September he wrote to Wagner: 'The whole opera being one indivisible wonder, I cannot stop to point out any particular passage . . . A pious ecclesiastic once underlined word for word the whole "Imitatio Christi"; in the same way I might underline your *Lohengrin* note for note' (*WL*, I, 87). In 1851, after the appearance of Wagner's article 'Das Judenthum in der Musik', Liszt wrote to Wagner: 'Can you tell me, under the seal of the most absolute secrecy, whether the famous article on the Jews in music in Brendel's paper is by you?' (*WL*, I, 142). Wagner replied: 'You must know that the article is by me. Why do you ask? . . . I felt a long-repressed hatred for this Jewry, and this hatred is as necessary to my nature as gall is to the blood' (*WL*, I, 145).

In November 1851 Wagner informed Liszt that he had changed *Siegfried's Death* into a cycle of dramas recounting the complete myth of the *Nibelungen*, and no longer contemplated a production at Weimar. In February 1853 he sent Liszt the text of *Der Ring des Nibelungen*, adding in a letter: 'Yea, in the fire of Valhalla I should like to perish. Consider well my new poem; it contains the beginning and the end of the world' (*WL*, I, 257). In April Liszt wrote a long letter to Wagner. Part of it touched on the consolations of religion:

Your letters are sad; your life is still sadder . . . Your greatness is your misery; both are inseparably connected, and must pain and torture you until you kneel down and let both be merged in *faith*!
'Lass zu den Glauben Dich neu bekehren, es gibt ein Glück'; this is the only thing that is true and eternal. I cannot preach to you, nor explain it to you; but I will pray to God that He may powerfully illumine your heart through His faith and His love. You may scoff at this feeling as bitterly as you like. (*WL*, I, 273)

Wagner's lengthy reply illuminates the fundamental difference between the two men; in it he rejects religious belief, replacing it by human will-power, which unaided must succeed in creating a world full of love, thus achieving 'the task of history'.

How ever could you think that I should 'scoff' at any of your magnanimous effusions? . . . Dear friend, I also have a strong faith, on account of which I have been bitterly scoffed at by our politicians and sages of the law. I have faith in the future of the human race . . . I have succeeded in observing the phenomenon of nature and of history with love and without prejudice, and the only evil I have discovered in their true essence is *lovelessness*. But this lovelessness also I explain to myself as an *error*, an error which must lead us from the state of natural unconsciousness to the *knowledge* of the solely beautiful necessity of love. To gain that knowledge is the task of history; and the scene on which that knowledge will be practically shown is none other than our earth, than nature, in which there are all the germs tending to this blissful knowledge . . . This . . . will in the future create on this earth a state of things from which no one will long to fly to a hereafter henceforth become unnecessary; for all will be happy . . . I believe in mankind, and require nothing further. (*WL*, I, 277)

This letter marks the beginning of the rift that increasingly grew between the two men. Liszt did not reply directly, but he did think Wagner was profoundly mistaken. In 1854 Liszt gave his answer to Wagner's objections in a letter to the Princess Wittgenstein:

During the journey I read some Brendel, who tries, in his own way, to justify Christianity in opposition to the theories of Wagner. His point of view is summed up in these words, to which I would put my own name: 'Christianity, taken at its innermost core, will endure (I for my part would say: to redeem the world and mankind!) until the end of the world. Its outer forms, however, will change inside certain chronological periods, since not one of them has been able to survive unchanged until now.' Wagner's idea that a new flowering and harvest of Art requires the link that joins Apollo and Jesus Christ is not false – but he falls into flagrant contradiction when later he uses this to strike a blow at Christianity by upholding in principle and practice Love and Brotherhood, which are the very essence of Christianity. (*Br.* IV, 184)

Having denied the possibility of the hereafter, Wagner then had somehow to come to terms with death. He found the answer in the philosophy of Schopenhauer:

I have of late occupied myself exclusively with a man who has come like a gift from heaven . . . into my solitude. This is Arthur Schopenhauer, the greatest philosopher since Kant . . . His chief idea, the final negation of the desire of life, is terribly serious, but it shows the only salvation possible . . . I have at least found a quietus which in wakeful nights helps me to sleep. This is the genuine, ardent longing for death, for absolute unconsciousness, total non-existence . . .

In this I have discovered a curious coincidence with your thoughts; and although you express them differently, being religious, I know that you mean exactly the same thing. How profound you are! (*WL*, II, 53)

Liszt, however, did not think much of Schopenhauer, or indeed philosophy in general. In 1859 he referred to 'that snarling old cur, Schopenhauer' (*WL*, II, 305). In 1874 Adelheid von Schorn was in Rome and wrote:

I visited the Princess and spent the evening with her and Liszt. The conversation turned to the subject of Schopenhauer. Liszt, out of principle, did not hold with any philosophical system, and loathed in particular the pessimism of Schopenhauer. As for the Princess, she detested Schopenhauer. To round off the evening, Liszt sat at the piano and played excerpts from his *Christus*. (*SFL*, 238)

In 1855 Liszt told Wagner about the commission to compose the *Gran*

*Mass.* Wagner replied: 'You write about this Hungarian commission. I can imagine how the invitation has pleased you; and I too am pleased and most curious to see your work' (*WL*, II, 72). In May Wagner told Liszt that he was reading Dante's *Divine Comedy*. This prompted Liszt to confide to Wagner his plan to compose a *Dante Symphony*, and to dedicate it to Wagner if he 'does not dislike it'. Wagner replied with a letter containing his advice not to set the Paradise, and a lengthy diatribe against Christianity and Catholicism. He admitted enjoying reading Hell and Purgatory, but could not stomach the Paradise, which was

done in order to confirm the Catholic doctrine of a God Who, for His own glorification, had created this Hell of my existence ... This problematic proof I rejected from the bottom of my soul, and remained dissatisfied accordingly ...

The misleading problem in these questions is always How to introduce into this terrible world, with an empty nothing beyond it, a God Who converts the enormous sufferings of existence into something fictitious, so that the hoped-for salvation remains the only real and consciously enjoyable thing.     (*WL*, II, 91)

Wagner then elaborates his own interpretation of the human condition. Man, he argues, embodies the 'will of life' which fashions his organs, among them the intellect. In men of genius the intellect detaches itself from the will and becomes 'aesthetic', which for Wagner equals 'will-less'. Such men, in common with the true saints, renounce the 'will of life':

This act of the 'negation of will' is the true characteristic of the saint, which finds its last completion in the absolute cessation of personal consciousness ... But the saints of Christianity, simple-minded and enveloped in the Jewish dogma as they were, could not see this, and their limited imagination looked upon that much-desired stage as the eternal continuation of a life freed from nature.     (*WL*, II, 97)

Wagner then advocates Buddhism, whose saints enter the state of Nirvana, 'the land of being no longer'. The doctrine of migration of souls shows the denial of the will of life; each soul comes back in the form of a creature on whom it has inflicted suffering. Only when it passes through a new-born life without inflicting suffering does the sorrowful migration cease. 'How sublime,' he wrote, 'how satisfying is this doctrine compared with the Judaeo-Christian doctrine, according to which a man . . . has only to be obedient to the Church during this short life to be made comfortable for all eternity, while he who has been disobedient in this short life will be tortured for ever' (*WL*, II, 99). At the end of 1855 he wrote to Liszt: 'Of your Christianity I do not think much; the saviour of the world should not desire to be the conqueror of the world. There is a hopeless contradiction in this in which you are deeply involved' (*WL*, II, 128).

At this time Wagner was working on an early version of *Parsifal*, called *The Victors*. In 1856 he told Liszt: 'I have again two splendid subjects which I must execute. *Tristan and Isolde*, you know, and after that the

*Victors*, the most sacred, the most perfect salvation. But that I cannot tell you . . . your music has given it to me, all but the close' (*WL*, II, 154). Liszt replied: 'You will speak to me about your *Victors*, the most sacred, the most perfect salvation . . . What will it be? The few hints in your last letter have made me very curious to know the whole idea' (*WL*, II, 155). Wagner, however, remained evasive: 'I shall perhaps lay my Victors before you, although this will be very difficult . . . you must first have digested my Tristan, especially the third act, with the black flag and the white. After that you will understand the *Victors* better' (*WL*, II, 161).

Between 1857 and 1859 plans were made to perform *Rienzi* at Weimar. Liszt also wanted *Tristan* and the *Ring* to be performed there, but after the death of the Grand Duchess in June 1859, no money was forthcoming for such unwieldy enterprises. Much of the financial support granted to Liszt by the Court was due to the Grand Duchess's enthusiasm for Wagner. *Rienzi*, though, was another matter; it was likely to prove popular. However, Wagner's need for money was urgent, and he wrote to Dingelstedt, the Intendant at the Court Theatre, demanding an advance. Dingelstedt had the reputation of being a difficult man to work with, and Liszt was anxious to preserve his support for Wagner's works. Liszt told Wagner to be polite in his letters to Dingelstedt. The Intendant, however, turned down Wagner's demand for money, and Wagner, furious, wrote to Dingelstedt to abandon the project. Liszt himself wrote back, in December 1858, saying that he was not continuing his activities in the theatre. Wagner, even more enraged, told Liszt he did not really *mean* to abandon the project; he had hoped it would push Dingelstedt into giving him the money. Eventually Wagner received the money in June 1860, and the opera was performed in December. Liszt did not conduct. Neither did he explain to Wagner why, or what his intentions were. He kept his contact with Hohenlohe secret, together with any plans he may have harboured to go to Rome.

In 1860 Wagner went to Paris, and during his visit met Agnes Street, who talked to him about Liszt. Wagner wrote from Paris:

Madame Street gave me to understand . . . that you had been very sad, although in very good health . . . this news has struck me very much, and Madame W., to whom I spoke about it, was quite frightened. There is something about you which causes you to appear surrounded by splendour and light, and makes it difficult for us to understand what could make you sad. Least of all am I inclined to discover the cause of your irritation in the stupid reception which your works have met with now and then, for it seems to me that . . . this animosity is caused not by your works, but by the false light in which you appear to the multitude . . . I think, therefore, you are right in withdrawing yourself from that illumination as much as possible, and in letting your works take their own course for a time without the least anxiety about them.                                      (*WL*, II, 328)

Liszt wrote back immediately:

# Revolution and religion

Truly, dear Richard, we belong together and must come together at last. Cordial thanks for your kind letter, which in these dreary days has been a great and noble joy to me. Amongst other things you have taken a fine and strikingly correct view of the totally passive attitude with regard to the reception and promulgation of my works which I shall observe for the future. Other people have somewhat misunderstood my conduct. What a blessing it is to be able to dispense with the explanation and discussion of certain things. (*WL*, II, 332).

In the summer of 1861 Wagner, who had been granted an amnesty in 1860, was able to attend the first Tonkünstler-Versammlung, held at Weimar. Liszt wrote to him: 'Your presence here, coming as it does at the end of my too much prolonged stay, will be a beautiful spiritual ray of sunlight . . . On 18 August I intend to leave Weimar for a longer period, and have made the necessary preparations for my removal . . . I want retirement and work above all' (*WL*, II, 339).

In 1863 Liszt's daughter Cosima, the wife of Hans von Bülow, decided to devote her life to Wagner. Towards the end of 1868 she left her husband and went to live with Wagner at Lucerne. On 1 January 1869 she started to keep a diary of her life with Wagner. The couple were married on 25 August 1870 in the Protestant church at Lucerne. Liszt learned of the wedding from the newspapers, and for two years held aloof from the household, even refusing to go to Bayreuth for the laying of the foundation stone in May 1872. In June he sent Cosima a copy of the score of *Christus*, which had just been published. Cosima recorded Wagner's reactions to the music in her diaries. On 7 June Wagner played passages from the work on the piano, and said: 'That one can so use the resources of a great and noble art to imitate the blubbering of priests, that is a sign of intellectual poverty' (*CWD*, 7 June 1872). Cosima adds: 'We deplore this development in my father, for which Princess W[ittgenstein] is certainly mainly to blame.' The following day she wrote: 'We talk again about *Christus*. "Fear of life after death [Wagner's words] places all such things as the *regnum coelorum* among the beatitudes. These people have never, either intuitively or consciously, grasped the ideality of time and space, which makes one aware that eternity and truth are always present"' (*CWD*, 8 June 1872). On 10 June: 'In the evening took up *Christus* again, with ever-mounting sorrow. A great talent has here been almost entirely destroyed' (*CWD*, 10 June 1872).

At the beginning of September Wagner and Cosima visited Liszt at Weimar. After this reunion, Liszt visited the Wagners in October, and during the visit played parts of *Christus*. Cosima wrote on 16 October: 'My father plays passages from his *Christus*, which certainly sounds different beneath his fingers' (*CWD*, 16 October 1872). Wagner and Cosima travelled to Weimar on 28 May 1873 to hear *Christus* conducted by Liszt himself the following day. Cosima described the performance:

# Weimar: Liszt, the Church and Wagner

During the very first bars R. said to me, 'He conducts splendidly, it will be magnificent.' It is a formulation of faith in the new church order, which dispenses with faith; the naive feeling of this highly unnaive creation; popular tendency toward pomp, although in the church this pomp is only a cruel net in which such feelings are trapped. The whole work thoroughly un-German, and only made possible by appealing to German sensibilities at their best; it could only be performed by Germans. R.'s reaction covers all extremes, from ravishment to immense indignation, in his attempt to do it both profound and loving justice.

(*CWD*, 29 May 1873)

The following day the Wagners returned home, and on 31 May Cosima wrote: 'I write to my father, telling him our feelings about *Christus* in detail, but I do not know if he will understand them properly' (*CWD*, 31 May 1873).

During Liszt's visit to the Wagner household in October 1872, Wagner had read aloud a sketch of the libretto of *Parsifal*. Liszt wrote to the Princess: 'The sketch of Wagner's *Parsifal* which he read to me recently bears the stamp of the purest Christian mysticism . . . I would even declare that several of our poets who are reputed to be religious and Catholic leave me with an impression far short of Wagner's religious feeling' (*Br.* VI, 368). When the Princess objected to *Parsifal* on the grounds that Wagner himself was not religious, and had made no secret of the fact, Liszt replied: 'My point of view remains unchanged – complete admiration, or excessive, if you like! *Parsifal* is more than a masterpiece – it is a revelation in musical drama . . . in *Parsifal* Wagner has gloriously depicted the highest canticle of divine love, insofar as the narrow limitations of the theatre permit' (*Br.* VII, 351).

Liszt's own musical path was determined in 1855, when he composed the *Gran Mass*, and moved away from the theatre. The same year he wrote:

If it be admitted that all the metaphysical arguments in support of the existence of God are reduced to nought by the reasonings of philosophy, there will always remain one which is invincible: affirmation by our cries to God, our need for Him, the yearning of our souls for His love. That is sufficient for me, and I need question it no further, remaining a believer until my dying breath. (*Br.* IV, 243)

# 5

# 1861: ROME, CARDINAL HOHENLOHE
# AND PRINCESS WITTGENSTEIN

I look forward greatly to learning when you are in Rome the details of the plan you have formed regarding religious music.          Hohenlohe to Liszt in 1859

In 1877 Princess Wittgenstein wrote:

I have dedicated my life to a man whom I consider a genius gifted with profound insight into his art. He has always been thought of . . . as a madman, a charlatan, a virtuoso practising his trade! For myself, I await patiently the time when he will be rendered justice . . . I myself have also been thought a fool for taking this man for a genius; but an era will come when all those who doubt will feel themselves elevated, ennobled, and touched in the depth of their souls by his works, which are noble, pure, and breathe eternity.          (*HSd*, 174)

Of Liszt the man, she wrote: 'Liszt is, above all else, the most noble-hearted, great soul that can possibly be imagined' (*SFL*, xvii).

Cosima Wagner described Liszt and the Princess thus:

In religion, which they both put above everything else, they differed in that the Princess, a fervent Catholic, adhered to the smallest external details of worship, believed in relics and miracles as much as in the dogma itself, not to mention her ardent proselytism, while Liszt, with a naïve and simple faith, confined his actual practice to attending Low Mass, and showed infinite tolerance towards other people's beliefs.          (*HSd*, 25)

There is, of course, no music at Low Mass, which is spoken. Liszt, who frequently voiced his disgust at Catholic church music, told the Princess that there may, at bottom, have been a musical reason for his limited church attendance: 'You know that in general my devotions do not go beyond Low Mass. Perhaps there is really a musical reason for that' (*Br.* IV, 96). In the same letter he describes his discomfort at having had to endure the dreadful music of the Weimar Catholic church for an hour on Palm Sunday.

In 1860 the Princess went to Rome, where she lived for the rest of her life. 'When she first settled in Rome,' remarked Adelheid von Schorn, 'she associated only with the *Black* party, that is to say those people in society who supported the Pope; but later she also saw *Whites* . . . these new associations were a sensitive issue in her relations with the Vatican.

## 1861: Rome, Cardinal Hohenlohe and Princess Wittgenstein

On this point she said: "I am riding two different saddles" ' (*SFL*, 238). The Princess at heart envisaged a fusion of Catholicism and republicanism – a vision which later gave rise to her 24-volume work *Causes intérieures de la faiblesse extérieure de l'Église en 1870*. In 1865 she wrote: 'Many believe that the Papacy is finished and that soon, very shortly, Rome will belong to those who do not wish to have anything to do with either the Roman Church, or Rome the holy city. I confess that, leaving aside my own involvement, I do not think it will happen' (*SFL*, 75). However, her fears increased in the autumn of 1870, after the outbreak of the Franco-Prussian war: 'Ah! how dreadful are the horrors of war ... The days of the Holy Father are numbered, and afterwards there will no doubt be stormy days here which no one will want to witness ... For myself, if I leave Italy my first journey will be to Weimar' (*SFL*, 166). However, things looked better by June 1871: 'Yesterday the Pope's 25th Jubilee was celebrated; tomorrow the King is to arrive and Rome will be celebrated as the capital of Italy. And so Providence *has seen fit to arrange everything for the best, in an unexpected manner*' (*SFL*, 169). The Princess remained in Rome, but, like Gregorovius, she felt its great days were over:

Ancient Rome, the city of desolate and majestic ruins, extolled by Byron as the Niobe of nations, is everyday passing further away, and will end by being gradually jolted into becoming a city like any other, its streets lined with fashionable shops and all the amenities of modern life which are to be found in Paris, New York, Berlin, or Rio de Janeiro! (*SFL*, 193)

In 1871 she declared her political affiliations: 'I am a supporter of the papal party, which in theory does not exclude republican opinions, but which renders them impossible in practice at present here, where the Italian government is itself seeking the support of the papal party against the republicans – who are considered as precursors of the *International*' (*Hsd*, 121). Years later she wrote: 'The upper classes are designated by God to preserve truth, beauty, and goodness in the world . . . One can well see that without religion we shall arrive at the Commune, as in France' (*SFL*, 309).

Soon after arriving in Rome, the Princess started writing. In 1860 her article on the Sistine Chapel was published. Gregorovius wrote: 'Princess Wittgenstein has written a description of the Sistine Chapel for the *Revue du Monde Catholique*; a brilliant article, genuine fireworks, like her conversation' (*GRJ*, 273). She enjoyed writing, as she told Adelheid von Schorn: 'I am so comfortable here, I am happy working in peace, living in this rich environment which provides so much nourishment for the mind and the soul . . . I see only interesting people, who come to Rome . . . ' (*SFL*, 91). Furthermore, she had no illusions about her talent:

You ask me what I am doing? I am writing . . . but having no artistic gift save for

49

the appreciation and love of art, and being in this respect outside the sphere of productivity and having no creative imagination, what I write is very dull and can find only a very few readers. I deal with morals, philosophy, and art criticism from the Catholic point of view.                                      (*SFL*, 98)

The list of her books runs to more than a dozen titles, and comprises 45 volumes, though they were never widely disseminated.[1] However, her ideas were given a posthumous lease of life by her friend Henri Lasserre, a French Catholic writer. One of her books, *Entretiens pratiques à l'usage des femmes du monde*, published privately in 1875, was reissued in a new form by Lasserre in 1895. After Lasserre's death, his biography was written by Étienne Laubarède,[2] and this was read by Princess Marie Hohenlohe, who asked Laubarède to continue Lasserre's work by further reworking the writings of her mother. The author agreed to do so, and his version of the Princess Wittgenstein's writings appeared under the title *La Vie chrétienne*, which ran into 20 editions by 1925. It included a preface by Henri Lasserre describing Carolyne Sayn-Wittgenstein as one of the greatest Catholic writers of her time.

For over a decade the Princess worked on her last book, *Causes intérieures de la faiblesse extérieure de l'Église en 1870*. Her ambition was to demonstrate that the Church had made a great historical error in failing to come to terms with, and take the leading rôle in, modern society. Her example was, of course, Lamennais; and that is why her books were eventually put on the Index in 1877 and 1879. Döllinger, the great Munich theologian, was sent copies, and said that to understand the work one would need the learning only to be acquired by someone who had studied in depth the history of the Church. Among some of the clergy, the Princess was in fact viewed with respect. The Bishop of Anthédon, Mgr Gay, wrote: 'The Princess Wittgenstein . . . is very interesting and erudite for a woman' (*HFL*, 215).

A longer opinion of her work was expressed by Émile Ollivier, Liszt's son-in-law, who wrote to the Princess:

I think you are very courageous. It is Lamennais' brand of Catholicism, and you will be put on the Index. You renew and give added strength to the liberal argument, but you go too far! Your conclusion is that the destruction of the temporal power is a good thing. The need, according to you, is for a spiritual '89 [i.e. 1789, the year of the French Revolution; *cf.* the similar ideas of Lamennais] . . . When we have finished with our earthly revolutions, the Church will commence with her own.                                                            (*HFL*, 276)

When in 1877 the threat of the Index proved imminent, Liszt wrote to Princess Marie Hohenlohe:

I wish now that . . . I hadn't neglected to warn her in time, several months before the start of the Council in 1869 . . . I wasn't able to combat her arguments, and I contented myself with the humble wish that I should like to see her wonderful

## 1861: Rome, Cardinal Hohenlohe and Princess Wittgenstein

intelligence and great knowledge employ themselves in less arduous regions than that of transcendental theology, and prophecies joined with disquisitions concerning the politics and administration of the Church. To my way of thinking, lay Catholics should have nothing to do with this . . . the wisest stand to take is the devoted conformity of silence. (*LMW*, 213)

Behind Liszt's avowal hovers a tacit agreement with the ideas of the Princess, if not with her diplomacy. Indeed, it is impossible to ignore the parallel between her literary work and what Liszt was striving to achieve in his church music. If anyone, throughout his musical life, had represented 'a spiritual '89', it was Liszt. The reason his music was rejected by the Church is largely the reason the Princess's books were put on the Index: Liszt's church works were too modern, too revolutionary. Furthermore, the only real link in the Princess's life between the ideas of Lamennais and her own ideas could have been the ideas of Liszt.

Liszt himself left no theoretical works expounding his ideas on music and the Church, as for example Wagner did on music and the theatre. Liszt's opinions have to be deduced from remarks made in letters, together with other pieces of circumstantial evidence. The Princess herself said she had drawn inspiration from the ideas of Liszt, as she acknowledged when she dedicated one of her books, *La Matière dans la dogmatique chrétienne*, to him:

It is to you, whose great soul, great heart and great spirit have seized with such rare perception the real point and vital nerve of the most sensitive questions which today centre round Christianity and non-belief, that I owe the fact that I have thought passionately about this subject . . . you have inspired in me a disinterested respect for and persevering love of work, not merely by what you have said, but by the shining example you have set me during the last 24 years.
(*Br.* VI, 293)

It should be remembered that Adelheid von Schorn, who knew both Liszt and the Princess, remarked: 'Intellectually the two were of such a similar nature that each complemented the other' (*SFL*, 58). In 1882 Liszt wrote to the Princess: 'Truly you stem from the line of St Augustine, St Bernard, St Thomas, St Theresa, St Catherine of Siena – and a little also of Joseph de Maistre; for, if I may say so, you share his militant sense of prophecy' (*HFL*, 281). On another occasion he wrote: 'I admire from the depths of my heart your grand militant spirit, which I follow timidly and not without a certain dread' (*HFL*, 278).

This 'grand militant spirit', together with a 'sense of prophecy', is found in *Christus*. The Princess wrote of the work:

*It is the glorious fulfilment of my heart.* For me, it is a work which the centuries have not seen the equal. Its hour has not yet come. It must rest yet awhile wrapped in obscurity. What greatness Liszt shows in his modesty with regard to it. Only

# Revolution and religion

I think that if someone voluntarily neglects himself, that is no reason for his friends to take the same attitude and contribute to his neglect.     (*SFL*, 200)

In 1874 she wrote: 'His genius is not yet understood – much less so than Wagner's, because Wagner represents a reaction for the present; but Liszt has thrown his spear much further into the future. Several generations will pass before he is really understood' (*SFL*, 212).

Of Wagner's *Parsifal*, the Princess wrote: 'I acknowledge that, thanks to his genius, he has in his music expressed religious feeling so well that the music might be used in any church. What more can I say?' (*Hsd*, 177). But in another letter she had a lot more to say:

It is natural that I disapprove of the theatrical action, not merely from a Catholic point of view, but . . . from that of all men who call themselves Christians. What is the purpose of all religion? . . . Is it not precisely to bring men nearer to their God through religious rites? You will never find a people who would have allowed their religious ceremonies to be seen on the stage . . . that has never existed on earth, because it can only diminish the religious rite. In the first instance, people take part in something *real*; in the other they see only make-believe, which nobody can take seriously . . . In *Parsifal*, there is no trace at all of God . . . only a parody!     (*SFL*, 417)

Liszt's biographers give the impression that in 1861, when Liszt went to Rome, he 'followed' the Princess Wittgenstein, who had left Weimar the previous year in order to obtain from the Pope an annulment of her marriage so that she could marry Liszt. Yet there is a strong possibility that when Liszt resigned his post at Weimar in 1858–9, he already intended to devote his best energies to the composition of religious works, and may even have had ideas about going to Rome. An examination of this episode in Liszt's life, largely neglected by the biographers, reveals that Liszt himself played a significant rôle in the Princess's attempts to secure a divorce, but only after the affair became ecclesiastical.

Princess Carolyne Sayn-Wittgenstein was born on 8 February 1819 into a Catholic family. Her father, Peter Iwanowsky, was an immensely rich landowner in the Polish Ukraine. On 7 May 1836 she married a German Lutheran, Prince Nicholas Sayn-Wittgenstein, aide-de-camp to the governor of Kiev. Their daughter Marie was born the following year. On the death of her father, Princess Wittgenstein inherited 14 estates, and became thereby an immensely wealthy woman. In 1847 she met Liszt, who had come to Kiev to give concerts. In September that year Liszt abandoned his virtuoso career, and stayed with the Princess at Woronince until January 1848, when he took up residence at Weimar as Grand Ducal Director of Music. In April the Princess left Russia, having liquidated enough of her property to raise three million roubles, met

# 1861: Rome, Cardinal Hohenlohe and Princess Wittgenstein

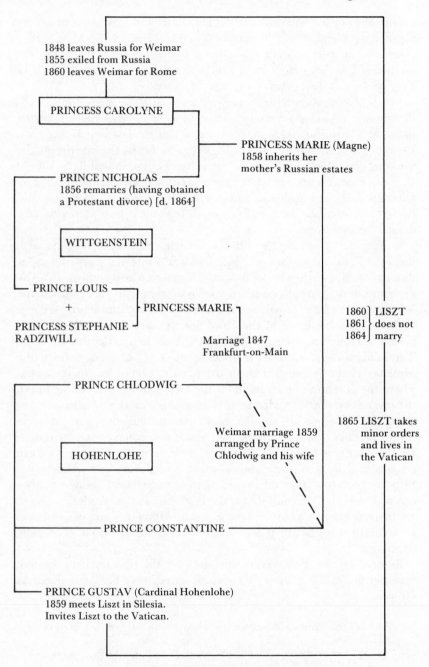

1848 leaves Russia for Weimar
1855 exiled from Russia
1860 leaves Weimar for Rome

PRINCESS CAROLYNE

PRINCESS MARIE (Magne)
1858 inherits her
mother's Russian estates

PRINCE NICHOLAS
1856 remarries (having obtained
a Protestant divorce) [d. 1864]

WITTGENSTEIN

PRINCE LOUIS
 +
PRINCESS STEPHANIE
RADZIWILL

PRINCESS MARIE

Marriage 1847
Frankfurt-on-Main

1860 ⎱ LISZT
1861 ⎬ does not
1864 ⎰ marry

PRINCE CHLODWIG

Weimar marriage 1859
arranged by Prince
Chlodwig and his wife

1865 LISZT takes
minor orders
and lives in
the Vatican

HOHENLOHE

PRINCE CONSTANTINE

PRINCE GUSTAV (Cardinal Hohenlohe)
1859 meets Liszt in Silesia.
Invites Liszt to the Vatican.

Figure 1. A chart showing Liszt's position in relation to the
Wittgenstein and Hohenlohe families

Liszt at the border, and travelled with him until June, when together they returned to Weimar. The Princess took up residence at the Altenburg, a property she rented from the Grand Duchess Maria Pavlovna, the mother of Liszt's patron Grand Duke Carl Alexander, and the sister of Tsar Nicholas I. Liszt moved into the Altenburg in 1849.

Before leaving Russia the Princess had left with the Metropolitan of St Petersburg a petition for the annulment of her marriage, alleging paternal constraint. This referred to a Polish custom of the time, whereby the bride's father struck his daughter across the face during the wedding ceremony in full view of the congregation, so that later, should she wish to seek a divorce, she could do so in a Roman court by alleging paternal constraint. At her wedding in 1836, the Princess's father had not failed to observe this custom. Even so, in 1848 the Princess's petition for divorce was refused.

In Russia at that time the ultimate decision in divorce cases lay with the Tsar. This was so for both Catholics and Protestants (as well as for those belonging to the Orthodox Church, of which he was the head). The decisions of the Catholic consistory were submitted to the Senate, to the Minister of the Interior, then to the Tsar, and theoretically to the Pope. However, the influence of the Holy See was practically nil; Catholic priests were nominated by and paid by the Tsar. In practice the will of the Tsar held law. Similarly the Protestant consistory was subordinate to the Minister of the Interior, then to the Senate, except in divorce cases, where the decision was reserved for the Minister of the Interior, and in the last resort, the Tsar. Hence the Tsar had absolute authority.

As a wealthy heiress, the Princess's petition for divorce centred on what should become of her property, and this may have been the reason for the Tsar's refusal. Also, Prince Nicholas enjoyed his wife's wealth only by marriage. A succession of legal wrangles ensued whereby the Princess tried to obtain a divorce and the Prince tried to obtain a property agreement. One solution for the Prince was to persuade his wife to settle her inheritance onto her daughter, and then to marry off the latter to a family with Wittgenstein connections. This is what eventually happened.

Before 1856 the affair was conducted by the Princess and her husband, together with their lawyers. Its various stages may be summarized as follows:

(1) In 1848 the Princess's petition for divorce was refused by the Russian authorities.
(2) In 1852 Prince Nicholas came to Weimar, and he and the Princess signed a protocol in the presence of their daughter Marie, Liszt and the Grand Chamberlain Baron Vitzthum. Under its terms, the daughter was placed under the protection of the Grand Duchess and inherited six-sevenths of

her mother's property. The Wittgenstein family consented to a divorce, but in the event of the Princess remarrying, the Prince should be entitled to a seventh share of the daughter's estates. However, the Princess later objected on the grounds that as the Catholic Church would not annul her marriage, the Prince had no right to claim any of her property.

(3)    The Prince summoned his wife back to Russia and received a refusal from her, saying that 'having decided to ask for a divorce and having the intention of marrying the musician Liszt, she wished to devolve her inherited property onto her daughter, reserving to herself enjoyment for life of its profits' (HFL, 175). The Russian Minister of Justice then proposed on 26 January 1854 that the full rigour of the law be applied to the Princess, and her estates be sequestered. She and her daughter were to receive an annuity of 15,000 roubles from their revenues. The daughter, thanks to the intervention of the Grand Duchess, could stay with her mother until her eighteenth birthday, which fell on 18 February 1855.

(4)    When she was 18 a marriage was proposed with Baron Talleyrand, French Minister at Weimar. The Princess asked the Tsar to return her estates to her daughter, which the Tsar agreed to do, allowing the Princess to settle her debts out of the daughter's estates. A marriage contract was drawn up, but the Princess meanwhile learned that the new Tsar, Alexander II, had condemned her to exile. She then opposed the marriage of her daughter, and instead the property was put in trust, the daughter receiving an annual income of 75,000 roubles until the age of 21.

(5)    In January 1856 Prince Nicholas, knowing that his daughter would inherit the Russian estates, obtained a Protestant divorce and remarried, but the marriage was not published. Not until 1861 did the divorce appear in the Almanac de Gotha, and then without any mention of a further marriage on the part of the Prince.

Thus in 1856 the only remaining obstacle to the Princess marrying Liszt was the Roman Catholic Church. Liszt now entered the fray with a letter to the Grand Duchess dated 6 May 1856:

Madame,
Whilst having forborne for several years to draw the attention of your Royal Highness to the constant thought of my life, the enduring and unchangeable wish of my soul, the destiny which I have it in my heart to accomplish, I venture to hope, however, that this silence demanded of me has not been wrongly interpreted by you, Madame, and that you have always judged me for what I am: simple, straightforward, and ardently devoted to what I consider to be the supreme goal of my existence. Deign to forgive me then if today I wish to recall to the memory of your Imperial Highness a passage in the letter of H.R.I. the Prince of Oldenburg, in which is announced the decree of the Imperial Council condemning Madame the Princess Carolyne Sayn-Wittgenstein to exile from Russian territory, and the deprivation of her estates. This letter, which your Royal Highness authorized M. de Maltitz [Russian chargé d'affaires at Weimar] to communicate to Madame the Princess Sayn-Wittgenstein, ends with these words: 'Regarding the divorce, I think it will be easier because, according to Russian law, exile and the loss of political rights dissolve the marriage.'
May I be permitted to ask your Royal Highness to have the grace to let me

know how and by what means it might be possible to pursue this matter, which is already much advanced, with antecedent decrees favourable to the Princess from the Russian Catholic consistories? At the same time I venture to place at the feet of your Royal Highness the entreaty of assisting, by your all-powerful intervention, in the settling of the local debt contracted by the Princess Sayn-Wittgenstein during the years preceding the decree with which she has been smitten, that is to say, to see that this sum soon be paid out of her fortune which, by imperial decision, has returned to her daughter.                (*HFL*, 177)

Earlier it had been suggested that Liszt and the Princess change their religion to facilitate marriage, but as early as 1848 Liszt had opposed the idea: 'We'll have to see how it works out. The Princess is bound on all sides in Russia, and they always forget here in Weimar that we are not Protestants, and we wouldn't dream, either of us, of a conversion' (*LZB*, 350). Later in 1860, when the Princess was bound on only one side in Russia, the religious side, Liszt insisted even more strongly that the marriage was a religious question:

The Grand Duchess . . . has not yet rid herself of her old mistaken notions regarding the manner of our marriage – and even though no longer insisting on the need to change religion, she admits that the sacrament administered by a Protestant priest would suffice – if it is the case that we should prefer not to limit ourselves simply to the State register. To suppositions of this nature only the strongest denials can be opposed. I did not fail in this respect, as you can well imagine.
(*Br.* V, 79)

Liszt's first involvement in the affair was to ask the Grand Duchess to use her influence with the Russian Catholic authorities. It was thus Liszt, and not the Princess, who made of the marriage an affair of the utmost seriousness, and took the matter to the highest religious authority, when even the Weimar Ducal family were suggesting acceptable alternatives to bring about their marriage.

Shortly after writing this letter to the Grand Duchess, Liszt travelled to Hungary in August 1856 to conduct the first performance of his *Missa solennis* at Esztergom. In September he wrote of his ambitions as a composer of church music: 'I am fully confident that in three years I shall have entirely taken possession of the spiritual domain of church music which for 20 years has been occupied solely by dozens of mediocrities' (*Br.* III, 51). In June 1857 the Franciscans at Pest made Liszt an honorary member of the brotherhood, although Liszt did not attend a ceremony to confirm this until April 1858. In 1857 the Princess wrote to Georg and Emma Herwegh: 'In Zürich you will also have heard . . . about Liszt's affiliation to the Franciscan Order. But you surely will not have thought that our marriage might be prevented by these spiritual reasons. Ah! no, it is still very much the temporal power which is involved!' (*Hsd*, 87).

In February 1858 Princess Marie had her twenty-first birthday, when according to the 1855 agreement her income came to an end, and she inherited the estates put in trust for her. Suddenly the Princess was no longer a wealthy woman. Suddenly Princess Marie became an important person with regard to whom she might be married. Suddenly the reason for Liszt prolonging his stay in Weimar as the Princess's consort had come to an end, as had the income that paid for the running of the Alten-burg. Liszt probably began to look for an opportunity to resign.

On 25 June Liszt drafted a letter which he persuaded the Grand Duke Carl Alexander to send to the Tsar:

Here, Monseigneur, is the substance of what the paragraph concerning myself should contain.

'My affectionate interest in Liszt having not diminished, but grown during the 18 years that he has been in the service of my household, I wish to give him a testimonial of the affection which his loyal conduct and attachment to my person have inspired, by at last regularizing his position at Weimar through his marriage with the Princess Wittgenstein. The marriage will become a simple and easy matter the moment you come, like myself, to cast a favourable eye upon it. To bring it to a conclusion it is only a question of lifting the inconsistent instructions given over the affair of the divorce of the Princess. In those which affect her, there is every reason to fear offending the authorities by assuming they conform impartially to the wishes of the Princess Wittgenstein, which are all the more legitimate now that Prince Wittgenstein, to whom she was married, has contracted a second marriage three years ago. I am expressing to you (adverb of Monseigneur's choice) my personal desire in entreating you to be favourably disposed towards this matter, so that measures may be taken in order that this case, at present entrusted to one of the Princess's lawyers, shall obtain from the Pope the instruction to the Metropolitan of St Petersburg to have her divorce revised.'

(*HFL*, 178)

The last words of this letter reveal that it was Liszt who caused the affair to reach the Vatican. The same year, on 15 December, Liszt conducted Cornelius's opera *The Barber of Baghdad*, which produced a riot in the theatre. The biographers say he resigned, but his first letter to the Grand Duke explaining his intentions was written in February 1859. A second letter followed in 1860. In the 1859 letter Liszt gives several clues to his state of mind at the time. The most revealing ones touch on his musical ambitions.

Monseigneur,
Your Royal Highness having not only asked me, but ordered me, to outline from this moment the conditions upon which the efficacy of my cooperation in his theatre depends, I obey as his servant, without being able to stop myself from adding that I am acting against both my wishes and my personal interests . . .

The few savings that I owe to my former successes will be enough for me to spend a couple of years in retirement where I can devote myself without trouble, without daily vexations, without the need of involving myself in local affairs, to the completion of several works which demand quiet contemplation and peace of mind . . .

# Revolution and religion

By continuing in office, Monseigneur, I would be giving you what no amount of money can compensate for, my time . . . The operas of Wagner [Liszt's period of activity at Weimar coincided, of course, with that of Wagner's political exile from Germany (1849–60)] already accepted in the repertoire (thanks to her Royal Highness, who accorded me the protection and support I needed, and which I will never forget) . . . have, however, no further need of me.     (*LCA*, 66–71)

The 'several works' which Liszt had been trying to find the time to compose included *St Elizabeth* and *Christus*.

The same month as this letter, Liszt met Prince Viktor Hohenlohe, Duke of Ratibor, who invited him to his estate at Rauden. The Duke's brothers included Prince Constantine, who married the Princess's daughter later that year, Prince Gustav (the future Cardinal) and Prince Chlodwig, who was Prime Minister of Bavaria at the time of Wagner's involvement with Ludwig II, and in 1894 became Chancellor of Germany. In 1847 he had married the daughter of Prince Louis Wittgenstein, the elder brother of the Princess's husband. At Rauden, Liszt met Prince Gustav, at that time Papal Chamberlain, and through him sent luxuriously bound copies of his *Missa solennis* to the Papal Secretary Cardinal Antonelli and to the Pope. In April he thanked Carl Alexander for 'that efficacious support which will remove obstacles that do not stem from theological scruples as people imagine, but very much from the passions and ways of the world, which consequently are anti-Christian' (*HFL*, 183). The same month Liszt received the Order of the Iron Crown, and was later raised to the Austrian nobility. On 24 April he wrote to the Princess:

The very serious rumours of war made me a little afraid that Prince Constantine might find himself prevented from keeping his promise. His presence alone at Munich is a sign that his heart lies in according these preliminaries some importance. I charge Magne [the Princess's daughter] with finding the best moment to tell him how much I am personally indebted and grateful to him for the part he took regarding my iron crown.     (*Br.* IV, 463)

The 'preliminaries' refer to the wedding of Prince Constantine and Princess Marie Wittgenstein, which was already being planned.

Meanwhile the Princess was being pushed into an increasingly isolated position. In June, the Grand Duchess, Liszt's protectress and owner of the Altenburg, died. The same summer one of the managers of the Russian estates, named Okraszevsky, came to Weimar. Okraszevsky

informed the Princess Sayn-Wittgenstein, in confidence, that the Bishops of Vilna and Kamenec believed the divorce possible with the sacrifice of a considerable amount of money. It was understood that Rome should be approached first, where matters are often dealt with more easily. The latest concordats include less rigorous rules. Unfortunately the Princess persists in not wanting to solicit Rome.     (*HFL*, 180)

# 1861: Rome, Cardinal Hohenlohe and Princess Wittgenstein

However somebody, presumably Liszt, changed the Princess's mind, and she told her daughter to pay Okraszevsky. Princess Marie wrote to M. Maltitz on 15 July 1859:

Your Excellency . . . I here express to you again my firm and unalterable resolution to conclude a contract with M. Okraszevsky whereby I undertake to pay him the sum of 70,000 silver roubles if he obtains the canonic divorce of my mother, the Princess Carolyne Sayn-Wittgenstein. I am hereby obeying my filial duty and in so doing am using rights which have been conferred upon me by law.

(*HFL*, 180)

The same month, Liszt had taken the opportunity to enlist the support of Carl Alexander's influence at Rome. Attached to Liszt's letter to him written on 8 July 1859 was a list of reasons why the Pope should be sympathetic towards Liszt as a religious artist and a champion of the Catholic Church:

Monseigneur,
You have been kind enough to tell me more than once that you would not refuse to lend me your support at Rome. A situation has arisen in which I come to have recourse to this promised protection. M. Okraszevsky, of whom Your Royal Highness will perhaps have heard spoken, has just brought the Princess Sayn-Wittgenstein a resolution from the Archbishop Metropolitan of St Petersburg concerning her divorce, according to which M. Okraszevsky must go to Rome to obtain the order whereby this case be taken up again, revised in Russia, and judged anew by his Grace the Metropolitan. This involves the court of Rome in hardly any liability, and it is to be hoped that the order can be granted without difficulty. Nevertheless, M. Okraszevsky cannot go to a foreign country with any hope of success in an affair of this importance unless equipped with a high recommendation. The petition he will present in the name of the Princess will be addressed to the 'Commission for Requests', presided over by Cardinal Antonelli.
    If Your Royal Highness deigned to promise to see me tomorrow or later, I would be in a position to explain verbally why it is urgent that M. Okraszevsky leaves as soon as possible, without losing a minute of time.

By way of claims to the particularly kind consideration of His Holiness on behalf of M. Liszt, one might point out: the number of donations made by Liszt to Catholic churches and religious foundations in all countries. The concerts given in Berlin and Cologne for the benefit of Cologne Cathedral, at Pest for the building of the Leopold church, at Brussels for the reconstruction of the Mont-Carmel church, etc., produced the sum of more than 8,000 écus, not counting a sum, at least as large, distributed by him to various charitable institutions, hospitals, nurseries, and other charitable works. M. Liszt was elected in 1841 an honorary member of the chief committee of Cologne Cathedral, an exceptional distinction at that time when the committee consisted of only a few members, and in 1857 the Franciscan monastery at Pest admitted him to the brotherhood, as attested by the enclosed document. (*HFL*, 183)

On 3 September Liszt wrote to Hohenlohe in Rome and received the following reply dated 28 September 1859:

# Revolution and religion

Sir,

If the few moments I had the pleasure of spending with you at Rauden with my brother Viktor have left memories of the most pleasant nature, which are still with me, then it was a real joy for me to receive your letter of 3 September from Weimar. However, before replying, it was incumbent upon me to communicate that letter, worthy of a true Catholic, to our Holy Father, and indeed yesterday I read to His Holiness your fervently expressed lines, which deeply moved his heart. I will quote to you the words of the Holy Father:

'In the midst of so many troubles it is a real consolation to hear these fine and truly Christian sentiments ("ces beaux sentiments de *vero christiano*"). Tell M. Liszt that I send him my blessing and that I have given his celebrated Mass to the Chapter of St Peter. Tell him also that it will be sung in the month of November at St Peter's, "in Die Dedicationis Basilicae S.S. Apostolorum Petri et Pauli", and that I shall be present. This Mass may not be able to produce the immense effect that it has elsewhere because we do not have instruments at St Peter's, but without doubt it will still be really beautiful, and I am very much looking forward to hearing it.'

The Lord has called you to glorify His name in the heavenly medium of sacred song, as do the Angels who glorify God with their Hosannah.

Nowadays opinions are much divided regarding sacred music and it is for your genius to decide the form it must take from now onwards. Your inspirations, which guide you by the grace of God, will be its soul, the delights of the faithful, a vigorous weapon to bring back the prodigal sons to our Holy Mother Church. I look forward greatly to learning when you are in Rome the details of the plan you have formed regarding religious music, and I offer you from this very moment, most sincerely, a modest abode with me in the Vatican, and I shall be happy to express to you personally that I am, Sir, with the very highest consideration, your very devoted servant.     Gustav Hohenlohe, Archbishop of Edessa.

(*HFL*, 181)

The words 'when you are in Rome' are evidence that Liszt had already spoken of his intention to go there. Now, in September 1859, Liszt had an invitation to go not only to Rome, but to the Vatican. Did the Princess know of this?

The wedding of Prince Constantine Hohenlohe and the Princess's daughter took place in Weimar on 15 October 1859, and the couple went to live in Vienna. The Prince was aide-de-camp to the Austrian Emperor, and the marriage was arranged by Prince Chlodwig Hohenlohe and his wife Princess Marie, née Wittgenstein. We know this from the memoirs of Prince Chlodwig, which contain a letter from the Princess's daughter: 'He [Chlodwig] devoted himself with fatherly care to his youngest brother, Constantine, who was hardly more than a boy at the death of their beloved mother. He and his wife arranged our marriage, and Marie was delighted to have a cousin in the intimate family circle.'[3] Not only had Prince Chlodwig's wife acquired a cousin for her brother-in-law's wife – she had gained access to the Princess Wittgenstein's Russian estates, which, through the marriage, also became part of the 'intimate family circle'. The marriage of the Princess's daughter, who henceforth became Princess Marie Hohenlohe, was an 'arranged' marriage; it brought back the wealth of the Princess Wittgenstein within the orbit of the Hohenlohe–Wittgenstein family connection. Any further objections to Liszt marrying the Princess were not likely to emanate from Prince Nicholas, or any other member of his family.

Immediately, Liszt began to find reasons for leaving Weimar. In December he wrote to Carl Alexander: 'I foresee that, in spite of the pain that separation from you will cause, Monseigneur, I must as soon as possible look for a life away from Weimar' (*LCA*, 84). He did not, however, mention Rome. Even as late as 1861, he continued to give the impression that his future was uncertain.

In the spring of 1860, Okraszevsky, having been successful in Rome and having returned to Russia, brought to Weimar the degree of annulment from the Archbishop of St Petersburg. Armed with this, the Princess herself left for Rome on 17 May, expecting to return to Weimar soon for the marriage. However, her petition was subject to endless delays, even though she gained more than one audience with the Pope. Liszt asked Carl Alexander to write to Cardinal Antonelli, which produced a favourable response, whereupon he again asked him to intervene by speaking to the Tsar a few words 'whose effect on the Russian Ambassador at Rome, who exercises considerable influence in this matter specially under his jurisdiction, ensuing straight from the St Petersburg decree, would be extremely decisive' (*LCA*, 97). Carl Alexander, during a visit to Russia, obliged this request. In September the affair was to be considered by the College of Cardinals. Before their verdict was known, Liszt wrote his Testament on 14 September 1860. In it, he betrays a very complex state of mind. Later he wrote: '14 September, the feast of the raising of the Cross, is a day when I think most about my inner life. My Weimar Testament was written on 14 Sept.' (*Br.* VI, 186). The document originated in the form of a Will deposited on 24 April and revoked on 15 August, when Liszt rewrote it as his Testament. Most of his property is left by him to the Princess, as might be expected. The opening lines, however, are of a personal nature:

I am writing this down on the 14th September, the day on which the Church celebrates the Festival of the Holy Cross. The denomination of this festival is also that of the glowing and mysterious feeling which has pierced my entire life as with a sacred wound.

Yes, 'Jesus Christ on the Cross', a yearning longing after the Cross and the raising of the Cross, – this was ever my true inner calling; I have felt it in my innermost heart ever since my seventeenth year, in which I implored with humility and tears that I might be permitted to enter the Paris Seminary.

(*L*, I, 439)

On 22 September the College of Cardinals decided in the Princess's favour, and a wedding should have been arranged to take place in

# Revolution and religion

Weimar. However, objections were raised. According to Princess Marie Hohenlohe:

Cardinal de Lucca, the nuncio at Vienna, received the instruction to authorize the Bishop of Fulda, whose diocese included Weimar, to allow my mother to remarry. The nuncio and the Bishop together put up a violent opposition. So once more the Pope was solicited. Liszt went to Vienna where just at that time my brother-in-law Monsignor Gustav was staying, who received Liszt very warmly, as did the nuncio. But Liszt did not attempt to change the nuncio's mind.[4]

This version must be compared with Liszt's own, given to the Princess in his letters. On 8 October he wrote:

Since the letters of 9–14 [September], I have received only the welcome lines of 22 September in which you tell me the decision of the Council, and now today comes your letter of 1 October . . . This morning I telegraphed you to ask you to stay in Rome – and to tell me if there is any possibility that I might join you there, never to be apart again. Whilst I know that anything you do will be for the best, and whilst I unreservedly and lovingly yield to it, I wish however to point out to you that Rome seemed to me much preferable to any other place for us at the moment; if only to spend just the whole winter there, during which I would like to collect my thoughts, pray, and, by the grace of our Saviour Jesus Christ, be spiritually renewed. You know that for me this is no empty notion, but really the aspiration and devouring need of my whole life. If it is possible, try to arrange it that we are together again in Rome . . .

Okraszevsky has sent me this telegram from Milan, which arrived yesterday evening . . . 'The Princess has completely won. I am going to Vienna, then to Fulda and Weimar. Do not worry, she is in good health.' I have replied to this by telegram to Magne: 'I venture to ask you to instruct Okraszevsky to call first at Weimar as I wish to go with him to Fulda.' . . . At Fulda I will follow your instructions word for word, and will acquire the necessary papers.     (Br. V, 72)

From Vienna Liszt wrote to the Princess on 17 October:

After arriving on Tuesday morning, I wrote immediately to Mgr Gustav asking for an audience. Mgr Gustav received me at 2 o'clock, and our interview lasted about an hour. He will not alter his arguments. You already know the incredible rigmarole that I had to listen to without protest.

Yesterday morning, I attended a Mass said especially for me by Mgr Gustav at 9 o'clock in the nuncio's chapel. There was nobody but myself in the chapel, attached to the nuncio's apartments. I saw Mgr Gustav again today at 2 o'clock. Princess Catherine told him that His Holiness had said to her regarding the decision of the Council: 'È una opinione, non è un giudizio.' [It is an opinion, not a verdict.] During my interview with Mgr de Lucca, Archbishop of Tarsus, who remembered me from former times, I strongly emphasized your Catholic conscience, and the numerous proofs you have given thereof. On the other hand, I also attempted to suggest that things might not go so easily as the opposition party perhaps imagine – that in any case there would be a very big scandal, and it is my duty to try and prevent it, if at all possible.     (Br. V, 77)

In this letter Liszt claims that Hohenlohe argued against the marriage, even though he is not pinpointed as the actual source of the opposition.

# 1861: Rome, Cardinal Hohenlohe and Princess Wittgenstein

Yet Liszt was inconsistent on the matter, as he later, according to La Mara, told the Princess that Hohenlohe was not hostile to the marriage (see *Br.* V, 120n). Even so, the Princess for many years remained convinced that Hohenlohe was the source of all her troubles. Whatever the real source of the opposition, it served to prevent a wedding taking place in Weimar in October 1860.

Between October 1860 and October 1861, Liszt devoted himself to winding up his affairs at Weimar and preparing to start a new period of his life, which he envisaged as being devoted chiefly to composition. A visit to Paris was planned for the beginning of 1861, Liszt having been made Officier de la Légion d'Honneur in August 1860. Plans were made in December 1860 to hold the first Tonkünstler-Versammlung at Weimar in August the following year. As Liszt wished to be present, he decided to leave Weimar for Rome in late August 1861, but told the Princess that he would keep this a secret. Officially, he appeared to be leaving his arrangements open-ended. For a time, Florence was spoken of between Liszt and the Princess as the preferred place for the wedding, but Liszt left the arrangements to the Princess. He himself had to obtain certain documents, as he told the Princess on 26 February 1861:

The necessary papers . . . are: the authentication of bachelorhood of one of the contracting parties by means of a certificate issued upon personal and verbal declaration. In German this is called *Ledigkeitszeugniss*. Civil permission is given by a *Trauschein*. The first certificate is issued by the parish priest. Afterwards, the burgomaster gives the second one, the *Trauschein*. (*Br.* V, 134)

Liszt obtained these documents in August.

At the beginning of 1861, he told the Princess:

I shall arrange somehow to spend the spring either at Fontainebleau, or perhaps at St Tropez in Ollivier's little home, which would bring me nearer to Rome. There I shall live alone with music paper and several books. Beforehand it is my heartfelt wish to pay my respects to Paris, and thus to belong to you still more completely in God. (*Br.* V, 122)

On 31 March he described how the Grand Duke lost patience with the situation:

Then he came back for the twentieth time to the question of whether there weren't any means of finding a priest who would put an end to this strange situation, since everything was sorted out, judged to be in order, and settled. 'That would be very dangerous,' I told him. 'But what would happen?' he asked. 'We must wait.' (*Br.* V, 148)

Liszt also refused the offer made by the Duke of a castle to stay in, telling the Princess that he wished to live in Rome in peace and solitude. On 16 April he complained about the expense of keeping up the Altenburg:

It is absurd from every point of view to keep up so many expenses with such slender means – It cannot go on this way, and if I had been able to foresee that things would have gone on for so long, I would have moved somewhere else six months ago, where half the amount spent here would easily have been enough.

(*Br.* V, 155)

In May Liszt went to Paris. From there on 12 May he wrote: 'All I desire and hope for is to settle down in Rome – for as long as possible' (*Br.* V, 167). On 16 May he wrote:

Antonelli would be mistaken if he thought that I would not appreciate what Rome offers . . . My task from now on shall consist in writing things which have some value – and not to parade them personally in the market places of Germany or France. The modest celebrity attached to my name will ensure that they do not pass completely unnoticed. To cite only one small instance in support of this opinion, I know that Verdi has several of my scores on his desk, at Genoa. I am even assured that he speaks of them with particular esteem. Rome will suit me therefore much better than any other city, from the moment you like the idea.

(*Br.* V, 168)

Back in Weimar, the Grand Duchess (after the death of Maria Pavlovna, now Princess Sophie, the wife of Carl Alexander), finding Liszt's replies to her questions evasive, demanded to know his plans:

As the Grand Duchess did not find my explanations clear enough, I summed up the situation more or less like this: 'From 1848 until the time of the marriage of Princess Marie in '59, it was she who formed the centre of gravity, the *Schwerpunkt* of our whole position. What would happen to her in the present and in the future necessarily became of first importance for us. Since then, my centre of gravity, without exactly changing, can only be Princess Carolyne. Therefore I have only her to consider above and before everything, and her alone. I know that she follows me blindly with such affection and devotion that there can be no question of any sacrifice between her and myself. It is by my wish that she has stayed in Rome until now – and will probably stay there some time longer. However, the time may come when I have to tell her to leave Rome . . . The obstacles that are put in the way of our marriage may go on for ever. I no longer think we can count on a favourable solution to our destiny.'

(*Br.* V, 100)

The following September, however, a 'favourable solution' was found: 'After a winter of uncertainty,' wrote Princess Marie, 'the Council of Cardinals of the Sacred College, convened during the summer of 1861, reaffirmed its decision in favour of Carolyne. The nuncio and the Bishop of Fulda were obliged to concur.'[5] Having already decided to leave Weimar, Liszt wrote to the Princess on 6 July:

What happens on 15 August depends entirely on the news I receive from you. In any case I am leaving Weimar. I have spoken of St Tropez, to name somewhere in accordance with my economic needs . . . It does not suit me to wrap things in mystery where their Highnesses are concerned, to whom however I cannot speak too directly about you.

(*Br.* V, 200)

On 17 August Liszt left Weimar and travelled to Löwenberg, and on 28 August told the Princess to instruct him whether or not to come to

# 1861: Rome, Cardinal Hohenlohe and Princess Wittgenstein

Rome, advising her on this point as on all others to follow the advice of Antonelli. On 16 September he gave his opinion as to whether 22 October, his fiftieth birthday, would be a suitable date for the wedding, and on 29 September told her to arrange everything necessary for that day. An undated letter from the Princess preserved in the Liszt Museum at Weimar says:

> At last! At last! At last! That is all my heart can exclaim at this supreme moment. It leaps, it bounds before you. In the meantime I am sending you Vincent with a passport which will avoid you any troubles at the customs ... he has prepared an apartment for you in the Via dei Fiori. What a strange coincidence, as it is in that street that you lived before [with the Comtesse d'Agoult in 1839]. Another coincidence. The lofty souls come together, and as a result of their uniting we are doing what you said we would, we are staying together in Rome quite simply.
>
> (*HFL*, 192)

On 4 October Liszt wrote: 'I am also happy at the coincidence by which the church in your parish is dedicated to your patron saint, St Charles. After him, it is indeed Antonelli who is our great patron in Rome' (*Br.* V, 235). Liszt arranged to sail from Marseilles on 17 October. On 12 October he assured the Princess: 'As for Blandine, Cosette and everybody else, they think that I am undecided in my plans, which will be finalized only later' (*Br.* V, 237). Another letter from the Princess preserved in the Liszt Museum reads:

> I have spoken to the priest. He will be ready to marry us on Tuesday at 9 o'clock in the morning at the altar of St Charles. 14 years of waiting. But what woman wants God also wants. I have had the luck to find a most comfortable apartment; by taking it for a year, we can economize quite considerably. I haven't decided on it. But I suggest it to you as worth considering. We can do without it until 1 November, and in the meantime I could stay with you in your little apartment in the Via Fiori. But tomorrow I shall wait for you in the Piazza di Spagna.
>
> (*HFL*, 193)

Liszt arrived in Rome probably on 19 October, and at midnight on 21 October the wedding was abruptly cancelled. The messenger who brought the news was sent by Cardinal Antonelli.

So ends the affair; or rather, not quite. The Princess drafted a Will dated Rome, 23 October 1861, the day after the wedding should have taken place. In it, she refers to Liszt as her husband:

> Je dispose . . . en toute conscience et liberté légale du peu que je possède maintenant en objets mobiliers . . . en faveur de mon mari, Mr. François Liszt, que j'institue mon légataire universel et mon exécuteur testamentaire.

The document is signed 'Carolyne Liszt'.[6] In it, the Princess speaks of Liszt's Weimar Testament, and in the event of Liszt dying before herself, leaves her possessions to her daughter.

Who was responsible for the cancellation? According to Liszt's own

# Revolution and religion

version of the story, given to August Göllerich,

> To prevent the fiancée from committing perjury [by claiming she was forced to marry against her will], the Princess Odescalchi [a relative of the Princess living in Rome] hurried to the Vatican . . . and obtained the adjournment of the marriage. During the night of 21 October, a messenger from Cardinal Antonelli came to the Princess and gave her a message according to which the Pope withdrew his permission and demanded that the dossier of the process of annulment be re-examined.[7]

However, a descendant of Liszt has said that 'according to Vatican records, no last-minute objection had ever been lodged, and would not have been, since from the Vatican point of view, everything was then in order'.[8] If this is the case, then the legend of the Pope's dramatic intervention at the last minute has no basis in fact. Either Liszt was told the story and believed it, or he invented the story himself. This latter view seems to be supported by a remark made by Adelheid von Schorn, who knew the Princess in Weimar, and later visited her in Rome. There she made the acquaintance of Cardinal Antonelli, and later wrote: 'Antonelli, as I later found out, would have found nothing incorrect in the accomplishment of the marriage with Liszt, but he regarded it as pointless' (*SFL*, 242). Who, then, prompted him to send a messenger on 21 October 1861?

Another question remains: why was the wedding cancelled? A search for motives on the part of those involved leads to either the Hohenlohe family, or Liszt himself. The Wittgenstein family would by now have had no objections; and the Tsar, once the question of the property had been resolved, would not have been called upon to exercise any influence. But the Hohenlohes, if they wished to be the inheritors of Liszt's estate through the Princess's daughter, may have tried to postpone the marriage until the Princess was past the age of child-bearing; in 1861 she was still only 42. Also, if the 1852 agreement still held, then Prince Nicholas would acquire a small portion of the Russian estates when the Princess remarried, and these estates were now in the hands of the Hohenlohes – although doubtless the connection between the two families by marriage would lessen the objections to this happening.

Finally, there is Liszt himself. If he had wished to, he had ample means at his disposal for organizing a cancellation whose actual source would remain forever unknown. He was the friend of both Hohenlohe and later Antonelli. He had been in contact with the Vatican since 1859, when he had received an invitation to go to Rome. After his resignation at Weimar, Liszt said the opposition to the marriage emanated from a 'secret and evil power' (*LCA*, 84). After the cancellation, he moved into the Via Felice and seemed quite undisturbed by the dramatic dénouement to years of waiting. On Christmas Day 1861 he wrote to Blandine: 'My life here is quieter, more harmonious and better organized than in Germany. Also, I am hoping that my work will derive some benefit and be successfully accomplished.'[9]

In 1864 Prince Nicholas Wittgenstein died, and the Princess was free to marry. Liszt paid a visit to Weimar, where Carl Alexander asked him about the change in his situation. Liszt reported his reply to the Princess:

Up till then I had not spoken about the situation as it now stands, and I very much counted on not breaking this silence from now on. Regarding the question of my position and where I live, there is no occasion to be troubled by it any more: everything I could wish for being contained in my inkstand, and the inkstand being where it could not be better placed, in the custody of the *Madonna del Rosario* at Rome.                                    (*Br.* VI, 55)

Liszt's final word on the marriage came on 31 March 1865 to Carl Alexander at Weimar:

The duration and the consequence of certain exceptional feelings do not at all depend on this or that external outcome. 'The heart has its reasons of which reason itself understands nothing.' Thus it is these reasons of the heart which have been, and always will be, supremely decisive for me.          (*LCA*, 128)

Less than four weeks later, Liszt received the tonsure at the hands of Mgr Hohenlohe, and took up residence in the Vatican.

Liszt could not have married and then taken minor orders. The fact that he could leave the Church afterwards is irrelevant. The post of *maestro di capella* at St Peter's was not given to laymen. Palestrina, for example, was debarred from the post on this account. In the nineteenth century it was generally considered that those who received minor orders were contemplating the priesthood. It was even possible to advance in the Church without passing through the intermediate stages. Cardinal Antonelli, for example, was the last Cardinal not to have been made a priest; he was only possessed of deacon's orders. The news of Liszt's entry into the Church took the world by surprise; it seemed a sudden and unexpected change of direction. But Liszt wrote afterwards to Agnes Klindworth: 'I think you will hardly be surprised by the carrying out of a resolution already made some time ago, but about which I preferred to inform only the three absolutely indispensable people a few days before-hand' (*Br.* III, 180).

Exactly how long 'some time ago' was can only be a matter of con-jecture. It is worth remembering that Liszt first determined on the idea of an oratorio on Christ in 1853, and the greater part of it was composed after he had entered the Church – in 1865 and 1866. He called the work 'my musical will and testament'.[10] In Liszt's mind, *Christus* was the climax of his career as a composer. In 1861 he could not know that he would live another quarter of a century and enter another remarkable period of composition.

We know that in 1859 Liszt told Hohenlohe of his plan to reform religious music, and that he received an invitation to go to Rome. We know that the Princess left for Rome in 1860 initially against her will. We know that the opposition to a wedding in Weimar in 1860 involved Hohenlohe, whom Liszt travelled to Vienna to see, and that Liszt told the Princess to stay in Rome. After settling in Rome, Liszt chose not to marry in 1864, presumably because he intended taking minor orders. For the last third of his life, one of Liszt's closest friends was probably Cardinal Hohenlohe, who had proprietorship of the Villa d'Este, where Liszt, thanks to the Cardinal's patronage, was able to retire annually and compose. The pattern is clear. Is it satisfactory to assume that the cancellation of the wedding in 1861 was merely fortuitous?

# 6

## 1865: MINOR ORDERS

My stay in Rome is not an accidental one.                    Liszt in 1863

If Liszt had an ulterior motive for taking minor orders, apart from the personal one, it may have been in connection with his eligibility for a musical post in Rome. There is a tradition that Palestrina, who held various posts there, was debarred from being appointed *maestro di capella* at St Peter's and put in charge of music in the Sistine Chapel because the post was not given to a layman. The nineteenth century viewed Palestrina as 'the saviour of church music', and in his later years he had been entrusted to produce a reformed version of the chant. Liszt himself in 1861 wrote that he was occupied 'with some researches relating to my liturgical work with d'Ortigue . . . You will understand, dear Carolyne, and will not disapprove of me in this at a later date' (*Br.* V, 166). This is listed among the planned works of the composer as *Liturgie catholique, liturgie romaine* (1860–1).

After Liszt had taken minor orders in 1865, the Princess referred to him as a modern Palestrina; Pius IX himself is also reputed to have called Liszt 'my dear Palestrina'. However, during Liszt's years in Rome, the choir of the Sistine Chapel was under the charge of Salvatore Meluzzi (1813–97), and Liszt himself disavowed any particular wish to direct the Sistine choir:

I have never expected or wished for any appointment or title of any kind at Rome. If the Holy Father had put me in charge of the Sistine Chapel, I would have accepted with veneration for his goodness, and through obedience – in the perhaps mistaken notion of rendering a service to religious art, but under no illusions as to the difficulty and vexations of such a task.          (*Br.* VII, 73)

Doubtless the Pope saw no reason to remove Meluzzi from his post.

According to Liszt himself, his reasons for taking minor orders were both personal and musical: 'It agrees with the antecedents of my youth,' he stated, 'as well as with the development that my work of musical composition has taken during these last four years, – a work which I propose to pursue with fresh vigour, as I consider it the least defective form of my nature' (*L*, II, 99). After finishing *St Elizabeth* in 1862, he wrote: 'I am now about to set myself the great task of an oratorio on Christ' (*L*, II, 39). This 'great task' took, all told, until 1868 to carry out. Liszt found that, as in Weimar, demands were made upon his time; he was involved in teaching and in Roman social life, and wished to escape. Part of *Christus* was composed in the Vatican itself, after Liszt had entered the Church: 'In certain cases, when the monk is already formed within, why not appropriate the outer garment of one?' 'Convinced as I was,' he wrote, 'that this act would strengthen me in the right road, I accomplished it without effort, in all simplicity and uprightness of intention' (*L*, II, 100).

An examination of Liszt's correspondence between 1862 and 1865 shows clearly that during this time he had one main aim: 'to try and lead a *natural* kind of life. I hope I may succeed in approaching more closely to my monastico-artistic ideal' (*L*, II, 50). Remembering the 1859 letter from Hohenlohe, we should not be surprised that the 'right road' led from 113 Via Felice to the Vatican.

The Princess Wittgenstein lived at 93 Piazza di Spagna until August 1862, when she moved to 89 Via del Babuino, where she lived until her death in 1887. Liszt's manservant Otto and the Princess's servant Auguste both returned to Weimar, the latter to the Altenburg to act as custodian until 1867, when the Princess's possessions were removed to another building in the town. An Italian married couple, Fortunato and Peppina Salvagni, looked after the needs of Liszt and the Princess respectively. In religious matters Liszt and the Princess were still in close accord; they shared the same confessor, a Dominican called Father Ferraris.

Something of Liszt's enthusiasm for ecclesiastical Rome finds expression in a letter of June 1862:

Grand, sublime, immeasurably great things have come to pass here lately. The Episcopate of the whole world assembled here round the Holy Father who performed the ceremony of the canonisation of the Japanese martyrs at Whitsuntide in the presence of more than 300 bishops, archbishops, patriarchs, and cardinals. I must abstain, dear friend, from giving you any picture of the overpowering moment in which the Pope intoned the Te Deum; for in Protestant lands that which I might call the spiritual illumination is wanting.                    (*L*, II, 11)

The following month he told Franz Brendel, editor of the *Neue Zeitschrift für Musik* and President of the Allgemeine Deutsche Musikverein, that he would send the manuscript score of *St Elizabeth* to the copyist at Weimar. 'It would certainly be pleasanter for me,' he wrote, 'if I could bring the things with me – but, *between ourselves*, I cannot entertain the idea of a speedy return to Germany' (*L*, II, 19). On 11 September his daughter Blandine died, and her husband Emile Ollivier went to Rome and stayed with Liszt until his fifty-first birthday on 22 October. On his departure Liszt was ill, and confined to his bed for a week. When he began to catch up on correspondence, he answered Brendel's invitation to attend the Tonkünstler-Versammlung planned for 1863 (but which eventually took place in 1864) thus: 'Unfortunately this question I am forced to answer decidedly in the *negative*. Owing to its being my custom not to enlighten others by giving an account of my own affairs, I avoid, even in this case, entering further into particulars.' Later in the letter he wrote: 'At my age (51 years!) it is advisable to remain at home; what there is to seek is to be found within oneself, not without' (*L*, II, 33). Ten days later he wrote:

I needed more than ever, and above all things, ample time to compose myself, to gather my thoughts, and to bestir myself. During the first year of my stay here I secured this. It is to be hoped that you would not be dissatisfied with the state of mind which my 50th year brought me; at all events I feel it to be in perfect harmony with the better, higher aspirations of my childhood, where heaven lies so near the soul of every one of us and illuminates it. I may also say that, owing to my possessing a more definite and clearer consciousness, a state of greater peacefulness has come over me. (*L*, II, 38)

However, Liszt could not avoid teaching and other commitments. In May 1860 he wrote again to Brendel:

The last months brought so many interruptions in my work that I still feel quite vexed about it. Easter week I had determined should, at last, see me regularly at work again; but a variety of duties and engagements have prevented my accomplishing this. I must, therefore, to be true to myself and carry out my former intention, shut myself up entirely. To find myself in a net of social civilities is vexatious to me; my mental activity requires absolutely to be free, without which I cannot accomplish anything. (*L*, II, 56)

The following month, a solution was found. 'The day after tomorrow,' he wrote, 'I quit my rooms in the Via Felice and move to Monte Mario (an hour's distance from the city). Father Theiner [the Vatican archivist] is kind enough to allow me to occupy his apartments in the almost uninhabited house of the Oratorian' (*L*, II, 49). After moving, Liszt taught his pupils in the city at the house of Mgr Nardi, not in the Oratory of Madonna del Rosario, which became a retreat where he could devote his time to composition. On 11 July he was visited there by the Pope himself – 'an extraordinary, nay, incomparable honour', in Liszt's words.

His Holiness Pope Pius IX visited the Church of the Madonna del Rosario, and hallowed my apartments with his presence. After having given his Holiness a small proof of my skill on the harmonium and on my work-a-day pianino, he addressed a few very significant words to me in the most gracious manner possible, admonishing me to strive after heavenly things in things earthly, and by means of my harmonies that reverberated and then passed away to prepare myself for those harmonies that would reverberate everlastingly. – His Holiness remained a short half-hour; Monsign. de Merode and Hohenlohe were among his suite – and the day before yesterday I was granted an audience in the Vatican (the

first time since I came here), and the Pope presented me with a beautiful cameo
of the Madonna. (*L*, II, 55)

Liszt was now clearly becoming accepted in ecclesiastical circles. He
wrote to Agnes Klindworth:

There is no need to tell you that no great change has taken place within myself,
still less any forgetfulness. It is merely that my life is organized more simply – and
the Catholic piety of my childhood has become a regular and guiding sentiment.
For some people piety consists of burning one's old loves. I am far from blaming
them – but for my part I am tending, and shall try even more so, to consecrate the
things I have loved, and if you will allow me this comparison of the very great with
the very small, I would say that in so doing I am following the method constantly
employed in Rome for Christian monuments. Do not the magnificent columns of
St Mary of the Angels come from the Baths of Diocletian, and has not the bronze
of the Pantheon been used for the altar canopy of St Peter's? – One could go on
for ever enumerating similar transformations; for at every step here, one is struck
by the concordance of the divine plan with what has been, and what is and will
be. Also, I am particularly attached to Rome, where I hope to leave my bones, and
I repeat along with St Bernard: 'Ibi aër *purior*, coelum *apertius, familiarior* Deus!'
[Here is the air more pure, heaven more open, and God more accessible!]
(*Br.* III, 161)

Shortly afterwards Liszt wrote to Brendel:

This much is certain, – that in the tiresome business of self-correction few have
to labour as I have, as the process of my mental development, if not checked, is
at all events rendered peculiarly difficult by a variety of coincidences and con-
tingencies. A clever man, some twenty years ago, made the not inapplicable
remark to me: 'You have in reality three individuals to deal with in yourself, and
they all run one against the other; the sociable *salon*-individual, the virtuoso and
the thoughtfully-creative composer. If you manage one of them properly, you
may congratulate yourself.' – Vedremo! [We shall see!] (*L*, II, 61)

In October he wrote: 'I am deep in my work. The more we sow a field the
more it spreads. One would need to live to the age of a Methuselah to
accomplish anything plentiful!' (*L*, II, 67).

In January 1864 Liszt reluctantly agreed to attend the Musical Festival
at Carlsruhe in the summer: 'Although it will be very difficult for me to
make up my mind to start, I will towards the beginning of June have my
passport *visé'd* for Carlsruhe' (*L*, II, 77). In May he wrote: 'Meanwhile
(after 4 months' incessant interruptions) I have again set to work and
cannot now leave it till the time comes for my journey' (*L*, II, 81). In June
he emphasized that his visit would be short: 'A variety of considerations
. . . compel me not to extend my absence from Rome beyond a month . . .
All mere reports about my remaining in Germany for some length of time
I beg of you to contradict most emphatically' (*L*, II, 82). In July Liszt
visited for the first time the Villa d'Este: 'Last week I visited Mgr
Hohenlohe at the Villa d'Este (at Tivoli) which he is in the process of

splendidly restoring and which the owner, the Duke of Modena, has transferred to him for the duration of his life' (*Br.* III, 175). From the Villa d'Este he wrote to the Princess on 14 July:

My course has been decided on for a long time, and, on arriving in Rome, I swore and resolved not to part from it any more. Only one thing is necessary and beneficial for me: to work hard and continuously at my little notes, in such a way that in total they will later do honour to 'bon Ecclésiaste' [a nickname for the Princess]. I do not wish for, look for, or desire anything else. Having appreciated the public many times over both in mass and in detail, I have arrived absolutely at the point where one not only does without the public – but what is more, one finds a real satisfaction in doing without them! Those who do not understand that, hardly understand music! *Ergo*, I shall work for 'bon Ecclésiaste', and a little for myself. Even if I do not succeed in doing something worthwhile, it will always be the best use to which I can put my time.                    (*Br.* VI, 25)

On 31 July he wrote from the Hôtel de Rome, Castel Gandolfo, 'where, thanks to the very kind pains of Hohenlohe, I am perfectly lodged, ten paces away from the Palace of His Holiness'. The Pope had heard Liszt play the piano the previous day, and

had deigned to receive me and tell me that it was very pleasant for him to see me, talk with me, and listen to me here. Soon afterwards, between one and two o'clock, before his meal, I played for him several pieces on a small piano that Mgr Hohenlohe had acquired. Today, at the same time, I continued to show him my small repertoire.                    (*Br.* VI, 26)

On 9 August Liszt set out for the Tonkünstler-Versammlung at Carlsruhe, accompanied by his servant Fortunato, and travelling via Marseilles, St Tropez, where he visited Blandine's grave, and Strasbourg. After the Festival, Liszt wrote in some surprise to the Princess: 'My works obtained complete success at Carlsruhe. It is almost the first time that such a thing has happened to me' (*Br.* VI, 37). During a visit to Wagner on the Starnberger See, Liszt played his 'Beatitudes'; he then travelled with Cosima to Weimar, where he had 'a long session at the organ in the Stadtkirche with Gottschalg' (*Br.* VI, 49) and handed over the score of *St Elizabeth* to Götze, his copyist. During a visit to Löwenberg he gave a performance on the piano of the 'Shepherds' Song at the Manger' and 'The Three Holy Kings (March)' from *Christus*, and wrote to the Princess: 'Oh, when will the time come that I belong to myself again – and can continue our *Christ* and finish it!' (*Br.* VI, 50). At Berlin he visited his son Daniel's grave with Cosima, and back in Weimar wrote: 'The German atmosphere oppresses me horribly – I am simply yearning to get away from it, and to embark as soon as possible at Marseilles' (*Br.* VI, 53). Before doing so, however, Liszt and Cosima travelled to Paris to see Liszt's mother, and then Liszt returned to Rome. Back in the church of the Madonna del Rosario, he wrote: 'I am once again at my table, which is all the space necessary for my career and my external ambition' (*Br.* VI, 63).

On 14 December, Liszt received an invitation from Hungary to attend the twenty-fifth anniversary celebrations of the Conservatory at Pest, to be held in 1865. Liszt replied in the negative: 'I have contributed to a certain extent to the founding of the Pest–Buda Conservatory, and therefore I would be very happy if we could celebrate the quarter-centenary jubilee together. Regrettably, a previously arranged and very binding commitment prevents me from being in Budapest in May' (*BruS*, 336). It was not until the end of April 1865 that the world learned of Liszt's entry into the Church. He did not even tell the Princess until the last minute: 'People almost blamed her for my having entered the Vatican, of which she had no suspicion, and which I simply announced to her, one month before, as settled' (*LOM*, 135).

Already on New Year's Eve Liszt seemed to be making veiled references to the impending event, which took place in Hohenlohe's chapel in the Vatican four months later:

Our excellent P. Ferraris heard my confession yesterday in Hohenlohe's chapel – and this morning my priest gave me communion. I will tell you how this came about – as you can well imagine that I had no ambition at all to go to confession in an archiepiscopal chapel! Nobody other than myself was present at my Communion Mass.                                        (*Br.* VI, 65)

From the beginning of the New Year 1865, Liszt started to prepare himself for the event. 'I have no wish to increase the amount of my correspondence', he wrote, 'as my whole day would be spent at it – and having no other traffic with this world, I also prefer to do without mental dealings, except in cases of absolute necessity' (*Br.* VI, 66). By April he had been allotted a priest named Salua, with whom to recite the Divine Office. 'He has also given me a book of *Meditations* taken from St Thomas,' Liszt wrote of Salua, 'which we read together. During this week of mission, it will be difficult for me to be occupied with anything other than *cose sante* [holy matters]. I have had the times of the carriage changed, in order to be present at prayers and spiritual exercises regularly each evening' (*Br.* VI, 67).

The ecclesiastical orders in the Latin Church are those of bishops, priests, deacons, subdeacons, acolytes, exorcists and *ostiarii* or door-keepers. Of these the last four constitute minor orders, and holders of these may leave the Church if they so desire. The tonsure (the shaving of the crown in a circle) does not in itself constitute an order, and is generally regarded as a mere introduction to the clerical state. To be ordained lawfully a person must have observed the interstices, which are the intervals which canon law requires between the reception of the various degrees of orders. An interval is required between the tonsure and the minor orders, and Liszt's activities between April and August 1865 were in accord with this requirement. After receiving the tonsure and donning the cassock in the Vatican on 25 April, he retired to the Villa d'Este in May, where he stayed until the end of July, when he passed the examination for minor orders.

A few days before receiving the tonsure Liszt retired to the monastery of the Lazzaristi, from where he wrote to the Princess:

*Et ego semper tecum!* I am very comfortable here, and these 3 or 4 days of transition are very harmonious for my soul! Nothing rigorous is imposed upon me. Over and above a few spiritual readings, which I willingly perform, it is practically the same as my life at Monte Mario. Here are the principal points of the *Orario*: Arise at 6.30 – meditation alone – my coffee in my room. Mass at 8.30 – tomorrow, Sunday, a Sung Mass at 9.30. Spiritual reading alone – a visit to the Holy Sacrament – dinner in the refectory at midday. The dinner is much better than my priest's dinner; there are about 35 of us. I am put at a separate table, alone. No one talks, which suits me very well. I cannot quite understand the reading which a brother gives, up in the gallery, from the beginning to the end of the meal. They had coffee with water served to me in my room yesterday, a gesture by which I was extremely touched. Rest 1.30. Spiritual reading, a visit to the Holy Sacrament, a walk in the garden *ad libitum*, 3.30 Meditation alone, *per un'ora*, 6.45. Supper 8 o'clock, silence and a reading, as at dinner. I returned to my room at 8.30 where the superior, Pater Guarini, very kindly kept me company until 9.30. At 10 o'clock the lights of the house must be extinguished. (*Br.* VI, 67)

The same day as this letter (22 April 1865), Liszt tried on his cassock in front of Hohenlohe in readiness for the ceremony the following Tuesday, 'for which I feel most perfectly prepared in heart, mind, and willingness'. He also added: 'The piano will be transported from Nardi's house to the Vatican in about ten days' time – Hohenlohe having assured me that it would in no way disturb his furniture. The Holy Father has spoken to him of the Latin studies I have to do – it is Solfanelli who will officially be in charge of them' (*Br.* VI, 68). On the Sunday, Liszt asked the Princess to send Father Ferraris to Hohenlohe's chapel on the Tuesday morning to hear his confession before the ceremony. On the Monday he asked her to send Fortunato with his certificate of baptism, adding: 'My three days at the Mission have been very soothing – I shall retain a more serene and profound memory of them than I do of my so-called successes of former times. In truth man is only what he is in the eyes of God' (*Br.* VI, 69). On the day of the ceremony, Mgr Hohenlohe fetched Liszt from the Lazzaristi at 7 a.m., and together they walked to the Vatican.

The ceremony preceded the Mass. The words that constitute the ceremony are taken from Ps. 15. I offered them up from my heart and lips at the same time as the bishop – while he was making the sign of the tonsure over me: 'The Lord is the portion of mine inheritance and of my cup: thou maintainest my lot.' – A few prayers, and Ps. 83: 'How amiable are thy tabernacles, O Lord of hosts!' complete the ceremony. At the end, Hohenlohe addressed a very moving speech to me. Mgr Corazzo and Don Marcello [priests in Hohenlohe's household] administered the Mass. Salua and our excellent Ferraris, who had received my last confession as a layman, were present – as were Fortunato and Antonio [Hohenlohe's servant].

As you know, the cut of the tonsure has to be in the shape of a crown – but you may have forgotten its significance. It is so that upon the head of the cleric, and of all the clergy, is imprinted the image of the crown of thorns of Our Saviour Jesus Christ. It also signifies the 'royal dignity' of those admitted into the ranks of the clergy.                                               (*Br.* VI, 70)

At 10 a.m. Liszt took possession of his rooms at the Vatican,

which are very comfortable, well furnished and arranged, and suit me very well. The view is *ad libitum*. If I go to the window, which will happen rarely, I can enjoy the whole façade of St Peter's. Otherwise I can see only a *buon pezzo* of the cupola which is visible from my writing-table. Apart from the bells, I hear almost no noise. Do you recall the remark of Felix Lichnowsky's father, which his son inserted in an article in the Augsburg Gazette in '41, I think: 'If Liszt had been an architect, he would have built the dome of St Peter's'?                  (*Br.* VI, 71)

During the morning, Liszt copied a letter, drafted for him by Hohenlohe, addressed to the Bishop of Raab (Györ), in whose diocese Liszt's birthplace Raiding (Dobr'jan) was situated. 'Hohenlohe had brought me the draft of this letter,' he wrote. 'It says: "Seit heute Morgen trage ich das geistliche Kleid – und wohne hier unter demselben Dache mit dem Statthalter Christi." I have copied it word for word, without changing a thing' (*Br.* VI, 72). After dinner, which was eaten in the company of Hohenlohe, his nephew Prince Nikolaus Hohenlohe-Waldenburg, and Don Marcello, Liszt offered the use of his rooms for smoking. His relations with Hohenlohe, he told the Princess, 'will be of long and steadfast duration' (*Br.* VI, 72). In the afternoon Liszt slept for an hour and, shortly before the Ave Maria, accompanied Hohenlohe to the Pope's quarters, where he was given an audience alone. 'Pius IX,' he wrote,

received me with great goodness and kindness. At my second genuflection, your recent prayer for the worker and his work came into my mind, and I said something to this effect: 'The Gospel for today teaches us that the harvest is plentiful ... I am, alas, merely a very small and feeble worker – but I am indeed happy to be yet a little more attached to you now, and beseech Your Holiness to ordain me.' The Pope then spoke to me: 'Now you have some theological studies to do' – 'I have not been entirely a stranger to them, and shall resume them with greater zeal and joy. It is indispensable also that I work at Latin.' Pius IX: 'The Germans have a lot of ability ... ' Ego: 'Particularly my compatriots, the Hungarians – my father was an excellent Latin scholar.' Pius IX: 'Recently a Hungarian spoke to me in Latin with a fluency and accuracy which surprised me, and which I could not possibly equal. I could not say as much for the Latin of Cardinal Scitovsky [Primate of Hungary] which is in *modo grosso*, as we say ... ' ... So as not to leave the area of Hungary, I added that I would probably be ... going to Hungary this year, where, during the week of the Feast of St Stephen on 20 August, they will be celebrating a musical jubilee at Pest. The occasion not presenting itself naturally to touch on Roman matters, I was quite happy to pass over them in total silence. It is important to me that people should be fully confident that I am not ambitious for, and do not covet, whatever might later be granted to me. But towards that end *bisogna dar tempo al tempo* . . . My audience lasted about ten minutes. At the end of it the Holy Father gave me his blessing *in extenso*.

(*Br.* VI, 70ff)

The day following the ceremony of the tonsure, Liszt and Hohenlohe went to visit Cardinal Vicaire, who proved to be not at home. Liszt therefore left a message: 'I wrote, at the dictation of Hohenlohe . . . "The Abbé Liszt, to present his respects to His Eminence." ' (*Br.* VI, 74). This is the first use of the title 'Abbé'.

On 1 May Liszt was asked whether he intended to enter the priesthood. 'I confessed,' he replied, ' . . . that I felt prevented from it primarily by virtue of unworthiness – and also by two or three works which it was in my heart to accomplish, and which claimed the greater part of my time' (*Br.* VI, 75). This musical emphasis appears again in the letter he wrote to Carl Alexander at Weimar on 3 May:

I have just carried out in all simplicity of purpose an act for which by deep conviction I have been preparing for a long time. On 25 April I entered the ecclesiastical state by receiving minor orders, and since that day have been living near Monseigneur Hohenlohe, who holds me in truly benevolent attachment.

This modification – or, as one person of high rank expressed it – this transformation of my life does not mean a sudden change. In a short time I shall resume my composing ('travail de composition musicale'), and shall try and finish the oratorio entitled *Jesus Christ* by Christmas. Other works, sketched in my mind, belonging to the same world of feeling, will appear as time goes by. Since my new state imposes no demands upon me, I am confident that I can live like this quite normally, observing the rules without any more disturbance to the mind than is caused physically by my soutane, on which subject I am being complimented that it fits me as though I had always worn one.          (*LCA*, 130)

On 4 May he informed the Princess of the progress of his Latin studies: 'For nearly three hours yesterday evening, Solfanelli made me practise declensions – we shall continue on Saturday' (*Br.* VI, 77). He added that Nardi's piano had been brought to Hohenlohe's rooms, and that he had got rid of the one from Monte Mario. A few days later he wrote: 'Hohenlohe returned early this morning, and told me that he has arranged for me to use three rooms in the Villa d'Este' (*Br.* VI, 79). Meanwhile, Liszt's mother had received her son's letter containing the news of his entry into the Church, and had sent her reply from Paris, dated 4 May 1865.

My beloved child!
People often talk about a thing so much that it actually happens – so it is with the

present change in your life. The newspapers here were repeatedly saying that you have entered into the ecclesiastical state. I tried hard not to believe it when people told me about it. Your letter of 27 April, which I received yesterday, gave me a shock – and I burst into tears. Forgive me – I was really not prepared for such news from you. After thinking about it – they say *la nuit porte conseil* – I surrendered to your will, and also to the will of God. I felt calmer – since all good resolutions come from God. This decision which you have now made is not one which is *vulgaire*. God gives you Grace in order to fulfil thereby his goodwill. It is a great thing – but you have been preparing yourself for it for a long time, on the Monte Mario. I have noticed it in your letters to me for some time. You sounded so beautiful, so religious, that I was often very moved – and shed a few tears for you. And now finally, my child – *tu me demandes pardon!* Oh, I don't have to forgive you. Your good qualities far, far outweighed the errors of your youth. You have always fulfilled your obligations stringently in every respect – whereby you have secured for me peace and happiness. I can live quietly and without worry, for which I have only you to thank.

So be happy, my beloved child. If the blessing of a fast-failing mother can be of any avail with God – then bless you a thousand times over. I commend your soul to dear God and remain your faithful mother.

Anna Liszt<br>(Br. VI, 78)

From the Villa d'Este Liszt wrote to the Princess:

Here everything is perfect, as initiated by my 'patron'. He has fitted up three rooms very nicely for my use – with piano, harmonium and several items of furniture which could not have been chosen better. My day was spent yesterday in reading 50 pages or so of the *Catéchisme de persévérance* in Italian – and in seeking out some ideas at the piano for the Indian jugglers in *L'Africaine*, of which I shall be the 'coq d'Inde', otherwise called the 'dindon de la farce'!

I started my studies for the duties of sacristan this morning by serving Mass to Hohenlohe. A short time from now I hope to fulfil this duty in a decent manner – but . . . I am promising myself to devote my modest *savoir-faire* as sacristan exclusively to Hohenlohe, as I have already expressly told Salua.     (*Br.* VI, 79)

Shortly afterwards he told the Princess that he was hard at work on the *Missa choralis*. Another letter says: 'It is not the *canonico* Martini, but in fact your friend Canon Audisio who will examine me on the four minor orders – probably it will not be until the day after tomorrow that the examination takes place' (*Br.* VI, 67). At the beginning of August Liszt left Rome for Hungary to attend the première of *St Elizabeth*. 'During the months of June and July', he wrote, 'I had to prepare for my examination (for minor orders), which I passed quite satisfactorily before my departure' (*Br.* III, 183). The certificate gives 30 July as the date on which Liszt received minor orders.

On his return, Liszt lived in the Vatican until June 1866, when Hohenlohe was made a Cardinal and left the Vatican. Liszt returned to Monte Mario until November, when he moved into an apartment in the church of Santa Francesca Romana near the Forum, for which he paid a yearly rent of 1500 francs, and which enabled him to spend the winter months living a more sociable life in the city. According to Haraszti,

he had in fact decided, in 1866, to prepare for the diaconate; an instructor had been chosen for him by the Pope; but he abandoned the project. A letter of Mgr Gay reports that Liszt was continuing his studies at Rome, but that he would probably not be able to advance any further, having been denied a thorough grounding in his youth. 'He told me [wrote Gay] that his whole ambition lay in being able to understand and to recite the breviary.'                    (*HFL*, 215)

The summer of 1868 Liszt spent with Solfanelli. 'We started with a pilgrimage,' Liszt wrote,

to the *Madonna della Stella*, a wild spot with a chapel carved out of the rock, where the grandfather of my friend – the Abbé Solfanelli – died a hermit at the age of 80 or so. Afterwards, we went to Assisi and Loreto, staying for a couple of days at Fabriano with his father, an excellent priest. Then his uncle, Count Fenili, rendered us the most charming hospitality from 14 July until 30 August, at Grotta Mare, beside the Adriatic. The principal occupation of our hearts and minds was to say our breviary together, sometimes on the beach, sometimes in an orchard of citron trees which we encountered on our way.            (*Br.* III, 202)

Enjoying the perfect tranquillity of this summer idyll by the sea, he told the Princess: 'I am now enjoying in my old age – with a perfectly easy conscience – the peace and contentment which were missing from my youth' (*Br.* VI, 177). 1868 was the last year of Liszt's permanent residence in Rome. During that year he completed *Christus* and composed a *Requiem*.

In January 1869 Liszt returned to Weimar to teach. The same year he stayed in Hungary in April and early May, and thus began the process that was to link him permanently to his homeland when he became President of the new Academy of Music in 1875. Rome became one of the three cities in his 'vie trifurquée'.

In 1879, when Hohenlohe became Cardinal Bishop of Albano and, on 12 October, Liszt was made a canon of Albano, Adelheid von Schorn reports seeing him after the ceremony: 'Liszt came to Rome, and when I went to see him, I saw in his room a purple mantle that I had never seen him with before. He then spoke to me of the dignity to which he had been raised. Afterwards, I heard no more spoken of it; I never again saw the mantle' (*SFL*, 329). Liszt often told the Princess that he had no ambitions for an ecclesiastical career: 'In taking minor orders in 1865 in the Vatican, at the age of 54 – the idea of outward advancement was as foreign to me as possible. I was only following, with a simple and upright heart, the former Catholic predilection of my youth' (*Br.* VII, 258). As Liszt wrote in 1865: 'I do not in the least intend to become a monk, in the severe sense of the word. For this I have no vocation, and it is enough for me to belong to the hierarchy of the Church to such a degree as the minor orders allow me to do' (*L*, II, 100).

Plate 2. The Abbé Félicité de Lamennais (1782–1854) (from an oil painting by P. Guérin)

Plate 3. Princess Sayn-Wittgenstein in about 1847, the year she met Liszt (from a daguerreotype)

Plate 4. Princess Sayn-
Wittgenstein dressed as she
was for her interview with
Pope Pius IX in 1860

Plate 5. Cardinal Gustav
Hohenlohe (1823–96)

Plate 6. The Abbé Liszt in the Vatican in 1866 in conversation with Pius IX and Cardinal Antonelli (sketch by Paul Thumann)

Plate 7. Liszt's Certificate of Ordination, dated 30 July 1865

Plate 8. The Basilica at Esztergom (Gran) (engraving by Rohbock)

Plate 9. Liszt conducting the first performance of *The Legend of St Elizabeth* in the Vigadó, Budapest, on 15 August 1865 (engraving by K. Rusz)

# PART II

Sacred music is scarcely cultivated at all, and it would take very little to make it
die of inanition.                                                    Liszt to Janka Wohl

# 7

# LISZT AND PALESTRINA:
# THE PLAN TO REFORM
# CHURCH MUSIC

'I look forward greatly to learning when you are in Rome the details of the plan you have formed regarding religious music.' This extract from Hohenlohe's letter to Liszt from the Vatican, written in 1859, is evidence that Liszt had a 'plan'. Yet Liszt's church music is not composed to a plan of what the Church should use; taken as a whole the pieces form a highly variegated group, drawing much of their character from the texts. In this respect their poetic qualities parallel those in the secular music.[1]

Liszt's article 'On Future Church Music' spoke of 'a pledge of greater things to come to influence the masses: we mean the ennobling of *church music*'. The same article says music 'must recognize God and the people as its living source; must hasten from one to the other, to comfort, to purify Man, to bless and praise God'. These words of the 23-year-old Liszt, though they reflect his enthusiasm for the Abbé Lamennais, reveal an aspiration that remained with him throughout his life. In 1865, after taking minor orders, Liszt wrote from the Vatican: 'And when [music] is joined with words, what more legitimate use could be made of it than to sing Man's praise of God, and to become thereby the meeting point between two worlds – the finite and the infinite? – This is its prerogative, for it partakes of both at the same time' (*Br.* VIII, 171). An important ingredient in the 1834 article is the idea that music should 'influence the masses'. When Hohenlohe invited Liszt to the Vatican, he wrote: 'Your inspirations, which guide you by the grace of God, will be . . . a vigorous weapon to bring back the prodigal sons to our Holy Mother Church.' This idea was later echoed by Cosima Wagner, after she and Wagner heard *Christus* at Weimar in 1873: 'Parts of *Christus* ought to be performed upon each of the feast days to which they belong, and the whole work on the great days of the Church. More than missions, more than religious propaganda, more than acting by means of terror, such performances would strengthen souls and win them over.'[2] Liszt himself wrote: 'The best part of my religious compositions is the emotion evoked by them in a few fine souls' (*LMW*, 227). Thus there was a continuity in Liszt's thinking on the subject. In *Christus* he in effect put into music feelings that in 1834 had found expression in words.

# Revolution and religion

From the start this formed the basis of his objection to the music used in his day by the Catholic Church. The article he wrote in 1835 for the *Revue et Gazette Musicale*, containing his diatribe against the Church's reactionary outlook (see above, p. 17) deals as well with its music:

Do you hear that stupid bellowing resounding beneath the valuted roofs of cathedrals? What is it? It is the song of praise and benediction addressed to Jesus Christ by his mystic bride . . .

And the organ, the pope among instruments, the mystical ocean that formerly washed so majestically against the altar of Christ and deposited there among its waves of harmony the lamentations and prayers of centuries – do you hear it now prostituting itself with vaudeville airs and even galops? Do you hear, at the solemn moment when the priest raises the sacred host, do you hear the wretched organist playing variations on *Di piacer mi balza il cor* or *Fra Diavolo*?

O shame! O scandal! When will these loud-mouthed drunkards be chased from the holy place? When shall we at last have religious music?

Church music! . . . We no longer know what that is: the great productions of a Palestrina, a Handel, a Marcello, Haydn, Mozart can hardly stay alive in libraries. (*Cpr*, 60)

To Liszt the two criticisms amounted to aspects of the same thing: the Church failed to read the signs of the times, while church music failed to express the feelings of the people. Characteristically, Liszt's starting point was the music, from which he argued his position, and how he saw that of the Church. It is remarkable that in 1835 Liszt should advocate revival as well as reform; the composers he mentions do not reflect the usual Romantic tastes.

Liszt's description of the prevailing musical conditions was not an exaggeration. In Italy and France opera was frequently used for Sung Mass. Throughout the century there were attempts at reform,

but reformers had to deal with Italian love of operatic expression and instrumental *concertato*. Even if the latter were merely represented by an organ the admired organist was he who best evoked the variety and colour of the theatre band . . . To secure the admired musical structures, from fugues to cavatinas, words might be repeated, sentences and paragraphs dissected and dramatic pauses introduced. Many choir directors made a practice of fitting the sacred texts to opera melodies.[3]

In his *Memoirs*, Berlioz gives an amusing description of this practice, as witnessed by him in Rome in 1832. He concludes:

I have often heard the overtures of the *Barbiere*, *Cenerentola*, and *Otello* in Church. They seemed to be special favourites with the organists, and formed an agreeable seasoning to the service. The music in the theatres is in much the same glorious condition, and is about as *dramatic* as that of the churches is *religious*.[4]

In 1862 Liszt wrote from Rome describing this same practice.[5]

One of the more surprising attempts at reform came from Spontini in

1838, who wrote to Cardinal Ostini of Jesi from Berlin after a visit to Italy, complaining about the state of Italian church music. The Cardinal sent out an edict against the 'abuse of operatic music in church',[6] which he sent to Spontini, who sent it to Pope Gregory XVI. The Pope replied: 'Let the diocese of Jesi begin. Others will follow; then I shall act.' A commission was formed under the presidency of Spontini, including among its members Baini (Palestrina's biographer) and Basili, *maestro di capella* at St Peter's. They quarrelled, however, and nothing came of it. In 1860 Liszt wrote from Weimar to the Princess in Rome: 'Perhaps you might find the means of sending to me, through Mgr Gustav, a copy of the memorandum presented by Spontini to His Holiness Gregory XVI at the beginning of the year 1839 concerning the reform of church music. Spontini did send it to me at the time, but I would like to read it again' (*Br.* V, 35). In the same letter Liszt speaks of a project he is engaged upon: 'For the work I have in mind, I should need above all to make use of the material already very well prepared at Ratisbon, through the publications of Canon Proske and of Mettenleiter, recently deceased.' This 'work' was nothing less than a compilation of plainsong harmonized for church use. 'In a year,' he wrote,

I should be ready to submit this work to His Holiness, which, if he should deign to accord it his approval, would be adopted by the entire Catholic world. When this happens I shall first lay out the plan, itself very simple, for it is above all a question of settling upon what is unalterable in the Catholic liturgy – and adapting it to the demands of the notation at present in use, without which there is no means of obtaining an exact and satisfactory performance.

This may be the 'plan' referred to by Hohenlohe. Liszt, like other musicians in the nineteenth century, felt that the basis of church music should be the chant. The problem was twofold: how to restore the practice of its widespread performance, and how to harmonize it. The latter seems incongruous today, when argument centres upon the rhythmic interpretations used in performing chant. Liszt's reference to 'the notation at present in use' itself shows an awareness of this problem, which led to the publication after the turn of the century of the Vatican Edition based upon the researches of the monks at Solesmes. But in Liszt's day, as well as using corrupt notation, musicians were in the habit of performing plainchant in harmonized versions, and it was therefore natural that Liszt and others concerned with reform should adopt this practice, but try to improve upon the harmony. Liszt's first piece of church music, the *Pater noster* of 1846 (S21), is essentially a harmonization of the chant, whose publication coincided with a change in the political outlook of the Church. By attaching his own harmony to the chant, Liszt gave parallel musical expression to the idea of 'renewal'.

The Liszt Museum in Budapest houses a collection of books which formerly belonged to Liszt. Among these are several which deal with the problem of harmonizing chant; some of them contain pencil markings that show Liszt's careful study. The *Nouvel eucologe en musique . . . avec les plainchants en notation moderne*,[7] published in 1851, was obviously used by Liszt. The book falls open at page 326, which quotes from the Second Epistle of Paul to the Corinthians, chapter 11, verse 25 to chapter 12, verse 10. This passage seems to have had a special significance for Liszt, as the page is darkened from lying open. Many of the chants in the book occur with the same notation in Liszt's religious music, including *Christus*, the *Hungarian Coronation Mass* and *Via Crucis*, as well as in certain of the instrumental works. The preface to the book reflects views then current regarding plainsong:

Le christianisme a sa musique qui lui est propre. Après avoir composé sa liturgie des textes sublimes de l'Écriture sainte et des accents les plus élevés de la poésie humaine, il sut aussi s'emparer du mode musical le plus propre à la populariser. En effet, le plain-chant est la mélodie de tous, intelligible pour tous, en même temps qu'il exprime fidèlement et avec plus de puissance que tous les autres chants, la longue *prière* de l'Église militante et les graves pensées des coeurs éloignés de leur patrie.

This was the Romantic view. The appeal of the chant lay in its twofold nature, at once religious and popular. In reality, the medieval picture was slightly different. Certainly the chant was widely known, and infiltrated popular song. But it was sung in church by specially trained singers, not by the congregation. The aim of nineteenth-century reformers of Catholic church music, and certainly of Liszt, was to bring religion close to the people; their historical error in viewing the chant as a vehicle for popularizing religion reveals their own aspirations.[8] Harmony was their own vehicle for achieving this, which is why they concentrated upon it. This practice is defended in another part of the preface:

Nourri et soutenu par les accords de l'orgue, qui, lui aussi, est un instrument éminemment chrétien, il s'harmonise, s'identifie avec les autres parties du culte, et forme avec lui cette unité imposante qui nous annonce la vérité divine.

Liszt, in his letter to the Princess, outlining his plan, says:

All orchestral instruments will be done away with – and I shall merely retain an organ accompaniment ad libitum, in order to support and strengthen the voices. It is the only instrument with a right to permanence in church music – and by means of the variety of its registrations, a little more colour could even be added. Even so, I shall use it with extreme reserve. As I have said, I shall write the organ part only *ad libitum*, in such a way that it could be entirely omitted without any trouble.

At the end of the book, Liszt has tabulated on two of the pages information gleaned from the book concerning the modes (see Table 1 and

# Liszt and Palestrina

Table 1. Liszt's manuscript table on p. 826 of his copy of
the *Nouvel eucologe en musique*

|   |        |     | Finale | Dominant |
|---|--------|-----|--------|----------|
| 1 | Auth:  |     | re     | La       |
| 2 | Plagal | *La* | re    | Fa       |
| 3 | Auth   |     | Mi     | Do       |
| 4 | pl–    | *ti* | mi    | La       |
| 5 | Auth   |     | Fa     | Do       |
| 6 | Pla:   | *Do* | Fa    | La       |
| 7 | Auth:  |     | Soh    | Re       |
| 8 | Plagal | *Re* | Soh   | Do       |

Ex. 1. Liszt's manuscript notation on p. 834 of his copy of the
*Nouvel eucologe en musique*

Ex. 1). It can be seen that in Ex. 1 Liszt has turned into notational form
the verbal information contained in Table 1. Already the elements of
modal theory begin to take on a harmonic appearance; the chief source
of puzzlement to nineteenth-century musicians was the search to find
'rules' for harmonizing the modes.

Another book bearing signs of use by Liszt is the *Traité théorique et
pratique de l'accompagnement du plain-chant* by Louis Niedermeyer and
Joseph d'Ortigue, published in 1859. D'Ortigue had known Liszt since
his adolescent years in Paris. Liszt wrote to him from Weimar in 1850:

> The work you mention concerning the liturgy will assuredly take its place
> amongst things most conscientious and valuable, and it pleases me even more to
> know about it as this matter is dear to my own heart. – Do you not think you could
> include some musical texts which might be chosen from the most lovely among
> the Catholic plainchants?[9]

D'Ortigue's preface to the *Traité théorique*, dated Paris 1856, recounts his
search for a theory of harmony derived from the modes and suitable for
plainsong. He acknowledges that the chants were in essence melodic, and
should not be harmonized, but argues that since they were daily
being sung in harmonized versions, then correct harmonizations were
needed. The answer came from Louis Niedermeyer (1806–61), who had

91

reorganized Choron's institute for church music in Paris as the 'École Niedermeyer':

Ce fut lorsque M. Niedermeyer m'eut démontré que non-seulement le plain-chant était susceptible d'une belle harmonie, mais encore que cette harmonie n'était que le développement naturel des lois mélodiques du plainchant lui-même, que je compris cette fécondité propre au système des modes ecclési-astiques, en vertu de laquelle, loin d'être déshérité des avantages du système moderne, il peut et doit engendrer aussi bien que ce dernier une théorie har-monique.

M. Niedermeyer détermina en moi cette conviction par le simple exposé de deux règles fondamentales:

1° Nécessité, dans l'accompagnement du plainchant, de l'emploi exclusif des notes de l'échelle;

2° Nécessité d'attribuer aux accords de *finale* et de *dominante*, dans chaque mode, des fonctions analogues a celles que ces notes essentielles exercent dans la mélodie.

La première de ces règles donne les lois de la *tonalité* générale du plainchant – la seconde donne les lois de la *modalité*, lois en vertu desquelles les modes peuvent être discernés entre eux.

L'énoncé de ces deux règles fut pour moi un trait de lumière; à l'instant les bases du système harmonique grégorien me furent révélées.

Markings were made by Liszt in the margin beside the two 'rules' in his own copy of the *Traité*.

D'Ortigue's search for the 'système harmonique grégorien' resembles to us the medieval belief in the philosophers' stone; nevertheless, by taking an erroneous view of the modes he was able to invent harmony that was characteristic. Trained to think of 'tonic' and 'dominant' as har-monic concepts, he applied them to the chant, thus producing new cadential formulas, for example by treating the 'dominant' (F) of the plagal dorian (no. 2 in Liszt's table) as a chord. In practice d'Ortigue's harmonizations of mode 1 and mode 2 are indistinguishable, both becoming in effect D dorian (see Exx. 2(a) and (b)). Nevertheless, this kind of harmony gained currency, and figures very strongly in Liszt's religious works. When given full choral and orchestral treatment, as in parts of *Christus* for example, the effect can be electrifying.

The work in which Liszt adopted this approach most thoroughly is the one he was referring to in his letter to the Princess Wittgenstein: *Responses and Antiphons* (S30), dating from 1860. These harmonizations of plain-song remained unpublished until 1936, when they were incorporated into the Collected Edition. They were never used for the purpose for which they were intended, and may have formed part of a work listed among those which Liszt planned but never carried out: *Liturgie catholique, liturgie romaine* (1860–1). Certainly in 1861 Liszt wrote of his 'liturgical work with d'Ortigue' to the Princess Wittgenstein. Göllerich, in his

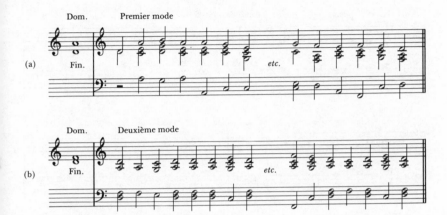

Ex. 2. Examples of the 'système harmonique grégorien' in Liszt's
copy of the *Traité théorique et pratique de l'accompagnement du plain-chant*,
p. 114

catalogue of Liszt's works, says that the *Responses and Antiphons* may have
been written for Cardinal Hohenlohe.[10]

The music occupies 60 pages and is written on two stages in four-part,
occasionally three-part, harmony. The rules of part-writing are
observed, but the impression it gives is that Liszt found the harmony at
the keyboard first. Liszt is more adventurous than d'Ortigue's method
would allow, but the influence is nevertheless evident. The words are
taken from the breviary, and belong to the following occasions:

> In nativitate Domini
> Feria V in coena Domini
> Feria VI in Parasceve
> Sab.° Maj. Hebd. (Sabbato sancto)
> In officio defunctorum

An extract from the last-named, in which Liszt manages to give the bare
style some expression, may be taken as representative (see Ex. 3). Liszt
here seems to be putting into practice the theoretical ideas outlined by
d'Ortigue.[11] The common aim of both men, and others like them concerned with the state of Catholic church music at the time, was to persuade the Church to adopt this 'revised' version of the chant along the
lines of Pope Gregory's reform. The fact that such harmonizations can
today be seen only as historical curiosities should not lead us to under-
value the contribution such attempts made to the general revival of
interest in plainchant. Perhaps their very error reveals the nature of the
problem; they wanted plainchant to be once again at the centre of a living
tradition.

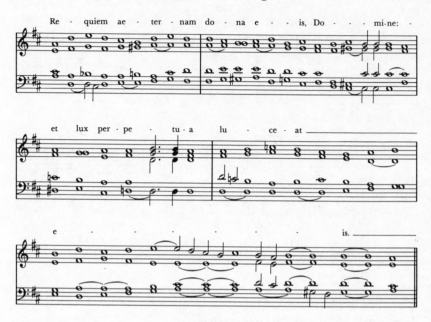

Ex. 3

Liszt's use of plainchant was not confined to his church music, and his use of it in other works shows that it was a religious symbol for him. His earliest use of plainchant was in the *De profundis* for piano and orchestra, in which 'transformation' technique is used (see above, pp. 20–2), and was obviously made for personal reasons – a use of plainchant characteristic of Liszt throughout his life. Thus in 1838 he sketched *Totentanz* (S126), a set of variations for piano and orchestra on the *Dies irae*; the 1846 *Pater noster* was arranged as a piano piece (no. 5 of *Harmonies poétiques et religieuses*); the *De profundis* reappears in *Pensée des morts* (S173, 4), written between 1847 and 1852;[12] the Gregorian hymn *Crux fidelis* is used in *Hunnenschlacht* (symphonic poem no. 11), planned in 1855; a plainchant associated with the feast of St Elizabeth is used extensively in the orchestral music of the oratorio, also planned in 1855; the *Magnificat* is used in the *Dante Symphony*, composed in 1855–6; the first *Episode from Lenau's Faust* (S110), dating from 1860, contains the *Pangue lingua*; much of the orchestral music of *Christus* is based upon plainchant; a piano piece using *Vexilla regis* (S185) appeared in 1864; the music of *Die Glocken des Strassburger Münsters* (S6) of 1874 is based upon the *Te Deum*; and in his last years Liszt wrote a piano piece based upon the *Stabat mater dolorosa*.[13] In addition Liszt's 'Cross motif' (see Ex. 178, p. 284), widely employed in his instrumental as well as his choral works, is an intonation taken from plainchant.

# Liszt and Palestrina

Thus during the Weimar period Liszt produced music which was simply a harmonization of the chant, for example the *Te Deum II* (S24) in 1853, while the *Male-Voice Mass* composed in 1848 quotes the plainsong Credo for personal reasons. The climax of this 'personal' use of the chant in church music came in 1865 with the composition of the *Missa choralis*, in which the Kyrie is based upon *Sacerdos in aeternam*; his choice of this chant is obviously connected with his entry into minor orders the same year. After 1865 there was a decline in Liszt's output of church music using plainchant, though not of religious music; for example the choral work *Die heilige Cäcilia* (S5) of 1874 is based upon *Cantantibus organis*, sung on the Feast of St Cecilia. There seems therefore to have been a connection between Liszt's use of plainchant in church music and his ambitions to reform church music, for although he used it throughout his life, there is a concentration upon its use in church works during the Weimar period, leading to the *Responses and Antiphons* in 1860. In 1860 Liszt was still in Weimar, but after meeting Hohenlohe in 1859 had persuaded the Princess to go to Rome. Liszt would not have poured so much energy into the task of harmonizing plainchant without a further end in mind.

Closely related to this is Liszt's interest in Palestrina, whose 'reformed' version of the plainsong of the Mass was published in the 'Medicean' Gradual of 1614. The nineteenth century accepted the story found in Baini's biography (1828) that decisions of the Council of Trent were affected by the *Missa Papae Marcelli*, and Palestrina was universally regarded as the saviour of church music. Liszt possessed a book in German based upon Baini's biography, entitled *Ueber das Leben und die Werke des G. Pierluigi da Palestrina. Nach den Memorie storico-critiche des Abbate Giuseppe Baini*,[14] published in 1834, the very year Liszt wrote his article 'On Future Church Music'. It is not known, unfortunately, when Liszt acquired the copy, but in all probability he did so before going to Rome. His markings in the book therefore indicate his particular interest in Palestrina.

Regarding the man, Liszt marks several passages. On page xix of the preface, the words 'dieses unermüdlichen Homers der Musik' are underlined. On page xx the author's remark that 'G. Pierluigi zwar zum komponisten nicht aber zum Maestro der päpstlichen kapelle gewählt werden konnte' has an elaborate mark next to it in the margin. In Chapter I, 'Jugend- und Bildungsgeschichte Pierluigi's', Liszt underlines the following passage (p. 3):

Leonardo Cecconi erzählt, dass Pierluigi noch als Knabe sich bei einer musikalischen Ausführung befand, wobei der Kapellmeister bemerkte, dass derselbe mit ausserordentlich richtigen Gefühle die Kadenzen begleitete.

In Chapter II the author tells how Palestrina dedicated a volume of Masses for four and five voices to Pope Julius III in 1554. Liszt marks the following (p. 6):

In der Dedikazion sagt *Pierluigi* unter andern: *Christianus summi Dei laudis exquisitioribus rhythmis cum cecinissem, nulli magis quam tuo nomini eas dicare visum est.* Er selbst also hielt diese seine Arbeit höher, als die gewöhnlichen seiner Zeitgenossen.

Later, Palestrina's expulsion from the papal choir on the grounds that he was married is marked in heavy double lines (p. 9):

Am 30. Juli 1555 erschien das päpstliche *Motu proprio* des Inhalts: dass die drei verheiratheten Individuen, die zum Skandal des Gottesdienstes und der heiligen Kirchengesetze mit den päpstlichen Kapellen-Sängern zusammen leben, aus dem Collegio ausgestossen werden sollten.

In Chapter V, the author gives the reason why Pope Pius IV created for Palestrina the special title of 'composer' to the papal chapel, instead of the usual *maestro di capella*; Palestrina was married, and the post was given only to a priest. Liszt underlines this (p. 53):

Diess muss dadurch erklärt werden, dass dieser Titel von je her einem Prälaten ... zukam.

Quite clearly, Liszt was interested in those aspects of Palestrina's life that might correspond with his own: Palestrina's musical precociousness as a child, his high regard for his own church music, and the fact that marriage prevented him from being put in charge of the Sistine choir.

Regarding the music, Liszt's markings are equally illuminating. In Chapter II the author refers to the third edition in 1591 of Palestrina's volume of Masses dedicated to Pope Julius III, to which the composer added another Mass, based upon plainchant: 'eine fünfstimmige Seelen-messe über die Melodien des Gregorianischen Gesanges'. Liszt marks this in the margin. Later occurs a passage referring to the banning of musical instruments in church, against which Liszt has put a marking (p. 20; the italics indicate his own underlining):

So bezeugt schon der h. Thomas, dass in seinem Jahrhunderte die Instrumente ganz aus den Kirchen verbannt worden wären. 'Instrumenta musica, sicut citharas et psalteria non assumit Ecclesia in divinas laudes, ne *videatur judaizare*'.

A later footnote by the editor (p. 21) states that in the time of Giovanni Croce, instruments played voice parts. He has seen a work 'wohin der dritte Chor aus einer obligaten Tenorstimme und *drei Posaunen statt* Stimmen besteht'. Another reference to instruments playing vocal music is marked by Liszt. The author says (p. 23) that Renaissance composers designed their works 'dass sie auch ohne Sänger *mit blosen Instrumenten ausgeführt* werden konnten'. Later, reference is made to the Renaissance practice of using secular melodies upon which to base religious works (p. 29):

Die Tonsetzter des 15. und 16. Jahrhunderts, um neu und beliebt zu sein, benutzen die genialen Melodien der Volksgesänge, der Romanzen, Sonette, Madrigale, und machten Sie nicht selten zum *Thema* ihrer Messen. Daher die profanen Titel solcher Komposizionen. Z.B. Mio marito mi ha infamato; baciatemi o cara; il Villano geloso; l'Amico o Madama; O Venere bella; che fa oggi il mio sole; io mi son giovanetta etc.

Liszt marked the last sentence of this quotation in his copy. The editor adds a footnote (p. 37) also marked by Liszt: 'Der Missbrauch, über Thema's weltlicher Lieder zu kontrapunkturen, hatte der Kunst nicht geschadet.' The footnote explains that the secular melodies were inaudible because they were turned into long notes, given Latin texts, and were hidden beneath the layers of counterpoint. Liszt marks a quotation from the Council of Trent regarding church music (p. 42):

Ab ecclesiis vero musicas eas, ubi sive organo, sive cantu lascivium aut impurum aliquid miscetur, (Ordinarii locorum) arceat, ut domus Dei vere domus orationis esse videatur ac deri possit.

Taken together, these passages represent Liszt's own practice when writing church music: the use of plainchant to base works upon, the exclusion of instruments save for the organ – the exception being wind instruments, which, for example, Liszt prompted Herbeck to use to accompany the *Male-Voice Mass* – and the occasional use of secular melodies to form the basis of religious works, as in the *Hungarian Coronation Mass*, which contains fragments of the *Rákóczy March*. The works by Liszt which use the full orchestra, and yet were intended for church use, were written for special occasions involving pomp and ceremony. The majority of Liszt's church works are for choir and organ, and of these many derive their character from the Palestrinian ideal. This is true for example of the *Pater noster* and *Ave Maria* composed in 1846. Liszt's last piece of church music, the *Salve regina* (S66) composed in 1885, is in the same vein. This ideal can be regarded as the foundation of Liszt's church style. Concerning the composition of the *Male-Voice Mass* in 1848, Liszt later wrote to d'Ortigue: 'While writing it, Rome and Palestrina came back into my mind' (*Br.* VIII, 62). The implication is that Liszt had heard Palestrina's music in Rome in 1839, the year of his first visit. His second was in 1861, when he went to live there. Shortly after his arrival, he wrote: 'The services and ceremonies of the Sistine Chapel and of St Peter's, to which I attached a special musical interest, have absorbed all my time during the last fortnight' (*L*, II, 11). It is clear that Liszt identified his task with that of Palestrina. Not only did his own church style derive from

Palestrina, but his position at Rome was to some extent parallel, an obsession that doubtless lay behind his taking minor orders in 1865.

Liszt's interest in reforming church music extended into the past as well as into the future. He was an active supporter of the Cäcilien-Verein, or Society of St Cecilia, founded by Franz Witt in 1867 to promote the revival of Renaissance church works, and to advocate the composition of church music in a similar style. Franz Witt (1834–88) took holy orders in 1856, and became a pupil of Proske at Regensburg, the centre for research into plainsong before the activities at Solesmes got under way. He founded the periodical *Musica Sacra*, published by the Society of St Cecilia. The successor to Witt as President was Franz Xaver Haberl, who in 1867–70 was organist at Santa Maria dell' Anima in Rome, where he met Liszt. During his stay in Rome, Haberl succeeded in gaining papal recognition for the Society, whose edition of the chant, based upon the Medicean Edition, was granted approval in 1870.

In 1869 Witt sent Liszt a copy of his *Litaniae lauretanae*, and Liszt wrote giving his opinion. Liszt held a high opinion of Witt, and in the 1870s, when the Hungarians were hoping to persuade Liszt to accept a permanent post in Budapest in connection with the proposed new Music Academy, he asked Witt to come and teach church music there.[15] At Liszt's instigation a special department for the subject was set up, though Witt, through illness, was unable to take up the post. In 1873 Liszt spoke of the idea in a letter to Baron Augusz:

I am especially pleased at the proposal of our exalted patron and president, Archbishop Haynald, to set up a 'special department' for church music. The absence of similar 'departments' in other conservatoires has proved detrimental alike to both Art and Worship. To what end are barrel-organ tunes so much used in church? . . . surely not, in divine service, to commit a sin against Art? Let Hungary now take the lead with better examples; I am ready to give them my support, but on my own I cannot do enough. We are in need of a strong and zealous personality who can grasp and solve both the musical and the ecclesiastical sides of this difficult problem. For this purpose I once again suggest to you the venerable priest and highly esteemed musician, conductor and composer, Franz Witt, President of the German Cäcilien-Verein etc., and I would ask you to recommend urgently to Archbishop Haynald and the Minister Trefort that he be appointed to the Music Academy at Pest.                    (*BruS*, 159)

The two main ingredients upon which Liszt based his idea of reforming church music were therefore (a) the adoption of plainchant, albeit in harmonized versions, and (b) the revival of the church music of the Renaissance, which should serve as a model for the composition of new works. These eventually became the two main recommendations of the 'Motu proprio' issued later, in 1903. Liszt's main concern, however, was for renewal. He did not envisage the future being usurped by the past. Although Palestrina's name heads the list of neglected church com-

# Liszt and Palestrina

posers mentioned in Liszt's 1835 article, the aim was to continue the tradition they represented. Liszt succeeded in doing this in so far as his attempts to emulate Palestrina are successful works of art, though they are not truly Palestrinian. They rely upon harmony rather than counterpoint, and evoke particular moods.

Liszt's church works were not widely used in his lifetime, and some remained unpublished. The works which were known, like the *Gran Mass*, aroused controversy, while others for modest resources remained in the background. Liszt summed up his situation in a letter to the Hungarian composer Mihalovich:

Everyone is against me. Catholics, because they find my church music profane, Protestants because to them my music is Catholic, freemasons because they think my music is clerical; to conservatives I am a revolutionary, to the 'futurists' an old Jacobin. As for the Italians, in spite of Sgambati, if they support Garibaldi they detest me as a hypocrite, if they are on the Vatican side I am accused of bringing Venus's grotto into the Church. To Bayreuth, I am not a composer, but a publicity agent. Germans reject my music as French, the French as German, to the Austrians I write gypsy music, to the Hungarians foreign music. And the Jews loathe me, my music and myself, for no reason at all.[16]

# 8

## THE MASSES

All of Liszt's settings of the Mass, including those with orchestral accompaniment, were composed for church use. Before 1903 there were no restrictions regarding the use of instruments in church, and both the *Gran Mass* and the *Hungarian Coronation Mass* were performed in church on other occasions than the ones for which they were specifically composed. On the other hand, they were also given concert performances, taking their place alongside those orchestral Masses usually heard only in the concert hall, chief among them of course Beethoven's *Missa solemnis*.

Liszt therefore had regard for practical considerations when composing these works. His general approach is summed up in these words: 'The Church composer is both preacher and priest, and what the *word* fails to bring to our powers of perception the *tone* makes winged and clear' (*L*, I, 316). On settings of the Mass in particular, Liszt gave the following advice to Saint-Saëns, who had submitted one for Liszt's opinion:

Bear with one more liturgical question, and, in addition, a proposition boldly practical in the *Kyrie*, the spire of your Cathedral. The inspiration and structure of it are certainly admirable . . . 'omnia excelsa tua et fluctus tui super me transierunt'. Nevertheless, during these 300 bars, or so, of a slow and almost continuous movement, do you not lose sight of the *celebrant*, who is obliged to remain standing motionless at the altar? Do you not expose him to commit the sin of impatience directly after he has said the confiteor? . . . Will not the composer be reproached with having given way to his genius rather than to the requirements of the worship?

In order to obviate these unpleasant conjunctures it would be necessary for you to resign yourself to an enormous sacrifice as an artist, namely, to cut 18 pages! (*for church performance only*, for these 18 pages should be preserved in the edition to your greater honour as a musician, and it would suffice to indicate the 'cut' *ad libitum*, as I have done in several places in the score of the Gran Mass).

Sacrifice, then, 18 pages as I said, and put the *Christe eleison* on page 6, instead of the *Kyrie eleison* . . .

From the musical point of view exclusively, I should blush to make such a proposition; but it is necessary to keep peace, especially in the Church, where one must learn to subordinate one's self in mind and deed. Art, there, should be only a correlative matter, and should tend to the most perfect *concomitance* possible with the rite.                                                  (*L*, II, 186)

# The Masses

Liszt composed five settings of the Mass and one of the Requiem. Two Masses, one with organ and one with orchestral accompaniment, were composed at Weimar, and two more – again, one with organ, the other with orchestra – in Rome, while the fifth was a reworking of the first. Before undertaking this reworking Liszt composed the *Requiem* in Rome in 1868.

## MISSA QUATTUOR VOCUM AD AEQUALES CONCINENTE ORGANO (*MALE-VOICE MASS*) (S8)

### Composition

The early version, according to Liszt, was composed in 1848, and this is the date given in the catalogues. However Liszt did occasionally make errors in this respect regarding other works of his; he says in a letter, for example, that the *Gran Mass* was composed in 1856 (*Br.* VI, 326), when it was composed in 1855. Therefore he may have been wrong about 1848, and the gestation period may have reached as far back as 1846. The quality of the work suggests a longer gestation than the period Liszt spent at Weimar before leaving in the spring to meet the Princess Wittgenstein. It was published in 1853 by Breitkopf und Härtel.

The second version of the work is known as the *Szekszárd Mass*. In 1865 Liszt visited the home of Baron Antal Augusz at Szekszárd, where a new church was being built. He promised Augusz a new Mass for the consecration of the church, but the work was not written. In July 1869 Liszt designated the revised version of the *Male-Voice Mass*, due to be published, as 'Messe sexardique'. This version, published in 1869 by Étienne Repos in Paris and in 1870 by Brietkopf und Härtel, is the one incorporated in the Collected Edition.

### Performance

The early version was first performed on 15 August 1852 in the Catholic church at Weimar on the occasion of the birthday of Louis Napoleon, President of the French Republic. The *Szekszárd Mass* was given a public rehearsal on 23 September 1870 in the castle church in Buda. The première was intended for Szekszárd, but did not take place due to the historical events at that time concerning the Ecclesiastical State. The first performance eventually took place in Jena in 1872.

In 1857 Liszt indicated his requirements for a performance of the early version:

I fear that the preparation of this work will cost you and your singers some trouble. Before all else it requires the utmost certainty in intonation, which can only be attained by practising the parts *singly* (especially the middle parts, second tenor and first bass) – and then, above all, *religious* absorption, meditation, expansion, ecstasy, shadow, light, soaring – in a word, *Catholic devotion* and *inspiration*. The *Credo*, as if built on a rock, should sound as steadfast as the dogma itself; a mystic and ecstatic joy should pervade the *Sanctus*; the *Agnus Dei* (as well as the *Miserere* in the *Gloria*) should be accentuated, in a tender and deeply elegiac manner, by the most fervent sympathy with the *Passion* of Christ; and the *Dona nobis pacem*, expressive of reconciliation and full of faith, should float away like sweet-smelling incense.                                    (*L*, I, 315)

## *Arrangements*

On the occasion of the Mozart centenary in 1856, Liszt conducted in Vienna, where he played portions of the Mass to Johann Herbeck (1831–77), director of the choir at the Piaristenkirche, later Hofcapellmeister (court conductor). Herbeck wished to perform the work, and Liszt wrote to him:

If the extent of the chorus allows of it, it might perhaps be desirable to add a few more wind instruments (clarinets, bassoon, horns, indeed even a couple of trombones) to support the voices more. If you think so too, please send me a line to say so, and I will at once send you a small score of the wind instruments.

(*L*, I, 316)

In the end, Herbeck undertook the arrangement himself, sending Liszt the sketches. Liszt replied:

I am *entirely in accord* with the various sketches you so kindly lay before me in your letter, and only beg you, dear sir, to complete this work according to your own best judgment.                                    (*L*, I, 341)

The arrangement, completed and performed at Jena in August 1858, remains unpublished.

The Liszt Museum at Weimar contains the manuscript of an arrangement by Raff of the Kyrie for mixed choir and orchestra.

Liszt's *Missa pro organo* (S264) composed in 1879 is based partly on the *Male-Voice Mass*.

The work is in the key of C minor, although only the Kyrie and parts of the Gloria (Glorificamus te and Quoniam tu solus sanctus) have a key signature of three flats. The Credo and the Dona nobis pacem are in C major, while the rest of the work has a key signature of one sharp. Philipp Wolfrum, the editor of the church music published in the Breitkopf Collected Edition, states that though the manuscript of this early version at Weimar contains no organ part, staves are left empty for one which Liszt must have added prior to its publication. Certainly the later

(Szekszárd) version could not be performed unaccompanied; neither could the early version, but one of the differences between the two versions is the greater independence of the organ part in the later one. Otherwise the two versions contain the same music; none of the sections of the Mass was recomposed in the sense that Liszt substituted different music. The differences are more a matter of lengthening or shortening phrases and sections – a genuine rethinking on Liszt's part of the actual material, some of which (e.g. in the Gloria and the Dona nobis pacem) is based on plainchant. The very opening shows the subtlety of these changes. The later version (see Ex. 4(a)) has an increased spaciousness, taking 25 bars where the early version (see Ex. 4(b)) has only 12 to reach the same point. The later version, though gaining in breadth and dignity, loses the dissonance in bar 11 of the 1853 version (E natural in the bass against F and D in the tenors). These are the kind of differences that make it difficult to choose between early and revised versions of many of Liszt's works. Although the early versions of most works tend towards rhapsodic prolixity, they often contain passages of originality and beauty omitted in the later version. There are a few such passages in the 1853 Mass which do not figure in the version performed today; on the whole though, this later version is the better of the two. Liszt made the other movements more concise (the Kyrie is the exception), at the same time bringing the emotional climaxes into greater relief.

The opening of the Gloria (see Ex. 5(a)) makes use of plainchant (see Ex. 5(b), which shows the chant as it appears on p. 134 of the *Nouvel Eucologe en musique*). The first three notes form Liszt's 'Cross motif' (see chapter 14) and the theme forms the basis of a fugal passage leading to the Laudamus te. The words 'Et in terra pax hominibus' are set to a phrase of Liszt's own invention (see Ex. 6), reflecting the polarity in his mind between heaven (the chant) and earth (a man-made theme). The two melodic fragments form the basic material of the Gloria movement. Thus the setting of 'miserere nobis' (see Ex. 7) clearly derives from the 'man-made' fragment, while the 'Cross motif' is singled out at the words 'Tu solus altissimus'.

The longest text of the Mass is the Credo, and Liszt approached the problem differently in each of his settings, avoiding it altogether in the *Hungarian Coronation Mass* by substituting someone else's setting. In the present work Liszt's desire that it should sound 'as if built on a rock' is achieved by making the choir declaim the text to repeated chords. A linear approach with imitation is introduced at the Crucifixus; at this point Liszt includes an *ossia* version in the score, using the same music, but without any imitation, relying on the Bachian flavour imparted by the falling diminished seventh to convey the spirit of the words (see Ex. 8). The declaimed style returns at the Et resurrexit.

103

Ex. 4(a)

Ex. 4(b)

Ex. 5

Ex. 6

Ex. 7

Ex. 8

Ex. 9

The Sanctus opens with a long-breathed melody for tenor solo. In the 1853 version there was no organ accompaniment at this point, but Liszt later doubled the voices with the organ, doubtless after experiencing difficulties of intonation in performance (see Ex. 9). A new theme appears at the Pleni sunt caeli, initially sung unaccompanied by a bass solo. The same theme is used to set the Benedictus, and there is also a return of the Sanctus theme, also set to the words of the Benedictus. Liszt does not do this in any of his other settings of the Mass, where the Sanctus and the Benedictus are clearly differentiated by their music; a recapitulation, if desired (as in the *Gran Mass*), is then effected by using the same music for each appearance of the Hosanna in excelsis.

The Agnus Dei opens with a passage remarkable both for the originality of the choral writing and the expressive power of the harmony. In the 1853 version this was entirely unaccompanied (see Ex. 10), but discreet organ chords were later added. The Dona nobis pacem is set to the plainchant 'Credo in unum Deum' (see Ex. 11). This late appearance in the work of another fragment of plainchant melody could only have had a personal significance, as it is not justified by either the words or the musical plan of the work. (The *Gran Mass*, *Missa choralis* and *Hungarian Coronation Mass* all become cyclic at this point by reintroducing the music of the Kyrie.)

The *Male-Voice Mass* is remarkable in many ways. The sheer quality of the music places it among Liszt's best works. This is all the more surprising considering that at the time of its composition Liszt had yet to embark upon the symphonic poems, the piano concertos and the symphonies. The quality of the choral writing in particular is to be admired. Already Liszt shows great resourcefulness in his writing for male voices, a medium for which he had a special predilection. The early version is full of imaginative touches regarding the layout of the voice-parts, the contrasting of solo and tutti passages, and an appreciation of the timbres of the different vocal registers. The organ part in the final version has

Ex. 10

Ex. 11

eliminated the few flamboyant passages of the early version, and is a judicious mixture of support for the voices to help chiefly in matters of intonation and independence in the musical structure, lending colour and animation at appropriate points. The neglect therefore of this setting of the Mass amounts to ignoring buried treasure. Also, its contribution to Liszt's development as a composer has not been recognized.

# The Masses

For whereas his early attempts at orchestral music betrayed a pianistic approach, the *Male-Voice Mass*, originally composed largely without accompaniment, shows an impressive, and therefore surprising, practical command of choral writing, together with original ideas as to its treatment.

## *MISSA SOLENNIS ZUR EINWEIHUNG DER BASILIKA IN GRAN*
## (*GRAN MASS*) (S9)

### Composition

On 27 January 1855 Liszt received a letter from Baron Antal Augusz informing him that Archbishop János Scitovsky wished to renew the commission he had made in 1846 for a Mass from Liszt (to be performed at the ceremony of the reconsecration of Pécs cathedral). In 1849, before the cathedral at Pécs had been fully restored, Scitovsky became Prince Primate of Hungary, and moved to Esztergom (Gran), seat of the Catholic Church in Hungary, where the cathedral was being rebuilt over the ruins of the Turkish devastations of the sixteenth and seventeenth centuries. Liszt's new Mass would be performed at the ceremony of reconsecration, and he set to work immediately. On 4 May he wrote to Agnes Street: 'I have completely finished the score of my *Mass* to which I might add the epigraph "Laboravi in gemitu meo . . . Sana me, Domine, quoniam conturbata sunt ossa mea"' (*Br.* III, 10).

Liszt revised the work after the performance at Esztergom in 1856, adding fugues to the Gloria ('cum sancto spiritu') and the Credo ('et unam sanctam catholicam ecclesiam'; see chapter 13). The *Gran Mass* occupies an extremely important place in Liszt's output; its initial success seems to have caused Liszt to entertain serious thoughts about the direction his career as a composer should take. It was this work he sent to the Pope in 1859 via Hohenlohe. In 1857 he wrote:

If I am not quite mistaken, the Church element, as well as the musical style of this work, will be better understood and more spiritually felt after frequent performances than can be the case at first in the face of the prevailing prejudice against my later compositions, and the systematic opposition of routine and custom which I have to meet with on so many sides. Thus much I may in all conscientiousness affirm, that I composed the work, from the first bar to the last, with the deepest ardour as a Catholic and the utmost care as a musician, and hence I can leave it with perfect comfort to time to form a corresponding verdict upon it.

(*L*, I, 334)

The score was published in 1859 by the Royal State Printing House in Vienna, at the expense of the State, and in 1871 by Schuberth, Leipzig.

# Revolution and religion

*Performance*

On 24 April 1856 a committee headed by Cardinal Scitovsky agreed to perform Liszt's Mass on the day of the reconsecration ceremony. Preparations for this were put in the hands of Count Leo Festetics, an old friend of Liszt's who, however, had misgivings about letting the 'music of the future' into the Church, and persuaded the Cardinal that he should not have his name associated with it. Scitovsky then wrote to Liszt saying that the Mass could not be performed as the size of the choir was too small at Esztergom, and he had heard that the work lasted more than two and a half hours. Liszt replied that the choir was adequate, the music lasted at the most an hour, and he was prepared to make cuts if necessary. It was then suggested that the Mass be performed at Esztergom, but in November, after the ceremony had taken place. Liszt replied that not to perform the work on the occasion for which it had been especially commissioned was an insult to his reputation as an artist. Baron Augusz then managed to persuade the Cardinal that these were unworthy intrigues against Liszt, and on 27 July Liszt learned that the Mass would be performed at the ceremony of the reconsecration. He left for Hungary on 7 August.

The choirmaster at Esztergom was Károly Seyler, and it was his music that Festetics wished to substitute for Liszt's. In 1855 Liszt had suggested that the Offertorium and Graduale – which belong to the Proper sections of the Mass – should be composed by Mihály Mosonyi, who consequently set to work and produced the requisite music. On the day, however, Mosonyi's music was replaced by Seyler's; Liszt made amends to Mosonyi by performing his music in the Pest inner-city church.

Mosonyi played the double bass in the orchestra at the performance of Liszt's Mass at Esztergom. Before that time, he had not been acquainted with Liszt's works. Years later, he wrote:

I got to know Liszt more closely when in 1856 he came to Pest to conduct the rehearsals for the performance of his Gran Mass. I must admit honestly that this work then meant the ray of light for me that once transformed Saul into Paul. Because until then, in the wake of general public opinion, I, too, spoke only volubly but idly in his interest, empty words which even though glorifying him as an outstanding virtuoso pianist did not want to recognize him at all as a great composer. But during the rehearsals of the Mass in question the scales fell from my eyes, and I beat my breast in mea culpa with a repenting heart.[1]

Public rehearsals were held on 26 and 28 August in the National Museum in Pest. On 30 August the musicians, together with Liszt, took a steamer up the Danube to Esztergom, and rehearsed in the cathedral, where they discovered that the new building had terrible acoustics.

# The Masses

(They have still today too much reverberation.) There were no lodgings for the musicians in Esztergom, so all including Liszt spent the night on the steamer without food, drink or lighting. The ceremony on 31 August took place before the Austrian Emperor, Hungarian magnates, and an audience of 4,000. The musicians, including the choir, numbered 140. Liszt conducted. A member of the choir later described the performance:

> I was in the choir facing him, and the play of his wonderful features so struck my childish soul, that it inspired me with the following lines:
> 'I cannot keep my eyes off his sublime face. There is nothing more interesting than to see Liszt conducting. His features always reflect the nature of the music he hears. Enthusiasm, beatitude, spiritual fervour, all can be read in his eyes. I could always tell beforehand what would be the dominant idea in any passage just begun; Liszt's features told me.'                                    (*WRC*, 4)

The music displeased the Emperor, however, and Liszt was not invited to the banquet held after the ceremony. He returned with his musicians to Pest, where the Mass was performed in the parish church on 4 September. This time the music was given an ovation. Liszt wrote to his cousin Eduard Liszt:

> Yesterday's performance of my Mass was quite according to my intentions, and was more successful and effective by far than all the preceding ones. Without exaggeration and with all Christian modesty I can assure you that many tears were shed, and that the very numerous audience (the church of the *Stadtpfarrei* was thronged), as well as the performers, had raised themselves, body and soul, into my contemplation of the sacred mysteries of the Mass . . . and everything was but a humble prayer to the Almighty and to the Redeemer!                (*L*, I, 288)

To Agnes Klindworth he wrote a slightly more self-revealing letter:

> On the one hand I have gained the full knowledge that the task I fulfil in this world forms an integral part of the nation's glory . . . And on the other I have occupied a serious position as a religious and *Catholic* composer. That indeed is a boundless field for art and I feel a vocation to cultivate it vigorously . . .
> The intelligent portion of the clergy immediately *adopted* me, after the first performance of my Mass, and the number of my enthusiastic *adherents* among the ecclesiastics grows all the time. The fact is, I think I can say in good faith and all modesty that among the composers known to me, none has such an intense and profound feeling for religious music as your most humble servant . . . Here, as elsewhere, it is a question of renewing from the foundations, as Lacordaire says, and of penetrating to the living source which springs into eternal life.
> (*Br.* III, 80)

An ambition had been awakened in Liszt which grew over the following years. In March 1858 he again wrote to Agnes Klindworth – while on board the steamer from Vienna to Pest:

> Indeed no, you are not mistaken, I cannot get rid of my affliction. At times my whole being is overcome by it. I suffer from an unquenchable thirst, which prayer makes even more ardent. This feeling for the impossible, it would seem, comes

out in my works, and one of my compatriots, on hearing my Mass, said: 'This music is so religious it would convert Satan himself!' (*Br.* III, 105)

On 15 March 1866 the *Gran Mass* was performed in the church of St Eustache in Paris, and brought a storm of critical abuse on Liszt's head. The occasion, a very grand affair, was attended by Princess Metternich and other members of the aristocracy, Cardinal de Bonnechose, Archbishop of Rouen, Berlioz, Gounod, Auber, and of course Liszt himself. An orchestra of 80 was assembled from various theatres, and the soloists with the choir were Warot and Agnesi from the Opéra. The conductor was a M. Hurand, chorus master at the Théâtre-Italien, and the organist of St Eustache, Batiste, took the organ part. The hostility directed afterwards at Liszt by his former friends, particularly Berlioz and d'Ortigue, left wounds which never healed. Liszt stayed away from Paris for years afterwards (his reason for being there in 1866 was the death of his mother in February), and as late as 1882 could write:

At the time when Berlioz was attacking the *Messe de Gran* and condemning it as 'the negation of art', my two old friends, he and d'Ortigue, were disowning me at their leisure in Paris (in the winter of '66), concluding with 99 percent of the public that I was very wrong to concern myself with composition, since I had no talent and should limit myself to my success as a pianist. Not to follow this peremptory advice amounts, in the religion of art, to final impertinence. My sincere Catholicism does not prescribe that I should seek the absolution of people who dislike my music, such as it is. Opinions and sensations are free and I make no claim whatever to imposing mine on anyone. To go on working is enough for me. (*LOM*, 423)

## Arrangements

The whole Mass was arranged for the piano (four hands) by Mosonyi and published in 1865 by Rózsavölgyi. The piano score included in the full scores of 1859 and 1871 was by Zellner. Liszt himself did not arrange any part of the work for either the piano or the organ.

The *Gran Mass* is Liszt's greatest setting of the Mass, and one of his masterworks. It is scored for full choir, four soloists, and a large orchestra including four trumpets, bass drum, cymbals, gong (used in the Credo only), harp and organ. The musical construction of the work is symphonic, along the lines developed by Liszt in his symphonic poems, though as well as thematic transformation there is a use of recurring themes. Some of these appear in different movements – the opening theme of the Gloria, for example, recurs at 'et resurrexit' in the Credo, and at 'dona nobis pacem' in the Agnus Dei. The effect of this is twofold: first it gives musical cohesion to the Mass as a whole, and secondly it provides emotional links between different sections of the text. Both features have been criticized, the one because Liszt seems to be copying Wagner, the other because it is asserted that there is no valid connection between the passages of text chosen by Liszt to receive the same music. English critics have taken their point of departure from Dannreuther, who wrote in 1905 in *The Oxford History of Music*, vol. VI:

Liszt . . . came to interpret the Catholic ritual in a histrionic spirit, and tried to make his music reproduce the words not only as *ancilla theologica et ecclesiastica*, but also as *ancilla dramaturgica*. The influence of Wagner's operatic method, as it appears in *Tannhäuser*, *Lohengrin*, and *Das Rheingold*, is abundantly evident; but the result of this influence is more curious than convincing. By the application of Wagner's system of Leitmotive to the text of the Mass, Liszt succeeded in establishing some similarity between different movements, and so approached uniformity of diction. It will be seen, for example, that his way . . . of repeating the principal preceding motives in the 'Dona nobis pacem' . . . has given to the work a musical unity which is not always in very clear accordance with the text.

It is very important to set the record straight on this matter. When Liszt composed the work in 1855 he had already conducted *Tannhäuser*, *Lohengrin* and *The Flying Dutchman*. In none of these works does Wagner apply his 'system of Leitmotive', though there are recurrent themes. In this respect, Liszt's use of recurrent themes in the *Gran Mass* is much more thorough, and we do not find the same thoroughness in Wagner until *after* its composition. Therefore, even if the procedure is acknowledged to be found in Liszt, there are no grounds for assuming that he took it from Wagner. The distinctive feature of 'recurrent themes' is that they recur in different movements (or, in the case of Wagner's operas, in different acts), and are not confined to one. Before 1855, Liszt had composed the *Faust Symphony*, whose third movement is based upon varied forms of themes from the first movement, and includes a theme from the second, while the closing 'Chorus mysticus' uses themes from both the first and the second movements. Similarly the Piano Concerto in E♭, which was in existence, if not completed, by 1850, makes use of recurring themes as its basic structure, though the work clearly divides into four movements, three of which are joined without a break. Liszt may have taken the idea from Schubert's *Wandererfantasie*, which he arranged for piano and orchestra in 1851. Alternatively he may have been influenced by Berlioz's *Symphonie fantastique*, in which case the idea was implanted in 1830. Certainly Liszt's *De profundis*, the unfinished work for piano and orchestra composed in 1834, uses the psalm theme as the mainspring of the work, turning it into a march for the finale.

It is evident that Liszt thought of the idea as being symphonic, and as such had put it to use *before* Wagner applied it to opera. Wagner's concern was similarly to make opera more symphonic in its musical construction.

The difference between the two composers is that Liszt combined the idea of recurring themes with the idea of transformation of themes, which Wagner makes little use of, as it would defeat his purpose if a leit-motif became unrecognizable. But often Liszt's transformations are sufficiently adroit as to give at first the impression of a completely new theme. This was part of his aim, for then the relationship would be unperceived, or unconsciously perceived; in either case it would remain 'secret' until repeated familiarity 'revealed' it. This for Liszt represented the programmatic process at work, and, paradoxically for a composer whose aim was to be popular, only the initiated were likely to discover the true significance of these transformations.

Liszt's application, therefore, of the idea of recurring themes was his own, and not a result of Wagner's influence. Indeed, since Wagner studied Liszt's symphonic poems in 1856 before embarking upon *Tristan und Isolde*, leaving the music of *The Ring* unfinished, it is possible that the influence was the other way round, as his 'system of Leitmotive' became increasingly the very basis of Wagner's composing process.

We are left with the claim that Liszt's use of recurring themes in the *Gran Mass* 'is not always in very clear accordance with the text'. Here a study of the music is illuminating. There are nine repeated themes in the *Gran Mass*, and their use in relation to the words is shown below. For the sake of clarity, the English words have been substituted.

Ia: Lord (Kyrie); give us peace; Amen (Agnus Dei). See Ex. 12.
Ib: have mercy (Kyrie); Pontius Pilate (Credo); who takest away the sins of the world, have mercy upon us (Agnus Dei). See Ex. 13.
II: Christ (have mercy) (Kyrie); who takest away the sins of the world, have mercy upon us; thou who takest away the sins of the world, receive our prayer (Gloria); Blessed is he who is coming in the name of the Lord (Sanctus); Lamb of God; give us peace (Agnus Dei). See Ex. 14.
III: Glory be to God on high; we glorify thee, we give thee thanks for thy great glory. Lord God, heavenly King, God the almighty Father. Lord Jesus Christ, only-begotten Son. Lord God, Lamb of God, Son of the Father; Thou, Jesus Christ, alone art the Most High; Amen (Gloria); And the third day he rose again according to the scriptures. And he ascended into heaven (Credo); (Thy glory) fills (all heaven and earth); Hosanna in high heaven! (Sanctus); give us peace (Agnus Dei). See Ex. 15.
IV: and on earth peace to men of good will. We praise thee, we bless thee, we adore thee; thou who sittest at the right hand of the Father, have mercy upon us. For thou alone art the Holy One. Thou alone art Lord (Gloria); begotten, not made (Credo); give us peace (Agnus Dei). See Ex. 16.
V: I believe in one God [= the theme itself], the almighty Father, maker

# The Masses

Ex. 12

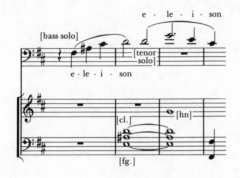

Ex. 13

Ex. 14

Ex. 15

Ex. 16

of heaven and earth, and of all things visible and invisible. And in one Lord Jesus Christ, only-begotten Son of God, born of the Father before all ages; of one essence with the Father; through whom all things were made. He for us men, and for our salvation, (came down from heaven,) and was incarnate by the Holy Ghost from the Virgin Mary; and is seated at the right hand of the Father. He will come again with glory; and of his reign there will be no end; who [the Holy Spirit] proceeds from the Father and the Son; who together with the Father and the Son is adored and glorified; And I believe in one holy, catholic, and apostolic Church. I acknowledge one baptism for the remission of sins (Credo). Amen (Agnus Dei). See Ex. 17.

VI: God from God, light from light, true God from true God; I believe too in the Holy Spirit, Lord and life-giver (Credo). See Ex. 18.

VII: and was made man (Credo); Lamb of God (Agnus Dei). See Ex. 19.

VIII: to judge the living and the dead; And I look forward to the resurrection of the dead; Amen (Credo). See Ex. 20.

IX: Holy, Holy, Holy Lord God of hosts; Hosanna in high heaven! (Sanctus). See Ex. 21.

# The Masses

Ex. 17

Ex. 18

Ex. 19

# Revolution and religion

Ex. 20

Ex. 21

The association of ideas presented here is clear and logical. It is noticeable how 'peace' figures prominently (see chapter 3, p. 30 for Liszt's enthusiasm for Lamartine's 1848 manifesto); Liszt associates the Lord (Ia), Christ (II), and his glory (III) with peace itself (IV). His placing of 'Pontius Pilate' in relation to 'the sins of the world' (Ib), and 'he was made man' in relation to the 'Lamb of God' (VII) is also revealing. The themes not included in the Credo – Lord (Ia), Christ (II) and Holy Lord God of hosts (IX) – have others to duplicate their rôle: Ia and IX are subsumed in VI ('God from God, light from light'), and the aspects of II in the Credo are Ib ('Pontius Pilate') and VII ('was made man'). The function of the excluded themes is to point Christ's divinity; in the Sanctus ('Blessed is he who is coming in the name of the Lord') by using themes II and IX, and in the Kyrie ('Christ have mercy') by using themes II and Ia. In the Credo, Christ is not addressed separately, and a new theme (VII) is introduced to represent the new element concerning Christ ('was made man'). When Christ is addressed again in the Agnus Dei, the two themes II and VII are joined together to lend full significance to the meaning of the words 'Lamb of God'. The same words in the Gloria, which precedes the Credo, have only theme II (Christ).

# The Masses

From the formal standpoint, Liszt achieves symmetry in the long movements (Gloria and Credo) by balancing his themes at each end of the movement. In the Gloria themes III and IV at the beginning are balanced by IV then III at the end. In the middle is a long passage where III is transformed, and then II is introduced from the Kyrie. The final fugue is in the nature of a coda, leading to the Amen built upon the main theme of the movement.

The Credo is the most complex in construction of all the movements. As in the Gloria, Liszt balances the opening themes (V and VI) with their repeat at the end. And again the middle contains a long passage where the main theme, V, is transformed. But there is then new material with theme VII and the whole of the 'Crucifixus' section, which is followed by theme III before the recapitulation of V. Thus Liszt continually introduces new music as well as reaching back to earlier material. Hardly has the recapitulation got under way when a startling new theme (VIII) interrupts the proceedings. The recapitulation then continues, leading to theme VI. After this, an energetic fugue once again dominates the ending of the movement, this time based upon its main theme ('Credo') and leading to a final vision of the Last Judgment. In spite of its seeming complexity, the structure is perfectly clear in performance, and the whole movement has energy and vision. Its grandeur parallels the dominating rôle in the Mass of the Credo, while the ingenuity shown in creating a symphonic poem around the text shows Liszt's powers at their best.

In the *Gran Mass* the themes are not leitmotifs which appear at significant points to alert the listener to something that is happening; they are rather the stones Liszt uses to build an edifice, and are wedded to the text in a relationship unlikely to be immediately perceived by the listener for the simple reason that they trace ideas, not feelings. Even so, Liszt achieved this result not through a cold calculation of textual relationships mapped out on a preconceived plan – he would not have sat down and made a list of all the words associated with a particular theme. Yet each theme pursues a clear line of thought through the text of the whole Mass; at the same time each contributes to the building of a satisfying musical structure. This feat could be achieved only by somebody for whom the words of the Mass formed part of the very fabric of his thought and feeling. On 14 November 1856 Liszt wrote to Dr Carl Gille, a close friend who after Liszt's death became head of the Liszt Museum at Weimar:

You may be sure, dear friend, that I did not compose my work as one might put on a church vestment instead of a paletot, but that it has sprung from the truly fervent faith of my heart, such as I have felt it since my childhood. '*Genitum, non factum*' – and therefore I can truly say that my Mass has been more *prayed* than composed. (*L*, I, 292)

On another occasion he wrote that 'the work is truly "of pure *musical water* (not in the sense of the ordinary *diluted* Church style, but like diamond water) and living *Catholic wine*" ' (*L*, I, 295).

Dannreuther's further condemnation of the work, however, placed it beyond the pale for English choral societies for nearly a century:

The music is made up of scraps of melody, of fragmentary counterpoint, and sudden changes of key; and . . . the prevailing restlessness and the theatrical character of some of its instrumental effects are not in just accord with the spirit of a religious ceremonial.

Its suitability for liturgical use is today no longer the issue; what is at stake is its reputation as a work of art, and there can be no doubt that it has been done an injustice. Certainly the *Gran Mass* is a mosaic rather than a painting, as are all Liszt's large works, but just as a mosaic becomes a picture if we stand back, so in performance the Mass impresses us as a unified experience, not a concoction. Its open-hearted lyricism, dramatic passion, and sheer ardour of the imagination place it among the outstanding choral works of the nineteenth century, a lone edifice between the symphonic settings of Beethoven and Bruckner.

## *MISSA CHORALIS, ORGANO CONCINENTE* (S10)

### *Composition*

Liszt probably finished the composition in 1865. In January of that year Liszt wrote to Agnes Street: 'My compositions at present are: (A) A mass (a capella – unaccompanied) which I intend to dedicate to the Holy Father. It will be completed in a fortnight's time . . . ' (*Br.* III, 177). Evidently the work was begun before January 1865, that is, before the end of 1864, and this is evidence that Liszt was already thinking of minor orders at that time (see my description of the Kyrie below). According to Wolfrum, the Credo movement in the manuscript at Weimar is dated '3. Mars 65 Madonna del Rosario'. Liszt, in a letter to the Princess written in 1870, referred to 'ma *Missa choralis* – celle que j'ai écrite au Monte Mario' (*Br.* VI, 245). However, after receiving the tonsure in April, Liszt spent May and June at the Villa d'Este, where he also worked on the Mass, as he told the Princess Wittgenstein: 'I'm back at my work – if things work out tomorrow I shall have finished my Jubilee Mass [Messe de Jubilé] before seeing you on Sunday. I shall still need a week or so to copy it out – after which I shall have it sent to the Holy Father' (*Br.* VI, 80). The reason Liszt intended to dedicate the work to the Pope was that in 1866 fell the 1800th anniversary (the 'Jubilee' in Liszt's letter) of the founding of the Holy See in the year A.D. 66. However when the work was published it bore no dedication. Liszt seems to have finished the composition in 1865, for in September he wrote: 'I have had to set it [*Christus*] aside for a year, as the *Vocal Mass* and other smaller works prevented my doing anything to it' (*L*, II, 108).

Although Liszt several times referred to the work as being 'without accompaniment', the version published in 1869 by Kahnt contained an organ accompaniment.

*Performance*

It is not known when or where the first performance took place. Certainly there was no performance in Rome. Liszt seems to have intended the work for one of the Vatican choirs, possibly the Sistine Chapel. In 1865 he wrote:

If Meluzzi's choir were not in too much disarray, it could be performed occasionally in the canons' chapel at St Peter's, where there is an organ to sustain the voices – as there was a bell at the Weimar Catholic church! As for the Sistine, I doubt whether they would be willing to take the trouble to rehearse sufficiently in order not to spoil some of the modulations – which I could not leave out without the risk of falling into an archaic style devoid of the feeling I want to evoke!
(*Br.* VI, 80)

In 1862 Liszt described performances of Palestrina's music given in the Sistine Chapel:

Up till now I haven't heard anything that made me want to listen more attentively – with the exception however of the Masses of Palestrina and his school whose sublime and enduring qualities are revealed completely in the Vatican chapel. The number of singers is relatively few; but the acoustics of the chapel are so excellent and the choir so well situated (near the middle of the nave, a little towards the altar) that the voices, at the most 24–30, produce a very impressive effect. It is incense in sound, bearing prayer upon clouds of azure and gold! ('C'est un encens sonore qui porte la prière sur ses nuages d'or et d'azur!')
(*BruS*, 111)

It is puzzling that in January Liszt referred to the *Missa choralis* as 'a capella', and later in the year acknowledged the need for an organ to support the voices, at the same time considering a performance in the Sistine Chapel, where the singing was unaccompanied. Both this Mass and the earlier one for male voices started life with no organ accompaniment, and just as Liszt said he thought of 'Rome and Palestrina' when he composed the early work, so when he was actually in Rome did he again think of Palestrina when composing the *Missa choralis*, this time surely hoping to follow more closely in the composer's footsteps. The organ part of the *Missa choralis* is independent only in the 'Pleni sunt coeli' of the Sanctus, where it breaks into figuration, and even this is really only to impart energy to the voices, whose music could be performed alone. Unlike the *Male-Voice Mass*, it would be possible to perform the *Missa choralis* unaccompanied, and the organ part shows every sign of having been added later, chiefly as an aid to problems of intonation.

It seems clear that Liszt's hope for a performance in the Sistine Chapel dictated the style of the composition, which is evidently meant as a tribute to Palestrina, though typically done in a free, quite unacademic manner, and not strictly similar to Palestrina's music at all. As so often with Liszt, it is important to establish his intention before assessing the achievement. When the work was to be performed in Budapest in 1872, Liszt wrote:

The day after tomorrow, Sunday, the ladies of the Liszt-Verein [Liszt Society], numbering about 40, together with about 20 tenors and basses, will perform my *Missa choralis* at the *Stadtpfarrei* [city presbytery]. It will only be a run-through, with some mistakes, but I approve of its being done – despite the small support given to church music. It is hardly listened to by an indifferent public, and neglected, even disdained, by the clergy – with a few exceptions, who have little influence upon the general *andamento* in these matters. Should my Mass have some effect on Sunday – I shall gradually think again about how to give new impetus to sacred music, withered and decayed in most of today's Catholic churches. (*Br.* VI, 329)

We are left to speculate why the work was not performed in Rome, and why it was not published with a dedication to the Pope. Perhaps this work was to be the one Liszt hoped would give him entry into the field of liturgical music, the area he really wanted to influence. If so, then following his usual practice the work would have been performed first, dedicated afterwards to the Pope, and then published. (All Liszt's other settings of the Mass were performed before they were published, but only the early version of the *Male-Voice Mass* carried a dedication.) In this case, everything depended upon a performance taking place. It has been assumed (by Wolfrum, for example) that Meluzzi would not allow its performance; certainly Liszt, in his letter quoted above, placed little confidence in Meluzzi. Wherever possible, Liszt preferred to rehearse and conduct the first performances of his religious choral works himself. He would not have been debarred as a layman, because he had just received the tonsure and minor orders. It is surely not a coincidence that the work was composed at the same time, though the fact that the anniversary of the Holy See fell in 1866 was evidently fortuitous, in so far as it provided a happy excuse for dedicating the Mass to the Pope. These intentions are clearly indicated in Liszt's letters written at the time, and his insistence on describing the work as 'a capella' points to the musical practice in use in the Sistine Chapel. Yet there is no subsequent mention of why these intentions were not carried out.

The clue may be the addition of an organ part. Liszt doubted whether

Meluzzi 'would be willing to take the trouble to rehearse sufficiently in order not to spoil some of the modulations'. The implications here are that (a) Liszt had an *a capella* performance in mind and (b) Liszt had himself in mind as musical director of any successfully executed rehearsal and performance. The organ part added later probably indicates his having to yield to the practical considerations of letting others perform the work, thus necessitating a reduction of the difficulties caused by the modulations. At this point he must have abandoned any hopes of hearing the work in the Sistine Chapel, at the same time losing sight of the opportunity he sought for dedicating the work to the Pope. Thus the history of the composition and performance of the *Missa choralis* points clearly to the moment of failure where Liszt's ambitions as a reformer of church music were concerned. The music, unlike the man, could not enter the Church.

This is because church music was a matter for church musicians, not the clergy. While it is true that reform in the Catholic Church would most likely take effect from Rome – for Liszt the 'headquarters' – it is also true that opera was not performed in the Sistine Chapel. In other words, there was no call for new music, whether by Liszt or anyone else, since the Palestrina performances had themselves become sacred by that time. The 'new impetus to sacred music' mentioned by Liszt refers not only to his own intentions in composing a work based upon Palestrina, but also to the continuing need for such an impetus. The clergy, he says, 'have little influence upon the general *andamento* in these matters'. The problem, in other words, belonged to the world of music.

Certainly Pius IX, who is reputed to have been musical, did nothing to help Liszt's cause. Neither did his successor Leo XIII, who called Liszt 'il compositore tedesco' ('the German composer'). Even Cardinal Hohenlohe was noted chiefly for his patronage of German artists in Rome. Thus Liszt was a foreigner, an outsider. Meluzzi, by contrast, was born in Rome, and was to die there more than a decade after Liszt's own death. He was guardian of a tradition, a bastion of conservatism against the 'music of the future' – most certainly where the Sistine choir was concerned. Against this, Hohenlohe, Antonelli and the Pope himself would have been powerless. It was not their province.

Yet of all Liszt's church works, the *Missa choralis* was least deserving of opprobrium. The emotions he ascribes to Palestrina's music in the letter quoted above (p. 121) are in reality his own, which find perfect expression in the music he himself composed, itself 'un encens sonore qui porte la prière sur ses nuages d'or et d'azur'. Though derived from his admiration for the Renaissance, the work is entirely a product of the nineteenth century, a musical parallel to the 'Nazarene' painters of Germany, or the Pre-Raphaelite Brotherhood in England. Today it is the

Ex. 22

most frequently performed of Liszt's Masses, partly because it is the only one for mixed choir and organ. But it also complies with the requirements of the liturgy, both in form and spirit. It is, in fact, a successful work of art that failed to start the reform it was intended to initiate. The fault of this may lie with Meluzzi; we cannot be sure. What is clear is that the fault did not lie with Liszt as a composer.

### Arrangements

Liszt did not arrange the work, or any part of it, for the piano or the organ.

The *Missa choralis* is scored for mixed choir and organ. Searle says that the work 'makes a considerable use of Gregorian themes' (*SML*, 107), though he does not identify them. The Credo uses the plainchant which appears in the Dona nobis pacem of the *Male-Voice Mass*, though the Gloria does not use the Gloria plainchant found in that work. Likewise the Sanctus, which outlines the chords of B♭ major and G minor, is based on an original theme, as is the Agnus Dei, which relies heavily on harmony for its expressive effect.

The key of the work is D; the beginning of the Kyrie is modal (D dorian), with no key signature, and the closing Amen is in D major, with a key signature of two sharps. The imitative opening Kyrie exemplifies Liszt's approach, in which there is a more determined effort at counterpoint than usual (see Ex. 164 on p. 270). The Christe (in F major) is homophonic (see Ex. 22), but counterpoint returns with the reprise of the Kyrie, which retains the new key signature of one flat. A change to D major occurs at the end, and the word 'eleison' is repeated many times. The Gloria, marked 'Animato', opens with a fortissimo unison phrase, followed by a quiet 'et in terra pax' in four-part writing. The fortissimo phrase returns, given imitative treatment, for the Laudamus te (see Ex. 23). Liszt introduces chromatic harmony at

# The Masses

Ex. 23

Ex. 24

'miserere nobis', and Ex. 23 returns for the Quoniam tu solus. This, the motto theme of the movement, dominates to the end.

The Credo consists of varied repetitions of the plainchant (*cf.* Ex. 11), for example at the Deum de Deo, and in B minor for the Crucifixus (see Ex. 24). There is more energy than counterpoint, in the sense that much of the time there are no more than two real parts. An exception is the music at 'qui cum Patre et Filio' (see Ex. 25).

The Sanctus opens with a dignified theme, followed by more energetic music at the Pleni sunt coeli (see Ex. 26). A series of progressions by fifths at the Hosanna takes the music from B major to B♭ major in a short space, at the same time changing the mood for the Benedictus, which is based upon a new theme (see Ex. 27). The music of this section has great beauty. After a return of the 'fifths' progression, the Benedictus theme is sung to 'Hosanna in excelsis', ending with two solo voices alone.

The Agnus Dei (in D minor) opens with a splendid example of 'painful' chromatic harmony (see Ex. 28). The repeated cries of 'Agnus Dei qui tollis peccata mundi miserere nobis' are given increasingly impressive chromatic harmony, so that the Dona nobis pacem, sung to a simple major third, provides a real sense of relief, at which point the Kyrie music returns, thus making the work cyclic.

# Revolution and religion

Ex. 25

Ex. 26

Ex. 27

Ex. 28

# The Masses

The whole work is concise in form, and restrained in expression, without being either perfunctory or weak. A wide harmonic range is employed, though free of the startling modulations found in some works by Liszt. The discipline and care that must have gone into its composition (Wolfrum says the manuscript is covered in crossings out and recomposed passages) are unusual for Liszt, who preferred to work with the heat of inspiration upon him. Yet behind the music lies a clearly focussed ideal, which gives it life, and is never lost sight of. Its companion piece, the *Male-Voice Mass*, is more poetic by comparison, though just as carefully composed. The *Missa choralis* manages to combine features normally considered incompatible, namely an asceticism derived from the Renaissance with the harmony and rhythm in use in the nineteenth century. That Liszt succeeded in this is due as much to technical skill as to imagination.

## HUNGARIAN CORONATION MASS (S11)

### Composition

Liszt composed the *Hungarian Coronation Mass* for the coronation on 8 June 1867 of Francis Joseph I of Austria as King of Hungary, in Budapest. Liszt expressed interest in writing a work for the coronation in 1865: 'You know my wishes . . . it is my loyal ambition to be appointed to write the coronation Mass, and to show myself worthy of it as a Catholic, a Hungarian, and a composer' (*LAA*, 101). The commission, however, was not confirmed until 1867. This was because in Vienna it was felt that the Austrian court should provide the music, while in Budapest it was felt the music should be by a Hungarian. The Kapellmeisters at the Austrian court were Johann Herbeck, an admirer of Liszt's church music (see above, p. 102) and Gottfried Preyer. The matter was settled by the efforts of eight Hungarians, the choirmaster Engesser, the composers Erkel and Mosonyi, the violinists Karl Huber and Reményi, Rosti, Kornél Ábrányi (founder in 1860 of the first Hungarian musical journal) and Baron Augusz, the friend who informed Liszt of the commission in March 1867. Raabe says Liszt then 'finished writing the Mass in great haste' (*RLL*, 213), and other writers repeat this. It is a mere assumption however, which is contradicted by the report of a visitor to Liszt in Rome in 1867:

I mentioned the report connecting his approaching journey with the grand festival of joy and peace, the coronation in Hungary. The popular maestro took this opportunity of giving me a detailed history of his Coronation Mass. He said that in the Prince Primate Scitovsky he had possessed a most kind patron. In the course of a joyous repast, as on many other occasions, the Prelate had given lively and hopeful utterance to the wish of his heart that he might yet be able to place the crown upon the head of his beloved king, and at the same time he called upon Liszt, in an unusually flattering and cordial manner, to compose the Coronation Mass, but it must be short, very short, as the entire ceremony would take about six hours.

Liszt was unable to resist this amiable request, he said, and, drinking a glass of fiery tokay, gave a promise that he would endeavour to produce some 'essence of tokay'. After his return to Rome he immediately set about the sketch. But the prospect of the desired agreement between the Emperor and the Hungarians had, meanwhile, become overcast, and his work remained a mere sketch. Some months ago, however, he was pressed by his Hungarian friends to proceed, and so he finished the Mass. It was a question whether it would be performed on the day of the coronation, since there was a condition that the monarch should bring his own orchestra with him. Liszt said he was perfectly neutral, and in no way wished to run counter to the just ambition of others; for, however the Abbé might be decried as ambitious, he added, with a smile, he was not so after all.[2]

The mention of Scitovsky provides a link with the *Gran Mass*, supported by a remark in one of Liszt's letters to his cousin Eduard in 1864:

You will not be vexed with me for . . . postponing till another year my transient visit to you at Vienna, which I accept in the same manner as you offer it, and for which the occasion will be found when I return to Hungary, supposing that they are inclined (as appears likely) to give me an order similar to that of the *Gran Mass*. (*L*, II, 86)

Liszt returned to Hungary in 1865 to conduct *St Elizabeth*, and this was when the meeting with Scitovsky described above took place. Liszt then sketched the work after returning to Rome, a process which may have spread intermittently over a whole year or more, and in 1867 brought the work to completion at the request of the Hungarians, writing in March:

When Cardinal Scitovsky deigned to notify me of his wish to have a Mass of my composition performed at the coronation of His Majesty the King of Hungary, I set to work immediately. The sketch of the work is ready, and I have only to add the orchestration. (*LAA*, 122)

The brevity of the work was due not to haste, but to the requirements of the ceremony. As Liszt himself told the Princess Wittgenstein:

The fact that I found myself obliged to make as small an amount of music as possible, so as not to prolong unnecessarily the very long coronation ceremony, absolutely forbade that I expand or develop the usual refinements and pro-cedures found in great works by the great masters. (*Br*. VI, 181)

The need to keep the music simple, together with the conditions under which the coronation was taking place, combined to produce in Liszt the idea of giving the work a strong national colouring by the use of themes and rhythms associated with Hungarian popular song, in particular the patriotic *Rákóczy March*. There had been no King of Hungary since the revolution of 1848, Francis Joseph having acceded to the Austrian throne in December of that year. 1867, known in Hungarian history as the Year of the Compromise, was seen by some as a defeat for national pride seeking self-determination, hence the feeling aroused by the issue of whose music should figure at the ceremony. Liszt wrote:

It seems to me that, inside these narrow limits, the *Coronation Mass* is concise rather than abbreviated – and that the two principal themes of Hungarian national feeling and the Catholic faith combine and support each other from end to end. (*Br.* VI, 181)

This mixture of religious and patriotic feeling, which Liszt in the above letter calls 'ce double caractère national et religieux', has been denigrated by English writers. Dannreuther wrote: 'The style of the entire Mass is as incongruous as a gipsy musician in a church vestment.' Such opinions reflect ignorance as well as prejudice. The Rákóczy March is not gipsy music, and even if it were, Liszt's well-known error in identifying gipsy music with Hungarian music has long ago been forgiven by the Hungarians themselves, who accept his patriotic intentions; while as for the work's suitability for use in church, that must depend upon the church in question. In Pressburg (present-day Bratislava, formerly Pozsony and the seat of the Austro-Hungarian Diet) Liszt's *Hungarian Coronation Mass* was performed liturgically during Mass 39 times between 1874 and 1910.

The work was published in 1869 by Schuberth, Leipzig, who also published separately the Benedictus, Graduale and Offertorium.

*Performance*

The coronation took place in the church of St Mathias, known as the Coronation church, in Buda (the old part of Budapest on a hill above the right bank of the Danube). The Austrians brought their own musicians, and the performance was conducted by Preyer. (Herbeck had refused, saying he was ill; he felt Liszt himself should conduct.) The singers from the court choir (added to the choir of the church) numbered ten boys and eight men (four tenors and four basses). Liszt was not officially invited to the coronation. It had been the intention of the Hungarians that Liszt should conduct, and that Reményi should perform the violin solo in the Benedictus, which in the event was performed by Hellmesberger. The directorate of the National Conservatory invited Liszt, who arrived in Budapest on 4 June. Liszt sat with the choir during the performance to hear his music, and left the church before the end of the ceremony. The road to his quarters in Pest crossed the Danube, and thousands were waiting to see the new King. An eye-witness described the resulting scene:

129

# Revolution and religion

The Emperor of Austria, after being crowned King of Hungary at the church of St Mathias, was to go and take the traditional oath on a hillock, formed of a heap of earth collected from all the different states of Hungary, which had been built up opposite the bridge on the left bank of the river.

When the feverish suspense grew intense, the tall figure of a priest, in a long black cassock studded with decorations, was seen to descend the broad white road leading to the Danube, which had been kept clear for the royal procession. As he walked bareheaded, his snow-white hair floated on the breeze, and his features seemed cast in brass. At his appearance a murmur arose, which swelled and deepened as he advanced and was recognized by the people. The name of Liszt flew down the serried ranks from mouth to mouth, swift as a flash of lightning. Soon a hundred thousand men and women were frantically applauding him, wild with the excitement of this whirlwind of voices. *(WRC, 19)*

To understand the emotions of this scene, it is necessary to recall that Liszt took the name of Hungary across Europe at a time when the country was all but unknown in artistic circles, and that he himself had been a hero of the revolutionary epoch before 1848. What this popular outburst meant to the disciple of Lamennais after just hearing his Mass, composed in the idiom of popular song, can only be imagined.

The *Hungarian Coronation Mass* quickly became popular. 'You know,' Liszt wrote, 'that the Coronation Mass has met with the most kind reception. None of my works up to the present time had been so favourably accepted' *(L, II, 123)*. Regarding future performances he wrote:

The Mass fulfilled its object in Pest on the Coronation Day. If it should be given on any future occasion, I would recommend the conductor to take the *tempi* solemnly always, but *never dragging*, and to beat the time throughout *alla Breve*. And the *Gloria*, more especially towards the middle and before the commencement of the *Agnus Dei* up to the Prestissimo, must be worked up brilliantly and majestically. *(L, II, 134)*

After the coronation, the Emperor made Liszt a Commander of the Order of Franz Joseph. Liszt wrote to Count György Festetics, grandson of the man who had attempted to prevent the performance of the *Gran Mass*, and master of ceremonies at the Austrian court:

It is a particular honour for me to have been allowed to take part in celebrating the great national day on 8 June by composing the Mass for the coronation of His Majesty the King of Hungary.

In deigning to show satisfaction with my work, His Majesty has granted me the highest reward.

Allow me to request, Monsieur le ministre, that you place at the feet of His Majesty my homage of deepest gratitude. *(BruS, 129)*

## Arrangements

Liszt arranged the following parts of the Mass for instrumental performance:

# The Masses

The Benedictus for violin and orchestra (S362). 1875
The Benedictus and Offertorium for violin and piano (S381). 1869
The Benedictus and Offertorium for piano (S501). 1867
The Benedictus and Offertorium for piano duet (S581). 1869
The Offertorium for organ (S667). After 1867.

Liszt wrote to Mosonyi in April before the coronation ceremony:

First of all I have to apologize for the extreme musical simplicity of this Mass; unalterable prescriptions compelled me to the utmost brevity and I had to renounce large proportions, but I hope that the two basic features, i.e. the liturgical and the national Hungarian, have clearly come into relief; incidentally you will notice the infinite care I have taken to ensure an easy and smooth performance in all circumstances; the voices move in the most comfortable registers, the instruments in the most even accompaniments; I renounced enharmonies to eliminate disharmonies, I confined myself to the usual means, discarding every offending instrument; neither kettle drums, nor bass clarinets or other innovations, not even the harp, have been allowed to interfere. In short, I have arranged the Mass so as to be acceptably sung and played at sight ('a vista'); and what is more, should the conductor admit but two horns, well, the two in excess may be simply eliminated, and if they like they may even eliminate the trombones, the organ and the drums too: the core of the composition resides in the feeling and shall produce its effect through the latter.                (LAA, 128)

The 'unalterable prescriptions' were Scitovsky's: 'In composing this Mass,' wrote Liszt, 'I think I have fulfilled the prescriptions given me by His Eminence Scitovsky: "not too long, and no difficulties of any kind"' (LAA, 132).

The work is scored for choir and four soloists, with an orchestra of double woodwind, four horns, two trumpets, three trombones and tuba, timpani, organ and strings. This is smaller than the one used in the *Gran Mass*, and Liszt was prepared, as he says in the letter quoted above, for it to be reduced further if necessary. There is no contrapuntal music at all, and the Mass relies for its effect upon block harmonies, orchestral colour, contrast between choir and soloists, and rhythmic variety. Searle says the *Hungarian Coronation Mass* is 'an effective ceremonial piece, with many dramatic passages, but not a work of very great musical importance' (*SML*, 107). This is less than fair, as two of the movements, the Sanctus and the Graduale, rank among Liszt's finest choral works.

A remark made by Liszt with regard to creating 'national Hungarian' features is recorded by Borodin in a letter to César Cui written in 1881 from Magdeburg, where Liszt was to conduct the Mass in the church of St John. Borodin attended the rehearsal:

The rehearsal of the 'Coronation Mass' had begun. Liszt listened with lowered head ... On reaching the Gradual, Liszt bent towards me to explain that this portion, which is often left out in other Masses, is obligatory in the 'Coronation

Ex. 29. *Hungarian Rhapsody* no. 15, bars 31–4

Ex. 30. *Hungarian Rhapsody* no. 15, bars 61–3

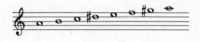

Ex. 31

Mass' [which is why Liszt added the Graduale to the published score], and that the use of fourths constitutes a characteristic feature of Hungarian music.[3]

Liszt here means melodic fourths, not harmonic, and these appear frequently in the work, though not, as it happens, very much in the Graduale. One of the phrases in the *Rákóczy March*, based upon fourths (see Ex. 29), occurs in the Mass. (It also features prominently in the choral work *Hungaria* written in 1848.) Another phrase from the March (see Ex. 30) is also used in the Mass. Use is made of the so-called 'gipsy scale', found in all Liszt's 'Hungarian' music (see Ex. 31). These elements combine to impart a strong and distinct flavour to the whole work.

The key of the work is E♭ major. The Kyrie is not in the usual ternary form, but a remarkably individual one invented by Liszt for the occasion. Starting with a majestic pronouncement of 'Kyrie eleison' by the choir in unison, the music passes to a 'praying' (*betend*) Christe for the soloists, given a Hungarian flavour at the cadence, which is completed in the woodwind accompaniment (see Ex. 32). A crescendo is built up as the full choir in unison sing 'Christe eleison' to a theme containing Ex. 30 and leading at the climax to a reprise of the words 'Kyrie eleison' sung by choir and soloists to a new theme in G♭ major (see Ex. 33). The tonality returns to E♭ major as the music quietens down.

The Gloria is a festive affair in C major, the melodic fourths appearing at 'in excelsis Deo' and at the Laudamus te, after which they continue in the orchestral accompaniment as a crescendo is built out of a new phrase (see Ex. 34), leading to more of the *Rákóczy March* at 'magnum gloriam

# The Masses

Chri - - - ste e - le - i - son

Ex. 32

Ky - - ri - e e - le - i - son

Ex. 33

glo - - - ri - fi - ca - mus te

Ex. 34

Mi - - se - re - - re

Ex. 35

tuam'. The 'Hungarian' scale appears at the Qui tollis in D minor, but is resolved magically onto a chord of D♭ major for the Miserere (see Ex. 35). The melodic fourths reappear in the orchestra at the Qui sedes, leading the music towards an immense climax in C major at 'in gloria Dei Patris amen'.

The Graduale, a setting of Psalm 116, 'Laudate Dominum omnes gentes', is described in chapter 9. It was added in 1869.

The *Messe royale* of Henri Dumont, from which Liszt took the Credo (*cf.* the *Missa regia* in the Liber Usualis) is composed in the style of plainchant. The whole Mass is found in Liszt's copy of the *Nouvel eucologe en musique*

(p. 127), where it is called *Messe de Dumont*. Beside the title in Liszt's handwriting are the words 'né à Liège 1610'. The music is written chiefly in breves and semibreves. In Liszt's copy of the *Graduale Romanum*,[4] also housed in the Liszt Museum at Budapest, the music appears (on p. 795) in minims and crotchets, and as this parallels Liszt's notation in the *Coronation Mass*, it was probably the source he used. Liszt adds an organ accompaniment, and Dumont's Credo is sung by the full choir in unison, with occasional passages of harmony along the lines described in chapter 7. The effect of this in performance is tedious, yet strangely it was the part of Liszt's Mass that most impressed Borodin:

The music of this Mass is enchanting almost throughout; the 'Credo' is superb in its depth and religious severity. It bears the stamp of the old Catholic liturgy, being in the Dorian mode with almost continuous unisons, as in the chants of our own Greek Church.[5]

Borodin's reaction was doubtless the one Liszt intended to provoke. His reason for not composing his own Credo was to do with the need for the maximum liturgical appropriateness.

For the Credo, I decided simply to use Gregorian chant. Its traditional, imposing style and excellent conciseness seemed better suited than any other to such a solemn occasion. However if it be feared that so much antique simplicity was not to present-day taste, it would be easy to replace this Credo by the one I had composed beforehand, in the same style as the rest of the Mass. (*LAA*, 133)

This is the only reference to another version of the Credo, which is otherwise unknown. In the context of the actual occasion for which Liszt provided the music, his choice of Dumont was obviously an inspiration, the solemnity of the event finding its echo in the music. By itself, it serves chiefly to lower the temperature in readiness for the ensuing Offertorium. A single example will suffice to illustrate Liszt's approach: compare Dumont's 'amen' (Ex. 36(a)) with Liszt's slightly altered version, harmonized for the choir (Ex. 36(b)).

The Offertorium is a short piece in E major, marked 'Lento assai e solenne', for violin and orchestra. It has a distinct Hungarian flavour, as Liszt pointed out to Baron Augusz:

I have just written an *instrumental* Offertorium for our Mass, which can be performed or not, ad libitum. It is a sort of *Magyar hymn* whose simple character will not displease you, I think . . . perhaps later some Hungarian words might be added to it. (*LAA*, 131)

It is based upon two themes, the first for the violin solo (see Ex. 37), the second for woodwind and strings (see Ex. 38). In the middle section the second theme in the woodwind appears with decorations from the solo violin, leading to a reprise of the first theme by the full orchestra with all

(a)

A   -   -    -    -    men

(b)

a  - - - - - - men.

[organ omitted]

Ex. 36

*sostenuto*    *f espressivo*

Ex. 37

*sempre espressivo*

Ex. 38

the instruments in their middle registers, producing a solemn and dignified effect.

The Sanctus in E major is the best movement (along with the Graduale) of the whole work. Again, it relies entirely upon immediacy of impact and an emotional approach to the words. The orchestra starts majestically with a rhythmic phrase, to which the choir add their harmonized cry of 'Sanctus'. This music is repeated continually, building up an immense crescendo at 'Dominus Deus sabaoth'. Everything stops except the organ's sustained ninth chord of F♯ major over a pedal B. Three beats of silence follow, and then the full choir, soloists, organ and orchestra enter with the Pleni sunt coeli. The Hosanna gradually dies away, leaving soprano and alto soloists 'suspended' over a chord of A major. This is the cue for the violin solo based on one of the 'Rákóczy' phrases that weaves its way through the Benedictus (see Ex. 39). The soloists enter quietly in pairs, echoing each other, these echoes being

Ex. 39

Ex. 40

joined soon by the choir. As in the Sanctus, a slow crescendo is built up, using a theme with Hungarian features, while the solo violin and later the orchestral strings weave their decorations around it. A magical change of harmony (see Ex. 40) leads to the climax, and the soloists, together with the violin, close the movement quietly. It is in this movement above all that the truth of Liszt's words emerges: 'The core of the composition resides in the feeling and shall produce its effect through the latter'.

The Hungarian scale returns for the Agnus Dei, followed by the music of the Qui sedes from the Gloria (the melodic fourths phrase from the *Rákóczy March*), and then the music of the Kyrie. The 'amen' outlines the chord of E♭, and the orchestra punctuates the interval of a fourth to end the work.

There is no denying the effectiveness of the *Hungarian Coronation Mass*. Liszt handles the forces with a sure hand, producing by essentially simple means music of colour and animation, extracting by turns pathos, drama, mystery and elation from the musical elements, chosen for their Hungarian associations. The form is rhapsodic, but succeeds basically because Liszt's emotional plan and sense of direction are clear, while the 'Hungarian' colour serves towards thematic unity. The unaffected lyricism of the work shows how far Liszt had moved away from the piano as a composer, while its popular appeal shows what amounts to a redeployment of the same talent that in 1840 roused Hungarian audiences to such fever pitch that the authorities banned him from playing the *Rákóczy March* in his concerts.

## REQUIEM (S12)

### Composition

Since the *Coronation Mass*, I have in fact only written one solitary work: a *Requiem* for male voices with simple organ accompaniment.                  (*L*, II, 151)

The letter from which this extract is taken was written in 1868, and as the phrase 'since the *Coronation Mass*' may be taken to refer to the early part of 1867, the date of composition for the *Requiem* is probably 1867–8. In a letter written in 1883 Liszt says the work was 'écrit à *Sta Francesca Romana*', though he gives no date. Liszt first moved into the church of Santa Francesca Romana in the late autumn of 1866, staying there periodically in successive years.

The sixth movement, Libera me, was composed in 1871 in Budapest, from where Liszt wrote to the Princess in February: 'I have written a *libera me, Domine* for four male voices and organ – a male voice choir, called *Begeisterung* [enthusiasm]' (*Br.* VI, 287). Speculation surrounds the identity of the person for whom the work was composed. According to Wolfrum, the Princess's daughter said that she heard Liszt himself say that the work was written for the Emperor Maximilian of Mexico, a brother of Francis Joseph of Austria, who was executed on 19 June 1867 (11 days after the Budapest coronation ceremony). He had been induced in 1863 to accept the crown of the Catholic Empire which Napoleon III was seeking to establish in Mexico. His power fell to the Mexican 'Liberals' when Napoleon III was forced to withdraw French troops in

# Revolution and religion

March 1867. The *Marche funèbre* from the *Années pèlerinage: troisième année* (S163, 6) was composed in 1867 for Maximilian. Certainly the ingredients of the situation – a Catholic monarch murdered by insurgents – were ones likely to have moved Liszt, but probably not to the extent of composing a whole Requiem. As late as 1882 Liszt wrote: 'Perhaps I shall yet write a Requiem at special command' (*L*, II, 410). La Mara, the editor of the letters, adds a footnote saying that a Requiem exists in manuscript, 'composed on the death of the Emperor Maximilian of Mexico'. No such work, however, has been traced.

Lina Ramann states that the *Requiem* was composed for Liszt's own funeral, and for the Princess's. Certainly the work was performed under the direction of Sgambati, Liszt's Roman pupil (pianist, composer and conductor), at the funeral of the Princess on 12 March 1887 in Santa Maria del Popolo at Rome. In 1862 Liszt wrote concerning the deaths of two of his three children:

> Blandine has her place in my heart beside Daniel. Both abide with me bringing atonement and purification, mediators with the cry of 'Sursum corda!' – When the day comes for Death to approach, he shall not find me unprepared or fainthearted. *Our* faith hopes for and awaits the deliverance to which it leads us. Yet as long as we are upon earth we must attend to our daily task. And mine shall not lie unproductive. However trifling it may seem to others, to me it is indispensable. My soul's tears must, as it were, have lacrymatoria made for them; I must set fires alight for those of my dear ones that are alive, and keep my dear dead in *spiritual and corporeal* urns. This is the aim and object of the *Art task* to me.
>
> (*L*, II, 38)

The following year he wrote:

> The melancholy familiarity with death that I have perforce acquired during these latter years does not in the least weaken the grief which we feel when our dear ones leave this earth. If at the sight of the open graves I thrust back despair and blasphemy, it is that I may weep more freely, and that neither life nor death shall be able to separate me from the communion of love.  (*L*, II, 69)

At the time of Wagner's death, three years before his own at the age of nearly 75, Liszt wrote:

> Ever since the days of my youth I have considered dying much simpler than living. Even if often there is fearful and protracted suffering before death, yet is death none the less the deliverance from our involuntary yoke of existence.
> Religion assuages this yoke, yet our heart bleeds under it continually! –
> 'Sursum corda!'  (*L*, II, 431)

Liszt's mother died in Paris at the beginning of 1866. Probably the accumulation of deaths led to the *Requiem* being composed.

The *Requiem* was published (without the Libera me) in 1869 by Repos, Paris, and in 1870 by Kahnt, Leipzig, new editions appearing in 1872 and

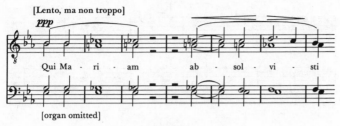

[Lento, ma non troppo]

Qui Ma - ri - am ab - sol - vi - sti

[organ omitted]

Ex. 41

later. The Libera me appeared separately in 1871 through Kahnt; from 1872 it was incorporated into the *Requiem*.

## *Performance*

It is not known when the first performance took place; according to Raabe it was probably in 1869 in Lemberg. Regarding practicalities, Liszt wrote in 1883:

In the three-part strophe
  'Qui Mariam absolvisti,
  Et latronem exaudisti,
  Mihi autem spem dedisti'
lies the fervent, tender accent, which is not easily attained by ordinary singers . . .
The execution is also made more difficult by the 2 semitones, ascending in the 1st
Tenor, and descending in the 2nd Tenor and 1st Bass [see Ex. 41]. Progressions
of this kind are indeed not new, but singers so seldom possess the requisite
crystal-clear intonation without which the unhappy composer comes to grief.

(*L*, II, 432)

## *Arrangements*

The *Requiem für die Orgel* (S266) is based upon the *Requiem*.

Liszt's *Requiem* is scored for men's voices (choir and four soloists) organ, two trumpets, two trombones, and timpani. It is possible to perform the work with organ accompaniment alone. It was intended for church performance, and is quite different in character from the Requiems of Berlioz and Verdi. Of the former Liszt wrote:

Yesterday in Leipzig I heard Berlioz's *Requiem* – a prodigious, nay sublime, work
– but in many places differing in feeling from what the words of the Requiem
evoke in me. The expression that moves me most in this gigantic work is found
chiefly in the Offertory, the *Sanctus* and the *Agnus Dei*.     (*Br.* VI, 345)

He held a high opinion of Verdi's *Requiem*:

Te de-cet hymnus, De-us, in Si on,

Te de-cet hy - - mnus [organ omitted]

Ex. 42

I have twice heard Verdi's *Requiem*, an important and deeply felt work. Its great success, insured by all who stand to gain by success, is no less deserving than that of Rossini's *Stabat mater* . . . Verdi's *Requiem* will bring good receipts to the theatres – for on some days of the year, the memory of an illustrious man needs to be celebrated in the country to which he belonged. Mozart's *Requiem* is become hackneyed, Cherubini's is too formal, and Berlioz's too difficult. So: *Viva Verdi*! He possesses the double merit of being a sincere composer and a profitable one!

(*Br.* VII, 177)

Liszt's lack of sympathy with these works concerned not the music but their religious sentiment, which was different from his own: 'Composers in general,' he wrote, 'both the great and less great, colour the Requiem black, quite unrelentingly black. From the start, I made use of a different light – it shines throughout, despite the terrors of the *Dies irae*' (*Br.* VII, 383). He explained the nature of this 'different light' ('autre lumière') thus: 'In my "Requiem" (for men's voices) I endeavoured to give expression to the mild, redeeming character of death' (*L*, II, 431). Consequently the work is for the most part restrained in expression. The brass and timpani are used for their solemn effect in the Dies irae ('Tuba mirum', 'Judex ergo', and 'Judicandus homo reus'), and to provide fanfares, albeit solemn, in the Sanctus and Benedictus ('Hosanna in excelsis'). The thematic material throughout is Liszt's own; there is no use of plainchant. In places Liszt uses harmony, including whole-tone chords, of the type found in the late works. The writing for the voices makes more use of the contrast between soloists and choir than is found for example in the *Male-Voice Mass*; occasionally, as in the Sanctus, the two groups are used simultaneously to achieve almost a double-choir effect.

The first movement, Requiem aeternam, opens in F minor with an unaccompanied solo bass voice. The soloists continue until the Te decet hymnus in A♭, sung by the choir (see Ex. 42). The return of the opening music at 'Requiem aeternam' is sung by the choir. The soloists sing the Kyrie, which starts in A♭, but soon passes to D major. The music of the opening returns for the final Kyrie, which closes the movement in A♭ major.

Ex. 43

Ex. 44

The Dies irae opens with a unison theme which functions as the motto theme for the whole movement (see Ex. 43). For example at 'Mors stupebit' it occurs *sotto voce*, while at 'Liber scriptus', whose theme outlines the Cross motif, it acts as the bass line. For the Lacrymosa Liszt writes a haunting theme over it in the organ part (see Ex. 44). This builds up to a fine climax at 'Huic ergo parce, Deus'. The Pie Jesu is sung in unison by the choir, while the organ has the harmony, which is at one point (bar 473) extremely dissonant.

The Offertorium opens in A minor, with an expressive passage for the soloists at 'libera animas omnium' (see Ex. 45), while whole-tone harmony appears at 'libera eas de ore leonis'. The Hostias makes use of the contrast between soloists and choir, and introduces movement into the

Ex. 45

Ex. 46

organ part. The Sanctus opens majestically in F major. Imitation is introduced at 'Pleni sunt coeli' (see Ex. 46). The Benedictus uses the two
groups of voices to beautiful effect, as the soloists sing 'Hosanna', while
the choir sing the words of the Benedictus (see Ex. 47). The Agnus Dei
opens in D minor, and at 'dona eis requiem' the opening music returns
in F minor. The ending of this movement repeats the consolatory ending
of the opening Kyrie, and originally the work ended here, in A♭ major.

The Libera me relies more than the preceding movements upon the
organ which, for example, is used to depict the words 'Quando coeli
movendi sunt et terra' (see Ex. 48). Much of the choral writing is in
unison, but harmony reappears at 'Requiem aeternam', though the

# The Masses

Ex. 47

Ex. 48

music is not a repeat of the first movement. Liszt repeats the opening strophe, ending with 'dum veneris judicare saeculum per ignem' and a diminished seventh chord on the organ; the final bars are for organ solo. It is to be regretted that Liszt chose to end the choral part with a cry for deliverance from eternal torment expressed so dramatically, as the effect of this is to disturb the 'mild, redeeming character' of the work as a whole. The previous five movements reflect well Liszt's declared aim.

The *Requiem* is an unusual work, primarily because of its liturgical function. It reflects, via the Lisztian theme of love triumphing over death, the Christian teaching on the after-life. A late illustration of this is the letter he wrote when Caroline de St Criq, his adolescent love in Paris, died in 1872: 'Her long suffering, endured with such Christian gentleness and resignation, made her ripe for Heaven. There she at last enters into the joy of the Lord . . . May God be pleased for having called her from this earthly exile' (*Br.* VI, 345).

# 9

# THE PSALMS

Liszt composed complete settings of Psalms 13, 18, 23 and 137 for independent performance. To these may be added Psalm 116, composed as a Graduale for the *Hungarian Coronation Mass*, Psalm 129, intended as the closing number of the unfinished oratorio *St Stanislas*, and part of Psalm 124. They are composed for various forces ranging from tenor solo, full choir and orchestra in Psalm 13 down to a single voice and piano (or harp and organ) in Psalm 23. Liszt himself said: 'My Psalms . . . are very diverse, both as regards feeling and musical form' (*L*, II, 71). Within this diversity Liszt maintains a consistent musical quality, and the Psalms must be counted among his most successful choral works.

Liszt, of course, follows the Catholic numbering; where appropriate the Protestant number is given in brackets together with the English title.

*Psalm* 13 (How long, O Lord, wilt thou quite forget me?) (S13)

### Composition

Referring to his intention to compose a setting of this Psalm, Liszt wrote to the Princess on 16 July 1855: 'I shall go through several of Mendelssohn's Psalms which I need to see again, and the volume of Bach Cantatas – before commencing the Psalm which is trotting through my head' (*Br.* IV, 225). A week later he wrote: 'I have begun my Psalm and shall try to finish it soon' (*Br.* IV, 233). On 28 July he wrote to Agnes Klindworth:

I shall stay alone in the Altenburg until 5 August. In a fortnight from now I hope to have just about finished the composition of Psalm 13: 'Herr, wie lange willst Du meiner so gar vergessen? – Wie lange verbirgst Du Dein Antlitz vor mir? Wie lange soll ich sorgen in meiner Seele und mich ängstigen in meinem Herzen täglich? Wie lange soll sich mein Feind über mich erheben? Schaue doch und erhöre mich!' etc.

I have left off scoring my Prometheus Choruses to write this Psalm which welled up from the depths of my heart. (*Br.* III, 37)

On 18 September he wrote to the Princess: 'I have done the piano arrangement of my Psalm, and am in the process of adding the expression marks, which is several days' work. After that I shall send it to Hans [von Bülow] to have copied by Conradi' (*Br.* IV, 267). In 1859 Liszt reworked the composition: 'I have . . . considerably enlarged and reorganized the Psalm 13 . . . which I shall publish this winter' (*Br.* III, 122). Originally there were several solo voices; the final version has a tenor solo only.

The full score, together with a piano part for rehearsal, was published in 1864 by Kahnt.

*Performance*

The first performance was given by the Sternschen Gesangverein under Liszt's direction in the Berlin Singakademie on 6 December 1855. It had little success, and Liszt described it as 'only a *first trial* performance' (*L*, II, 30).

Liszt was specific about his performance requirements for this work:

The tenor part is a very important one; – I have made *myself* sing it, and thus had King David's feelings poured into me in flesh and blood! (*L*, II, 30)

Were any one of my more recent works likely to be performed at a concert with orchestra and chorus, I would recommend this Psalm. Its poetic subject welled up plenteously out of my soul; and besides I feel as if the musical form did not roam about beyond the given tradition. It requires a lyrical tenor; while singing he must be able to pray, to sigh and lament, to become exalted, pacified and biblically inspired. – Orchestra and chorus, too, have great demands made upon them. Superficial or ordinarily careful study would not suffice. (*L*, II, 72)

The work is scored for full orchestra, mixed choir and solo tenor, and lasts half an hour in performance. Liszt wrote: 'The [13th Psalm] is one of those I have worked out most fully, and contains two fugue movements and a couple of passages which were written with tears of blood' (*L*, II, 71). The work is constructed along the lines of the symphonic poems, in which sections of differing character and tempo are based upon transformations of a theme. The theme, virtually the motto of the work, is first stated in unison by the orchestra, then sung by the tenor (see Ex. 49). A second theme makes its appearance at the commencement of the first fugal section, which is orchestral (see Ex. 165 on p. 271). This theme contains the Cross motif, and its fugal treatment corresponds to Liszt's 'psychological' use of fugue in his instrumental works. The rôle of the choir at this point is to add interjections of 'Wie lange?'; it does not participate in the fugue, whose chromatic yearning expresses the character of the words.

# The psalms

Ex. 49

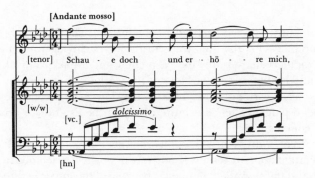

Ex. 50

The first transformation occurs at the words 'Schaue doch und erhöre mich, Herr mein Gott!', the mood being established at the outset by the use of a dominant ninth chord over a tonic pedal in the key of A♭, the key associated by Liszt with the subject of love (see Ex. 50). Another transformation expresses the words 'dass nicht mein Feind rühme, er sei meiner mächtig geworden, une meine Widersacher sich nicht freuen, dass ich niederliege' ('lest my adversary say, "I have overthrown him", and my enemies rejoice at my downfall').

At the psychological turning point of the work Liszt introduces a new long-breathed lyrical theme for the tenor which upon examination can be seen to combine features from Ex. 49 (the falling interval) and Ex. 165 (the Cross motif), set to the words 'Ich aber hoffe darauf, dass du so gnädig bist, mein Herz freuet sich, dass du so gerne hilfst' ('But for my part I trust in thy true love. My heart shall rejoice, for thou hast set me free') (see Ex. 51). This beautiful theme, in conjunction with the 'Schaue doch' theme, brings the work to its climax, a fugal section sung to the words 'Ich will dem Herrn singen, dass er so wohl an mir gethan' ('I will

147

Ex. 51

sing to the Lord, who has granted all my desire'). The fugue subject (see
Ex. 166 on p. 271) is the final transformation of the motto theme. This
time the fugue is shared fully between choir and orchestra in a mood of
triumph and jubilation. At the close of the work the motto theme is used
in the bass as an ostinato over which, in the slower tempo of the opening,
an extended plagal cadence is built, bringing the Psalm to a broad and
splendid conclusion.

*Psalm 13* is a quintessential Liszt work. Like the *Faust Symphony* and the
Piano Sonata it constitutes a self-portrait in music carried out in a most
complete and unrestrained manner. The style of the music is the same as
that found in Liszt's orchestral and piano music: romantic, operatic,
histrionic, the style natural to Liszt. Technically, Liszt transferred this
style to the choral medium in a masterly fashion, sweeping away
completely any suggestion of fusty ecclesiastical decorum or rigid
academicism. The work roams freely, yet in a cogent manner, taking its
inspiration from the text, the leading rôle being given always to the
tenor, supported by the choir as the crowd supports the hero in an opera.
The whole piece is a drama executed in music by a consummate actor.

This of course touches on the controversy surrounding Liszt's
religious music: how can we be sure he was sincere? The question of
sincerity is generally not considered important today when judging
works of art, but in Liszt's case it is central to several objections of those
who criticize his music, and is almost certainly the reason why the music
receives hardly any performances, especially in England.

It is important to relate the emotional plan of the work to Liszt's other
music. The piece is a simple prayer, starting in despair and ending in joy,
Liszt's favourite musical pattern found for example even in the *Hungarian
Rhapsodies*, which, however, are not programme music. The development
of the scheme took time, starting with the 1833 piano piece *Harmonies
poétiques et religieuses*, Liszt's first programmatic piece, and which is clearly

meant as a prayer. Prayer became the basic emotional plan behind Liszt's serious works, including the symphonies. The characteristic feature of *Psalm 13* is that it uses transformation of themes in a choral work to reflect the message of the text. In his letter to the Princess affirming his belief in God (see above, p. 47) Liszt refers to 'our cries to God, our need for Him, the yearning of our souls for His love'. This is really the programme upon which the music of *Psalm 13* is built. The question of sincerity must therefore allow for the conscious element, since the music, like the letter, is about himself. Liszt habitually does in church what other composers do in the theatre or the concert hall: he uses music to dramatize himself. In opera this is done by means of the story and the libretto. In *Psalm 13* the libretto came from the Bible, and Liszt, as he said, 'made [*himself*] sing it', adding that the singer must be a tenor who 'must be able . . . to become . . . biblically inspired'. As programme music, the work is the composer's intellectual commentary on the rôle he here casts for himself. Significantly, its structure and form parallel those of the best of Liszt's symphonic works, thereby inadvertently revealing the guileless nature of his characteristically Romantic self-preoccupation.

## PSALM 18 (No. 19: THE HEAVENS TELL OUT THE GLORY OF GOD) (S14)

### Composition

Liszt composed the work in the summer of 1860, finishing it on 21 August. The following day he wrote to the Princess in Rome:

> While you were listening to the Psalm 'Coeli enarrant' in Sta Maria Maggiore, I was working at mine for male-voice choir. I finished it yesterday, and it seems to have turned out not at all badly. There are just over 300 bars, 30 pages of full score distinctly hieratic in character. I have made two versions, one in Latin, the other in German. I still have to arrange the instrumentation in various forms, in such a way that it may be performed with small resources, with organ alone if need be, or else with full orchestra, or furthermore in the open air, during some festival of male-voice choirs – a very frequent occurrence in Germany, Holland and Belgium. In the latter event it needs only brass instruments, horns, trumpets and trombones, together with a few clarinets. I hope to produce the 'Coeli enarrant' for you in these three versions.                                        (*Br.* V, 42)

The work was published, in the three versions outlined by Liszt, in 1871 by Schuberth.

### Performance

The first performance took place at Weimar on 25 June 1861. In a letter to Herbeck, who performed the work in Vienna in 1868, Liszt gave some advice for conductors:

The Psalm is very simple and massive – like a *monolith*. And, as in the case of other works of mine, the conductor has the chief part to play. He, as the chief *virtuoso* and *artifex*, is called upon to see that the whole is harmoniously articulated and that it receives a living form. In the rhythmical and dynamical climax, from letters B to E (repeated from H to L), as also in some of the *ritenuti*, especially in the passage:
>    'The law of the Lord is perfect,
>    Converting the soul;
>    The testimony of the Lord is sure,
>    Making wise the simple', etc.,

you will find substance to prove your excellence as a conductor.     (*L*, II, 148)

Liszt's description of the work as 'hieratic' sums up its qualities. The word means 'priestly', especially in connotation with Egyptian and Greek art, and this, together with Liszt's choice of male-voice choir, his favourite choral medium, may link it with his Testament written the following month. His use of the word 'monolith' also seizes upon its musical essentials, in that there is no contrapuntal movement until the final 'Hosanna', the bulk of the work being in a kind of grand and dignified 'marching to glory' mood, marked 'Allegro maestoso assai, ma sempre animato (e alla breve)'.

The music is in the key of F major, rarely used by Liszt, but significantly chosen also for the *Cantico del sol* (see chapter 12), another hymn to Creation. The orchestra opens the piece with unison Cs, then repeats them with inner notes of the C chord added one by one, outlining the Cross motif. The choir enters in unison with the main theme, after which an attractive rhythmic accompaniment gets under way in the orchestra, leading via a long accelerando to a climax at letter E, the passage referred to in Liszt's letter to Herbeck. The return to Tempo I is for the first line of the text quoted by Liszt sung by the full choir. The second line introduces simple harmony for four soloists, accompanied by strings and low woodwind (see Ex. 52). It is marked 'ritenuto' eight bars after the Tempo I marking, and is followed by an 'a tempo' for the return of the choir for line three, then a repeat of the 'ritenuto'. This use of tempo change as a structural feature is found often in Liszt, and derives from his desire to reflect changes of mood. The danger of course is a too great disruption of momentum. It should be said in praise of the composer that these tempo changes, in this and other works, are part of an overall sense of timing which is masterly, and lies at the foundation of his approach to musical form. Shape and size derive significance from the variety of passing events, each part of a drama, however small the piece, whether sacred or secular.

The return to the first tempo is gradual, again via the long 'accelerando'. At the 'Hosanna' the tempo doubles, introducing in the

Ex. 52

Ex. 53

voices an imitative effect based upon the opening theme over dominant harmony, though interestingly Liszt uses the seventh of the chord as an orchestral harmonic pedal (see Ex. 53). The work ends with a jubilant 'Hosanna Halleluja!' sung to a plagal cadence constructed from the opening unison idea.

## PSALM 23 (THE LORD IS MY SHEPHERD; I SHALL WANT NOTHING) (S15/1)

### Composition

Liszt composed the work in the summer of 1859. In 1867 he wrote to the Princess: 'The Psalm . . . is a paraphrase by Herder of the Ps.: "The Lord is my shepherd – I shall want nothing". I composed it at Weimar, a little before Magne's marriage [the marriage of the Princess's daughter, 15 October 1859]' (*Br.* VI, 154). It was published in 1864 by Kahnt. A second version (S15/2), dating from 1862, remains unpublished.

On page 13 of the 1864 score Liszt refers to 'der Partitur mit vollem Orchester', but this must be lost since no orchestral version is known.

# Revolution and religion

In the letter to the Princess quoted above Liszt says she heard the work 'in the Weimar church, after your return from Paris'. If this was the first performance, then it must date from about November 1859.

The work is described on the cover as 'für eine Singstimme (Tenor oder Sopran)' but Liszt in a letter from Rome wrote of 'the 22nd [i.e. 23rd] Psalm which, in reality, I composed for a tenor' (*L*, II, 90). The accompaniment is for harp and organ or harmonium, but there is a piano part as well, and the work can be performed just with voice and piano, i.e. as a song. The music is in the key of E♭ major, and in style somewhere between Schubert and Wagner, in that the vocal line carries the melody, but there are recitative-like interruptions. The piece is operatic, and the melodic phrases are long-breathed, a rarity in Liszt, the outlines not spoilt by declamation (see Ex. 54). The lyrical vein is halted at the words 'Even though I walk through a valley dark as death I fear no evil', the recitative-like style making an appearance (see Ex. 55). The opening style then returns, giving the piece an overall ternary shape.

## *PSALM 116* (NO. 117: PRAISE THE LORD, ALL NATIONS) (S15a)

### *Composition*

Liszt composed the work as a Graduale for the *Hungarian Coronation Mass* two years after the coronation performance in 1867. On 19 September 1869 he wrote to Baron Augusz that he had made several revisions of the score, including 'Psalm 116, "Laudate Dominum omnes gentes", as a Gradual' (*LAA*, 155).

The score of the whole Mass was published in 1869 by Schuberth, who also published the Graduale separately in a version with piano accompaniment under the title *Psalm 116*, adding at the foot of the title-page 'Einzeln aus der ungar. Krönungs-Messe' ('Taken from the Hungarian Coronation Mass'). A further note informs us that the work may also be performed with orchestral accompaniment.

In its orchestral version Liszt's *Psalm 116* is one of his most effective choral works. The music relies entirely on energy and colour, the choral writing being either in unison or homophonic. The unison opening shows the style, the harmony residing in the orchestra (see Ex. 56). This choral entry is preceded by two bars of introduction in which the horns and woodwind announce the theme, while the strings have a lively figuration whose triplets conceal the Cross motif. The key is C major, Liszt's

# The psalms

Ex. 54

Ex. 55

Ex. 56

153

'worldly' key, and the marking 'Allegro pomposo' points to the work's festal origins. Much of the effectiveness of the music derives from the independence of the orchestra from the choir. This relationship changes at the words 'Quoniam confirmata est super nos misericordia ejus' ('For his love protecting us is strong'), where the rhythmic activity quietens down, and Liszt gives the word 'misericordia' to a quartet of solo voices. The opening mood returns via a gradual accelerando to the words 'et veritas Domini manet in aeternum' ('the Lord's constancy is everlasting'), which is rendered in long notes by the choir while the opening rhythmic activity is used in the bass of the orchestra.

At the climax the choir sing repeatedly 'Laudate laudate' in full C major harmony, while the orchestra have the opening theme. The brass and string writing at this point shows Liszt's use of the orchestra at its best. The mood of jubilation is sustained through a repeat of the complete text, stopping only for the 'misericordia ejus', which allows the very opening orchestral introduction to recur before a solemn close to 'et veritas Domini manet in aeternum'. The influence of plainsong is felt here, though it is given full-blown harmony together with an organ part in the orchestra, and takes on a characteristically Lisztian hue. *Psalm 116* is concise and to the point throughout, qualities rare in Liszt's works.

## QUI SEMINANT IN LACRIMIS (FROM PSALM 126: THOSE WHO SOW IN TEARS SHALL REAP WITH SONGS OF JOY) (S63)

### Composition

Liszt composed the work in 1884, writing to the Princess on 11 September: 'I have just written for choir and organ what used to be called a motet, on the verse from Ps. 125: "Qui seminant in lacrimis, in exultatione metent"' (*Br.* VII, 412). It remained in manuscript until after Liszt's death, when it was incorporated into the Complete Edition, first appearing in 1936.

There is no record of the work having been performed in Liszt's lifetime.

Liszt's late works are characterized by brevity and harmonic exploration. *Qui seminant in lacrimis* is no exception, and is of interest in that its 61 bars form a miniature 'lamento e trionfo', constituting a microcosm of the Lisztian emotional world. Liszt manages to use the whole text in repetition, rather than, as one would expect, the 'lacrimis' part first and then the 'exultatione' to finish. This is achieved by using chromatic harmony for the opening words (see Ex. 57) followed by unaccompanied chant-like passages, until D major is reached and the rising chromatic

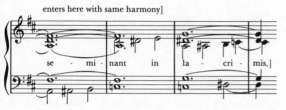

Ex. 57

Ex. 58

scale of the introduction reappears in a mood of exultation (see Ex. 58). Liszt maintains this mood for the whole second half of the piece, ending with jubilant octaves in the organ part.

PSALM 129 (NO. 130: OUT OF THE DEPTHS HAVE I CALLED TO THEE O LORD) (S16/2)

### Composition

Referring to the publisher of this work, Liszt wrote in 1882: 'He is taking . . . the Psalm *De profundis*, written at Rome, Nov. '81. It is very simple, with neither choir nor orchestra, or nonsense of any kind. I don't know

Ex. 59

Ex. 60

whether it will find a singer who can express its feeling of intimacy and prostration' (*Br.* VII, 358). It was published in 1883 by Kahnt. Another version (S16/1) with a part for male-voice choir appeared also in the 1880s.

This is a very important late work because its title refers back to 1834 and Liszt's work for piano and orchestra written for Lamennais entitled *De profundis* (see chapter 2). Whereas the earlier work ended in triumph, this ends in resignation, though not without hope, expressing the attitude found in certain letters of Liszt's old age, for example one to Baroness von Meyendorff in 1872: 'As for me, I have only reached the stage of a kind of sad resignation regarding men and events, sometimes tempered and as though illumined by faith in divine providence and invincible hope in Christ's redemption!' (*LOM*, 43). The early work was, of course, connected with Liszt's revolutionary hopes, though it had a religious theme. This late work shows the nature of the change that took place in Liszt: the revolutionary element has become purely musical.

The work is scored for bass voice with organ accompaniment. The score suggests the piano as an alternative, but the sustained chords of the music sound better on the organ. The text is given in Latin and German, but Liszt's title is 'De profundis'. The revolutionary element lies in the harmony of the opening bars (see Ex.59). The juxtaposition of fifths to make a discord arises from the rearrangement of the preceding rising sevenths F to E and C to B. If these notes are placed in alphabetical order, which is the music in reverse, we see that they outline BCEF (see Ex. 60), the four notes that begin the *Crux fidelis*, and contain the Cross motif. It is in this order that Liszt presents these notes at the entry of the voice (see Ex. 61).

The absence of a key signature points to C major as the tonal base, corresponding with Liszt's use of the key to represent man on earth (*cf.*

# The psalms

Ex. 61

Ex. 62

*Les Préludes*, etc.). The key changes to E major, Liszt's 'religious' key, at the words 'Quia apud te propitiatio est' ('But in thee is forgiveness'), and the vocal line makes a more direct reference to the Cross motif (see Ex. 62). The vocal tessitura reflects the text, starting low down for the opening 'De profundis', and reaching its highest at 'ipse redimet' in the phrase 'et ipse redimet Israel ex omnibus iniquitatibus ejus' ('He alone will set Israel free from all their sins'), which is repeated alone at the close of the setting, where Liszt emphasizes the word 'redimet' as the message of the work. Thus redemption is the theme, as it was in the earlier work, but it is expressed differently. At the end, the voice sinks back into the depths, and the organ comes to rest alone on the E major chord, avoiding any suggestion of a conventional cadence.

Liszt planned to use the music in the oratorio *St Stanislas*, but the work remained unfinished. It was the last of the Psalms to be composed, just as the 'De profundis' of 1834 constitutes the first, since Liszt gave it the title 'Psaume instrumental'. The two works encapsulate Liszt's musical progress from Catholic revolutionary to revolutionary Catholic.

PSALM *137* (BY THE RIVERS OF BABYLON WE SAT DOWN AND WEPT) (S17)

### Composition

On 20 August 1859 Liszt wrote to Agnes Klindworth: 'I have just finished two Psalms: "Der Herr ist mein Hirt" (the German translation by

Herder) and the well-known one "An den Wassern zu Babylon" ' (*Br.* III, 121). In 1862 he wrote from Rome to Gottschalg, cantor and organist in Tieffurt, later court organist at Weimar: 'I beg you most particularly to make *no* further use of the two Psalms "By the waters of Babylon", of which you have a copy, because I have undertaken to make two or three *essential* alterations in them, and I wish them only to be made known and published in their present form' (*L*, II, 7). The following year he wrote again: 'In the Psalms I have made some important alterations, and shall shortly send Kahnt the manuscript. A few passages (especially the verse "Sing us one of the songs of Zion") which had always appeared awkward to me in the earlier version, I have now managed to improve. At least they now pretty well satisfy my soul's ear' (*L*, II, 45). Liszt refers to two settings, of which only one is published; the manuscript of a second exists in the Weimar Liszt Museum. According to Lina Ramann Liszt based the music on a picture of the lamenting Jews by Eduard Bendemann.

The score was published in 1864 by Kahnt.

*Performance*

Liszt attached great importance to the performing rôle of the singer, writing that 'mind and soul are indispensable in it' (*L*, II, 98).

*Psalm 137* is scored for solo voice and women's choir, with violin, harp, piano and organ. This strange combination of instruments is used effectively by Liszt, the rôle of each being clearly defined. The organ sustains the harmony, the piano punctuates the beat with arpeggiated chords, the harp has a rippling figuration suggestive of water, and the violin weaves an independent obbligato round the vocal lines, a use of the violin almost unique in Liszt's choral works (another example occurs in the Benedictus of the *Hungarian Coronation Mass*). It lends the Psalm a distinctive, perhaps Hungarian, colouring, a feature used deliberately by Liszt, who exploits the lower register of the instrument in the first half and the high register in the second. He was equally insistent on the type of voice to sing the solo, though curiously this is not specified in the score. Referring to the psalms in this respect Liszt wrote: 'The 137th is meant for a mezzo-soprano' (*L*, II, 90). The range is from B below middle C to B♭ above the stave, the contrast between low and high notes following their use in the violin part.

The work opens in C minor and ends in C major. The unharmonized opening line, constructed from Liszt's 'Hungarian' scale, suggests the Cross motif (see Ex. 63). The violin enters with the theme, the harp, piano and organ providing harmony. The voice then sings the opening lines of the psalm to the theme. The music progresses in the manner of

# The psalms

Ex. 63

Ex. 64

a 'lamentoso' aria. At the words 'Des Zion's Lieder singet uns doch eins!' ('Sing us one of the songs of Zion') the style changes to recitative. The violin and voice follow each other with mournful phrases, until the violin introduces a rising sixth over the chord of G♯ minor, echoed by the voice singing 'Jerusalem!'. This introduces the note of hope required to mark the turning point. Liszt marks the voice: 'aus tiefster Seele'. The phrase is repeated over an E major chord – the 'religious' key – and then a dominant progression leads to C major and the entry of the women's choir with 'Jerusalem!'. This comes as something of a surprise after the long wait, a typically dramatic touch on Liszt's part. The solo voice, as if taking courage, sings 'If I forget you, O Jerusalem, let my right hand wither away' to a phrase of operatic dimensions stretching across the vocal range (see Ex. 64). The music settles into a mood of transfigured calm, as the violin weaves a line around the upper register of the voice, accompanied by the choir and other instruments.

The opening C minor music recurs after the solo's words 'Let my tongue cling to the roof of my mouth if I do not remember you', the violin reintroducing the opening theme. This time it mounts ever higher, arriving at C major and the entry of the full voices, 'pp dolce', with 'Jerusalem!'. Liszt reserves the purest sound of unaccompanied voices for the very end, employing a modal cadence very similar to the one that ends the *Male-Voice Mass*, the second soprano outlining the Cross motif.

*Psalm 137* is dramatic in conception, and belongs to the large category of Liszt works inspired by painting, as for example the symphonic poem *Hunnenschlacht*. Liszt does not set the whole text of the psalm, stopping at the vision of Jerusalem. In this way he confines his music to the characteristic idea of 'lamento e trionfo', the promise of redemption.

# 10

# THE ORATORIOS *ST ELIZABETH* AND *CHRISTUS*

Shortly after moving to Rome, Liszt wrote to Franz Brendel:

> I am firmly resolved for some length of time to continue working on here undisturbed, unremittingly and with an object. After having, as far as I could, solved the greater part of the *Symphonic* problem set me in Germany, I mean now to undertake the *Oratorio* problem (together with some other works connected with this) . . . To other people this anxiety on my part may appear trifling, useless, at all events thankless, and but little profitable; to me it is the one object in art which I have to strive after, and to which I must sacrifice everything else.
>
> (*L*, II, 33)

Liszt's solutions to this problem were *The Legend of St Elizabeth* and *Christus*, works which themselves became central to what is commonly called the 'Liszt problem'. The two oratorios are entirely different in conception and form, the first being 'symphonic' and organized into six scenes, with characters and dialogue, the second being in 14 independent 'numbers', but without the usual division into choruses, arias and narration by a 'testo'. Instead there are orchestral pieces, choral pieces with organ accompaniment only, full-scale 'ensemble' pieces for orchestra, choir and soloists, and one piece for solo voice and orchestra, the soloist being identified as 'Christus'. What is the explanation for these peculiarities?

As far as Liszt's music is concerned, there is a close link between symphony and oratorio, since the *Faust* and *Dante Symphonies* were originally planned as operas. One of the main criticisms of *The Legend of St Elizabeth* is that it is operatic, one writer going so far as to say that 'basically, one feels, Liszt was not quite certain what kind of a work he was writing. Sometimes, it has the character of a Concert Opera, while at others it has the essentially static character associated with Oratorio.'[1] This opinion is extreme, since it may be assumed that Liszt did know what kind of a work he was writing. The issue at stake troubles Protestants and Englishmen more than it does Catholics, who are less inclined to associate opera with sin and oratorio with virtue. Historically there is no distinction between the two musical forms, an oratorio being an opera on a biblical or religious subject. The rôle of the chorus became amplified, particularly when it became customary not to stage oratorio. But originally an aria in an oratorio was identical in form and character to one in opera. By the nineteenth century, however, this was no longer true, as it was assumed that 'religious' music was somehow different from other music. Liszt's fundamental challenge to this idea was to treat it as the nonsense it was, and to write full-blooded music in both his oratorios, though in *Christus* he made a distinction between church music and other music, since parts of the work were intended for church use.

The common element in Liszt is that opera, oratorio and symphony each serve the same function, which is to tell a story. The issue therefore centres upon his view of programme music, which in turn raises the question whether music should be programmatic. This question did not exist for other composers, for example Dvořák, who wrote operas, oratorios and non-programmatic symphonies without obvious qualms. But Liszt belonged to the circle that surrounded Wagner, and while he lived in Germany he felt obliged to explain his views on what music was all about, which basically meant a defence of programme music in the country that produced Beethoven and was critical of Berlioz. Wagner neatly side-stepped the issue by claiming that the symphony had died with Beethoven's *Choral*, and that its natural successor was opera, which was Wagner's sole concern. Liszt, however, had to justify the notion of associating instrumental music, formerly considered self-sufficient, with words, thus seeming to limit rather than expand its significance. His apology came in the form of an article, 'Berlioz and his Harold Symphony',[2] published in 1855, the year of Berlioz's second visit to conduct at Weimar, and the year that saw Liszt's *Gran Mass*, *Psalm 13*, *Dante Symphony* and *Hunnenschlacht*. In the course of his defence of Berlioz, Liszt manages to mention oratorio, and to give a clear indication of his own views and preoccupations during that year.

The article is long and diffuse, and the argument presented by Liszt, who was no theoretician, has to be uncovered and the ideas put into their logical order. The result is clear, if flawed. Liszt makes eight basic points:

(1) 'Music . . . is the embodied and intelligible essence of feeling.'

Here Liszt states the premise upon which his whole output rests as a composer.

(2) 'The programme asks only acknowledgement for the possibility of precise definition of the psychological moment which prompts the composer to create his work and of the thought to which he gives outward form.'

The key word here is 'psychological'. Liszt argues that the composer has the right to explain his reasons for composing a particular piece. He therefore immediately links music with literature.

(3) 'In the modern epopoeia [epic poem] . . . the action acquires a symbolic lustre, a mythological basis . . . No longer does the poem aim to recount the exploits of the principal figure; it deals with affections active within his very soul. It has become far more important to show what the hero thinks than how he acts . . . The stage is always more receptive to the transplanting of motives from the classical epos than it is to those modern poems which, for the want of a better name, we shall call *philosophical epopoeias*; among these Goethe's *Faust* is the colossus, while beside it Byron's *Cain* and *Manfred*, and the *Dziady* of Mickiewicz constitute immortal types.'

Liszt here attempts to justify programme music by invoking the similarity of music to modern literature, which is unsuitable for the stage. He then moves away from opera, on the assumption that the stage cannot convey the workings of the mind, being constrained to depict external action, which is found in Classical epic poetry.

(4) 'Is music unsuited to cause such natures to speak its language? . . . But could music do this in the drama? Scarcely. The interest which they arouse attaches itself far more to inner events than to actions related to the outer world . . . The function of the programme then becomes indispensable, and its entrance into the highest spheres of art appears justified.'

Here the relationship between the music and the programme in a work like Liszt's *Faust Symphony* is explained.

(5) 'Through song there have always been combinations of music with literary or quasi-literary works; the present time seeks a *union* of the two which promises to become a more intimate one than any that have offered themselves thus far.'

Liszt here attempts to justify why music based upon literature should be played rather than sung. In pointing the connection between the text of a song and the character of its music, Liszt implies that since music must have character, then a prior stage to its composition has to be to decide what kind of piece it shall be. An obvious link then arises between the desire to compose 'great' music and the availability of suitable literary foundations.

(6) 'Aside from dialogue, held together by a certain continuity in the action it presents, oratorio and cantata have no more in common with the stage than has the epos; through their leaning towards the descriptive, instrumentation lends them a similar frame. Episode and apostrophe play almost the same rôle in them, and the effect of the whole is that of the solemn recital of a memorable event, the glory of which falls undivided on the head of a single hero. If we were asked which musical form corresponded most closely to the poetic epos, we should doubt whether better examples could be brought forward than the *Israel, Samson, Judas Maccabaeus, Messiah* and *Alexander* of Handel, the Passion of Bach, the *Creation* of Haydn, the *St Paul* and *Elijah* of Mendelssohn.'

# Revolution and religion

This is important since Liszt explains that oratorio (a) is superior to opera, (b) derives its superiority from a resemblance to epic poetry (the heroic ideal), and (c) constitutes the highest form of vocal music, thus warranting a departure from programmatic instrumental music. There is no question of musical style at issue here; the argument is entirely about music and words. Here the flaw in the argument appears. Liszt first claims that epic poetry depicts external action – hence its themes have been plundered by opera – then he justifies the superiority of oratorio to opera by invoking its resemblance to epic poetry, this time the heroic ideal. Thus epic poetry is first condemned because it is not 'philosophical' like *Faust* etc., of which modern programme music is the equivalent, and by implication its superior; then it is praised because it provides a Classical precedent for the heroic ideal found in oratorio. The curious thing is Liszt's omission of his central assumption – that oratorio is religious. Clearly he was invoking literature in support of a musical argument whose real nature remained hidden even from himself.

(7) 'Man stands in inverse relations to art and nature; nature he rules as its capstone, its final flower, its noblest creature; art he creates as a second nature, so to speak, making of it, in relation to himself, that which he himself is to nature. For all this, he can proceed, in creating art, only according to the laws which nature lays down for him, for it is from nature that he takes the materials for his work . . . for all that it [art] is the creature of man, the fruit of his will, the expression of his feeling, the result of his reflection, art has none the less an existence not determined by man's intention, the successive phases of which follow a course independent of his deciding and predicting.'

Here Liszt is writing about himself as an artist. His views derive from the experience common to all composers concerning the separation of form and content, or construction and ideas. Where do ideas come from? To Liszt the question was synonymous with 'where do feelings come from?' since music expressed feeling. There is nothing a composer can do about the effect music has upon the emotions, except use it to fashion his art. In this sense, the composer is the 'single hero'.

(8) 'In art and in its oscillation between sterile, outworn forms which continue to vegetate, bearing no new types, and the progress of evolving forms which are still imperfect there is revealed *the finger of God* which Newton speaks of.'

This is the idea Liszt imbibed in his youth at the feet of Lamennais. It unites the historical and the religious in its attempt to account for creativity in man. Liszt's citing of epic poetry was an appeal to history, which in passing to oratorio became an appeal to God. The choice of 'hero' in Liszt's oratorios shows this preoccupation. His circular argument shows clearly that the reason he composed oratorios instead of operas was religious, since oratorio represented the programmatic

164

expression of how he viewed himself as a composer. This explains the operatic style of the music; to Liszt it was not style that was religious – his oratorios are operatic music outlining religious programmes to do with himself. Thus we see that in Liszt the religious question centres upon the man.

## THE LEGEND OF ST ELIZABETH (S2)

### Composition

Between Weimar and Eisenach lies the Wartburg, the ancient castle of the Kings of Thuringia, where in the thirteenth century Elizabeth, the daughter of King András II of Hungary, was brought as a child to be the future bride of Ludwig, the son of Landgrave Hermann of Thuringia. In 1855 frescoes by Moritz von Schwind depicting scenes in the life of St Elizabeth were installed in the Wartburg, and these formed the basis for the oratorio. In 1879 Liszt wrote to Olga von Meyendorff: 'I'll send you . . . the Wartburgerinnerungen by Philipp Freytag, with drawings by Schwind . . . They served as the programme for my *Legend of St Elizabeth*' (*LOM*, 347). Shortly after their installation, Liszt took the sculptor Rietschel to see the frescoes. 'He wanted,' wrote Liszt, 'to see Schwind's paintings in the Wartburg, and we set out this morning for Eisenach' (*Br.* III, 25). In August 1855 the Princess Wittgenstein gave her daughter a present of Schwind's drawings for the frescoes: '15 August is also Princess Marie's birthday,' wrote Liszt. 'Her mother gave her a magnificent present today of the cartoons of Schwind's paintings in the Wartburg. Often it happens that the cartoons of German painters are better than their pictures, and so it is with these *seven deeds of charity* of St Elizabeth' (*Br.* III, 39). This reference to seven paintings is important since the oratorio contains six scenes, each based upon a single painting. The author of the text, Otto Roquette, together with Liszt and the Princess, decided which to include. In 1865, after the first performance of the work, which took place in Hungary, Liszt wanted to send a copy of the pictures to Baron Augusz, and wrote to Franz Brendel from the Vatican on 28 September:

Request Kahnt to purchase for me the steel-plates (or wood-cuts) of Schwind's *Elisabeth-Glaerie* in the Wartburg, published in Leipzig by Weigel or Brockhaus . . . If I am not mistaken, the drawings are published in *two* parts. The first part contains the pictures of St Elizabeth's arrival at the Wartburg, the miracle of Roses – up to her death. The second part gives the medallions depicting her *works of charity*. (*L*, II, 108)

Otto Roquette, who from 1896 was Professor at the Polytechnikum in

Darmstadt, was well known as a writer and poet. On 14 April 1856 he informed Liszt that the fifth and sixth scenes were nearly completed and in a few days would be handed to the copyist. He was however finding it difficult to write the third scene. On 28 April he wrote that he had heard from the Princess that 'the first part of the Elizabeth is at least not unusable for composing' (*BrZ*, 72), and he had therefore completed the following part in the same manner. The third scene, however, was still missing. Entitled 'The Miracle of the Sick', Roquette could not find the right poetic expression for it, and asked: 'Is it perhaps the Catholic element, with which I as a Protestant have no inner rapport?' By contrast, 'The Miracle of the Roses' had caused him no trouble. 'All the other situations,' he wrote, 'struck me purely as poetic, and so also is the Rose miracle a poetic idea, without any elaboration. I am therefore, in doubt as to whether this particular scene is absolutely necessary' (*BrZ*, 73). Eventually the scene in question was abandoned, leaving five scenes completed by Roquette, who gave Liszt the following ideas for the ending of the oratorio: 'I thought of the ending as ceremonial, perhaps a solemn Mass, and am therefore of a mind to put it into Latin, ready made. I have compiled the Latin verse from various hymns to do with Saint Elizabeth which I found in Montalembert' (*BrZ*, 72). Montalembert's *Vie de Sainte Elisabeth* was evidently known to Liszt as well as Roquette, since the scene of 'The Miracle of the Roses' contains details both musical and textual not found in Schwind's painting. Roquette's idea for Latin texts was paralleled by Liszt's own request in 1858 from Hungary for liturgical music associated with St Elizabeth. The original plan would have been six scenes followed by this ending. With the omission of Roquette's problematic third scene the plan became six scenes altogether, including the ceremonial ending in Latin. The oratorio thus fell neatly into two halves, each of three scenes, the actual third scene being 'The Crusaders'.

In June 1857 Liszt wrote that he hoped to work on the oratorio in the autumn. 'I am greatly attracted to this work,' he commented, 'to which I shall apply myself wholeheartedly. The libretto of the legend which Otto Roquette has prepared for me leaves me plenty of scope, and I hope to succeed in sustaining the interest and piety of the artist without monotony, strain or triviality' (*Br.* III, 92). It is unlikely, therefore, that Liszt composed any of the music before 1857.

On 11 April 1858 Liszt met János Nepomuk Danielik, Canon of Eger, who was one of the guests invited to the meal given in Liszt's honour by the Franciscans at Pest when he visited the order. The previous year he had published *Das Leben der heiligen Elisabeth von Ungarn*, and he presented Liszt with a copy. In his letter of thanks, Liszt wrote: 'I hope, moreover, on my own modest part to contribute also a little to glorifying St

Elizabeth by composing an oratorio for which the life of the beloved Saint has provided me the subject, and which will be finished during the course of this year' (*BruS*, 101). In June Liszt wrote from Weimar to seek Danielik's help in finding musical material for the oratorio:

It is to be presumed that among the liturgical hymns and prayers relating to St Elizabeth that you consulted during your work, there must be some notations of ancient plainsong belonging to the liturgy which it is important for me to know and make use of in the Legend (for choir, soloists and orchestra) which I am composing at the moment in honour of the same saint.                    (*BruS*, 101)

Danielik, however, was not a musician, and through Baron Augusz passed Liszt's request to the composer Mosonyi, who copied many liturgical melodies from various sources and sent them to Liszt, who later acknowledged Mosonyi's help in his note at the end of the score.

Liszt seemed to be making slow progress in composing the work during 1858. In April he wrote to the Princess's daughter: 'This year I *have* to keep my promise and *finish* Elizabeth, of greater concern to me than anything else since this work was specially planned for *Minette*: Johanna-Karolyne Elizabeth' (*LMW*, 99). ('Minette' was a nickname for the Princess Wittgenstein.) In June he extended his deadline: 'By winter ('59) I should like to have finished *the Elizabeth* on which I am now working. There will be approximately two and a half hours of music, which means at least six months' work for me. The text made for me by Otto Roquette seems very well done, and there will be several *pleasing* numbers' (*Br*. III, 111). At the end of the year Liszt resigned as court conductor, and in January 1859 wrote explaining to Wagner his 'negative attitude', adding: 'I feel sure that you will see in it no neglect of my artistic conviction, much less of my duty as a friend to you' (*WL*, II, 269). In May Wagner wrote asking Liszt to visit him: 'Come to me and play all your things to me, especially the Crusaders' chorus (splendid!!)' (*WL*, II, 299). This is the first mention of any of the music from the oratorio, and it seems probable that Liszt tackled first the third scene. This is significant because the music for the Crusaders is based upon the Cross motif.

In 1860, the work was still far from complete. In July Liszt wrote to his cousin Eduard: 'I shall . . . work at the Oratorio *St Elizabeth*, exclusive of all else, and get it completely finished before the end of the year. May God in His grace accept my endeavours!' (*L*, I, 433). In 1861 Liszt moved to Rome, where he continued to work on the oratorio, composing 'The Miracle of the Roses' and the storm in the fourth scene: 'When I awoke I returned to the *Tempest* in *Elizabeth* – which I was determined to reduce for piano. After trying 20 versions, I finally managed reasonably well' (*Br*. VI, 7). In July 1862 he wrote to Franz Brendel: 'Already more than 140 pages of the score of my *Elizabeth* are written out complete (in my own little cramped scrawl). But the final chorus – about 40 pages – and the piano arrangement have still to be done. By the middle of August I shall send the entire work to Carl Götze at Weimar to copy' (L, II, 18). On 10 August 1862 Liszt wrote: 'The *Legend of St Elizabeth* is written out to the very last note of the score' (L, II, 20). The work was not given to the copyist, however, until 1864. Liszt was unwilling to send his manuscript through the post, and there was not a decent copyist to be had in Rome:

The postal arrangements are so little safe, under present circumstances, that I do not care to send manuscripts by this means. In despatching parcels to Vienna or Paris I could, of course, make use of the courtesy of the embassies; but it is more difficult with Weimar . . . and so the parcel with the *Legend of St Elizabeth* . . . must remain in my box till some perfectly reliable opportunity presents itself. If the worst comes to the worst I shall bring the whole lot myself.     (L, II, 36)

In the event he did in fact take the manuscript with him when he visited Weimar.

After the first performance of the work Liszt sent the still unpublished score to Hans von Bülow at Munich for a performance to be given at the request of King Ludwig II of Bavaria. This took place on 24 February 1866. A performance followed the same year under Smetana in Prague. In October 1866 Liszt wrote to Brendel:

I have made up my mind to wait another year before publishing the *Elizabeth*. In the first place it is necessary that I should correct the frequent errors in the copy of the score – a piece of work that will take a couple of weeks. – Then, before its appearance, I should like an opportunity of quietly hearing the work once in Germany, and this perhaps might occur next year.     (L, II, 114)

Such an opportunity did occur when Liszt conducted a performance of the *Legend of St Elizabeth* on 28 August 1867 in the Wartburg itself as part of the celebrations marking the 800th anniversary of the castle. At the beginning of the year Liszt yielded to pressure to have the work published by Kahnt: 'You know that I should have preferred to postpone the publication of the *Elizabeth* for some time longer – still I understand Kahnt's difference of opinion, and desire to prove myself willing' (L, II, 119). The vocal score appeared in 1867, the full score in 1869.

*Performances*

Liszt replied to the Hungarian letter of invitation to give the first performance of the work in Hungary, sent by Baron Prónay, that he was willing for this, since the work was part of his artistic tribute to his homeland. The libretto was translated into Hungarian by Kornél Ábrányi. The performance in the Vigadó (Redoute) on 15 August 1865 was conducted by Liszt. Erkel helped with the preceding rehearsals. Reményi and

Mosonyi played in the orchestra – expanded from the National Theatre (Opera). Cosima, Hans von Bülow and Eduard Liszt were among the audience. Articles by Bülow appeared in the *Pesti-Napló* and the *Pesth-Ofener Zeitung*. No other work by Liszt was so well received and frequently performed in his lifetime. The composer's visit to England in 1886 was expressly to be present at a performance in London, as he told Walter Bache, the organizer of the performance: 'The *accented point* of my coming to London is to be present at the *Elizabeth* performance. It was this that decided my coming, and it is to be hoped it will be a success' (*L*, II, 479). The work was translated into English for the occasion, and published by Novello.

The 'legend' of the title of the work is the miracle of the roses, which Liszt makes the musical and dramatic pivot of the whole work. The episode is described by Montalembert in his *Vie de Sainte Elizabeth*:

Elizabeth loved to carry to her poor, clad in the attire of a simple lady, not only money, but food, and other objects which she destined for them. Thus burthened, she made her way by the rocky and winding paths that led from her castle to the town and the cottages of the neighbouring valleys. One day, as she was walking down a narrow and very rough path, which is shown to this day, accompanied by one of her favourite attendants, carrying, in the folds of her mantle, bread, meat, eggs, and other food, to distribute amongst the poor, all of a sudden she met her husband, returning with a party of young noblemen from the chace. Astonished to see her quite bending under the weight of her burden, he said: 'Let us see what this is you are carrying'; and, at the same time, opened, in spite of her, the mantle, which she, quite timid, was holding tight to her bosom; but he found nothing within but white and red roses, the most beautiful he had ever seen; this surprised him the more, as it was no longer the season for flowers. Perceiving the confusion of his Elizabeth, he wished to calm her by his caresses, – but he stopped short all at once, on seeing a luminous cross appear over her head. He then told her to continue her walk, and not to be troubled at him; after which, he himself climbed up to the Castle of Wartburgh [*sic*], meditating in silence on the wonders God wrought in her, and carrying away one of those marvellous roses, which he preserved for the rest of his life.[3]

The evidence that this description was known to Liszt lies in the reference to the cross, which does not appear in Schwind's fresco, but does in Liszt's music in the form of the Cross motif played by the trombones after the miracle has taken place. The music of the succeeding scene, 'The Crusaders', is based upon the Cross motif, which makes a programmatic point all Liszt's own, the implication being that Ludwig goes to Palestine as a result of the miracle granted to his wife. In other words the first part of the oratorio ends with a conversion. It should be noted that Elizabeth does not perform the miracle herself; the words of the chorus are 'A wonder God himself hath wrought'. The reason for this miracle is that she was on her way to give food to the poor. Montalembert's Latin subtitle to his book is 'Sancta Elisabeth Hungarica, patrona pauperum'.

The emotion Liszt is here dealing with is Elizabeth's compassion, but the implications of his programmatic approach are much more far-reaching. The abolition of poverty is at once a human, religious, social, political, and economic issue, and harks back to Liszt's youth, his interest in Christian Socialism, and his devotion to Lamennais. Even Louis Napoleon, be it remembered, wrote a book entitled *The Extinction of Poverty*, and was praised after his death in Saint-Simonian terms by Liszt.

The second part shows Elizabeth's persecution, death and canonization. During the absence of her husband, she and her children are driven out of the Wartburg at night by Ludwig's mother, Landgravine Sophie, who seizes power on the death of her son in Palestine. Liszt portrays her as the embodiment of evil, using the interval of an augmented fourth, the 'diabolus in musica' found in the 'Inferno' movement of the *Dante Symphony*, the second *Mephisto Waltz*, the late piano piece *Unstern* (*Evil Star*) and elsewhere. Its significance here is obvious, particularly when, after the expulsion of Elizabeth, a terrific storm destroys the castle. In terror, the elderly Seneschal cries: 'That is the wrath of Heaven.'

Elizabeth, now homeless and alone, is shown wandering among the poor. Before she dies, she is granted a vision of Ludwig in Paradise, and her soul is carried up to Heaven by a choir of angels. Her burial is solemnized by Emperor Frederick II of Hohenstaufen, together with a Mourning Chorus of the Poor and of the People generally, and a Procession of Crusaders. The Latin text given to the Church Choristers and the Hungarian and German Bishops at the end of the work signifies the canonization of Elizabeth.

The only scene, therefore, in which Elizabeth does not appear as a saint is the first one, depicting her arrival as a child to live at the Wartburg. The journey from childhood to sainthood, though, in Lisztian terms, is the circular one he portrayed in *From the Cradle to the Grave*: from innocence through love and the struggle against evil to God. By making the miracle scene Elizabeth's first appearance as an adult, we see Elizabeth as the symbol of God's love, against which the whole of the story takes place, each event serving to illustrate the single programmatic idea. This single idea in Liszt's mind made the work religious, and as such unfit for the stage, despite its operatic structure. In 1874 he gave his reasons for not wishing to see the oratorio staged: 'Whether it is advisable to put on a second [performance of *St Elizabeth*] in Düsseldorf so soon I leave entirely to your judgment; similarly the matter of a "staged performance", which up to now I have not been able to consider right, and which I forbade in Pest and Weimar' (*Br.* VIII, 276). Clearly the issue centred upon the miracle scene, which it was not 'right' to stage. To symbolize the sacred in music was entirely characteristic of Liszt, even in an operatic form with dialogue between characters. But to turn the singers into actors and the roses into a stage effect he would not allow. The point was psychological, and, as with all Liszt's music, its province was the ideal world of the mind.

Here Liszt's problem was his habit of being literal in music. In *Christus* the storm brought to a calm by Christ is the most vivid orchestral evocation of a storm he ever composed, and the voice of Christ that stills it is unaccompanied. The structure of *Christus* makes it unsuitable for the stage – it has been staged, for example in Budapest between the wars, but the intention was clearly to make it totally unsuitable for the theatre – and Liszt's reason for not wanting it staged is the same as in the case of *St Elizabeth*. What determined the different form of the work is its subject matter, and the need to give the characters who appear in the legend words to utter.

This posed a problem which Otto Roquette did not quite solve. As in Wagner, the characters in *St Elizabeth* have a symbolic function; they are not primarily of interest as people, but for their relationship to Elizabeth. To set the scenes, however, Roquette was obliged to resort to standard operatic procedure, and there are passages of banality and tedium. The miracle scene, for example, is preceded by a standard hunting song simply because Ludwig happens to be out hunting when he meets his wife in the woods. Liszt's music makes the best of the situation by providing an efficiently crafted aria in the manner of mid-nineteenth-century German opera, but it is too long, and musically untypical of its composer. The dramatic improvement in the quality of inspiration as soon as Elizabeth appears shows where his interest lay, and the ensuing scene is a masterpiece. All the scenes except two suffer from these tedious beginnings. The exceptions are the fifth – entitled simply 'Elizabeth', which begins with Elizabeth alone, for whom Liszt provides ravishing soprano writing right up to her death, continuing the inspiration through to the choir of angels that closes the scene – and the third, which begins with the 'March of the Crusaders'.

At the end of the score Liszt gives a list of the musical themes used in the oratorio, a feature unique to this work. The list is prefaced by a letter of thanks, dated 'Rome, October 1862', to those who helped find the themes. Four themes are then identified, the last of which is the Cross motif (see Ex. 178, p. 284), which is followed by the comment: 'It is used in this particular composition of the Legend of St Elizabeth likewise as a tonal symbol of the Cross, and as the basic theme of the Crusaders' Chorus and the March of the Crusaders.'

The use of these themes falls midway between the leitmotif technique

Ex. 65

of Wagner and Liszt's own transformation of themes. Thus the plain-chant used to represent Elizabeth, which is the dominant musical theme of the work, appears in conjunction with Elizabeth herself much as it would in opera, and is also used as building material for choral and orchestral passages. The method follows Liszt's symphonic poems and *Tannhäuser* rather than the Wagner of the *Ring* cycle; that is to say, *St Elizabeth* is partly a 'number' opera and partly 'symphonic'. Each scene is separate, but largely continuous within itself. To achieve continuity Liszt tends to avoid a closing cadence at the end of each 'number', although the opening 'Chorus of Welcome', the Hungarian Magnate's aria and the 'Children's Chorus', for example, all in the first scene, start like self-contained pieces. The only choral part of the entire work which can be performed separately occurs in the 'March of the Crusaders' that closes the third scene. The structure of this scene parallels the history of the composition of the work as a whole, since the 'Old Pilgrim Song' does not appear in the opening 'Chorus of Crusaders', praised by Wagner in 1857, but does appear in the closing piece, which recapitulates the same music. Liszt did not begin his investigations into relevant musical material until after his visit to Hungary in 1858. The result is that the music of the march (see Ex. 65), built out of the Cross motif, appears too often (five times) during the scene. At the end of the scene Liszt includes a page of music to act as an introduction, 'should the "March of the Crusaders" be performed separately'. This is the same music, consisting of the Cross motif over a dominant pedal, that opens the scene. It must be concluded that the music was composed twice, the second time incorporating the 'Old Pilgrim Song' as an interlude in the middle, at the end recapitulated by men's voices and orchestra, in a 'number' entitled 'March of the Crusaders', which is purely orchestral for the first 18 pages of score.

The imbalance of this scene reflects Liszt's enthusiasm for the Cross motif. The music of the Crusaders deserves Wagner's praise, for it has all the makings of a popular concert item, full of energy and colour. It illuminates Liszt's attitude to the work as a whole, since it was the first music to be composed. It is self-contained also in that it makes no reference to any of the characters involved in the legend, not even Elizabeth herself. In that sense it functions as the 'message' of the oratorio. Elizabeth's function, by contrast, is to bring about this 'message' by means of the miracle that converts her husband. Musically this is done by using a 'transformation' of Elizabeth's plainchant theme.

Here the story serves to illuminate Liszt's musical thinking. The music of 'The Miracle of the Roses' is among the best Liszt wrote, and shows the strength of his skill in making a theme serve extra-musical ends. The task was simple: to create an atmosphere of wonderment and beauty. The result, it must be strongly emphasized, is unique to Liszt. Technically it may be inferior to Wagner, but Wagner never caught this mood; at a stroke Liszt achieves a total change of atmosphere, changing the time-scale of the previous half-hour of the oratorio. What follows amounts to the only love-duet that Liszt composed, 'Praise Him who us His blessing gave', while the choir in the background quietly sing 'Thou shalt the joys of the angels share, who art the rose's emblem so fair!' (see Ex. 66). From this flows the drama of the rest of the oratorio. Liszt's problem was how to follow such music without creating a sense of disappointment. His 'March of the Crusaders', already composed, serves to return the mood to one of energy and optimism, but Roquette's dialogue for the central farewell scene between Elizabeth and Ludwig returns the couple to the world of operatic commonplace. Elizabeth assumes the rôle of a mother weeping at being left alone with her children, which is ludicrous after the miracle scene. Also, Roquette indulges in the trick of operatic foreboding when he makes Elizabeth anticipate the banishment scene:

> What thoughts shall bring me peace?
> Her sable pinions Hatred hath
> Spread for dismal flight,
> No star of hope shall lead me,
> Nor comfort me at night.

The interruptions of the Crusaders, urging departure, are musically effective, but the episode as a whole is tedious, Liszt's efforts doomed by the libretto.

The real test of Liszt's skill as a dramatist was posed by the fourth scene, which is the most operatic one of the whole work. The music reveals clearly the opera-composer *manqué* in Liszt, and a craftsman in the theatrical style. The libretto, which is a gothic horror, this time failed to prevent success on Liszt's part. His theme representing the wicked Landgravine Sophie is full of 'diabolical' energy (see Ex. 67). A second

Ex. 66

Ex. 67

Ex. 68

Ex. 69

theme, containing the augmented fourth, represents her greed for power
(see Ex. 68). Sophie's sorrow at the death of her son is short-lived, and
she immediately determines to seize power and banish Elizabeth, whose
'offstage' entry is suggested by the orchestral introduction to what
sounds like the beginning of an aria: 'Oh day of sorrow, day of anguish'.
This ends with a Wagnerian progression to the words: 'Oh God! . . . hast
thou withdrawn from me thy hand?' (see Ex. 69). Elizabeth's plainchant
theme appears in an attempt to touch Sophie's heart, but to no avail. A

Ex. 70

trio follows for Elizabeth, Sophie and the Seneschal based upon the 'day of sorrow' theme, followed by the most Wagnerian passage in the whole work, perhaps in all Liszt, for Elizabeth alone to the words 'Thou too art a mother . . . have pity.' Elizabeth takes her children and leaves, the score carrying the stage direction 'Elizabeth goes away with dignity.' The orchestra starts the storm, which increases in fury when Sophie exults in having seized power. The music of the storm uses Sophie's themes and Elizabeth's 'day of sorrow' theme, while Sophie and the Seneschal sing their cries of fear. The storm dies away, and in a beautiful transition to the following scene low oboe and English horn play Elizabeth's theme in D minor, capturing the mood of refreshed calm that follows the storm. This leads via the augmented fourth on isolated timpani strokes to the key of F♯ major for Elizabeth's prayer.

The two parts of this long solo, 'Prayer' and 'Dream and Thoughts of Home', are based respectively on the plainchant theme and the Hungarian folk melody. The first part is addressed to her dead husband, ending with a plea to God to unite them:

> But Thee, my God, I thank Thee, ere I die,
> For trials sent, from sin us to deliver!

The music to this is purposeful and declamatory (see Ex. 70). The 'Elizabeth' theme forms the climax, 'Rejoin our hearts in love no Death shall sever!' (see Ex. 71). The harmony used here, transposed into E major as a full choral and orchestral tutti, ends the oratorio. The 'Prayer' ends with a short 'coda' referring to Elizabeth's children whom she says 'strangers took away'. A change to B♭ major introduces the Hungarian melody as a violin theme. The mood changes to agitation at 'I see my parents' tears fast flowing, They're weeping for their absent child', and an orchestral crescendo leads to another passage of Wagnerian expansiveness that closes Elizabeth's solo.

A long passage of quiet orchestral music acts as an interlude before the

Ex. 71

'Chorus of the Poor'. This commences with woodwind music that reappears immediately after Elizabeth's death. It resembles part of the final section of the symphonic poem *From the Cradle to the Grave*, and may be taken to represent the soul of the saint (see Ex. 72). Its repetition by the strings alone is ravishing. The key changes to G minor, and immediately we hear part of the music from the chorus that is to follow, where it is sung to the last two lines of the first reference to Elizabeth as a saint:

> Behold her in a cottage dwelling,
> The Saint, an Angel to the needy,
> Sad hearts of heavenly comfort, telling,
> At the sickbed's watching full of pity!

The orchestra then plays the music to the first two lines, which 'announces' the chorus and vividly suggests their gradual entrance 'on stage' as a tattered crowd. The dorian mode of the melody contributes to the atmosphere (see Ex. 73). The chorus sing this in unison, then change to harmony for the second two lines (see Ex. 74). This music later appears 'transformed' when Elizabeth has a vision of her husband in Paradise just before she dies.

Ex. 72

Ex. 73

Ex. 74

The music for the poor is the most original in the oratorio. Liszt alternates the 'dorian' theme there with passages of his own preserving the same flavour (see Ex. 75). Elizabeth herself speaks to the poor:

> Take all and fear not for the morrow,
> My cloak take, and this loaf of bread!

The chorus then sing 'Elizabeth, thou Saint, who helped the poor and needy' against an orchestral transformation of the 'dorian' theme. The 'Deeds of Charity' section ends with this chorus, whose 'exit' is suggested by the 'dorian' theme played alone by pizzicato strings. Left alone, Elizabeth sings unaccompanied 'darkness deep o'erveils my yield-

Warm clothes thou gavest for the poorly clad, and in thy presence all were glad.

Ex. 75

Thy hand hath led me, Lord, I praise Thee. Thou call'st and earthly sorr-ows end,

Ex. 76

ing senses', and this is followed by the reappearance of the 'soul' music in the orchestra. This is the beginning of 'Elizabeth's Death'. At the words 'I wake to new-born light', the plainsong theme receives a new transformation and Elizabeth sings 'Lo! radiance bright, breaks thro' the clouds of night!' followed by a vision of Ludwig: 'In heav'nly glory clad thy form I see'. A new theme appears, later to form the basis of the 'Angels' Chorus' (see Ex. 76). A climax is reached, and the 'saint' theme appears as a full tutti. This is the moment of death: 'To Thee, who doth upraise me, my spirit I commend!' The orchestra then quietly repeat the 'soul' music that preceded the 'Chorus of the poor'. Women's voices enter with the 'Angels' Chorus', accompanied by a harmonium which Liszt directs 'is to be placed in the centre of the singers'. The effect intended is one of distant voices. The 'saint' theme is sung in F♯ major, and the plainsong theme reappears at the words 'heav'nly roses fair are blowing where once but thorns of anguish grew'. At this point the orchestra enters upon the seventh chord of C♯, which begins a chain of dominant sevenths and ninths suggesting the passage of the soul to Heaven (see Ex. 77).

Ex. 77

The 'Orchestral Interlude' that follows sums up the whole oratorio. It begins with the 'dorian' theme from the 'Chorus of the Poor', passing to a full tutti statement of the 'Elizabeth' plainsong theme. Music from 'The Miracle of the Roses' follows, then the Hungarian theme and the 'Pilgrim Song'. A return of the 'Miracle' music leads via the 'Pilgrim Song' to a superb full tutti statement of the 'Hungarian' theme, a splendid piece of orchestration. The 'Elizabeth' theme, in the form that closes the oratorio, ends the piece, which is a fine example of Liszt's mature orchestral technique.

The oratorio ends in ceremonial. Emperor Frederick, in Wagnerian style, informs us that 'The robbers of her empire, they have fallen, By Heav'n's high vengeance they're for ever banned', and leads what one imagines to be an immense crowd to Elizabeth's grave. The funeral procession is built out of the 'dorian' theme from the 'Chorus of the Poor' (see Ex. 78). This section is effective mourning music. The Cross-motif music from the 'March of the Crusaders' returns to accompany the men's voices addressing Ludwig:

> Thou, who in holy lands
> Lost thy life, thy God adoring,
> Now see'st her heav'nward soaring.

The key changes from the Crusaders' Bb major to Elizabeth's E major, and the whole choir representing the Church enter in Latin, accompanied by the organ for the first time:

> Decorata novo flore
> Christum mente, votis, ore,
> Collaudet ecclesia.

Liszt maintains a mood of enthusiasm and splendour to the end of the

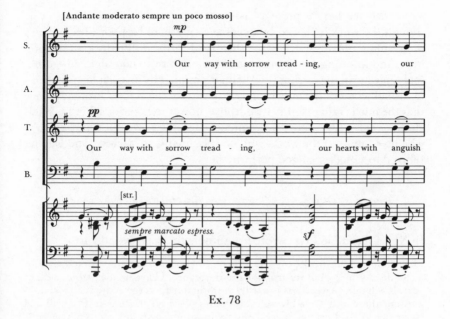

Ex. 78

work, which culminates in a terrific burst of the 'Elizabeth' theme. The final 'Amen' uses the closing music of the 'Introduction'.

The *Legend of St Elizabeth* shows above all Liszt's operatic skill. Although the work is not for the stage, its scenes are organized along theatrical lines, and require music that does the same job as in a stage work. The 'Chorus of Welcome' that opens the work illustrates this, exactly capturing the 'curtain-up' atmosphere that starts an opera. Also the dialogue is well set by Liszt, who captures the inflections and moods of the speakers in a simple and direct manner. Above all, Liszt's sense of dramatic timing operates throughout the work, rescuing Roquette's tedious passages and saving the best music for the big moments. Musically there are many surprises, the greatest being perhaps the 'Children's Games and Children's Chorus' in the first scene, which is delicate and vivacious in a manner that recalls Berlioz, yet preserving an independent, Lisztian character. Since the scene represents, from the programmatic point of view, the childhood of Elizabeth, it is apposite that this should be the best music. The same is true of later scenes viewed in direct relation to the 'programme'. Thus in no. 2 it is the 'Miracle' that impresses, in no. 3 the 'March of the Crusaders', in no. 4 the 'Storm', in no. 5 the 'Chorus of the Poor', and in no. 6 the 'Church Chorus'. Taken alone, these outline the legend itself, and it is to Liszt's credit that the very best music is that of the 'Miracle', which is the point of the whole story. We see here a perfect fusion of mind and music in Liszt, even though the work is flawed by excessive length and a poor libretto. It is programme music that takes a theatrical form to illustrate a religious idea, and in doing so illuminates Liszt's failure to complete any of his real operatic plans during the Weimar period. His interest lay primarily in the subject, not the music, and certainly not the stage. One may object that the music is histrionic. Its purpose, however, is serious. For Liszt the character of St Elizabeth represented something very important, which is why he composed the work, why he classified it as 'sacred', and why he refused to sanction staged performances.

### CHRISTUS. ORATORIO ON TEXTS FROM THE HOLY SCRIPTURE AND THE CATHOLIC LITURGY (S3)

In November 1866 Liszt wrote from Rome to Agnes Klindworth:

I have finished this work ['my Oratorio on Christ'], after having worked on it for a couple of years; – but regarding its performance, I have no idea either *when* or *where* it will take place. Paris is hardly oratorio territory; the genre is almost non-existent there and probably will not gain a place for itself as in England and Germany. Also, I am on several counts in an unusual and very unfavourable position personally. I can neither push myself forward, nor retire into the background. What is perfectly alright and of use to other composers no longer applies to my position. Organizing concerts, for example, seeking the means to produce my works, accepting favours for certain advantages, are things absolutely out of the question. Hence, since I am off the beaten track, I shall probably make no headway. No matter; I have taken my stand – and for a long time. While my exterior activity at Weimar lasted, I saw to it that several of my works were performed – because I needed to hear them in order to assess their merits, and it was far more to that end than to present them to the public that I undertook it. Otherwise, as you know, it is never without a very special and *specific* invitation that I have agreed to perform them whether in Weimar itself, or in a score of other German towns, where I needed to get to know and try out the various orchestras. Now my experience is acquired, and I hold it sufficient to compose with absolute security. I also am content to profess total disinterest with regard to the fate of my compositions. If they are worth anything then this will show itself in time without my worrying about anything other than writing them to the best of my ability. The *Elizabeth* was completed in May '62 – and was only performed in August '65, first of all in Pest. I shall publish the score in a year's time. The *Christ* can wait yet awhile, perhaps until after my death. It is not going into the market place begging vulgar applause! (*Br.* III, 188)

Liszt planned the work in 1853, writing in July to the Princess: 'I mentioned to Herwegh the matter of the "Christ", and how I would like to compose it – it is not impossible that he will undertake the work' (*Br.* IV, 147). In 1857 the problem of the text still troubled him: 'As soon as my *Elizabeth* is finished,' he wrote to Princess Wittgenstein, 'we must compose the *Christ*, in the manner we consider the work should be. If you take charge of the layout, Cornelius will make a good job of the verse, taking the Gospels and Rückert as a basis' (*Br.* IV, 366).

The first music to be written was 'The Beatitudes', which Liszt began in 1855: 'My poor Beatitudes!' he wrote to the Princess. 'I shall have to snatch a few hours before your return in order to complete them' (*Br.* IV, 249). They were completed in 1859:

I didn't write to you at all yesterday, though I did nothing but think of you while preparing for you a little surprise – which I will tell you about right away. From 9 until 1 o'clock the *Beatitudes* were composed almost in their entirety – there remains only the ending to work out, which will not give me much trouble'.

(*Br.* IV, 461)

The music was finished on 28 April: 'The Beatitudes are finished, and I sang them yesterday to Scotland [Miss Anderson, the Scottish nanny] and Bronsart [a pupil of Liszt's]' (*Br.* IV, 469). The oratorio is in 14 numbers, composed separately and at different times. 'The Beatitudes' is no. 6.

After his removal to Rome in 1861, Liszt completed *St Elizabeth* before re-embarking upon *Christus* in 1862. The greater part of the work was composed in 1865 and 1866, after Liszt took minor orders. The order of composition in Rome is as follows:

1863 Shepherds' Song at the Manger (no. 4)
   Stabat mater speciosa (no. 3)
   Pater noster (no. 7) [The Latin version; the Weimar version is a setting
    of the German text.]
   The Three Holy Kings (March) (no. 5)
1865 Introduction (no. 1)
   Pastorale and Annunciation (no. 2)
   The Miracle (no. 9)
   The Entry into Jerusalem (no. 10)
1866 Tristis est anima mea (no. 11)
   Stabat mater dolorosa (no. 12)
   Resurrexit (no. 14)
1867 The Foundation of the Church (no. 8) [A setting of *Tu es Petrus* to music
    from 1865 entitled *Inno del Papa*.]
1868 O filii et filiae (no. 13)

When Liszt wrote in 1866 that he had finished the work, it had only 12 numbers. The addition of 'The Foundation of the Church' made this 13, which Liszt doubtless found an unsatisfactory number, and which he increased to 14 in 1868.

The work as a whole was first performed on 29 May 1873 in the Protestant church at Weimar with Liszt conducting. Wagner attended the performance, and his comments were noted by Cosima in her Diaries:

Lunch with my father; afterwards many Hungarians, who have come to hear *Christus*. At 6 o'clock to the church, the performance goes on until 9. Remarkable, peculiar impression . . . the naive feeling of this highly unnaive creation; popular tendency toward pomp . . . After the performance, went with my father to the Bürger-Ressource – very popular. R. wanted to make a speech, but is unable to say a word before all these beer mugs and knitting women. 'They are poor people,' says my father, of whom R. declares that one can understand him only if one sees him as he is here, a thoroughly popular and friendly German figure.

*(CWD*, 29 May 1873)

Earlier, parts of the work had been performed separately, including 'The Beatitudes' on 15 October 1859 at Weimar on the occasion of the marriage of the Princess's daughter, and the 'Stabat mater speciosa' in Rome on 4 January 1866. The first part of the work, the 'Christmas Oratorio', consisting of nos. 1–5, was performed in Vienna on New Year's Eve 1871, conducted by Anton Rubinstein. The organist in this performance was Anton Bruckner.

The Weimar performance included cuts authorized by Liszt, and the first complete performance took place in Budapest on 9 November 1873, conducted by Hans Richter. This performance was judged to be better than the Weimar one by musicians who attended both.

The score was published in 1872 by Schuberth, later by Kahnt. 'The Beatitudes' appeared previously in 1861, published by Kahnt with Latin and German text; the 'Pater noster' followed in 1864.

It is understandable that writers who persist in presenting Christianity as a historical fact, more or less complex but natural and devoid of any miracles, should find that St Paul is not free of the faults which are shocking in sectarians, and that 'his style is ponderous'. His rôle was not to sit 'weary on the side of the road, or to waste his time in noting the vanity of established opinions'. His faith in Our Lord Jesus Christ was not an 'opinion'; he preached of Jesus crucified, resurrected, risen into Heaven; he fought the good fight and awaited 'the crown of justice which Our Lord will confer in the full light of day on those who love his coming'. Fine and great minds may understand nothing about all this; nevertheless millions of souls are illumined and fired by the words of St Paul.   *(LOM*, 93)

No other work of Liszt is surrounded by as much controversy and incomprehension as the oratorio *Christus*. It would be true to say that the neglect of this work constitutes the greatest injustice suffered by any composer of the nineteenth century, since it is without doubt the greatest musical composition of its time based upon the life of Christ. The remedy for this state of affairs is obvious, but is more likely to take place if we can understand how the situation has arisen in the first place.

It would be fair to say that *Christus* has suffered neglect not from musical, but from religious prejudice – not from the usual kind of prejudice that exists between Protestant and Catholic or Jew and

Christian, but from the simple fact that the nineteenth century, as a secular age, could not take seriously a mammoth work devoted ostensibly to religion and the Church, particularly from a man as worldly as Liszt was supposed to be. Two conclusions were immediately drawn: first that Liszt's music must be feeble when compared with opera and symphony, and secondly that his religion must be insincere, a mere theatrical gesture made by a hypocrite. Both are profoundly wrong. The music is strong and passionate, while nothing could be more representative of the man than his decision to devote his 'musical will and testament' to the subject of Christ. The failure to understand Liszt that persists to this day stems absolutely from a refusal to accept *Christus* as a masterpiece and to study it seriously for what it tells us about Liszt's mind as man and musician. The so-called 'Liszt problem' cannot be solved without an explanation of *Christus*, which is unusual in conception, form and style when compared with other oratorios, including Liszt's other work in the same field. *Christus* is in fact unique in the history of music. Furthermore it contains Liszt's best single choral piece for mixed choir and organ ('Pater noster'), his best piece for solo voice and orchestra ('Tristis est anima mea') and his best piece for soloists, choir and orchestra ('Stabat mater dolorosa'), the last-named belonging alongside the famous settings of the text. 'The Beatitudes', the first music to be written, has a claim to pride of place among Liszt's choral works for beauty and originality combined.

Humphrey Searle says of *Christus*: 'Here he had no need to write "effective" ceremonial scenes, and was able instead to express his own reaction to the Bible story' (*SML*, 106). Many exceptions might be taken to this assessment. The life of Christ hardly constitutes a 'Bible story', being the substance of the entire New Testament. Also, Liszt did not share Searle's misgivings about 'effective' ceremonial scenes, since 'The Entry into Jerusalem' is exactly such a piece, the most theatrical and vivid representation imaginable.

Searle is mistaken in using the word 'story' for the simple reason that for Liszt it was not a story: it was true. Strictly speaking, none of Liszt's programme music 'tells a story' in the conventional sense. Instead it uses the programmatic approach to illustrate a moral principle. We should distinguish at this point between the intention and the result; not all of Liszt's orchestral music achieves the desired end. But his best music does match the aims of the programme, as in the two symphonies, and most decidedly in *Christus*. For *Christus* is programme music just like all the rest of Liszt's serious works. That does not make it any the less religious; indeed it demonstrates by its programmatic approach what Liszt's religion was.

The key to an understanding of the work lies in its motto, placed at the head of the score:

Veritatem autem facientes in caritate,
crescamus in illo per omnia qui est
caput: Christus.

(Let us speak the truth in love;
so shall we fully grow up into Christ.
He is the head.) (Paulus ad Ephesos 4, 15)

This is Liszt's choice of 'programme' and the reason why the oratorio, instead of being a mere setting of a Bible story, represents the quintessence of the musical Liszt, most of whose music portrays in various forms the theme of redemption through love. In *Christus* we see the living process at work, demonstrated by Liszt's choice of events from the life of Christ and his musical organization of the work. Liszt accepted the historical Christ in an age that increasingly questioned Christ's divinity. For Liszt the direct connection existed between Christ's life on earth, his message to St Peter, and the founding of the Church of Rome. All this symbolized an idea sacred to him as a Romantic artist, the divinity of love, seen as God's gift to mankind.

The association of love and Christ is the earliest idea outside music that we find in the letters of the young Liszt, who praised Lamennais because

He is a marvellous man, prodigious, absolutely extraordinary . . . loftiness, devotion, passionate ardour, an acute mind, profound judgment, the simplicity of a child, sublimity of thought . . . I have yet to hear him say: I. Always, Christ, always sacrifice for others and a voluntary acceptance of opprobrium, of scorn, of misery and death! (*PL*, 107)

One sees already in 1834 what the figure of Christ meant to Liszt. The oratorio is in reality a self-portrait, resulting from the fact that Liszt was able later to identify himself with the Church, and to use this as the source of his musical material. Much of *Christus* is built upon plainsong, and some of the pieces are meant as actual church music. So completely did Liszt fuse his musical ideal with the history and contemporary reality of the Roman Church that he was unable to distinguish in his mind between an oratorio about Christ and the performance in church of settings of some of Christ's words, for example the 'Pater noster'. This is why the 14 numbers into which the work falls are separate, not connected by recitative, and for the most part unrelated musically. Each is the musical portrayal of a real event, whether it be the Sermon on the Mount or the Resurrection. Above all, it was of paramount importance that the oratorio as a whole should not be able to be performed on stage. Thus it represents the ultimate ideal, the final resting-place, of programme music as conceived by Liszt, a fusion of music, religion, drama and the Church.

This also accounts for the absence of thematic transformation in *Christus*. In *St Elizabeth* the symphonic approach and the use of thematic transformation reflect the nature of the story; Elizabeth's progress is from the human to the divine. Christ, by contrast, represents the divine made human. Thus Liszt's usual pattern of 'lamento e trionfo' is reversed in *Christus*, two thirds of which are a 'trionfo'. The 'lamento' occurs at the end, with the Agony in the Garden and the Crucifixion. But there is no thematic connection or development. Liszt states, as it were, the bare facts. Christ's moment of suffering and trial came when he had to shed his mortality. Thus the musical approach reveals Liszt's mind and illuminates the attitude that lies behind other works.

The oratorio divides into three parts: 'Christmas Oratorio', 'After Epiphany' and 'Passion and Resurrection'. Of the 14 numbers, five make up the first part, five the second, and four the third. The quality of the music matches the intensity of the drama, with the result that, unusually for Liszt, the work improves as it progresses, the third part being the best. The progression within each part shows a masterly sense of proportion and dramatic timing, even though the work as a whole is rather long. The climax of the first part is 'The Three Holy Kings', representing the earthly recognition of Christ's divinity. This is followed by the first appearance of the voice of Christ in 'The Beatitudes' at the opening of part 2. The climax of this part is Christ's 'Entry into Jerusalem', which in turn is followed by another appearance of the voice of Christ in 'Tristis est anima mea', which begins the third part. The 'Resurrexit' that ends the work quotes the main theme from 'The Entry into Jerusalem', where it is sung to the words 'Hosanna, qui venit in nomine domini'. The closing 'amen' is sung to the theme that opens the whole work, part of the plainsong 'Rorate coeli desuper et nubes pluant justum: aperiatur terra et germinet Salvatorem' ('Rain righteousness, you heavens, let the skies above pour down; let the earth open to receive it, that it may bear the fruit of salvation'). The shape of the work is of course not Liszt's own, being that of the life of Christ. But the choice of texts is Liszt's own, and they reflect his attitude not only to religion, but to music as well. It is because he took a religious view of music that he set *Christus*, not the other way round. In this as in other works, the programme illustrates the music as much as the music the programme.

The manuscript of *Christus* is in the British Library (Add. MS 34182). Many of Liszt's markings are not reproduced in the published score, and a study of these throws more light onto his musical intentions. Most significantly, the title is written on the cover by Liszt as 'Xtus'. The letter 'X' here symbolizes the Cross, and this has a musical reference destroyed

# Revolution and religion

Ex. 79

Ex. 80

later by the expansion of the work into 14 numbers instead of the 12 found in the manuscript, where no. 10 is 'Tristis est anima mea'. Liszt numbers the movements with Arabic numerals until ten, when he uses the roman X. Other markings include details resembling stage directions for 'The Entry into Jerusalem'.

The oratorio begins with the orchestral 'Introduction' based upon the *Rorate coeli* plainsong, which appears at the outset (see Ex. 79). The rhythm, which determines so much of its character, is found in Liszt's copy (1857) of the *Graduale Romanum*, where the chant appears on page 25 (see Ex. 80). The scoring is for strings and woodwind, in a contrapuntal style. The rising fifth of the opening forms the chief single musical feature of the whole oratorio; Liszt uses fifths to form bare harmony as well as melodically. The fugue that closes the work has a subject constructed entirely of rising fifths.

At their first entry the brass instruments are used alone, playing a harmonized version of the middle of the plainsong set to the words 'Coeli enarrant gloriam Dei' (see Exx. 81(a) and 81(b)). The second part of the 'Introduction' is an Allegretto moderato in 12/8 time, opening with the woodwind alone, marked 'pastorale'. In the manuscript at this point, though not in the score, Liszt has written 'Angelus ad pastores ait: Annuntio vobis gaudiam magnam: quia natus est vobis hodie Salvator mundi.' This text is sung at the beginning of no. 2 to the plainsong, which appears in Liszt's *Graduale Romanum* on page 58 (see Ex. 82). The material of this section of the 'Introduction' is based upon the plainsong, rhythmically altered by Liszt, who makes much of the rising fifth (see Ex. 83). The woodwind writing here is masterly. Throughout the oratorio Liszt's handling of the orchestra is skilful, imaginative and musical, without any of the bombast that mars some passages in the orchestral works, as well

Ex. 81

Ex. 82

Ex. 83

as the oratorio *St Elizabeth*. In *Christus* the climaxes are expansive rather than forced, with a correspondingly more satisfying musical result.

No. 2, 'Pastorale and Annunciation', is really misnamed, since it commences with the Annunciation, a soprano solo singing unaccompanied the *Angelus ad pastores* plainsong (see Ex. 84 and *cf.* Ex. 82). The gradual entry of the choir, beginning with unaccompanied women's voices, leads to a full choral and orchestral texture, and the entry of the tenor solo at the words 'Gloria in excelsis, et in terra pax hominibus'. The mood is one of transfiguration, helped by the string figuration which suggests the beating of many wings. The return of the rising fifth in the orchestra at letter U, together with the marking 'Animato' lends new purpose, and an

189

Ex. 84

'Alleluja' climax is reached where choir and orchestra state part of the plainsong in unison, followed by an effective passage using bare fifths harmony. A quiet coda for solo violin and woodwind, based upon the plainsong, ends the movement with music of ethereal beauty.

No. 3, 'Stabat mater speciosa', for mixed choir and organ, constitutes the first piece in the work considered by Liszt to be actual church music. Gregorovius, who attended the first performance of the piece on 4 January 1866, wrote: 'Last Wednesday Liszt conducted a cantata [*sic*] in Ara Coeli, the *Stabat Mater Speciosa* of Fra Jacopone, set to a composition of his own. It was rather tame; leaning over towards me, he whispered, "Church music! Church music!"' (*GRJ*, 7 January 1866). Gregorovius may have found the music disappointing, but could not know of Liszt's youthful ideals for 'church music', which explains the enthusiasm of his exclamations. The piece is chordal throughout and gentle in mood. On the piano it is nothing, but sung in a church succeeds through the beauty of the vocal sound and the acoustics of the building. In this respect it has something in common with Palestrina's music, which influenced so much of Liszt's church music. What Liszt copied was Palestrina's sound, not his technique. The attempt to express a mood of sustained calm and joy Liszt makes through static repetition of chord sequences whose musical life depends essentially upon their rhythm. Liszt realized this, and changes the time signature from four to three at each occurrence of what amounts to a musical refrain (see Ex. 85). Occasionally the melodic interest is given to the bass voices, as it might be given to the left hand in a piano piece.

No. 4, 'Shepherds' Song at the Manger', is an orchestral piece, scored for a small orchestra of strings, woodwind, trumpets, horns, harp and

Ex. 85

timpani, but without trombones. Saint-Saëns, who heard *Christus* at Heidelberg in 1912 as part of the Liszt centenary celebrations, praised the piece. 'It is very simple,' he wrote, 'but in an inimitable simplicity of taste which is the secret of great artists alone. It is surprising that this interlude does not appear in the repertoire of all concerts.'[4] It opens with woodwind alone, using the figuration that appeared in the 'pastorale' section of the 'Introduction'. The outline of the succeeding melody recalls the *Angelus ad pastores*. A new melody follows, the German tune 'Es flog ein Täublein weisse von Himmel an', whose metre attractively alternates two and three beats to a bar (see Ex. 86). A third, chorale-like theme, marked 'religioso', appears first on woodwind and solo horn, then in a decorated version using the 'pastorale' rhythm of the opening, scored for solo viola and woodwind (see Ex. 87). These three themes form

Ex. 86

Ex. 87

Ex. 88

the basis of the piece, which rises to a fine climax towards the end before subsiding into silence.

No. 5, 'The Three Holy Kings (March)', concludes the first part of the oratorio. The magnificence of this piece is a good illustration of the connection in Liszt's orchestral works between the quality of the music and the programme that inspired it. In this case, as in others, the 'real' programme is latent, and has to be revealed.

The piece opens in C minor with the rising fifth 'motto' in march rhythm. This proves to be the opening notes of a theme, first given to pizzicato strings and staccato woodwind. After much repetition the mood changes with a modulation to D♭ major, illustrating the Latin text added by Liszt at this point: 'Et ecce stella quam viderat in Oriente antecebat eos, usque dum veniens staret supra ubi erat puer' ('And, lo! the star, which they saw in the east, went before them, till it came and stood over where the young child was!') (Matthew II, 9). The new theme that appears at this point is a real inspiration (see Ex. 88). It appears many times in a mood of increasing jubilation. Then another change of mood and key occurs with an 'Adagio sostenuto assai' richly scored for strings in B major, to illustrate the words 'Apertis thesauris suis, obtulerunt Magi Domino aurum, thus et myrrhum' ('And when they had opened their treasures, they presented unto Him gifts; gold, and frankincense, and myrrh') (Matthew II, 11). The 'star' theme reappears in F♯ major, a key with 'divine' associations for Liszt, again increasing in fervour and excitement, leading to a full tutti statement of the 'treasures' theme and a coda combining a phrase of this with one from the opening melody in quickening tempo. Brass fanfares bring the piece to a resounding conclusion.

It may be seen from this that the bulk of the music illustrates two texts from the Bible. The exception is the opening part, which has no text. If we label the opening theme 'A', the 'star' theme 'B', and the 'treasures' theme 'C', then we see the piece has the following form: A; B; C; B; Coda based on a fragment of A transformed, a fragment of B, and most of C. This constitutes a version of Liszt's 'progressive' form, in which there is no direct repetition of A. In other words, the feeling of ternary form includes only B and C, A forming a long introduction. Yet this is the only music in the piece that resembles a march proper. Clearly its programmatic function is antecedent in the quoted biblical texts.

The journey of the Three Kings was in two parts, separated by a visit to Herod, of whom they asked the whereabouts of the child 'who is born to be King of the Jews'. Herod told them to find the child and to 'report to me, so that I may go myself and pay him homage'. The next verse from Matthew says: 'They set out at the King's bidding.' Then follows Liszt's quotation, after which Matthew has: 'At the sight of the star they were overjoyed.' This is what Liszt's theme B describes. Theme A never returns, just as the Bible has: 'And being warned in a dream not to go back to Herod, they returned home another way.'

This represents the archetypal Lisztian idea, the journey from the human to the divine. Furthermore, the symbolism of earthly princes bowing down before Christ reaches back to Lamennais and *Words of a Believer*; all of which explains Liszt's thinking behind the composition of the music.

Part 2 opens with the Sermon on the Mount, a setting of the Beatitudes and the Lord's Prayer. Both pieces are meant as actual church music, apart from their place in the oratorio. Liszt thought very highly of his music for the Beatitudes, and rightly so. After completing the music in 1859 he wrote:

The piece is completely simple – poor in spirit and humble at heart. The baritone solo intones each of the first three lines which are repeated once only by the choir. To avoid monotony and to gain some movement – in the 4th, 5th, 6th and

7th lines – 'hunger and thirst to see right prevail, mercy, purity of heart and bless-ing of the peacemakers', the baritone solo says only half the lines: 'How blest are those who hunger and thirst to see right prevail!', 'How blest are those who show mercy', etc., and the choir completes them: 'they shall be satisfied', 'mercy shall be shown to them'. Finally in the 8th line: 'How blest are those who have suffered persecution', I first repeat with choir and solo voice the word 'Beati, beati', and several times the whole line that ends with 'regnum coelorum'. In all it contains about 80 bars, unaccompanied. Towards the middle I may add a few chords on the organ to support the voices. The whole thing will last only 5 or 8 minutes.

(*Br.* IV, 461)

Liszt eventually accompanied the choir almost throughout with the organ, doubtless because the distant modulations proved impracticable for singers unaided, a problem he found in other 'unaccompanied' works like the *Male-Voice Mass* and the *Missa choralis*. 'I have written few things that have so welled up from my innermost soul,' he wrote. These words show the connection between the text and the music. In 1881 Liszt spoke of his attitude in a letter to Baroness Meyendorff:

The gentle and wise Marcus Aurelius seems to me to have uttered a truly imperial stupidity in counselling us to *divide* up each thing in our thoughts so as to become imbued with the emptiness of everything. To reduce music to single sounds, to isolate the features of a beloved person, is this to philosophize? Away with this method; let us look for the whole, the harmony. It is there we will find beauty and truth. I far prefer Job's heart-rending lamentations and resignation to the vanity of Solomon's *Vanitas Vanitatum*, and especially the sublime gentleness of the Sermon on the Mount, which sheds a divine light on our sufferings here below.

(*LOM*, 409)

The key words here are 'beauty and truth', 'sublime gentleness' and 'divine light'. Liszt's music is in E major, his 'religious' key, and the antiphonal treatment of solo and choir mirrors the idea of Christ preach-ing to the multitude, and that of priest and congregation. The Beatitudes represent Christ's message to the world, a message as much social as religious. If we compare the music with the early work *Le Forgeron*, whose text deals also with poverty and injustice, we find a new beauty in 'The Beatitudes', apart from its style as church music. The early work is all action, urging reform. The church work is meant to alleviate suffering by the promise of salvation. The key word is 'beati', from which the music takes its whole character. The state of blessedness arrives after the removal of suffering. We see here the clear link in Liszt's mind between morality and beauty, this being the fundamental reason Liszt thought of music not as mere decoration, but as an active force in the lives of men.

The piece opens with an organ introduction based upon the *Rorate coeli* that opens the oratorio, together with the phrase to which Liszt sets the words 'regnum coelorum'. Hence the function of the piece in the struc-ture of the oratorio is made clear. The writing for solo baritone is in the

Ex. 89

Ex. 90. The 'Gregorian intonation' quoted in Liszt's letter

highest degree expressive of the words; Liszt uses modulation not simply to change key, but as the shaping force of the whole piece (see Ex. 89).

No. 7, 'Pater noster', for mixed choir and organ, is in A♭, the key used by Liszt in association with 'love' (see chapter 15). The music is based upon plainsong, as Liszt says in a letter from Rome written in 1867:

As a slight musical indication observe that in the *Pater Noster* I simply modulate and develop somewhat, – in the somewhat confined limits of a sentiment of trusting and pious submission, – the Gregorian intonation as sung in all our churches [see Ex. 90], following the traditional intonations for each verse. This framework was naturally adopted to the arranging of my Oratorio – *Christ*, – in which I employed two or three other intonations of the plainsong, without considering myself guilty of a theft by such a use. (*L*, II, 121)

The musical style is for the most part harmonic, with occasional touches of imitation to lend impetus (see Ex. 91). The piece has a large sound and a sustained inspiration, making it a worthy companion to 'The Beatitudes'.

No. 8, 'The Foundation of the Church', is the first choral and orchestral piece in the oratorio of real splendour. The text is taken from Matthew, chapter 16, verses 18–19 ('You are Peter, the Rock; and on this rock I will build my church, and the powers of death shall never conquer it') and John, chapter 21, verses 15–17 ('Simon, son of John, do you love me more than all else? . . . Then feed my lambs . . . Feed my sheep'). The

Ex. 91

latter quotation was spoken after the resurrection, and is held by
Catholics to vindicate the authority of the papacy, since they argue that
in these words Peter was given charge of the Church. Liszt's music was
composed originally to an anonymous Italian text in praise of Pius IX,
'Dall' alma Roma sommo Pastore', published in 1866 as *Inno del Papa*.
This Liszt arranged for organ in 1867 as *Tu es Petrus*, writing in July to the
publisher E. Repos in Paris:

> The day after tomorrow I will send you four or five small pages which, if I mistake
> not, will suit you – and which may be propagated. It is a simple and easy version
> for Organ of the hymn 'Tu es Petrus', lately performed here on the eighteen-
> hundredth anniversary of St Peter.                           (*L*, II, 126)

The celebrations in Rome for this anniversary were of immense and
splendid proportions, and doubtless spurred Liszt to use his music in

praise of Pius IX as the basis for 'The Foundation of the Church' in *Christus*. The description he gave Baron Augusz of the event shows his enthusiasm:

You ask me what has been happening in Rome? As follows: On 29 June, the 18th centenary of the martyrdom of the Apostles St Peter and St Paul was commemorated with the supreme pomp and majesty reserved for the Apostolic Roman Catholic Church.

The religious and social importance of such a manifestation of Catholicism is increased still more by the announcement of an immense occurrence which will dominate all others in affirming more completely than ever this century the imperishable authority of the Holy See: *the Ecumenical Council* to be convoked in Rome in December 1868 . . .

Shall I tell you about the celebrations for the week of St Peter? There were magnificent illuminations, popular fetes, academic gatherings, a splendid *ricevimento* on the *Capitole*, and music of a sort everywhere . . . above all the motet for three choirs 'Tu es Petrus' by Maestro *Mustapha* [Raimondi], sung in St Peter's on 29 June. The positioning of two choirs (of about a hundred voices in each) up in the cupola at the end of the church above the entrance doorway excited much curiosity from the audience. Music coming from so high and so far away must inevitably seem sublime, celestial and angelic to people little familiar with the *spiritual* in art. But I don't want to carp, and you can imagine what effect this quite brilliant acoustic effect had upon me.                                                 (*LAA*, 133)

Liszt's own music sounds like the celebration of a grand occasion, and he may very well have had this scene in St Peter's before him when he composed it.

The opening 'Tu es Petrus', sung by the men's voices, is set to music of rock-like firmness. The first note is A♭, following on from the 'Pater noster', but this proves to be part of the whole-tone chord which Liszt uses to give a keyless air to the pronouncement. Eventually E major is reached, and a hymn-like mood succeeds for the 'Simon Joannis diliges me?' The lyricism of this section is attractively simple (see Ex. 92). It is repeated with full orchestra, and at the climax the 'Tu es Petrus' returns, though now cloaked in orchestral splendour and full harmony, with declamatory notes from the trombones, lending an even more rock-like quality to the grand peroration.

No. 9, 'The Miracle', is the best orchestral storm in all Liszt's music. A Latin text above the music, taken from Matthew, gives the programme: 'All at once a great storm arose on the lake, till the waves were breaking right over the boat.' Before the storm gets under way a quiet passage for woodwind and horn describes another text: 'But he went on sleeping.' Then Liszt builds up an immense crescendo, a mere noise without key signature cleverly constructed from snippets of arpeggios and brass calls. The use of whole-tone harmony rescues the music from banality and raises it to the highest level of Lisztian originality (see Ex. 93). At the height of the fury the men's voices call out 'Save us, Lord; we are sinking!'

# Revolution and religion

Ex. 92

Ex. 93

A terrific crash from low brass, woodwind, strings and timpani on unison C stops the music, and the unaccompanied voice of Christ sings 'Why are you such cowards? How little faith you have!' The mood then changes as the strings alone, without harmony, play the 'Regnum coelorum' theme from 'The Beatitudes', taking the music to E major and a key signature of four sharps. The whole choir quietly sing 'And there was a dead calm', followed by an orchestral coda in C♯ major with a key signature of seven sharps depicting the 'tranquillitas magna'. This is a rare use by Liszt of this key signature (another example is the late piano piece *Recueillement* (S204), whose programmatic significance must be considered. The storm is keyless, representing chaotic energy. The voice of Christ leads the music to E major, Liszt's 'religious' key, of which C♯ is the relative minor. Liszt used C♯ minor rarely, most notably in the piano piece *Il penseroso*, whose programme is a quotation from Michelangelo: 'I am thankful to sleep, and more thankful to be made of stone. So long as injustice and shame remain on earth, I count it a blessing not to see or feel; so do not wake me – speak softly!' This music Liszt later orchestrated as no. 2 of the *Trois odes funèbres* entitled *La Notte*, and he wrote that he wished it to be performed at his funeral (which it was not). The idea

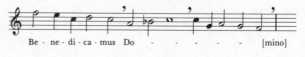

Be - ne - di - ca - mus Do - - - - - [mino]

Ex. 94

of oblivion lies behind the music, a kind of sorrow for the world's suffering. The storm in *Christus* represents a trial of faith and the 'miracle', represented by Christ's rebuking the wind and the sea, is really the abolition of fear. It is not sleep, death or oblivion that Liszt describes, but a transfigured awakening. Hence the unique use of the key C♯ major; in the cycle of fifths it is the furthest from C major, used consistently by Liszt to represent ordinary life, the human without the divine. Divinity is usually represented by F♯ major, whose dominant C♯ here signifies the unification of God and Man represented by Christ. Significantly, the further dominant, G♯, notated as A♭, is the key used by Liszt to represent love.

No. 10, 'The Entry into Jerusalem', forms the climax of part 2. Saint-Saëns found this the single most impressive piece in the oratorio:

Nothing in the whole work impressed me more than Christ's entrance to Jerusalem (orchestra, chorus and soloist) for the reading alone gives no idea of it. Here the author reached the heights.[5]

The remark about 'the reading alone' applies equally to other music in the oratorio, which must be heard in a full performance to realize its effect (as distinct from playing it on the piano, where much of it is misleadingly tame – itself evidence of Liszt's progress as a composer towards independence from the sound of the piano). 'The Entry into Jerusalem' is based upon part of the plainsong *Benedicamus Domino* found on page 53 of Liszt's copy of the *Graduale Romanum* (see Ex. 94). Liszt preserves the rhythmic shape of the chant, casting the whole movement in E major, and commencing with an orchestral introduction. This opens with the chant in unison, leading to music that suggests the gathering together of a large crowd, an effect obtained by the active quavers in the bass. The choir enter with 'Hosanna qui venit in nomine Domini, Rex Israel'. The mezzo-soprano solo sings 'Benedictus' to the plainsong theme, above the choir who sing 'pax in coelo et gloria in excelsis'. A quiet passage for the choir with string and harp chords begins a long build-up leading to a fugue, 'Filio David Hosanna'. The harmony of this passage is particularly effective, the bass line being derived from the opening phrase of the plainsong. The fugue subject is also derived from the plainsong (see Ex. 167, p. 272). At the climax the orchestra has the 'crowd' theme against the choir's fortissimo version of the 'Benedictus' theme (see Ex. 95). A quartet of vocal soloists, soprano, alto, tenor and bass, enter

Ex. 95

to function as a kind of cadenza, mostly unaccompanied, until, with their 'Hosanna in altissimis', the choir return, this time bringing the music to a splendid conclusion.

The musical form is thus of the utmost clarity and simplicity. What its description fails to convey is the atmosphere of a public event conveyed by the music. Liszt's manuscript contains many markings omitted in the printed score which reveal clearly what he had in his mind's eye when composing the music. At the head of the music Liszt quotes from Matthew in Latin:

Crowds of people carpeted the road with their cloaks, and some cut branches from the trees to spread in his path. Then the crowd that went ahead and the others that came behind raised the shout: 'Hosanna to the Son of David! Blessings on him who comes in the name of the Lord! Hosanna in the heavens!'

During his days as a virtuoso pianist, Liszt was no stranger to scenes of public acclaim, and it is easy to see the atmosphere he tried to depict in the music. This explains the vividness and sense of contemporaneity that characterizes *Christus*, which is modern in spirit, though built out of archaic material. In this manner the Romantic puts himself into his art, which is not to say that the music is not intended as an act of homage.

The choir at their first entry are described as the 'populus' ('the people') and later as the 'discipuli' ('the disciples'). At the start of the fugue, they are called the 'populus (turbae)' ('the people (the crowds)'). Over the mezzo-soprano solo is written the word 'Madeleine'. In other words the singers, far from being anonymous, are characters much as they would be in an operatic scene. In this way Liszt depicts the earthly triumph of Christ, the moment when the world acknowledged the coming of the Messiah.

Part 3 opens with the voice of Christ singing 'Tristis est anima mea', no. 11. This solo for baritone and orchestra is the only aria in the oratorio, and the most Tristanesque music Liszt ever wrote. The text, from Mark's Gospel, consists of Christ's words in the Garden of Gethsemane: 'My heart is ready to break with grief; Father, all things are possible to thee; take this cup away from me. Yet not what I will, but what thou wilt.'

The original numbering 'X' for 10 may indicate the special approach Liszt took when composing the music. Christ's suffering represents his reaction to his impending crucifixion, and in Liszt's Testament we find his own feelings about the Cross during his adolescence in Paris:

At that time I hoped it would be granted to me to live the life of the Saints and perhaps even to die a martyr's death. This, alas, has not happened – yet, in spite of the transgressions and errors which I have committed, and for which I feel sincere repentance and contrition, the holy light of the Cross has never been

Ex. 96

entirely withdrawn from me. At times, indeed, the refulgence of this Divine light has overflowed my entire soul. – I thank God for this, and shall die with my soul fixed upon the Cross, our redemption, our highest bliss.                    (*L*, I, 439)

The words 'a martyr's death' typify the Romantic state of mind, and Liszt was no exception. The paradox is that Liszt, in an oratorio, makes Christ sing of his suffering as a man, much as Wagner in opera makes Tannhäuser and Tristan. The explanation highlights the psychological difference between Liszt and Wagner. Whereas much of Wagner's music depicts suffering directly, hardly any of Liszt's does. One of the functions of his programmatic approach is to externalize suffering, which is seen as something to be fought against and overcome. But when Christ faces the moment of death he is at his most human, allowing Liszt to identify with his predicament musically in the knowledge that, in surrendering to God's will the divine element parts from the human. This, for Liszt, solves the anguish of human suffering, to which only Christ is allowed to give voice.

The music, marked 'Lento assai', starts without key signature until the voice enters, whereupon it changes to four sharps. The extreme ingenuity of the chromatic harmony keeps tonality at bay, though C♯ minor is intended. In this respect the use of C♯ minor in *Il penseroso*, whose music is also Wagnerian, may be said to have sprung from the same psychological source. The main 'theme', a mere fragment, is stark and full of pain (see Ex. 96). The vocal line, instead of falling, seems to struggle upwards away from the painful harmony. The central part of the piece is a long orchestral passage depicting Christ's agony. The chromatic yearning is here at its most Tristanesque, rising to a furious climax. When this has subsided, the voice repeats the 'Tristis est', but

Ex. 97

Ex. 98

the music is cleverly changed very slightly to incorporate the Cross motif in the bass part (see Ex. 97). The key changes to D♭ major, obviously meant to be heard as C♯ major, for the 'Father, all things are possible to thee' section. Liszt now repeats the 'take this cup away from me' music in D♭ major, altering the melodic line to incorporate the Cross motif, but maintaining the original harmony. A terrific vocal climax is created at the words 'not what I will, but what thou wilt', and the music subsides gradually to a peaceful close. The orchestration here is Berliozian, though the emotional world is Liszt's own. Nothing shows musically more clearly than this piece what Liszt could have achieved in opera, and at the same time psychologically why he decided against making the attempt.

No. 12, 'Stabat mater dolorosa', is the dramatic and musical apex of the oratorio, consisting of a huge set of variations for soloists, choir and orchestra on the plainsong (used later again in *Via Crucis*) which appears on page 55 of Liszt's copy of the *Nouvel eucologe en musique* (see Ex. 98). The compositional technique Liszt applied to this theme is without doubt the finest to be found in his choral music. This, wedded to the vivid imagination and sense of drama found everywhere in Liszt, makes it by far his greatest choral work, which, as it stands as an independent number in the oratorio, could be performed separately, and deserves to be better known. In the oratorio, of course, it carries the supreme dramatic function, a portrayal of the Crucifixion. Not surprisingly, it is the longest of the work's 14 numbers, lasting about 20 minutes in performance. The key is F minor, used rarely by Liszt, only once, for example, in his orchestral music, in the symphonic poem *Héroïde funèbre*, a piece in memory of those who died in the revolutions of 1848–9. The common idea seems to be martyrdom, strengthened by the relation of F minor to A♭ major, the key Liszt associated with love.

The text printed as a preface to the score consists of ten verses of six lines each. The musical climax occurs at the ninth verse, 'Inflammatus et accensus', where the poet asks the Virgin to protect him from eternal fire on the Day of Judgment. The soprano and tenor soloists in unison sing the opening fragment of the plainsong, marked 'con somma passione'. This is followed by a full choral and orchestral tutti statement in the major key, the only one Liszt gives. This climax is flanked by two Verdian full tuttis using different material from the plainsong, a theme invented by Liszt first set to the words 'Eja mater fons amoris' ('O thou mother! fount of love!'). The first is at verse 6, 'Crucifixi fige plagas' ('In my heart each wound renew Of my Saviour crucified'), the second at verse 10, 'Morte Christi praemuniri' ('May the death of Christ protect me, Lending mercy to my soul'). The build-up to these is gradual and handled skilfully by Liszt, their unusual spaciousness reflecting the overall scale of the 'Stabat mater'.

The placing of these points of climax determines the architecture of the piece, which is a broad A B A B A form, A being the plainsong, B the 'love' theme. The balance of this structure allows room for many felicitous episodes. The first of these occurs near the beginning, with the repetition of 'mater' together with a swelling choral crescendo at verse 2, 'O quam tristis et afflicta' ('Oh, how sad and sore distressed'). The contrasting of soloists and choir is operatically effective. A bass solo introduces verse 3, 'Quis est homo?' ('Is there one who would not weep?') to an altered version of the plainsong in triple time. The suspensions between alto and tenor in the following repeat of the theme are characteristic of Liszt's pictorial and italianate use of harmony in the piece. This is followed by a superb passage of imitative writing in the choir leading towards a climax (see Ex. 99). The almost savage violence of the ensuing tutti reflects the words 'She beheld her tender Child All with bloody scourges rent'. All of the music so far has been derived from the plainsong.

The new 'love' theme now follows as an alto solo in E major (see Ex. 100). When it is taken up by the choir, Liszt adds short interlocutory phrases for each soloist in turn, before settling into the slow build-up to the first Verdian tutti. The harmonic sequence, taking the music quite imperceptibly from E major to F, is typical of Liszt, here wedded to an

Ex. 99

impressive choral and orchestral sound. The music subsides to an unaccompanied timpani ostinato figure heralding the return in 'cellos and bassoons of the plainsong theme. A choral passage with free cadenza-like interruptions for the tenor soloist leads to a reprise of the opening orchestral introduction, this time with choral and solo parts added, to the text of verse 7, 'Fac ut tecum pie flere' ('Let me mingle tears with thee'). The mezzo-soprano solo returns for 'Juxta crucem' ('By the

Cross with thee to stay') followed by the choir, but leading immediately to a return of the 'love' theme, now in G major, for verse 8, 'Virgo virginum praeclara' ('Virgin of all virgins best'). The ostinato rhythm recurs and the music begins to gain momentum, using the opening phrase of the plainsong. Repeated chords in the woodwind plus tremolando strings serve to heighten the temperature, leading to the main 'inflammatus et accensus' climax, stated in D♭ major, followed by an

Ex. 100

orchestral epilogue. Verse 10 begins with the 'love' theme for 'Fac me cruce custodiri' ('Let the Cross my soul sustain'), leading to the repeat of the 'Verdi' tutti. The closing lines 'Quando corpus morietur' ('While my body here decays') use the plainsong, beginning in F♯ minor, passing to A major. The 'Paradisi gloria' ('Safe in Paradise with thee') uses Liszt's 'Palestrina' progression to take the music back to the tonality of F (see Ex. 101). The antiphonal effect of choir and soloists is effective here as Liszt alternates the chords of B♭ and D♭. The final quiet 'amen' retains the harmonic originality to the very end.

The fact that this long piece manages to counterbalance the whole first two parts of the oratorio, at the same time containing the best music in the work, is explained by its dramatic rôle. In the overall drama of Christ it represents the Cross. We see here how in *Christus* Liszt put into musical form the substance of what elsewhere is represented by the Cross motif.

No. 13, 'Easter Hymn', is a setting for women's voices and organ of an anonymous Latin hymn together with its plainsong melody. Only the harmony is Liszt's own. The melody, in the rhythmic form used by Liszt, is found on page 475 of the *Nouvel eucologe en musique* (see Ex. 102). It alternates verses for solo voice without harmony and for choir. Liszt uses the choral voices throughout, mostly in unison, but preserves the

Ex. 101

Ex. 102. The melody of Liszt's *Easter hymn* as it appears on p. 475 of
Liszt's copy of the *Nouvel eucologe en musique*

musical format by adding harmony in the organ part only for alternate
lines. Liszt's harmony avoids the sharpened seventh, producing a modal
effect (see Ex. 103). A note in the score instructs that the singers, of
whom '8 or 10 soprano and alto voices are sufficient', should be out of

Ex. 103

sight. The intended effect is of course a dramatic one, heralding the Resurrection. The 'Easter Hymn' was the last piece to be added to *Christus*, and in performance its effect is quite magical, coming after the immense upheavals of the 'Stabat mater dolorosa'. It arouses a feeling of expectancy.

No. 14, 'Resurrexit', starts with pianissimo tremolando strings. Clarinets and bassoons state the opening of *Rorate coeli*, with its rising fifth. A crescendo leads to the entry of the choir with 'Resurrexit tertia die', and horns and trombones fortissimo state the 'Hosanna' theme from no. 10, 'The Entry into Jerusalem'. In this way Liszt sums up the whole oratorio. A fugue follows, to the words 'Christus vincit, Christus regnat, Christus imperat in sempiternam saecula.' The fugue subject is constructed out of rising fifths (see Ex. 168, p. 273).

At the climax the soloists enter one by one with long phrases taken from the 'Hosanna' theme, until the music quietens down with choral interjections of 'imperat'. The quartet of soloists alone then sing 'Hosanna in excelsis', followed by a return of the pianissimo tremolando strings, leading this time to the return of the 'crowd' music from no. 10, and full choral and orchestral Hallelujas based on the *Angelus ad pastores* plainsong from no. 2. Bells and cymbals are added to the orchestral part to reinforce the mood of militant jubilation. The music stops dramatically, and after four bars of silence, the choir enter quietly with 'Hosanna' based upon the 'fifth' motive, swelling to an immense fortissimo statement in E major of the 'Hosanna' theme. At the close the orchestra states the *Rorate coeli* fortissimo against the choral 'amen', ending in a blaze of E major.

Liszt obviously intended the 'Resurrexit' as a blinding flash to dispel all gloom. Certainly it gives the impression of straining every nerve to create an apocalyptic effect. Musically it represents a summing up of the work, while dramatically it must go beyond even the splendours of 'The Entry into Jerusalem'. Here Liszt faced a problem he could not solve, since he could not excel his own portrayal of the earthly triumph of Christ, the divine made human. This is how Liszt thought of music itself, and explains his attitude to *Christus*. The work is programme music, composed for music's sake, representing an act of faith on Liszt's part. Hence he made immense efforts to complete it, but was prepared, if need be, for it to rest neglected and unperformed.

# 11

## THE SHORTER CHORAL WORKS

Liszt's church music is inspired by the sound of Palestrina, which he first heard in Rome in 1839. The evidence for this lies first in the music itself, secondly in the reference to Palestrina in Liszt's letter of 1850 to d'Ortigue discussing the composition of his *Male-Voice Mass* (see above, p. 97), and thirdly in the fact that his attempt to save church music was itself modelled upon the legend of Palestrina's influence upon the decisions of the Council of Trent, which earned him the title 'saviour of church music'. The desire for a similar title doubtless accounts for Liszt's claim that Pius IX called him 'my dear Palestrina'.

It is important to emphasize that Liszt's church style was his own invention, and has nothing to do with the Cecilian movement, which was not founded until 1867. The basis of this style was plainchant and the approach to harmonizing it. His first church composition was a harmonization of the *Pater noster* chant. The melodic lines of his free compositions for the Church are clearly influenced by plainchant. The most interesting feature of both types of composition, however, remains the inventiveness Liszt applied to the harmony. This explains the lack of counterpoint, usually the primary criticism levelled at Liszt's church works. Here it should be said that when Liszt did use counterpoint, it was perfectly effective, and it cannot be said that he lacked technical competence. But he associated it with dry academicism, and went out of his way to avoid it.

The problem for Liszt, therefore, was how to sustain vocal music without using a linear approach. One answer was to have a series of repeated chords (see, for example the 'Stabat mater speciosa' in *Christus*). Another was to contrast choral writing with unisons. This Liszt did to great effect, and he deserves the credit for inventing a quite individual, and for his time bold, choral style. By applying a commonplace of piano music, parallel octaves, to vocal music, and deriving his use of it from the practice of singing plainchant unaccompanied, he achieved at a stroke an ecclesiastical sound which allowed freedom of movement to the composer. Here it must be pointed out that a number of such passages are very weak when played on the piano, yet full of atmosphere when sung.

In this respect Liszt learned from opera, where countless similar passages only spring to life when sung, and are banal or worse on the piano. This shows the sureness of Liszt's aural imagination, which grew from the experience of conducting choral works at Weimar. Many of these church works are musicianly miniatures of real quality, the level of craftsmanship being generally even higher than in the piano music. There can be no rhetoric, no cadenzas, no histrionics or sleight of hand in choral music. Every note must count. This is where the strength of Liszt's originality lay. By choosing the harmonic rather than the contrapuntal approach, he had to solve unaided the problem of structure, and this he did by the same means, greatly reduced and intensified, that we find elsewhere in Liszt. He relied upon a sense of drama.

Drama is not the first element usually associated with church music, and in many respects that has been its downfall. Liszt's church music is refreshingly free of the tedious ecclesiastical commonplaces that existed in his day. He uses silence, for example, even in the shortest piece, whereas nearly all composers of church music fought shy of actually stopping, feeling that at all costs, and by any means, the music must keep going. This attitude, implanted in the conservatories by professors of harmony and counterpoint, served to paralyse the imagination of many composers. Liszt understood how to capture the attention of the listener, and then how to hold it instead of lapsing into mere note-spinning. Every chord, every note, has its effect. Common cadences are avoided, Liszt's inventiveness in this field alone making him one of the great originators of his age. Harmonic cliché is likewise nowhere to be found. Instead Liszt uses chromatic alteration in a new and subtle way, as well as triadic progressions and modal harmony, both avoiding the basic dominant–tonic relationship. This gives the music a free-floating quality, which is exactly what Liszt wanted. His 'incorrect' use of the 6/4 chord contributes to this feeling. There is nothing heavy or four-square about Liszt's choral music; it is thoroughly un-German in that respect. Liszt treats the bass line as a free voice, not as the foundation upon which the superstructure rests. The result is an improvisatory quality which succeeds in charming without being aimless.

Liszt described Palestrina's music as sounding like 'incense in sound' (see above, p. 121). He gave a similar description to the closing bars of his symphonic poem *Orpheus*. ('Leur élèvement graduel comme des vapeurs d'encens', he wrote in his preface to the score.) Here we see how the subjective approach of the Romantic is at once his doom and his salvation. Listening to Palestrina, Liszt marvelled not at the technique, but the state of mind that produced such music. The music provoked an intensely personal response from Liszt, and in setting out to copy it, he falsified it completely so as to create something new. He did not study

Palestrina's technique, but instead searched for harmonies that would evoke the world of enchantment conjured up in his imagination. At the same time, he paid great attention to the word-setting, his approach being the opposite of a contrapuntal composer in this respect. A surprising result is that Latin emerges as the language most suited to Liszt's style, its lack of national colour together with its ecclesiastical and perhaps declamatory associations fitting his music perfectly, a not unimportant factor contributing to the success of *Christus*. The shorter church works are poetic and individual. The church music may or may not be suitable for liturgical use – the question is not really relevant. It is part of the Romantic dream, in Liszt's case the very heart of it, and such is its relation to his other music.

## PATER NOSTER *II* (S21) AND AVE MARIA *I* (S20)

These works were published together by Haslinger in 1846. Later, in November 1852, Liszt sent them to Breitkopf und Härtel, suggesting that they appear with the *Male-Voice Mass*, all three works bearing a dedication to Father Albach. He expressly told the publisher: 'I have no other wish in the matter but that the *Pater should not be* separated from the *Ave*, on account of the former being so small a work' (*L*, I, 144). They appeared together in 1852, the Mass in 1853.

Some confusion exists over the versions of the *Pater noster*, since the full title of the 1853 version is *Pater noster quattuor vocum adaequales concinente organo secundum rituale SS. ecclesiae Romanae* (no. 21, 2 in Searle's catalogue), while the title of the earlier version, which is described by Searle as 'Male chorus unacc[ompanied]', is simply *Pater noster* (S21, 1). The Collected Edition includes only one work, for men's voices and organ, with the information 'komponiert 1845(?). Neu bearbeitet 1852.' It carries the dedication to Father Albach. We are therefore left in the dark as to whether this is based on the original version or the later version; also, no explanation is offered as to why we are not given both versions, whereas both versions of the *Ave Maria* are given, the earlier one in B♭ major (S20, '1st version'), the later one in A major (S20, '2nd version'). The suspicion remains that there is really no 'second version' of the *Pater noster*, and that Searle has given two numbers to one work which had a different title on its second publication.

We know from Liszt's letter that the two pieces were 'written at the same time', and that they were published in 1846. Hence the queried date 1845 in the Collected Edition. A clue to the precise date of composition exists on the manuscript of the *Ave Maria*, where Liszt has written: 'Écrit Paris I–Juillet'. In 1846 Liszt was in Vienna in July, and his movements at that time of year in the preceding years were as follows:

1845   July in Switzerland
1844   April to about July in France
1843   Summer on Nonnenwerth (an island on the Rhine) with the Comtesse
          and the children
1842   June and July in Paris.

We do not know exactly when the music was composed, merely that it originated in the 1840s; it could have been as early as 1842, less than half way through the virtuoso period (1838–47). Both pieces were arranged for the piano, appearing as nos. 2 and 5 of the *Harmonies poétiques et religieuses*.

These pieces are Liszt's first church music, and represent the style which he retained basically unchanged until his death. In the *Pater noster* Liszt takes the chant and adds the type of harmony he considered appropriate to express the mood, whilst the *Ave Maria* shows the kind of music he thought should be sung in church, the composer being free to choose the style. It is noteworthy how both pieces show a command of the choral medium, being more effective sung than in their piano versions.

The opening of the *Pater noster* (see Ex. 104) shows how the simple harmony travels away from the original C major key using related triads rather than traditional modulation, clearly in imitation of a Renaissance sound, but unmistakably nineteenth-century in effect. It is no more than an exercise in the 'unexpected' ambiguity found everywhere in Liszt.

The *Ave Maria* is an impressive piece, solidly built and lyrically sustained. There is no real counterpoint, though play is made between the different vocal parts. The opening (see Ex. 105) 'imitates' imitation. A melody ensues in the soprano line (see Ex. 106), later appearing in the tenors. The 'imitation' opening recurs twice in the minor mode, B and E♭ respectively. The E♭ minor section leads back to B♭ major via expressive harmony for 'peccatoribus' (see Ex. 107). The tempo changes to 'Quasi adagio' for 'et in hora mortis nostrae, amen', the harmony making use again of the triadic progressions found in the *Pater noster*.

What both pieces show is the attention Liszt applied to the harmony. This accords with his desire to reform church music via a 'renewal' of its content, which for a Romantic meant capturing the right feeling. This accounts for the deceptively uninteresting appearance of the music, since the texture lacks contrapuntal movement. Liszt's achievement was to sustain a mood, and impress it upon his hearers, by direct and simple means.

Ex. 104

Ex. 105

Ex. 106

Ex. 107

Ex. 108

### DOMINE SALVUM FAC REGEM (S23)

This piece, for male-voice choir, tenor solo and organ, was composed on 2 August 1853 at Carlsbad for a ceremony held in August at Weimar to mark the accession of Carl Alexander as Grand Duke, which had taken place on 8 July that year. The manuscript contains indications for wood-wind instead of organ accompaniment, and the work was scored by Raff for two clarinets, two oboes, four horns, two bassoons, two trumpets, three trombones, tuba, timpani and double basses, possibly for an out-door performance. The work is published in both versions, the organ score containing Liszt's added ideas for woodwind and timpani.

The music exemplifies Liszt's ceremonial style, in miniature, at its best. It is really a short coronation anthem. It opens with a fanfare-like passage (see Ex. 108). The tenor solo 'Et exaudi nos in die qua invocaverimus' rises operatically above the choir (see Ex. 109), and this leads to a short fugal peroration in the Handelian manner (see Ex.110).

### MIHI AUTEM ADHAERERE (S37)

On 8 August 1868 Liszt wrote to the Princess Wittgenstein from Grottamare:

I have written two short pages of music in three days. It is an Offertory for four men's voices, with a few accompanying chords on the organ, for the Mass of St Francis of Assisi. The text was given to me by maestro Boroni, a Franciscan religious, composer, and director of the choir at the church of St Francis at Assisi.

Ex. 109

Ex. 110

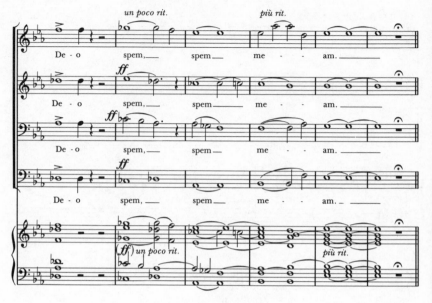

Ex. 111

The text is taken from a single verse of Psalm 72, and is extremely simple. A literal translation reads: 'For me it is good to belong to God – and to put my trust in the Lord!' The two final words, *spes mea*, have cost me much trouble, in order to find the expression that matches my feelings. I did not want it to be too restful, nor too agitated – just simple and full of feeling, tenderness, and gravity, ardent yet chaste, all at the same time!                                       (*Br.* VI, 179)

This remarkable verbalization of the composing process shows that Liszt gave pride of place to the mood of his church music, not the style. The piece is in E♭ major, and marked 'Andante con divozione'. Much attention is given to the words 'spem meam', which are stated four times in succession. The closing chord progression passes in a short space from the minor to the major, the A♭ in the tenor part being the highest note in the piece (see Ex. 111).

INNO A MARIA VERGINE (S39)

Liszt composed this setting of an anonymous text in 1869 in Rome, and it remained unpublished until 1936. The work is scored for mixed choir, organ and harp, and the reason for its remaining unpublished for so long may be the subject matter of the text, which is a hymn asking protection for Pius IX, at a time when the temporal power was threatened. In this sense the piece is a casualty of politics, like *Le Forgeron*, the *Arbeiterchor* and the choral *Hungaria*.

The music is of a high quality, suggesting a strong involvement on Liszt's part. The opening 'gloria' is festive and ceremonial. The time signature changes from ₵ ('Allegro solenne') to 3/4 ('Andante maestoso assai'), ushering in the lyrical middle section, 'Dalle stelle su l'ali d'amore', the key changing to A♭. The mood changes again at 'Vedi fra quanti perigli si dibatte la nave di Pier', the opening mood returning at 'per te regga sicuro il gran Pio'. The climax occurs at 'pieghi l'alme al suo giusto voler' ('bends souls to his just will') (see Ex. 112).

## O SALUTARIS HOSTIA *I* (S40)

Liszt composed two settings of this text, both probably in 1869. The better of the two is the first, for women's voices and organ, in B♭ major.

In his 1835 article 'De la musique religieuse' Liszt rails against the use of operatic music in church, mentioning particularly the sacred host:

Do you hear, at the solemn moment when the priest raises the sacred host, do you hear the wretched organist execute variations on *Di piacer mi balza il cor* or *Fra Diavolo?*
O shame! O scandal! (*Cpr*, 61)

Liszt's own music for this point in the liturgy answers this criticism made 30 years before its composition. It is restrained and musicianly. Much play is made of the contrast between the major and the minor mode, while the organ, used sparingly, injects a little movement into the music by means of a short quaver figure, which within the overall 6/4 time signature is rapid enough to act as an ornament preceding the chordal entry of the voices (see Ex. 113). A pictorial effect of the raising of the host is given in the closing bars.

## TANTUM ERGO (S42)

The two versions of this work, both probably composed in 1869, are for women's voices and organ and for men's voices and organ. The organ part for the first is mostly in the treble clef, while for the second it is extended downwards to cover the usual keyboard range. The vocal part of the second is simply an octave transposition of the first.

In 1822 Liszt composed a *Tantum ergo* for Salieri, which is lost. According to Lina Ramann (*RAM*, 61) the 1869 *Tantum ergo* was said by Liszt to express the same 'feeling' as the former piece. The manuscript of the version for women's voices, dated 'Santa Francesca Romana, 20–21 August '69', is found on the reverse side of that of *O salutaris hostia*. Both

# Revolution and religion

Ex. 112

# The shorter choral works

Ex. 113

pieces are in B♭ major, and may be said to explore the same emotional vein.

The music is chordal throughout, except for two passages in unison. The contrast of unison and harmony is used to good effect, not having the ring of cliché it has in the piano music. The closing bars illustrate the style (see Ex. 114).

## AVE VERUM CORPUS (S44)

Liszt's *Ave verum corpus*, for mixed choir and optional organ accompaniment, was composed in 1871. It is a short piece, but in a small space explores wide harmonic territory. It would be difficult to perform without the support of the organ, though its function is purely supportive, and it has no independent music.

Simplicity is combined with beauty and expressive power. The opening is innocuous enough (see Ex. 115), but the wounds of Christ are reflected in the harmony (see Ex. 116). This gives way to a passage, marked 'dolciss.', in the major mode. A reference to death produces the triad of D♯ minor, returning to D major ready for the closing bars, the 'amen' repeating the harmony of the opening bars, transposed into D major.

## ANIMA CHRISTI, SANCTIFICA ME (S46)

There are two versions of this setting of the prayer of St Ignatius Loyola, both for male-voice choir and organ, both commencing in E minor and ending in E major. The better of the two is the first, which is a masterpiece of compression and harmonic richness. The second, though commencing with the same material as the first, passes into a sparse texture relying too much upon unison writing and recitative-like pauses.

The manuscript of the first version carries the dedication: 'Au très révérend Père Mohr S.I. son très respectueux et reconnaissant F. Liszt 25. Juin 74 (Villa d'Este).' Mohr was a Jesuit priest whose efforts on behalf of church music were warmly welcomed by Liszt, who wrote in 1878:

> The ecclesiastics Witt, Haberl, and Father Joseph Mohr of the Society of Jesus are the real leaders and masters of Catholic music now. Mohr recently published two important works which I shall tell you about some other time. (*Br.* VII, 210)

St Ignatius was, of course, the founder of the Society of Jesus. The music is a model of Liszt's writing for men's voices, and seems to grow out of the very sound of the medium. He structures the piece to follow exactly the meaning of the words, in one place repeating material used earlier in the

# The shorter choral works

Ex. 114

Ex. 115

Ex. 116

piece, thereby giving it some musical form. The key structure is E minor, G major, a keyless chromatic scale, E major. The transition to E major via a lengthy piece of unison writing is masterly, since the absence of harmony suits the words 'Intra vulnera tua absconde me' ('Hide me within thy wounds'), while musically it conveys a sense of progress towards an impending 'salvation' – which takes the form of a repeat of earlier music transposed to the tonic major, plus an extension into a codetta. The repeated music occurs at the words 'O bone Jesu, exaudi me' ('O kindest Jesus, hear my prayer') and 'Et jube me venire ad te' ('And summon me into thy presence'), the sixth and eleventh lines respectively of a prayer of 12 lines. The first statement is in G major (see Ex. 117). Then, starting on a unison D, the chromatic scale creeps slowly upwards, arriving at the note C for 'in hora mortis meae voca me' ('call me at the hour of my death'). Such a passage, in 1874, would have been pregnant with atmosphere and harmonic suggestiveness – the chromatic scale was not just an

Ex. 117

easy solution to the problem of modulation. Its background of ambiguity and associativeness is used to the full by Liszt as the music gropes slowly and painfully upwards. The return of the G major music here in E major leads to the climax, a setting of the final line of the prayer, 'Ut cum sanctis tuis laudem te' ('There to praise thee with thy saints'). This copies the rising shape of the chromatic scale, but is diatonic and harmonized, the basses repeating the rising scale at the high point (see Ex. 118). This concluding section sustains the feeling of splendour through to the final 'amen', the rising scale appearing in the right hand of the organ part. Liszt's achievement in this piece is to give the bare essentials of his 'lamento a trionfo' pattern, compressed to miniature proportions, and containing an element of development and recapitulation. The fact that this is possible musically and psychologically in such a small piece is not without relevance to Liszt's use of these formal procedures in larger works, where the programme and the form must be seen to match.

### CHORALES (ZWÖLF ALTE DEUTSCHE GEISTLICHE WEISEN) (S50)

Much confusion surrounds these harmonizations by Liszt of various chorale melodies. A letter from Liszt to the Princess dated 16 February 1879 says:

The publication of the Chorales – notated at the Villa d'Este, for use by my most eminent *Padrone* [Cardinal Hohenlohe] – requires that a copy or even two copies be made beforehand. They will not be ready until the end of March – and

227

# Revolution and religion

Ex. 118

[der    hat    auf    kei - nen    Sand    ge - baut,]

Ex. 119. *Wer nur den lieben Gott*, bars 25–9

consequently I cannot send them before then. I should like to request that he bring me immediately, through your help, the three or four Chorales remaining in manuscript at Sta Maria Maggiore, in order to include them in the same publication of about 15 or 18 chorales.                                      (*Br.* VII, 243)

In the event they were not published. Seven were included in the Collected Edition, where they appear for organ (without pedal) and voice, except for no. 1, *Es segne uns Gott*, which is for SATB and organ. This is the only one for which Liszt himself actually wrote out the vocal parts. The manuscripts of all the others are for keyboard alone, the voices having been added by the editor.

Although described as German, three are Latin, the full list of titles that exist in manuscript being as follows:

| | | |
|---|---|---|
| 1 | *Gott sei uns gnädig* | |
| 2 | *Nun ruhen alle Wälder* | |
| 3 | *O Haupt voll Blut* | |
| 4 | *O Lamm Gottes* | |
| 5 | *Was Gott tut* | |
| 6 | *Wer nur den Lieben Gott* | keyboard score only |
| 7 | *Nun danket alle Gott* | |
| 8 | *O Traurigkeit* | |
| 9 | *Vexilla regis* | |
| 10 | *Crux benedicta* | |
| 11 | *Jesu Christe* | |
| 12 | *Es segne uns Gott* | (keyboard and SATB) |

Nos. 3, 8, 9 and 10 were added to *Via Crucis*. The seven included in the Collected Edition are nos. 12, 1, 2, 3, 4, 5 and 6, of which only the first is printed as Liszt wrote it. Even so, most of the keyboard writing is clearly in four-part harmony (see Ex. 119). Thus when Liszt wrote out his harmonization of *O Haupt voll Blut* for four voices in *Via Crucis*, he needed to make very few changes to the piano version.

Cardinal Hohenlohe was a good amateur pianist, and the likelihood is that Liszt thought of these arrangements as domestic music for private use, rather than for church performance by a choir. The exception, *Es segne uns Gott*, has a melody which is clearly in G major, though Liszt

229

Ex. 120

treats it modally, based on E minor (see Ex. 120). After a modulation to
D major in the middle, it ends in E major.

### Ossa arida (S55)

This is Liszt's most extraordinary piece of church music. The text is
Ezekiel 37, verse 4: 'O dry bones, hear the word of the Lord.' The setting
is for unison men's voices and organ with two players, the organ score,
which includes a pedal part, covering five staves. It was composed in
October 1879 at the Villa d'Este, and first published in 1936.

In 1883 Liszt mentioned the work while discussing Raff's oratorio
*Weltende, Gericht und neue Welt* (World's End, Judgment and New World):

Raff has included in it the famous horsemen of the Apocalypse, so impressively
portrayed by Cornelius [the painter, not the composer]. I myself at the time
intended to compose music to them, but I have contented myself with the *vision
of Ezekiel* concerning the dry bones which hear the word of God. Unfortunately,
my composition is just about impossible to perform, and will not fail to make the
critics grind their teeth!
(*Br.*VII, 393)

On the manuscript, a note by Liszt reads:

# The shorter choral works

Ex. 121

Professors and students in the conservatories will doubtless thoroughly disapprove of the unusual discords built from a succession of thirds in the first 20
bars: this notwithstanding scripsit F. Liszt, Villa d'Este, 18–21 October 1879.

There exists in manuscript an orchestral version of the work not in
Liszt's hand, but containing his remarks and alterations.

It is difficult to see why Liszt thought the work would be difficult to
perform, since it makes no technical demands upon either singers or
organists. He probably felt that the actual sound of the music would
frighten all but the intrepid. The opening succession of thirds grows from
a single note, suggesting a piling up of dry bones (Ex. 121). As the work
ends in A major, this is to be considered as a supertonic chord of A minor,
confirmed by the entry of the voices on the tonic, together with the
terrific discord produced by the simultaneous sounding of all the notes
in Ex. 121. After a silence, the key changes to three sharps, and the chord
of C♯ major accompanies a quiet 'audite'. Then a fortissimo chord of
F♯ major, followed by A major, accompanies 'verbum Domini'
(see Ex. 122). The choice of F♯ for the word of God is not fortuitous. The
music stays in A major to the end, an effect of heterophony being
obtained, the organ's crotchets elaborating the long notes in the voices.
The two parts of this piece are in the greatest possible contrast. The
weird sound of the organ introduction, together with the startling entry
of the voices, gives way to a mood of broad splendour. The directness and
simplicity of the music illustrates Liszt's instinct for sureness of effect.
But only a performance reveals the visionary element not apparent from
the score, a tribute to the quality of Liszt's aural imagination.

## MARIENGARTEN (S62)

This short motet was sent in 1884, together with *Via Crucis*, *Septem
sacramenta* and *Rosario*, to the publisher Pustet, who did not accept it. It
first appeared in 1936.

The text ('Quasi cedrus exaltata sum in Libano'), which describes the
garden of Our Lady with its cedar trees, is set for a choir of sopranos,

231

Ex. 122

altos and tenors, with organ accompaniment (manuals only). The beauty of the piece resides in its harmony (see Ex. 123).

## SALVE REGINA (S66)

The manuscript of this motet for mixed choir is dated '11 Janvier '85. Rome, F. Liszt'. There is no organ part, and the piece is therefore the only example of unaccompanied church music Liszt wrote. It is also one of his most successful short choral pieces.

The text is simply 'Salve regina, mater misericordiae' ('Hail Queen, mother of mercy'). The style is truly vocal (see Ex. 124). The beauty of this piece places it alongside 'The Beatitudes' from *Christus* and the *Ave Maria* of 1846. It also illustrates the continuity of style and approach maintained in Liszt's church music. There is not the marked difference in this late work that appeared in his piano and orchestral style. For 40 years Liszt tried to capture a mood in his church music which was important to him. Into this effort he put some of his most original and skilful harmonic inventiveness, with musical results that have been unjustly neglected.

Ex. 123

# Revolution and religion

Ex. 124

# 12

# THE LATE RELIGIOUS WORKS
# AND *LES MORTS*

## DIE GLOCKEN DES STRASSBURGER MÜNSTERS
### (THE BELLS OF STRASBURG CATHEDRAL) (S6)

### Composition

The text of this work is taken from poems by Longfellow, who visited
Liszt at the church of Santa Francesca Romana on New Year's Eve 1868.
The composition was completed on 19 July 1874, Liszt writing the
following day to Baroness von Meyendorff:

Yesterday I finished the instrumentation of the *Cloches*: you will find Longfellow's
poem in the volume of his *Légende dorée* [The Golden Legend] (I forget the spelling
of the English title), whose prologue, pages one to three, *Les cloches* [sic] *de la
cathédrale de Strasbourg*, served as a text for my composition, which is preceded by
a prelude of some thirty bars entitled *Excelsior*, after another poem by Longfellow
(whom I occasionally saw in Rome). *Excelsior* is synonymous with the *Sursum
Corda*; we repeat it daily at mass, and the faithful reply: *Habemus ad Dominum*!
(*LOM*, 150)

Liszt started the work in 1869, writing to the Princess in February: 'I shall
try and compose Longfellow's *Excelsior* for you on my return to Rome' (*Br.*
VI, 203). The work was published in 1875 by Schuberth. Liszt arranged
the *Excelsior* as an organ solo (S666).

### Performance

The first performance took place under Liszt at a concert in Budapest
given on 10 March 1875 to raise funds for Bayreuth. In the same concert
Liszt played Beethoven's 'Emperor' Concerto with Richter conducting.

This is the only choral work by Liszt in which a devil figure sings, which
is why it is important. The Prologue to Longfellow's *Golden Legend* gives
the following scenario:

The spire of Strasburg Cathedral. Night and storm. LUCIFER, with the Powers
of the Air, trying to tear down the Cross.

235

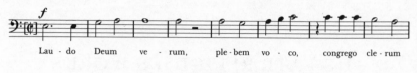

Ex. 125

Ex. 126. The plainchant *Te Deum*

Liszt's musical approach to the drama derives from Longfellow's note to the poem:

The Consecration and Baptism of Bells is one of the most curious ceremonies of the Church in the Middle Ages. The Council of Cologne ordained as follows:

'Let the bells be blessed, as the trumpets of the Church militant, by which the people are assembled to hear the word of God; the clergy to announce his mercy by day, and his truth in their nocturnal vigils: that by their sound the faithful may be invited to prayers, and that the spirit of devotion in them may be increased. The fathers have also maintained that demons affrighted by the sound of bells calling Christians to prayers, would flee away; and when they fled, the persons of the faithful would be secure: that the destruction of lightnings and whirlwinds would be averted, and the spirits of the storm defeated.'

In Longfellow's poem the bells declaim in Latin, contrasting with the English of Lucifer and the Voices. Liszt sets this Latin to the plainsong *Te Deum laudamus*, which is his musical starting-point, and from which he derives the musical material of the whole work. The programmatic idea is thus identical with the symphonic poem *Hunnenschlacht*, in which the Huns try to destroy Rome, and the Christians, represented by the *Crux fidelis*, are victorious. In Longfellow's poem, Lucifer is 'trying to tear down the Cross'. It is perhaps relevant to recall that during the years Liszt composed the work, Rome was itself being threatened from outside. Certainly, after the completion of *Christus* in 1868, this is the only large-scale choral work of force and imagination to come from Liszt's pen, albeit of much shorter duration; the total performance time is about a quarter of an hour for a work requiring full choir, soloists and orchestra.

The 'Te Deum' theme appears in its basic form only in the second part of the work, entitled 'Die Glocken'. It is sung by the bass voices of the choir accompanied by trombones and deep bells (see Ex. 125), and is Liszt's version of the plainsong (see Ex. 126). Reduced to its essentials,

Ex. 127. Liszt's thematic ideas derived from the plainchant

Ex. 128

we see an outline which for Liszt contained two thematic ideas (see Ex. 127). The first of these he used to construct the opening theme of the prelude, following the rhythmic shape of the word 'Excelsior' (see Ex. 128). This theme was later used by Wagner in *Parsifal* (as the 'Last Supper' motif). Translated from the Latin, 'Excelsior' means 'mounting higher and higher', or as Liszt described his own life 'ever striving upwards' (*L*, II, 65). The fact that he equated it with the 'Sursum corda' ('Lift up your hearts') of the Mass points to the religious thinking behind the work. Longfellow's poem describes how a youth carrying 'A banner with the strange device, Excelsior' climbs an alpine mountain, disregarding warnings of danger given by people on the way. The next day he is found dead in the snow by the monks of St Bernard, 'And from the sky, serene and far, A voice fell like a falling star, Excelsior!' Liszt sets only the word 'Excelsior'.

In the context of the ensuing drama, Liszt's 'Excelsior' prelude functions as the theme of the work, its subject matter. To achieve the desired end, Satan must be overcome. Here we return to the very beginning of Liszt's career as a serious composer, with the vision of God followed by despair in *Harmonies poétiques et religieuses* and the invention of the 'curse' theme in the *Malédiction Concerto* to represent the Devil. 'Excelsior' shows the goal, 'Die Glocken' how to get there. The rôle of Lucifer in this part is the most dramatic in the entire choral output of Liszt. Written for a baritone, it is the musical complement to the solo 'Tristis est anima mea' in the oratorio *Christus*, also for baritone.

The music is in the key of Eb major, and opens with a solo trumpet playing the 'Excelsior' theme. The strings enter with a quicker version, leading to a chord progression of unrelated triads against which the choir

Ex. 129

sing in unison. A climax for full orchestra returns to the tonic key of E♭, using the second idea (b) derived from the plainsong. The mezzo-soprano then enters with repetitions of the opening theme in a gentler tempo, Liszt making effective use of solo violin, harp and woodwind. The rhythmic music returns, together with the full choir, leading to a climactic plagal cadence as an ending. At the foot of the score, a note by Liszt reads: 'Dieses *Preludio* kann auch von dem Orchester allein, ohne Singstimmen, aufgeführt werden' ('This *Prelude* can also be performed by the orchestra alone, without the voices').

The succeeding part, in C minor, opens in a violent mood. The orchestral deep bells sound low E♭ repeatedly, the strings then entering with a phrase derived from part (a) of the plainsong. A climax quickly subsides, but immediately the orchestral fury is built up again, the basses outlining the (a) theme, the horns divided into pairs alternately playing fortissimo quavers, a striking orchestral effect (see Ex. 129). At the height of the fury, Lucifer enters: 'Hasten! Oh ye spirits! From its station drag the ponderous Cross of iron, that to mock us is uplifted high in air!' The score contains separate staves for the English and German versions, Liszt recasting the vocal line for each language. The women of the choir reply: 'Oh, we cannot! Oh, we cannot!' Then in the key of E major using the (b) part of the theme they sing: 'For around it all the saints and guardian angels throng in legions to protect it; they defeat us ev'ry where!' The 'bells', sung by the basses, then enter with the 'Te Deum' theme.

The drama consists of the contrast and opposition of the three elements, Lucifer and the storm, the Powers of the Air under his command, sung by women's voices, and the bells, represented by choral basses, trombones and orchestral bells. Finally Lucifer abandons the attempt to destroy the church, and retires, saying 'Baffled! Baffled! Inefficient, craven spirits! Leave this labour unto Time, the great

Ex. 130

Destroyer!' These words produced from Liszt the most dramatically effective music in his entire output. The voice declaims in fury, while the orchestra punctuates with chords of terrific violence (see Ex. 130). Here we feel more than ever in Liszt the opera-composer *manqué*, the man who turned his natural sense of theatre to Catholicism and the drama of redemption.

The chorus reply 'Onward! Onward! with the nightwind, over field and farm and forest', the orchestra carrying them away on the storm, at the height of which the music gives way to the 'Te Deum' theme in C major, marked 'Un poco meno allegro e maestoso', with for the first time a part for the organ. The closing section, for full choir and orchestra, is of the utmost beauty, Liszt using the (b) theme together with modal and chromatic harmony. Finally the choir sing 'Laudamus Deum verum, Deum verum' while the trumpets, horns and tenor trombones intone the 'Te Deum' theme, ending in a blaze of light with organ and choir on the chord of C major and triadic flourishes on brass, woodwind and strings.

The work had an effect upon Wagner, who heard it in March 1875, having received a copy in January from Liszt. According to Cosima, the initial impression was unfavourable: 'Arrival of my father's *Die Glocken von Strassburg* [*sic*], a curious work; done with great effect, but so alien to us' (*CWD*, 28 January 1875). Two years later, though, Wagner was repeatedly studying the work while composing *Parsifal*: 'R. works on the "Holy Grail March", he has cut out the crystal bells; he looked again at my father's *Die Glocken von Strassburg* [*sic*] to make sure he has not committed a *plagiarism*' (*CWD*, 28 December 1877).

### DIE HEILIGE CÄCILIA. LEGENDE (ST CECILIA. LEGEND) (S5)

#### Composition

In July 1874 Liszt wrote to the Princess from the Villa d'Este:

Be good enough to send me the volume of poems by Mme Girardin – the one which contains *the ode to St Cecilia*. I have composed music to it before – and I think that in taking it up again I shall make something of it.     (*Br.* VII, 78)

In August the music was complete:

For a long time I was obsessed by a hymn to St Cecilia. Händel has sung one in his grand manner, and Gounod has followed after him *al modo suo*. I look for a more Roman Catholic expression – and that *certa idea* which inspired Raphaël in his picture of St Cecilia. I liked the poetry of Mme de Girardin – and it has made me write a piece lasting a quarter of an hour or thereabouts.     (*Br.* VII, 80)

The earlier version referred to by Liszt is lost, but may have originated as early as 1839, when he wrote an article published in the *Gazette Musicale* entitled 'La Sainte Cécile de Raphael' (*Cpr*, 250). In it he describes his own reaction to the painting, outlining the 'idea' that lies behind it:

The painter has chosen the moment when St Cecilia prepares to sing a hymn to almighty God. She is about to celebrate the glory of the Most High, the expectation of the just, the hope of the sinner, her soul quivers with that mysterious thrill which gripped David when he improvised upon his sacred harp. Suddenly her eyes are flooded with light, her ears with harmony; the clouds part, the choirs of angels appear before her, the eternal *hosannah* echoes across eternity, the maiden turns her gaze toward heaven; she is in an attitude of ecstasy, her arms fall stretched out by her side, leaving hold of the instrument with which she is singing the sacred songs. We feel that her soul is no more upon the earth; her beautiful form seems about to be transfigured . . .
   Can you not say that like me you have seen in that noble figure the symbol of music at its most powerful? the art in which there is the most that is insubstantial, the most that is divine? This maiden taken out of reality by ecstasy, is she not inspiration as it comes from time to time upon the heart of the artist, unblemished, true, a revelation untarnished by any impurity?

For me, who have seen in St Cecilia a symbol, the symbol exists in reality.

Liszt dedicated the work to Cardinal Haynald, Archbishop of Kalocsa. It was published in 1876 by Kahnt.

Can - tan - ti - bus Or - ga - nis Caeci - - lia Domino decantabat dicens Fi - at

cor me - um im - ma - cu - la - tum

Ex. 131

## Performance

The first performance took place on 17 June 1875 at Weimar.

The music is scored for mezzo-soprano solo, choir and orchestra. An alternative version with piano accompaniment, or harmonium and harp, was also published. Liszt's note at the foot of the score tells us that this work is based upon the Gregorian chant for Antiphon I on the Feast of St Cecilia, which he then quotes (see Ex. 131). The vocal part is given with French, Italian and German texts, each having its own stave incorporating necessary variants of the vocal line. The original French version of the text is the one Liszt initially set, and which the music fits best.

The poem has 12 verses. The first eight describe how St Cecilia led a pious life and died a martyr's death in church while at prayer. The remainder tell how each winter concerts are given in her honour, and how 'Tous les arts lui rendent hommage.' She is 'la patronne des inspirés'. Liszt is therefore able to follow his usual 'lamento e trionfo' pattern.

The key signature at the opening is two flats, but this is a conceit, since the music is clearly in C minor, and the modulatory harmony is far removed from anything truly modal. The mezzo-soprano sings for the most part unaccompanied, the end of each verse being marked by a fragment of chant in the orchestra (see Ex. 132). A note of pathos is introduced after the fourth verse describing her murder, reflecting the words 'Dans ses douleurs elle succombe'. At the ninth verse, describing the annual winter concerts given in her name, the chant appears in the voice, doubled by orchestral woodwind, while an atmosphere of expectation is created by the use of tremolando strings. At the words 'on va célébrer cette sainte par des concerts' a full tutti follows leading to an expansive tune in C major for the words 'Tous les arts lui rendent hommage', itself derived from the plainsong. The mood of exultation is sustained through long-breathed phrases passing through various keys, leading to a climax at the words 'Sainte Cécile est la patronne des inspirés', followed by the first entry of the choir with part of the plainsong. The harmony of the suc-

# Revolution and religion

qui ja - dis pour la foi chré - tien - ne    don - na son sang.

De    Dieu

Ex. 132

sym - bo - le d'har - mo - ni - e    el - le

dic - te    les    chants

Ex. 133

ceeding passage, 'Vierge symbole d'harmonie', makes effective use of unrelated triads, a typically Lisztian device (Ex. 133). The rest of the work repeats the 'Tous les arts' theme with the choir, as well as the 'Vierge symbole d'harmonie', this time with an effective line above the choir for the solo, who is left alone to introduce the final peroration. This juxtaposes the chords of C major, A major and F♯ minor to form an unusual cadential progression, taken from the 'symbole d'harmonie' music. These three chords, considered as keys, polarize the most distant relationship; C major is used frequently by Liszt for the human, whereas F♯ represents the divine. This reflects the final words, 'elle répond du haut des cieux'.

Though Liszt saw St Cecilia predominantly as a musical symbol, his own music is a hymn to all the arts, and the divine inspiration of the artist. In performance the work is surprisingly effective, the structure being in essence one long gradual crescendo. The writing for the solo voice is expressive and idiomatic, while the many felicitous touches of orchestration lend colour, part of which consists in the use of the choir as a textural feature rather than as a musical foundation.

## CANTICO DEL SOL DI FRANCESCO D'ASSISI (S4)

### Composition

Liszt referred to this work as 'my *Cantico di S. Francesco*, written in Rome in '62, Via Felice' (*Br.* VII, 194), but his interest in the poem dated from long before the composition of the music. In 1853 he wrote to the Princess Wittgenstein's daughter, then a girl of 15:

At Mayence I bought two charming little volumes which are a part of the Railroad Library ... 'Joan of Arc', by Michelet, and 'Saint Francis and the Franciscans' by F. Morin. The latter volume delights me. The dream, the parables, the prayers, the teachings of the Saint all strike me as tender and impressive. Although you already know his famous Canticle, I wish to write it to you just as I found it in my little book:

'Highest, most powerful, and gracious Lord God, to You all praise, all glory and honour! To You all thanks! Everything comes from You alone, to You alone all returns – and no man is worthy to call upon You.

Be praised, O Lord, with all creatures, and above all for His Grace our brother Sun; through him the day shines that illuminates You; he is beautiful and beams in his splendour; he is Your emblem O Lord! –

Be praised, O Lord, for our sister the moon and for the stars; You made them in the heavens, clear and beautiful!

Be praised, O Lord, for our sister the water; she is useful and lowly, precious and pure!

Be praised, O Lord, for our father the fire; he lightens the shadows; he is beautiful, pleasing, vigorous, and ever-ready!

Be praised, O Lord, for our mother the earth, who sustains us; she begets the fruits and the herbs and the multiform flowers!'

The Franciscan's Chronicle says that St Francis 'rejoiced heartily when he saw this Canticle sung with grace and fervour; after hearing it, his spirit ascended wondrously up to God' – At the moment when the fight was the liveliest, he added the following strophe:

'Be blessed, O God, for those who pardon in the name of Your love, and who bear misery and tribulation! Happy are those who live in peace! heaven will crown them!'

At the moment of leaving for France, he made an admirable short speech to his brethren, of which I will only quote these lines to you: 'No matter where we may be, we always have our cell with us. This cell is our brother the body; and the soul is the hermit, who dwells therein to think upon God and to pray to Him; thus if the soul of him who is religious rests not at peace within the cell of the body, the outward cell serves him little' – and further: 'Our mission is to cure the injured, and to console the afflicted; to lead back those who have strayed; and, mark you, many are those who appear to be in the ranks of the Demon, who one day will be among the followers of Jesus Christ!'                                    (*LMW*, 54)

The music was 'composed in the spring' of 1862 (*L*, II, 19). In 1880 and 1881 Liszt revised the work in Weimar, writing in September 1881 to the Princess:

For a fortnight I have worked passionately at the *Cantico di S. Francesco*. As it stands finally improved, enlarged, embellished, harmonized and fully scored – I consider it one of my best works.                                    (*Br.* VII, 327)

This final version was published in 1884 by Kahnt. An organ prelude based upon the work (S665) was composed by Liszt in 1880, and a work entitled *Hosanna* for organ and bass trombone (S677), composed for Grosse, a trombonist in the Weimar court orchestra, and dating from 1862, is also based upon the work. A piano solo version (S499) dates from 1881.

### Performance

The 1862 version was performed that year in the Palazzo Altieri in Rome. A further performance was given in 1877 in Jena. There is no record of a performance of the later version in Liszt's lifetime, though one was planned to take place in Freiburg in the winter of 1880–1.

The work is scored for baritone solo, male-voice choir, organ and orchestra. As a preface to the score Liszt quoted a passage from a book by Antoine Frédéric Ozanam on Italian Franciscan poetry of the thirteenth century, describing the genesis of the *Cantico del sol*. The same passage is paraphrased by Liszt in a letter of 1862 to the Grand Duke Carl Alexander, and seems to have determined his approach to the music:

In the eighteenth year of his penitence, the servant of God, after spending 40 nights of vigil, fell into an ecstasy, following which he ordered brother Leonard to take a pen and write. He then recited the first seven verses of the *Canticle of the Sun*, glorifying God for brother Sun, sister Moon, brother Fire, sister Water, brothers Wind, Cloud and Air. (The title of the old Cologne edition is: *Cantico delle Creature, communemente detto de lo Frate Sol*.)

A few days later a great dispute arose between the Bishop of Assisi and the magistrates of the city. The Bishop inveighed against them and suspended them; the magistrates placed the prelate outside the law, and forbade all commerce with him and his supporters. The saint, distressed at such discord, grieved that no one intervened to restore peace. He therefore added to his Canticle the following eighth verse:

> Laudato sia, mio Signore,
> Per quelli chi perdonono per lo tuo amore
> E sostegneranno infirmitate e tribulazione!
> Beati quelli che sostegneranno in pace,
> Che da Te, Altissimo, saranno incoronate!

Then he instructed his disciples to go and earnestly seek the chief personages of the town and to beg them to go before the Bishop and, having arrived there, to sing in double chorus the new verse. The disciples obeyed, and at the sound of these words, to which God seemed to have lent a secret power, the adversaries embraced each other in repentance and asked forgiveness.

It is with this verse that my composition of the *Canticle of St Francis* ends.

(LCA, 117)

The emphasis upon this verse should be compared with its presentation in the 1853 letter quoted above; here the effect upon the hearers is important, and, certainly from Liszt's viewpoint, the fact that it was sung. Liszt omits the ninth verse of the Canticle, though the full text is quoted in the preface to the score. The music, wrote Liszt, 'is a development, or as it were a blossoming and flowering, of the chorale "In dulci jubilo" '.[1] The basic form of the work is thus a set of variations, the chorale theme carrying the text, the orchestra portraying water, fire, etc. However there is nothing extravagant in the accompaniment, the whole work having a dignified and simple air.

The key is F major (*cf. Psalm 18*) and the basic tempo 'Allegro giùbilando', though this is preceded by a recitative-like setting of the first verse, marked 'Lento solenne'. The chorale theme appears at the words 'Laudato sia Dio mio buon signore Con tutte le tue creature', which open the second verse (see Ex. 134). The rhythm in the orchestra is a persistent feature, used by Liszt to give momentum, and to provide contrast with a more static, hymn-like style, as at the words 'Laudato sia per Messer lo frate sole' (see Ex. 135). This music, put into the key of A♭ major,

Ex. 134

Ex. 135

returns for verse 7 at the words 'Laudato sia mio Signor per nostra madre terra'. The key of A♭ is used generally by Liszt to represent love, and it is followed here by the best music of the piece, the setting of the eighth verse. An atmosphere of mystery and awe is created by changing the rhythmic accompaniment, and by long-held chords on the woodwind. The voice creeps gradually upwards, breaking into a long-breathed melody for 'laudato per quelli che perdonano per tuo amore', marked 'con somma espress, e dolcezza', reaching its highest point at 'saranno incoronati', significantly in the 'religious' key of E major (see Ex. 136). Two trumpets in unison break through the texture with an arpeggio of E, then a full tutti sounds unison C, leading back to F major for a coda full of splendour, the solo voice echoed by the choir.

The *Cantico del sol* is Liszt's longest work for a solo male voice, and the fact that its composition spanned nearly 30 years, receiving great attention in Liszt's last years, places it among the composer's most personal

Ex. 136

utterances. It is certainly the only musical setting of stature to be given to St Francis's celebrated poem during the nineteenth century.

### AN DEN HEILIGEN FRANCISCUS VON PAULA (S28)

#### Composition

The first mention of this work occurs in Liszt's 'Testament' written in 1860:

A supplement to my Testament – containing the list of several manuscript works which I request Carolyne to have edited should I die before their publication –

. . .

4. Das Franciscus-Lied (Für Männerstimmen).
  N.B. On the title-page I want a reproduction of the picture by Steinle which I have spoken of in my testament. (*Br.* V, 61)

The passage referred to reads:

To my daughter Cosima I bequeath the sketch by Steinle representing St

# Revolution and religion

François de Paul, my patron saint; he is walking on the waves, his mantle spread beneath his feet, holding in one hand a red-hot coal, the other raised, either to allay the tempest or to bless the menaced boatmen, his look turned to heaven, where, in a glory, shines the redeeming word 'Caritas'. – This sketch has always stood on my writing-table. (*L*, I, 440)

Two questions present themselves regarding this work. First, when was it composed? Secondly, who is the author of the text?

There is a strong possibility that Liszt himself wrote the text, which is of no great literary value, and describes exactly the picture by Steinle. It begins:

> Über Meeres Fluten wandelst du im Sturm!
> und du verzagest nicht!
> In dem Herz die Liebe, in der Hand die Gluten,
> durch des Himmels Wolken schauend Gottes Licht.
>
> (Over the waves you walk through the storm!
> and you maintain courage!
> In your heart love, in your hand the glowing embers,
> through the cloudy sky shines God's light.)

This is a very Lisztian idea, of course, portrayed for example in one of his best piano works composed in Rome, *St François de Paule marchant sur les flots* (the second *Legend*, S175), as well as in a more general way in countless works. If Liszt required a text for a choral work about his patron saint, then without doubt he would have needed the stimulus of a picture to write one, as he did to produce the music for many of his programmatic works. In the Catholic Calendar the Feast of St Francis of Paola falls on 2 April, which is when Liszt chose to draw up the first version of his Testament. Liszt's full title for the work describes it as a 'prayer [Gebet] for men's voices – soloists and choir – with organ accompaniment and three trombones and timpani ad libitum'. Perhaps the music and the Testament originated at the same time. A connection with Rome lies in the fact that the music to the closing words, 'O lasse uns bewahren heilger Lieb' ('O let us safeguard holy love'), was used by Liszt to end the piano piece on the subject of St Francis of Paola.

The work was published in 1875 in Budapest by Táborszky and Parsch in both German and Hungarian, translated by Count Albert Apponyi. Liszt's wish regarding Steinle's picture was not followed, and the title-page bears another, by Gustave Doré. The work is dedicated to P. de Ferraris, Liszt's confessor in Rome. There is no record of a performance.

The music begins in E minor and ends in E major. The opening invocation to the saint (see Ex. 137) alternates with an agitated unison idea describing the stormy waves (see Ex. 138), with calmer, harmonized

Ex. 137

Ex. 138

Ex. 139

music depicting 'in dem Herz die Liebe' and a passage in grander mood for 'Gottes Licht', at which point the trombones and timpani enter (see Ex. 139). A fine climax is built up, leading to the theme used in the second *Legend* for piano (see Ex. 140). The piece is strong and concise, a tightly packed little drama for Liszt's favourite medium of men's voices, organ and brass, the sturdy sound he chose for the *Requiem*, the work that closed his Roman period in 1868.

Ex. 140

*VIA CRUCIS. THE 14 STATIONS OF THE CROSS FOR MIXED CHOIR,
VOCAL SOLOS AND ORGAN OR PIANO* (S53)

*Via Crucis* is one of Liszt's best and most original church works, written in
the style characteristic of his late years. Together with the *Septem
sacramenta* and the *Rosario* it was rejected by the Regensburg publisher of
church music, Pustet. *Via Crucis* received its first performance in
Budapest on Good Friday 1929, and first appeared in print in 1936 in the
Collected Edition.

Most of *Via Crucis* was composed at the Villa d'Este during the summer
of 1878. However, Liszt had been planning the work for many years. In
1874 he wrote of the 'little work I have been thinking about for a long
time: *Via Crucis*' (*Br.* VII, 49). It would not be 'learned or ostentatious',
but 'simple reflections of my youthful emotions – which remain
indestructible across all the trials of the years!' In 1875 he wrote of *'Via
Crucis* – which I started at the Colosseum when I lived very close by, at
Santa Francesca Romana' (*LOM*, 214). Liszt first moved into his quarters
there in the winter of 1866. The texts used in the work were assembled by
the Princess Wittgenstein, to whom Liszt wrote in October 1877: 'You

250

have arranged admirably the texts for the *Via Crucis*. I shall try to thank you by my composition, which I would like to undertake straightaway – but which I must adjourn, alas! until next summer' (*Br.* VII, 203). A year later he wrote on 16 October from the Villa d'Este: 'The *Via Crucis* has grown quite long . . . I am hoping to finish the manuscript the day after tomorrow' (*Br.* VII, 234). The completed manuscript bears the inscription 'F. Liszt Budapest 26. Février '79'.

Liszt sent the work to Pustet in 1884, and, when it was rejeected, wrote to the Princess:

My *Via Crucis* and *the 7 Sacraments* as well as the *Rosary*, will not be published by Pustet in Ratisbon, the Catholic editor of my choice. He excused himself politely, greatly to my displeasure – finding that the format of these works goes beyond that of his usual numerous publications. Another, and worse reason lies at bottom – my compositions of this sort do not sell, which will not prevent me from being fair to those of Witt, Haberl, etc., and contributing as much as I can to the propagation of the German society of St Cecilia. But in some things my rule is fixed: 'I will not do as you do.' (*Br.* VII, 427)

The title *Via Crucis* (The Way of the Cross) refers to the practice in the Middle Ages of erecting pictures or carvings at various positions around the church to represent the 14 Stations ('Station' here meaning 'standing still') where worshippers could gather in a spiritual pilgrimage in the wake of Christ. In many Roman Catholic churches there are paintings (derided as inferior by Liszt) on the walls depicting these. Prayers and meditations were said at each stopping point. Liszt intended his music to accompany such occasions, as he makes clear in his preface to the score:

The devotion to the Stations of the Cross, called Via Crucis, having received from the Sovereign Pontiffs many sanctions in respect of the souls of the dead, has spread to all countries, becoming very popular in some of them. In many churches the Stations are to be seen painted onto or attached to the walls. The faithful say the prayers consecrated to each of them, sometimes individually, sometimes sharing the words in small groups. On occasion, the priest attached to the church, having arranged a particular day and time for the devotion, himself leads the faithful. In the first instance the organ cannot take part, as it cannot in those places where the Stations of the Cross are in the open air, like at S. Pietro at Montorio in Rome. One may well imagine that the most solemn and moving of these devotional occasions took place in former times on Good Friday in the Colosseum, in the very place whose soil is stained with the blood of martyrs.

Perhaps one day the paintings, which are quite inadequate, might be replaced by the admirable Stations of the Cross modelled by the sculptor Galli, and a powerful harmonium be transported to play hymns, the voices being supported by the portable organ. I would be happy if one day these pieces might be heard, which only too feebly capture the emotions that filled me when more than once I repeated, kneeling with the procession of worshippers: O! Crux Ave! Spes unica!

The music therefore is both liturgical and programmatic, in so far as it is

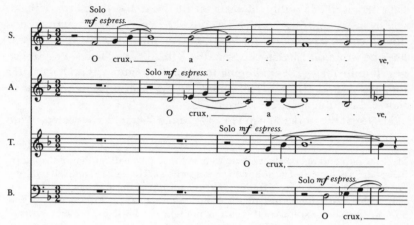

Ex. 141

meant to be used at such an occasion, and serves to describe the events of the Stations. Some of the pieces are organ solos, others are choral, and vocal soloists represent Pilate and Christ. Liszt's approach is direct and simple, attempting a literal evocation of what took place. The result is quite startlingly effective, since the 'programme' is medieval, and the harmonic style is modern. The pictorial element in the work's programmatic origin places *Via Crucis* alongside other works of Liszt like *Sposalizio*, *Hunnenschlacht* and *St Elizabeth*, all of which have a religious basis. Of *Via Crucis* Humphrey Searle says: 'The result is not a mere experiment, but a very deeply felt and moving work' (*SML*, 119).

The work opens with the Latin hymn *Vexilla regis* sung in unison by the choir, accompanied by the organ. To the plainsong melody Liszt adds the type of triadic harmony he associated with plainchant. The music irresistibly conjures up a slow procession. Before the entry of the choir the organ introduction refers to the Cross motif. After the hymn, four soloists sing, unaccompanied, 'O crux, ave, spes unica' in imitative entries based on the Cross motif (see Ex. 141). This ends the introduction. The first Station then follows.

*Station I. Jesus is condemned to death*
This is an organ solo, ending with an unaccompanied bass voice singing the words: 'Innocens ego sum a sanguine justi hujus.' The voice is identified as 'Pilatus'. The organ music is violent in mood (see Ex. 142).

*Station II. Jesus bears His Cross*
Another organ solo, marked 'Lento', is interrupted in the middle by an unidentified baritone solo singing unaccompanied the words 'Ave crux!' Pre-

Ex. 142

Ex. 143

Ex. 144

sumably this is the voice of Christ. The organ music is keyless and suggests weariness (see Ex. 143). The voice sings the Cross motif (see Ex. 144).

*Station III. Jesus falls for the first time*
Violent chords on the organ introduce the men's voices in unison, singing 'Jesus cadit' (see Ex. 145). This is followed by a trio of women's voices (two sopranos and an alto) singing 'Stabat mater dolorosa' to the same melody used in *Christus*.

*Station IV. Jesus meets His blessed mother*
This is a moving and highly original organ solo marked 'Lento'. The chromatic lines and whole-tone harmony are Tristanesque (see Ex. 146). A note of consolation enters with a more diatonic theme (see Ex. 147).

*Station V. Simon of Cyrene helps Jesus to carry the Cross*
Another organ solo, marked 'Andante'. There is a similarity in outline between this music, describing an offer of help to Jesus, and the end phrase of the 'love' theme (see chapter 14) in the Piano Sonata (see Ex. 148). After a chordal passage resembling a hymn-tune, the music of *Station II* returns.

# Revolution and religion

Ex. 145

Ex. 146

Ex. 147

Ex. 148

Ex. 149

Ex. 150

Ex. 151

*Station VI. St Veronica wipes Jesus' face with her veil*
The organ plays an unharmonized theme suggestive of compassion, which contains the Cross motif in reverse (see Ex. 149). This introduces the choir singing the chorale 'O Haupt voll Blut und Wunden'. The harmony is Liszt's own, but inevitably recalls Bach.

*Station VII. Jesus falls for the second time*
The music of *Station III* returns, a semitone higher.

*Station VIII. The women of Jerusalem weep for Jesus*
The organ opens with thirds descending chromatically to suggest weeping (see Ex. 150). A climactic chord stops the music, and St Veronica's theme from *Station VI* introduces the unaccompanied baritone solo singing Christ's words: 'Nolite flere super me' ('Weep not for me, but weep for yourselves and for your children'). The 'weeping' music returns, but gives way to a martial passage, ending startlingly on a diminished seventh chord (see Ex. 151). The word 'Tromp.' indicates the organ registration, the only one marked by Liszt in the score. There must be a programmatic reason for his use of the trumpet sound at this point. A possible explanation is that it refers to the 'Tuba mirum' of the *Dies irae*, Liszt

Ex. 152

Ex. 153

here using music to make the point that Christ's words refer to the Day of Judgment.

*Station X. Jesus is stripped of His clothing*
The music of *Stations III* and *VII* returns, with a slightly altered tonal basis.

*Station X. Jesis is stripped of His clothing*
This is perhaps the best of the organ solos. It has the key signature of F minor, a key which has programmatic significance in other works of Liszt in that it is related to A♭, which the composer associated with 'love'. The texture is contrapuntal, with continuous running quavers as an inner part, while the harmony is chromatic and often whole-tone. Halfway through, the St Veronica theme is added (see Ex. 152). At the end of this piece Liszt wrote in the manuscript: 'Durch Mitleid Wissend – Parsifal Wagner' ('Knowledge through compassion').

*Station XI. Jesus is nailed to the Cross*
Violent fortissimo organ chords introduce the men's voices in unison, singing 'Crucifige'. The first chord is C♯ minor over the dominant G♯, which survives into the succeeding harmony, producing extreme discords (see Ex. 153). The closing bars, marked 'piano', outline the Cross motif unharmonized.

*Station XII. Jesus dies on the Cross*
The unaccompanied baritone solo sings Christ's words: 'Eli, Eli lamma Sabacthani?' The organ plays pianissimo a succession of whole-tone chords descending chromatically, and the unaccompanied voice sings: 'In manus tuas commendo spiritum meum.' A organ solo follows, based upon the Cross motif,

# The late religious works and *Les Morts*

[Andante non troppo lento]

Ex. 154

which blossoms into *Crux fidelis* before the death of Christ (see Ex. 154). The voice then sings 'Consummatum est', sparsely accompanied by quiet chords. An organ postlude, again based upon the Cross motif, leads to the trio of women's voices repeating unaccompanied the last words of Christ. The choir then sing the chorale 'O Traurigkeit, o Herzeleid' unaccompanied until the second verse.

*Station XIII. Jesus is taken down from the Cross*
This fairly lengthy organ solo recapitulates preceding music, namely the *Stabat mater*, Jesus's mother, and St Veronica.

*Station XIV. Jesus is laid in the tomb*
This opens with a setting for mezzo-soprano solo, choir and organ, of the Latin hymn 'Ave crux, spes unica'. The organ accompaniment, with its off-beat chords, suggests a slow procession, providing a musical counterpart to the introductory *Vexilla regis*. When the procession has 'left the stage', the key changes to D major, and the choir sing long quiet chords to 'Ave crux' while the organ refers to the diatonic theme from *Station IV* (Jesus's mother) (see Ex. 155). The choir end with unharmonized statements of 'Ave crux', followed by the organ alone, which closes the work quietly with the Cross motif.

Because this work is about the Cross, it provides a microcosm of Liszt's religious and musical thinking. In particular, his use of unusual harmony, which is the chief cause of his late works being described as 'prophetic', takes place in a specific psychological and emotional context. In this respect it is not modern at all, being the single feature most characteristic of Romanticism, the search for personal expression. By 1878 Liszt had turned his attention almost exclusively to his private thoughts and feelings, not caring for public acceptance in the ordinary sense. This is partly why the pieces are so short, and so 'experimental' in form. In his search for direct expression, Liszt became at once concise and radical. But the thinking remains the same. The difference between a huge work like *Christus* and a series of miniatures like *Via Crucis* is more apparent than real, since in the late work Liszt puts himself under a kind of musical microscope, reducing what formerly took pages down to a single chord progression or a bare succession of notes. Liszt's interest lay in capturing a mood, not in discovering new tonal systems or laws of composition. His approach was empirical, and his starting-point was

Ex. 155

himself. In this sense he achieved 'freedom' of expression only by adhering to the fixed assumptions of his age. The impressive originality of *Via Crucis* resulted from Liszt's attempt to compose 'simple reflections of my youthful emotions', the music of 1878 describing the moods of 1828. It is important to see what had changed in that half-century, and what had not.

*SEPTEM SACRAMENTA. RESPONSES WITH ORGAN OR HARMONIUM ACCOMPANIMENT* (S52)

In November 1878, Liszt wrote from Tivoli to his cousin Eduard:

The *Via Crucis* (now finished) has brought me back to a long-cherished ideal – namely, the composition of choruses to be made use of at Church festivals during the giving of the 7 holy sacraments; thus 7 pieces of music of about a hundred bars each. These have now been 8 days at the copyist's, and, according to my thinking, are not quite a failure. (*L*, II, 344)

Two of the *Sacraments*, 'Eucharist' and 'Marriage', were sung in the Royal Chapel in Vienna on 8 April 1879, conducted by Hellmesberger, the court music director. The complete work was performed for the first time in the Catholic church at Weimar on 10 July the same year. It remained unpublished until 1936.

# The late religious works and *Les Morts*

In a preface to the score, Liszt gives an account of the work's origin:

One day when Overbeck [a German painter of the Nazarene school] was explaining to me his composition based upon the Seven Sacraments, in which he had included a number of (hidden) symbols, allusions, historical and mystical facts, the whole fresco a concordance between the Old and New Testaments, I was seized with admiration for his work and promised to reproduce the same subject in my own art, music. As he seemed extremely pleased at this, I refrained from telling him that my treatment of it would be diametrically opposed to his. He portrayed the workings of divine grace and human cooperation in these divine gifts. I intended to give expression to the feeling by which the Christian takes part in the mercy that lifts him out of earthly life and makes him aspire to the divine atmosphere of heaven.

The following compositions may be sung in churches and chapels shortly before or during the administering of the Holy Sacraments. The music for Penitence may immediately precede, together with a long pause, the music for Communion. The music for Extreme Unction will perhaps find a place during the period of silence before absolution at a funeral.

Once again we see how painting fired Liszt's imagination not to a literal portrayal, but to a corresponding musical idea of his own based upon his own feelings.

The seven pieces are 'Baptism', 'Confirmation', 'Eucharist', 'Penitence', 'Extreme Unction', 'Holy Orders', and 'Matrimony'. The first two are for men's voices and organ, with optional parts added occasionally for women's voices. 'Eucharist' is for full choir and organ. The rest are for men's voices and organ, with the exception of 'Matrimony', which also includes a mezzo-soprano solo.

The style of the music is simple, but avoids monotony by contrasting different voice combinations, and mixing unison writing, homophony and counterpoint. This last, though short-lived, is effective, and something of a surprise, in 'Eucharist' for example (see Ex. 156). In 'Holy Orders' there is a short fugato (see Ex. 157). The choice of key is significant also. 'Baptism' is in C major, while 'Matrimony' is in F♯ major. The accompaniment recalls the piano piece *Sposalizio* based upon the *Marriage of the Virgin* by Raphael. The tone of the work is more directly ecclesiastical than that of *Via Crucis*. Nevertheless the originality and beauty of the music match the subjects it serves to depict.

### IN DOMUM DOMINI IBIMUS
(LET US GO TO THE HOUSE OF THE LORD. FROM PSALM 122) (S57)

### Composition

The date of composition of this work is not known, but it is clearly a late work, probably composed in the 1880s. The manuscript was in the

Ex. 156

possession of August Göllerich, who published Liszt's arrangement for organ solo entitled *Praeludium* as an appendix to his book *Franz Liszt* in 1908. The score first appeared in the Collected Edition. There is no record of a performance during Liszt's lifetime.

The music is scored for mixed choir, organ, two trumpets, two trombones and timpani. It is marked 'Lento assai', but the 'Göllerich' organ version is marked 'Allegro', which suits the music better. The key is E♭ major, and the mood is one of fierce exultation. The fragment of Psalm 122 that constitutes the text is repeated several times, the choral writing being for the most part in unison. The harmony is bold, juxtaposing chromatically altered triads like splashes of unmixed colours (see Ex. 158). Towards the end a fanfare-like figure appears in the organ part. The piece is short and fortissimo throughout.

## *LES MORTS* (S112)

### *Composition*

*Les Morts* is the first of a set of three funeral odes catalogued among Liszt's orchestral works. The second and third are for orchestra only, but

Ex. 157

the first has an important part for male-voice choir, and is really a choral work. It was composed in 1860 in memory of Liszt's son Daniel, who had died the previous year at the age of only 22.

On 4 July 1860 Liszt wrote to the Princess:

Have I told you that I have been busy with an instrumental composition which I have been thinking about for a long time, and which will be entitled *Les Morts*? Each verse concludes with some chords representing the line: 'Heureux les morts qui meurent dans le Seigneur!'  (*Br.* V, 23)

The title *Les Morts* is that of a poem by Lamennais in which each verse ends with the line quoted by Liszt. In 1866 Liszt added the part for male-voice choir, setting the same line, but in Latin. Liszt's mother died in February 1866 and the music may have been added in her memory, as Liszt wrote in a letter:

After having received the last rites, my mother *Anna Liszt* died in Paris on 6 February 1866. Audivi vocem de coelo dicentem mihi: 'Beati mortui, qui in Domino morientur!' [I heard a voice from Heaven saying to me: 'Blessed are those who die in the Lord!']  (*LAA*, 16)

Ex. 158

### Performance

The work was not published or performed until after Liszt's death. In his Testament of September 1860 Liszt asked the Princess to take care of its publication, but it first appeared in the Collected Edition. A note on the manuscript of the second ode asks that *Les Morts* should be performed on the occasion of Liszt's own funeral, a request that was not carried out. The first performance took place in Weimar under Raabe on 21 May 1912.

Liszt arranged the work for organ under the title *Trauerode*, though this

Ex. 159

version also was published only after his death, in 1890 (S268, 2). A version for piano solo (S516) was published in 1908 as an appendix to *Franz Liszt* by August Göllerich.

In the letter informing the Princess of his composition of the work, Liszt discussed the subject of death:

Without being, as people commonly say, afraid of death – you yet do not share in my feeling of radiant calm towards the mysterious messenger, the august patron of our deliverance. But, believe me: it will be a supreme delectation for you – who have suffered so much, prayed, wept, and fought so hard, and have been so deserving and loving! Love triumphs over death here on earth – and in heaven, death is no more!
(*Br.* V, 24)

The 'feeling of radiant calm' spoken of by Liszt corresponds to the music he wrote for the words 'Beati mortui, qui in Domino morientur!' The 'chords' he speaks of in the earlier part of the letter outline the 'Cross motif' (see Ex. 159; this and the following examples are taken from the piano score in Göllerich's biography).

The key signature of A♭ major is not the key of the work, which begins with one sharp and ends with four, obviously suggesting the passage from E minor to E major; it is used deliberately to introduce the Cross motif, probably with a musical reference to the idea of love (see chapter 15). The opening of the work is remote from the suggested E minor tonality of the key signature (see Ex. 160), and the harmony throughout represents Liszt at his most original (see Ex. 161). The mood of the work oscillates between the violent and the visionary, and this is characteristic of the late works and some of the early ones. Here the connection with Lamennais is of key importance. The groping gloom of the opening alternates with the radiant calm of the Cross motif, and, becoming progressively energetic, passes into a triumphant but stormy passage in E major. This reflects the outline of Lamennais' poem, which is not a

Ex. 160

Ex. 161

gloomy meditation on death, but asks the question 'Où sont-ils? Qui nous le dira?' ('Where are they? Who can tell us?'). Lamennais paints a picture of life on earth familiar from *Paroles d'un croyant*, full of misery and oppression. The Cross, he says, was ignored by man, yet therein lies his salvation. The final verse portrays two voices coming from heaven; the first recites the 'De profundis' ('Out of the depths have I cried to thee, O Lord'), the second the 'Te Deum' ('We praise thee, O God'). We too are going there, he says, and concludes 'Où serons-nous? Qui nous le dira?' ('Where shall we be? Who shall tell us?').

Liszt's music captures the extraordinary atmosphere of the poem exactly. The use of the Cross motif in a work based on Lamennais links his earliest period to his latest, La Chênaie to Rome. At the time of its composition, Liszt was contemplating his whole life, which in his Testament he summed up as a vocation for the Cross. In the same document he disposes of his worldly goods, leaving them to the Princess. The work was thus of the utmost personal importance to Liszt, telling us more in music than the Testament does in words about the composer's musical and religious thinking. Above all, the originality and force of the composition are striking, just as the works composed for Lamennais in 1834 were also. *Les Morts* is not just a piece of music, but a psychological document, a key to the understanding of Liszt as man and musician.

# PART III

Music can be said to be in essence religious, and, like the soul of man, 'Christian by nature'.

Liszt in Rome, 1865

# 13

## LISZT'S PROGRAMMATIC
## USE OF FUGUE

Liszt's interest in fugue commenced in 1842, when he transcribed for the piano six of Bach's organ preludes and fugues (S462). By 1871, when he transcribed for the piano his own organ fugue on the name BACH, written in 1855 and revised in 1870 (S260), he had composed all his major works, namely the Piano Sonata, the symphonies, the concertos, the Masses, the oratorios and 12 of the 13 symphonic poems.

Fugal sections occur in 14 of Liszt's works. In order of composition these are:

1  *Missa quattuor vocum* (*Male-Voice Mass*). S8. 1848
2  *Fantasy and Fugue on the Chorale 'Ad nos, ad salutarem undam'* (from Meyerbeer's *Le Prophète*) for organ. S259. 1850
3  Piano Sonata in B minor. S178. 1852–3
4  *A Faust Symphony*. S108. 1854 ('Chorus mysticus' added 1857)
5  *Prometheus* (symphonic poem no. 5). S99. c. 1855 (first version 1850)
6  *Psalm 13*. S13. 1855 (revised 1859)
7  *Prelude and Fugue on the name BACH* for organ. S260. 1855
8  A symphony to Dante's *Divina Commedia*. S109. 1855–6
9  *Missa solennis zur Einweihung der Basilika in Gran* (*Gran Mass*). S9. 1855 (revised 1857–8)
10  *Hunnenschlacht* (symphonic poem no. 11). S105. 1856–7
11  *Totentanz* for piano and orchestra. S126. 1859 (planned 1838; composed 1849; revised 1853 and 1859)
12  *Missa choralis*. S10. 1865
13  *Christus* (oratorio). S3. Planned 1853; completed 1868
14  *Septem sacramenta*. S52. 1878

The 1848 *Male-Voice Mass*, revised in 1869 and published again in 1870, opens and closes Liszt's period of composing fugue, with the exception of one late example, the sixth of the seven pieces that constitute *Septem sacramenta*. Not by coincidence is this 'Holy Orders'.

The above works are listed in order of the composition of their fugal sections, so far as this can be ascertained. For example, although nos. 5–9 originated in 1855 (to which may be added *Hunnenschlacht*, which was planned the same year), *Prometheus* must have been completed first, since in March Liszt wrote in a letter: 'The engraving of my Symphonic Poem is in progress' (*L*, I, 234). In August he referred to the fugal ending of *Psalm 13*: 'I must end my Psalm with a brilliant fugal peroration' ('Il faut que je termine . . . mon Psaume par une éclatante péroraison fuguée') (*Br.* III, 39). The organ fugue on BACH was intended for a performance in September 1855, but the 'Ad nos' fugue was substituted because the piece was not finished in time. The *Dante Symphony* was completed on 8 July 1856, and although the *Gran Mass* was by then ready for its première in August, the fugal part of the Gloria was added after the performance. *Hunnenschlacht*, which contains a brief fugal passage, was completed in the early months of 1857. As *Psalm 13* and the *Gran Mass* each contain two fugal episodes, this means that, counting the *Faust Symphony*, which was finished in October 1854, Liszt composed eight passages of fugue in a little over two years (1854–6).

Of the 14 works, three are settings of the Mass; three are religious choral works; four are instrumental works with a programme; and four (including the organ pieces) are instrumental works without a programme. Do these varied works have anything in common apart from their use of fugue? Given that Liszt could write a fugue when he wanted to (even though none of his examples constitutes a fully worked-out specimen), it is worth considering what other factors governed his use of the style, beginning with the church music.

Most nineteenth-century church music employs fugal technique in some shape or form. The Church was viewed as the natural home of counterpoint. Yet few of the examples produced have survived; most of them were arid wastes of paper music. Liszt voiced strong opinions against this sort of music. In April 1855, when the composer Friedrich Kühmstedt, Director of Music at the Eisenach Seminary, came to Weimar to conduct his oratorio *The Transfiguration of the Lord*, Liszt attended the rehearsals, and wrote:

Having heard it at three rehearsals, I found no satisfaction in it either for my ears or my mind: it is the old frippery of counterpoint – the old unsalted, unpeppered sausage etc., rubbish to the ruin of eye and ear! I will try to leave it out in my Mass, although this style is very usual in composing Church music. (*L*, I, 239)

The Mass in question was the *Gran Mass*, but Liszt had already composed fugal passages in his first setting of the Mass. Liszt's first attempt at fugal composition, the Gloria of the *Male-Voice Mass*, has a fugue subject that contains his Cross motif (see Ex. 5, on p. 106 above). Hence its programmatic significance lies in the symbol of the motif – the Cross symbolizing redemption. We may say that for Liszt the idea represents the path to God.

In the note at the end of *St Elizabeth* Liszt tells us that the fugal 'cum sancto spiritu' which he added to the Gloria of the *Gran Mass* (see Ex. 162)

## Liszt's programmatic use of fugue

Ex. 162

Ex. 163

is also built upon the notes of the Cross motif. After composing this, Liszt wrote: 'I think I have considerably improved [the Mass] in my last revision, especially by the concluding Fugue of the Gloria and a heavenward-soaring climax of the subject' (*L*, I, 295). There are two fugues in the *Gran Mass*, the other one occurring in the Credo (see Ex. 163); this fugue subject is in fact the motto theme of the whole Credo. Only in the fugal version is it sung, rather than played. Liszt uses the Credo theme to sing of his belief in the Church, the tempo marking, 'Allegro militante', itself being a pointer towards his attitude. The Mass, let us remember, was composed especially for the consecration of a former ruined cathedral, newly restored – a potent symbol for Liszt.

The Kyrie of the *Missa choralis* is not so much fugal as imitative, but we may fairly assume that to Liszt the two styles were barely separate. It is obviously an attempt to emulate the Renaissance style (see Ex. 164). Nevertheless, the use of fugal technique to open the work was to some extent determined by outside considerations, since the music is based upon the plainchant *Sacerdos in aeternam* (*Liber Usualis*, p. 956). This is an obvious reference to Liszt himself in 1865, as is confirmed by his use of fugue in the piece 'Holy Orders' from *Septem sacramenta* in 1878 (see Ex. 157 on p. 261 above).

Two of the religious choral works that contain passages of fugue were not intended for church performance; namely *Psalm 13* and the oratorio *Christus*. Both works are regarded as being among Liszt's most personal creations.

The first fugal passage in *Psalm 13*, occurring at the words 'Wie lange soll ich sorgen und mich ängstigen?' ('How long must I suffer anguish in

Ex. 164

my soul, grief in my heart, day and night?'), is given over to the orchestra, while at first voices from the choir, then the tenor solo, cry 'Wie lange!' through the chromatic harmony and wayward rhythms of the contrapuntal texture. The fugue subject has an upward-surging character, as if trying to break free of oppression; significantly, its initial three notes form the Cross motif (see Ex. 165). The second fugal passage occurs at the words 'Ich will dem Herrn singen, dass er so wohl an mir gethan' ('My heart shall rejoice, for thou hast set me free'). It forms the emotional climax of the work (Liszt's 'éclatante péroraison fuguée'); see Ex. 166. This time, after the initial statement of the subject by the orchestra, the fugue is sung, the subject itself being a transformation of the gloomy motive that opens the work.

The emotional plan of the work is the one usually found in Liszt, which

Ex. 165

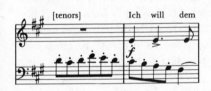

Ex. 166

the composer himself aptly characterized in *Tasso* (the second symphonic poem) as 'lamento e trionfo'. Later, this simple journey from lamentation to triumph became considerably modified in Liszt's serious works. In *Tasso* itself he added a middle section to provide a transition. Eventually the scheme grew to include four sections – though this is often disguised by the apparent number of the movements, as in the Piano Concerto in E♭, where the last three movements are joined together to form one continuous piece. In *Psalm 13* the second fugue represents the

Ex. 167

moment of triumph, its subject using a theme which appears initially as a lament. In between these two extremes it appears as a prayer to the words 'Schaue doch und erhöre mich, Herr, mein Gott' ('Look now and answer me, O Lord my God'). Thus the tripartite scheme consists of lament–prayer–triumph. But the piece is itself a prayer – a prayer which is supposedly answered. The rôle of the sung fugal ending is to celebrate this event, while the instrumental fugue incorporating the Cross motif at the beginning expresses struggle – what Liszt called in the *Gran Mass* a 'heavenward-soaring' quality. In that sense it is purely programmatic, the idea of struggle playing an important rôle in the instrumental fugues of Liszt.

In *Christus*, it is the third section which contains the lament. The first two sections of the oratorio, describing Christ's earthly mission, end with the triumphal entry into Jerusalem. It is at this point that Liszt introduces a fugue sung to the words 'filio David, benedictus qui venit in nomine Domini' (see Ex. 167). The words are significant: the entry into Jerusalem symbolized the Messiahship of Jesus, the public acclamation of the Son of God.

Part 3 of the oratorio contains the triumphant 'Resurrexit', where Liszt again introduces a choral fugue at the words 'Christus vincit Christus regnat Christus imperat in sempiterna saecula' (see Ex. 168). The fugue is preceded by a fortissimo statement of Ex. 167 by the trombones, while the choir sing the word 'resurrexit'. Thus even the dullest of listeners is made aware of the earlier fugue's programmatic intention: the triumphal entry into Jerusalem foreshadowed the return of Christ into Heaven. All Liszt's choral fugues are addressed to God.

The four programmatic works by Liszt that include fugal sections are the *Faust Symphony*, the symphonic poem *Prometheus*, the *Dante Symphony* and the symphonic poem *Hunnenschlacht*. The fugue in the *Faust Symphony* occurs in the 'Mephistopheles' movement. As might be expected, it is full of diablerie, and the fugue subject seems writhing and contorted (see Ex. 169). This whole movement constitutes a stroke of genius on Liszt's

# Liszt's programmatic use of fugue

Ex. 168

Ex. 169

part, in that its themes are distorted versions of those used in the first movement to characterize Faust. By this means Liszt symbolizes the Spirit of Negation. The fugue subject is a distorted version of the Affettuoso poco andante (letter K), which is usually taken to represent the amorous side of Faust. This is important, as the story, particularly in Liszt's interpretation, concerns the nature of Faust's love for Gretchen, and how this serves to redeem him. The addition of the 'Chorus mysticus' in 1857 gave the work a fourth section, thus completing the lamento–trionfo pattern. Originally there was no triumph; applying the emotional scheme of *Psalm 13*, we could say that the 'Faust' movement represents the lament, the 'Gretchen' movement the prayer, and the 'Chorus mysticus' the triumph. We are left with the 'Mephistopheles' movement, which represents the struggle between Man and the Devil. Thus emerges a new four-part scheme: lament–prayer–struggle–triumph. In psychological terms this represents Liszt's most fully worked out form, the sum of what he had to say.

In the 'Faust' movement the 'amorous' theme is followed by a theme in E major marked 'Grandioso, poco meno mosso' (letter O). Its rhythm fits these words from Goethe's *Faust*, Part One: 'Im Anfang war die Tat!' ('In the beginning was the Deed!'). At this point in the story, Faust is in his study alone save for a companion in the form of a black poodle, which later transforms itself into Mephistopheles. Faust feels moved to translate the New Testament into German, 'In simple honest will to understand the sacred codex, and its truth translate'. He ponders the opening of St John's Gospel: 'In the beginning was the Word', and tries three versions: 'In the beginning was the Thought'; 'In the beginning was the Power'; 'In the beginning was the Deed'. The dog starts to whine, and begins to change into 'a hybrid brood of hell'.

Liszt's theme is stated four times, paralleling Goethe's text, and may be taken to represent Faust when he says: 'We learn to cherish here immortal things, And look with longing hearts for revelation.' At the end of the 'Chorus mysticus', as the choir sings 'Das Ewig-Weibliche Zieht uns hinan' ('Eternal Womanhood Leads us above'), the same theme appears in the orchestral bass-line. The implication, clearly, is that Faust's soul returns to God, having escaped the Devil's clutches. This refers back to the 'Faust' movement, and explains why Liszt preceded the 'grandioso' (God) theme with the 'affettuoso' (love) theme.

The significance of the fugue now emerges. It is preceded by the only theme in the 'Mephistopheles' movement (apart from Gretchen's) which is not a parody of one of the Faust themes. This theme occurs in another work by Liszt, the *Malédiction Concerto* for piano and string orchestra, and over it in the manuscript Liszt wrote the word 'orgueil'. Thus before the fugue starts Liszt points to the Devil's pride. The fugue then commences, using a twisted version of Faust's 'love' theme, leading with furious energy to a brilliantly satirized version of the 'grandioso' theme, hideously decked with trills and shrieking woodwind. It is the first appearance of the theme in this movement. In this way Liszt portrays Mephistopheles' attempt to defile Faust's aspiration towards God. Liszt here brilliantly parodies his own use of fugue: the Devil's fugue too is directed at God, but with malicious intent.

Liszt composed the symphonic poem *Prometheus* after he had completed the 'Mephistopheles' movement of the *Faust Symphony*, but before he had added the 'Chorus mysticus'. As *Prometheus* exhibits the four-part emotional scheme lament–prayer–struggle–triumph, it may have prompted Liszt to round off the symphony, as the fugal part of *Prometheus* occurs also in the 'struggle' section.

Liszt said the work represented 'ein tiefer Schmerz, der durch trotzbietendes Ausharren triumphiert' ('a deep suffering which triumphs by defiant endurance'). In the myth, Prometheus was punished by Zeus for bringing fire to mankind. He was tied to a rock, and his liver

## Liszt's programmatic use of fugue

Ex. 170

Ex. 171

devoured daily by an eagle. Ultimately Zeus allowed him to be rescued by Hercules. The Greeks honoured Prometheus as the benefactor of mankind and the father of all the arts and sciences. Some of the themes of the symphonic poem are taken from the choruses Liszt wrote in 1850 for Herder's play *Entfesseltem Prometheus*, to which the work originally figured as an overture. Thus the 'prayer' section uses the theme of Prometheus's prayer to Themis, the goddess of justice. This is followed by the fugue subject (see Ex. 170), whose descending crotchets are taken from the main theme of the final chorus, sung to the words 'Was Himmlisches auf Erden blüht . . . Ist Menschlichkeit!' ('From Earth aspiring towards Heaven . . . is Mankind!'). After the fugue Liszt includes an optional cut which would leave out the recapitulation of the stormy Allegro molto appassionato, thus passing directly to the 'triumph' music, which itself combines the descending crotchets of the fugue subject with a jubilant version of the 'prayer' theme. Thus the fugue represents the transition between the prayer and its fulfilment, Prometheus as it were willing his own salvation (*cf.* the first – instrumental – fugue in *Psalm 13*). This is why Liszt chose as its subject a theme he had composed to the words 'aspiring towards Heaven'.

The fugue in the *Dante Symphony* (see Ex. 171) occurs in the second movement. The symphony is in two movements, but the 'Purgatorio' ends with a setting for women's voices of the 'Magnificat' – representing a vision of Paradise. Thus there is an implied three-movement pattern: 'Inferno', 'Purgatorio', 'Paradiso'. The function of the fugue is to provide a transition between the last two. This creates an extra section, making four altogether. We thus arrive at the lament–prayer–struggle–triumph pattern, in which the 'Inferno' movement figures as the lament, the open-

Ex. 172

Ex. 173

ing of the 'Purgatorio' as the prayer, the fugue as the struggle and the 'Magnificat' as a triumph. Significantly, the fugue subject is clearly derived from a theme in the 'Inferno' movement composed to the words 'Nessun maggior dolore Che ricordarsi del tempo felice Nella miseria' ('There is no greater pain Than to recall the happy days In time of misery'); see Ex. 172. This theme introduces the Paola and Francesca episode. Purgatory is, of course, a place of transition, a time for cleansing and preparation. The fugue represents this process of purification – the journey of 'dolore' from 'la miseria' towards the 'tempo felice' when the soul will return to God.

There is no fugue as such in *Hunnenschlacht*, but at letter H the theme representing the Huns (who are fighting the Christians) breaks into a fierce fugato passage (see Ex. 173). This represents the climax of the struggle between the two sides, and precedes the moment of salvation for the Christians, represented by the appearance of the plainsong *Crux fidelis*. (In the score Liszt describes the tune as a 'Choral' – 13 bars after letter C – but the German word is used in its original, pre-Reformation (i.e. Roman Catholic) sense to refer to that part of the plainsong sung by more than one voice.) Earlier in the music, Liszt had put the direction 'Immer stürmischer bis zum Buchstaben H' ('Increasingly stormy as far as letter H'). Thus the fugato passage plays a rôle analogous to the

'Mephistopheles' fugue in the *Faust Symphony*: the climax of a struggle between good and evil. In *Hunnenschlacht*, the implication is that the Christians are saved by their belief in God.

Taken by themselves, the fugues of these four programmatic works themselves outline a programme: the Devil's attempt to deny God (*Faust Symphony*), Man's aspiration towards God (*Prometheus*), the passage of the soul towards God (*Dante Symphony*) and the struggle between good and evil resolved by (belief in) God (*Hunnenschlacht*). Significantly it was during the years that these works were composed (1854–7) that Liszt resolved to carry out his ambition to reform church music.

We are left with four instrumental works which have no programme: two for organ, one for piano and orchestra, and one for piano solo. Of the organ works, we may pass over the BACH fugue, since its 'programme' is a homage to Bach, the great master of fugal composition.

The 'Ad nos' fugue is another matter altogether. It is Liszt's greatest composition for the organ, and also his first. The chorale tune which forms its basis was taken from Meyerbeer's opera *Le Prophète*. Critics have expressed surprise that Liszt expended so much labour on an artificial hymn-tune – for the music is Meyerbeer's own, and not a genuine chorale. The earliest of these critics was probably Raff, who wrote to Liszt in 1850:

Do you know, it is a mystery to me how you could bring yourself to expend so much painful labour on a theme of this kind? With the same expenditure of invention you could easily have produced an original composition of the first importance, and then people would not be saying that you have to fasten upon Meyerbeer because of a lack of original invention.                (*BrZ*, 154)

Raff here fails to understand Liszt's programmatic cast of mind. Something had obviously fired his emotions to bring about this mammoth work, with its fusion of technique and imagination found only in his best works.

The work was composed in 1849 and 1850. The opera had received its first performance in Paris in 1849, but Liszt had not seen it, and at the time possessed only a vocal score of the work. The chorale is sung by the three Anabaptists who urge the people to be rebaptized in the healing waters.

The Anabaptists (or Rebaptizers) were a radical left-wing movement of the sixteenth-century Protestant Reformation. They held that infants were not punishable for sin until an awareness of good and evil emerged within them, and that only then could they exercise their own free will, repent, and accept (adult) baptism. The movement opposed the use of the sword by Christians, and were intent upon restoring the spirit of the primitive Church, being confident that they were living at the end of all

Ex. 174

ages. John of Leiden (the 'prophet' of Meyerbeer's opera) was a Dutch Anabaptist (*c.* 1509–36) who led a Protestant rebellion in the north-German city of Münster in 1534, and ruled as king.

The appeal of this should be obvious when placed in the context of a Europe torn by the revolutions of 1848–9. The symphonic poem *Héroïde funèbre*, a funeral ode for those killed in the revolutions, was composed at the same time. The organ work contains Liszt's first instrumental fugue, which was only the second fugue he had written. The first was in the 1848 Mass.

In outline, the *Fantasy and Fugue on 'Ad nos, ad salutarem undam'* resembles the 1833 piano piece *Harmonies poétiques et religieuses*, which was Liszt's first instrumental work. In both pieces a chorale-like theme is anticipated during the first half, and then stated quietly. The anticipations are often stormy, and consist of transformations of parts of the theme. The main difference between the two pieces, however, is the fugue in the organ work. The chorale in the piano piece never reaches triumph; the music ends in despair. The fugue in the organ work, however, which occurs after quiet ruminations on the chorale, leads to its triumphant statement at the end of the work. The emotional scheme is the four-part one: lament (the Fantasy); prayer (the first appearance of the chorale, which is quiet); struggle (the fugue); triumph (the last appearance of the chorale). It is significant that this scheme, which was later to be used in Liszt's greatest works, appears first in an organ work written at the very beginning of the Weimar period. It points clearly to the rôle religion was to play.

Meyerbeer's chorale (see Ex. 174) is in 6/4 time. Liszt changes the time signature and alters the mode from minor to major, significantly choosing the 'mystical' key of F♯ (often used by Liszt in religious pieces, for example the piano pieces *Bénédiction de Dieu dans la solitude* and *Jeux d'eau à la Villa d'Este*, which contains the quotation from St John 'The water that I shall give him shall be in him a well of water springing up into everlasting life' – *cf.* the 'healing waters' idea behind Meyerbeer's chorale) for the initial statement of his own version of the chorale (Peters Edition, p. 22).

# Liszt's programmatic use of fugue

Moderato

Ex. 175

Thus in Liszt's organ piece the 'real' chorale is not Meyerbeer's at all, but his own version, itself more like a genuine chorale than Meyerbeer's. In that sense the title of the work is misleading. The 'programme' is quite simply the process of change whereby the 'mystical' version achieves substance in its triumphant statement that ends the work. This is in C major, the real world as compared to the world of F♯ major. To arrive at this stage it has to pass through the fugue.

In his study of Liszt's organ music, Peter Schwarz writes: 'Die Fuge der "Ad nos-Fantasie" . . . ist nicht Ersatz eines Finalsatzes, sodern eine bewusste Konzentration des vergangenen musikalischen Vorgangs auf einer anderen, höheren Ebene.' ('The fugue of the "Ad nos–Fantasy . . . is not in itself a closing section, but a conscious intensification of the earlier musical procedures towards another, higher plane.').[1] From the programmatic point of view, the C major statement of the chorale is not so much on a higher plane as a more immediate one. The distant vision is the F♯ major version; the fugue represents the effort needed to raise ourselves up to that level, so we see God face to face, as it were.

Liszt starts the work in Meyerbeer's key of C minor, but gives the music an air of restless gloom, retaining something of Meyerbeer's rhythmic shape in the 'anticipations' of the chorale which form the work's first (lament) section (see Ex. 175). The smooth crotchets of the chorale's (unharmonized) first appearance in F♯ introduce a mood of serenity to the second (prayer) section. This mood is maintained for several pages, all in the key of F♯, until a dramatic outburst returns the music to C minor ('Allegro deciso'; Peters Edition, p. 32) and introduces the fugue subject. This takes its rhythm from the opening (lament) section of the work (see Ex. 176). Its effect is to introduce a new purposefulness into the music. In that sense Liszt equates 'struggle' (in the four-part scheme) with effort. Thus in Liszt's first use of fugue in an instrumental work he assigns to it an emotional significance that corresponds to the peculiarities of fugal technique. On the one hand, because fugue is difficult to write, he used it to represent effort or struggle; on the other hand, what is usually called the 'working out' of a fugue Liszt imbued with his religious belief. Fugue represents purposefulness, and God is

Ex. 176

our purpose. In this manner Liszt gives a unified programmatic purpose to all his fugues, both choral and instrumental.

*Totentanz* is a set of variations on the *Dies irae* plainchant, for piano and orchestra. It was initially inspired by the frescoes at Pisa depicting the Triumph of Death. We may prefer to assume that Liszt simply let his imagination roam freely, paying attention to the demands of coherence rather than story-telling. Yet Vladimir Stasov wrote of a visit to Liszt in 1869: 'He refused to tell us the programme of the *Totentanz*, saying he felt that this was one of those works "whose content must not be made public". Thus, it remains an enigma to everyone.'[2] Bartók, whose admiration for Liszt was the result of deep and prolonged study, wrote of *Totentanz*:

This composition, which is simply a set of variations on the Gregorian melody 'Dies irae', is astonishingly harsh from beginning to end. But what do we find in the middle section? A variation hardly eight bars long, of almost Italianate emotionalism. Here Liszt obviously intended to relieve the overwhelming austerity and darkness with a ray of hope. The work as a whole always has a profound effect upon me, but this short section sticks out so from the unified style of the rest that I have never been able to feel that it is appropriate.[3]

The passage in question (Eulenburg Edition, p. 24) is in B major, and Liszt marks an optional cut which would result in its omission and lead the preceding variation straight into the fugato. This is a furiously energetic affair whose subject is simply the 'Dies irae' tune turned into semiquavers (see Ex. 177). It leads to a grand statement by the piano of the 'Dies irae' tune in B major which, although brief, is really the emotional climax of the work, occurring at about the mid-point. (The optional cuts of course make the exact proportions of the work rather flexible.) Now, B major is at the farthest remove from D minor; it corresponds to the F♯–C relationship used in the 'Ad nos' piece (regarding D minor as the subsidiary of F major), but in this case the emotional pattern is reversed. The 'mystical' key is chosen for the climax, and the 'reality' is in D minor. All the preceding music (the theme and three

Ex. 177

variations) is in D minor. Variation IV is still in D, but without the key signature – in other words it is modal. Liszt marked it 'Lento (canonique)'. The optional B major nocturne-like section then leads to the fugato.

Bartók objected to the 'ray of hope' in this section, but he at least acknowledged what he found. Both canon and fugue are particularly associated with the Church. Anyone who reads the words of the 'Dies irae' sequence will find exactly this ray of hope towards the middle: 'Salva me, fons pietatis'; 'Mihi quoque spem dedisti'; 'Voca me cum benedictis'. If the B major section before the fugato is a ray of hope, then the B major conclusion of the fugato is certainly a triumph. The fugato itself starts in D minor. For all its energy it has an element of caricature about it; when the orchestra joins in it is marked 'Marcato scherzando', a rare use by Liszt of the word 'scherzando'. He here uses a Mephisto technique, but in reverse; this time it is death itself that is mocked. With elation, Liszt describes in a brief but blinding flash the possibility of triumph over death. This is why he chose to treat the theme fugally at this point.

The Piano Sonata conflates the movements of a sonata with sonata form itself to produce one gigantic first-movement structure. It is therefore of interest to note that the fugue is strategically placed: it corresponds to the scherzo. The four main sections of the work are the exposition (which goes into a development section), the slow movement, the fugal scherzo, and the recapitulation, which functions as a finale. The fugue subject itself is fashioned by dovetailing two themes heard previously. It is Liszt's only example of fugal writing for the piano, and is widely regarded as his most successful fugue. Its position in the structure of the work corresponds to that in which Liszt uses fugue in the lament–prayer–struggle–triumph scheme in his programme music. Although the fugue subject has no tangible connection with words, it clearly performs a major rôle in the unfolding drama of the work. Critics praise the Sonata for its grand and ingenious design, its dazzling use of thematic transformation, its sense of heroic struggle – and above all because it is 'absolute' music. If this really is the case, is it not odd that out of Liszt's 17 fugues, 16 of which are demonstrably programmatic in both origin and intent, the best constructed, most strikingly characterized and dramatically effective example should occur in a work with no programme? Should we not rather assume that the Sonata does have a programme, and see if it cannot be deduced from internal evidence to be found in the music?

# 14

# LISZT'S CROSS MOTIF AND THE
# PIANO SONATA IN B MINOR

The Piano Sonata is unusual in that it makes use of sonata form. This might be expected in a work with this title, but Liszt's symphonies and concertos generally avoid the form. The E♭ Piano Concerto has an improvisatory first movement, while the A major Concerto has no first movement as such, being a set of variations. The 'Inferno' movement of the *Dante Symphony* is in a ternary form; what sounds like the second subject of an exposition (the Paola and Francesca episode) is not recapitulated, and proves to be a lyrical middle section surrounded by the stormy music depicting Hell. The first movement of the *Faust Symphony*, whilst following the outline of sonata form, has no development section. This section is replaced by the first subject, transposed from C minor into C♯ minor, and the music of the introduction.

In the symphonies, these peculiarities of form are determined by the programme. Liszt wished to depict Paola and Francesca in Hell; obviously once was sufficient, and to repeat the music would have made no sense. His portrayal of Faust is described as 'a character portrait'; but what 'happens' to Faust occurs in the 'Gretchen' and the 'Mephistopheles' movements, and there is no 'development' of his character in the Faust movement itself. For Liszt, the whole story is itself the 'development'. That this was indeed Liszt's approach to composition emerges in a letter to Louis Köhler written in 1856:

It is a very agreeable satisfaction to me that you, dear friend, have found some interest in the scores. For, however others may judge of the things, they are for me the necessary developments of my inner experiences, which have brought me to the conviction that *invention* and *feeling* are not so entirely *evil* in Art. Certainly you very rightly observe that the *forms* (which are too often changed by quite respectable people into *formulas*) 'First Subject, Middle Subject, After Subject, etc., may very much grow into a habit, because they must be so thoroughly natural, primitive, and very easily intelligible.' Without making the slightest objection to this opinion, I only beg for permission to be allowed to decide upon the forms by the contents. (*L*, I, 273)

Obviously the programme of a work in sonata form would have to allow for both the development and the recapitulation. The problem for Liszt

# Revolution and religion

Ex. 178. Liszt's Cross motif

was that he preferred his music to tell a story that 'progresses': a recapitulation represents going over the same ground twice. In works which do
approximate to sonata form, like *Les Préludes* (symphonic poem no. 3), the
recapitulation is 'transformed' so that the recurring themes are given a
different character, usually one of energy and optimism. In the Piano
Sonata, however, the recapitulated themes are unchanged.

There are only two programmatic works by Liszt which bear this
feature: the first movement of the *Faust Symphony* and the symphonic
poem *Prometheus* (no. 5). Both pieces follow the outlines of sonata form,
and their first-subject themes, in *Faust* marked 'Allegro agitato ed
appassionato' and in *Prometheus* 'Allegro molto appassionato', are very
similar in character. But, as mentioned in the previous chapter, in
*Prometheus* Liszt marks an optional cut after the fugue, which would leave
out the recapitulation of the 'Allegro' theme. Here, clearly, the claims of
the programme were at variance with the musical form he wished to
follow (the piece originated as an overture); given the dilemma, in Liszt's
mind the programme clearly won the day, even though he left the cut as
an option for the performer. The deciding factor was the fugue, in which
Liszt portrays Prometheus's effort to will his own salvation (whereas in
Herder's play he is rescued by Hercules). This has to lead straight into
the salvation itself, rather than back to the restlessness of the opening
material. In the *Faust Symphony* the first movement – which does not contain a fugue – recapitulates normally because Faust's salvation occurs in
a later movement – the one that does contain a fugue.

In the Piano Sonata there is no optional cut; the fugue leads to a full
recapitulation. This unique feature provides one clue to the nature of the
programme. Another clue is the use of a theme that corresponds in outline to *Crux fidelis*. Liszt mentions *Crux fidelis* in his note at the end of the
full score of *St Elizabeth*, where it is one of two examples he gives of
Gregorian melodies which he used in various works, and which contain
the 'tonisches Symbol des Kreuzes' (see Ex. 178). The other melody is
the *Magnificat*, which also occurs at the end of the *Dante Symphony*. *Crux
fidelis* is also used in *Hunnenschlacht* (symphonic poem no. 11); see Ex. 179.
Here it must be remarked that Liszt evidently associated *Crux fidelis* with
the deepest and strongest feelings. This is revealed in the description of
*Hunnenschlacht* which he wrote in 1879:

# Liszt's Cross motif and the Piano Sonata

Ex. 179

Kaulbach's world-renowned picture presents two battles – the one on earth, the other in the air, according to the legend that warriors, after their death, continue fighting incessantly as spirits. In the middle of the picture appears the *Cross* and its mystic light; on this my 'Symphonic Poem' is founded. The chorale 'Crux Fidelis', which is gradually developed, illustrates the idea of the final victory of Christianity in its effectual love to God and man.                    (*L*, II, 352)

Another letter, written to his cousin Eduard Liszt in 1876, refers to the chorale in a personal context:

Your letter has deeply affected me. I preserve it in the secret cell of the heart, where the last words of my dear mother remain – and give me consolation. I cannot thank you in words. My thanks rise in prayer to God. May his blessing ever be with your generosity and constancy in all that is good.

  I absolutely wrote the 'Hunnenschlacht' for the sake of the hymn 'Crux Fidelis'.                    (*L*, II, 292)

As the words of the hymn are addressed to the Cross, this melody, more than any other, would seem to have been associated in Liszt's mind with the Cross. Liszt quotes it in his note at the end of *St Elizabeth* because it contains the Cross motif of three notes. Thus the linear version, without harmony, functioned as a symbol for Liszt. The harmony of Ex. 179, though, is characteristic. If the tonic pedal is removed, then the roots descending in thirds of the triads I, VI, IV, II give the music its character. This progression, in conjunction with the Cross motif, occurs elsewhere, for example in the piano piece *Il sospiro* (see Ex. 180), and the song *Über allen Gipfeln ist Ruh* (see Ex. 181), both composed in 1848. The linear version is everywhere in Liszt. Consider the slow movement of the E♭ Piano Concerto and its transformation into a march for the finale. It can be found in all the symphonic poems, including the last one, *From the Cradle to the Grave*. And is not the opening, so-called 'yearning' theme of the *Faust Symphony* (see Ex. 182) the three-note motif (see Ex. 183) in disguise? And does this not illuminate Liszt's use of the Faust story as simply another parable of redemption – in particular redemption through love?

  At the end of his life, in 1884, Liszt commented on his use of the motif.

# Revolution and religion

Ex. 180. *Il sospiro*, bars 69–70 (reduced score, omitting arpeggios)

[from the opening bars of the piano part]

Ex. 181. *Über allen Gipfeln ist Ruh*, opening (piano part only)

Ex. 182

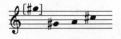

Ex. 183

One of his pupils performed Liszt's transcription of the *Solemn March to the Holy Grail from Parsifal* (S450) in one of his lessons. August Göllerich, who kept a diary of these lessons, recorded Liszt's reaction to the music:

Vom Gralthema sagte er, 'das sind uns sehr wohlbekannte Intervalle, die habe ich oft und oft geschrieben! Z.B. in der "Elisabeth". – Wagner sagte auch, "nun,

286

Ex. 184

Ex. 185

du wirst schauen wie ich Dich bestollen habt!" – Übrigens sind das Katholische, alte Intervalle und also hab's auch ich es nicht erfunden.'

(Of the Grail theme he said, 'Those intervals are very well known to me, as I have written them time and time again! for example in the "Elizabeth". – Wagner himself said, "Now you can see how I have stolen from you!" – However, they are old Catholic intervals, and so even I did not invent them myself.')[1]

The theme from *Parsifal* in Liszt's piano arrangement (see Ex. 184) should be compared with Liszt's *Crux fidelis* chord sequence. Liszt's comment above was recorded after Wagner's death, and Wagner may well have taken this music from him. It is usually called the 'Dresden Amen', but when Mendelssohn incorporated this Amen into his 'Reformation' Symphony in 1830 it did not include the opening three notes of Wagner's theme, which give the music its noble character, and which correspond exactly to Liszt's Cross motif with Liszt's own favourite harmony.

The linear version of the Cross motif occurs in the fugue subject of the Piano Sonata (see Ex. 185). The subject is constructed by joining together two themes (marked 'A' and 'B') heard separately beforehand, theme A containing the three note Cross motif (marked 'x'). Herein lies the first indication of the contents of the programme. The second lies in

287

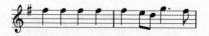

Ex. 186. Themes from the Piano Sonata quoted in Liszt's letter

Ex. 187

theme B, about which Liszt has something to say in one of his letters:

Of pianoforte music I have nothing more to send you . . . except the little 'Berceuse' . . . The thing ought properly to be played in an American rocking-chair . . . so that the player may, willy-nilly, give himself up to a dreamy condition, rocked by the regular movement of the *chair-rhythm*. It is only when the B♭ minor comes in that there are a couple of painful accents . . . But why am I talking such nonsense with you? – Your very perspicuous discovery of my intention in the second motive of the Sonata [Liszt quotes Ex. 186] in contrast with the previous hammer-blows [Ex. 187] perhaps led me to it.               (*L*, I, 190)

Liszt here points out the connection beetwen the two themes: one is a transformation of the other. In the Sonata they function as separate identities, however, whereas other themes are recognizably themselves even when 'transformed'. Thus, though 'the same', these two themes must represent different things in the programme. The first of the two themes is marked 'cantando espressivo' at its first appearance in the work, and has the character of a romantic nocturne, exactly corresponding to Liszt's words 'the player may . . . give himself up to a dreamy condition'. At its second appearance, in the 'slow movement' section of the work, it is marked 'dolcissimo con intimo sentimento'. Fairly obviously it belongs to the general category of 'love' themes. The other theme Liszt describes as 'hammer-blows', and at its first appearance, it is indeed marked 'f marcato'. It could not be more different in character from the 'love' theme, yet it is a version of that same theme. Where else do we find in Liszt's programme music a similar use of a distorted 'love' theme? The answer is: in the 'Mephistopheles' movement of the *Faust Symphony*.

As noted in the previous chapter, the subject of the fugue in this movement is a distorted version of Faust's 'love' ('affettuoso') theme. Much of the movement is based on this theme, which is chosen to represent the Devil's attack upon God in the fugue. Liszt portrays the Devil in terms of a 'love' theme because the Devil's function is to turn Man away from the love of God. If the 'hammer-blows' theme represents Satan, this leads us

Ex. 188

to another clue about the programme. The first appearance of the 'love' theme is preceded by, or rather introduced by, the 'Satan' theme. To be exact, the 'Satan' theme turns itself into the 'love' theme (see Ex. 188). Does this 'transformation' not immediately recall the words of chapter 3 of Genesis, 'The serpent was more crafty than any wild creature that the Lord God had made'? And if so, why should Liszt turn the serpent into a 'love' theme? In the Garden of Eden Eve listened to the serpent: 'Of course you will not die. God knows that as soon as you eat, your eyes will be opened and you will be like gods knowing both good and evil.' The serpent seduced Eve, who seduced Adam, and brought about the Fall of Man. Could this be part of Liszt's programme? The possibility certainly goes some way to explaining its secrecy. If so, what do the other themes represent?

Here we return to theme A. In the fugue it is linked to theme B (the 'Satan' theme) to make one continuous line. But in the exposition of the Sonata the two themes are combined, theme A in the right hand, theme B in the left, to act as the first-subject material (see Ex. 189). Nevertheless, the separate characters of the themes are preserved; theme A is

289

Ex. 189

'agitato' and theme B is 'marcato'. The effect is of two adversaries locked in mortal combat. In theme A the Cross motif is prominent. Later in the work, the recapitulation states the same material unchanged. The adversaries remain locked in combat. Somehow, the programme must allow for this feature. Drawing on the *Faust Symphony* for assistance, we may note that Mephistopheles is depicted as an aspect of Faust himself; but in that work Liszt was concerned to create a psychological portrait. In the Sonata the 'Satan' theme has an identity of its own. The parallel would be to give Faust an identity of his own. So does theme A represent Faust? Is the Sonata simply another Faust work?

Critics like to refer to it as such; they sense that some kind of great drama is being played out along the lines of the symphony. But the 'Faust' theme, if such it is, quite clearly contains the Cross motif. As noted earlier, this motif is used by Liszt to represent the path to God, the symbol of redemption. The first-subject material therefore represents the eternal struggle between Satan and an adversary containing within itself the power of redemption. Liszt appears to be thinking along theological lines. If so, theme A must represent Man, and the first-subject material therefore depicts the struggle between Man and the Devil.

Certainly this is a favourite theme of Liszt's. His 'Mephisto' music is generally agreed to be immensely effective, and there are many examples. Yet the Sonata as a whole is not Mephisto music. We have already seen how the 'Satan' theme is related to, and at one point transforms itself into, the 'love' theme. It has been suggested that this might depict the Fall. If so, is there a theme representing God? The *Faust Symphony* contains the 'zum Anfang' theme which clearly refers to Faust's 'longing for revelation'. The equivalent in the Sonata is the splendid theme in D major, marked simply 'Grandioso' (Ex. 190). This is certainly one of the most impressive passages in all Liszt, if not the most impressive. For our purposes though, the real clue is that it corresponds in

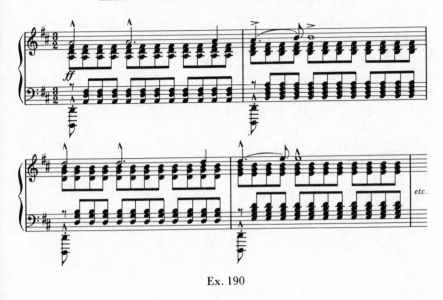

Ex. 190

harmony and outline to the chorale *Crux fidelis*, and that it not only contains the Cross motif, but *is* the Cross motif, magnified to immense proportions. The ingredients of the programme identified so far are therefore Man, Satan, God and the Fall. How many further unidentified themes remain?

The work as a whole is remarkably economical in its use of basic material; Liszt makes a little go a long way. So far, four themes have been identified, two of which ('love' and 'Satan') are versions of each other. There remain two others, one at the beginning of the work, and one in the middle. The form of the work, as noted in the previous chapter, combines sonata form with the basic four-movement plan found in symphonic works, all within a single-movement work. Thus the Sonata contains a 'slow movement' section. It is here that we find a completely new theme, significantly in Liszt's 'mystical' key of F♯ major (see Ex. 191). Clues to its programmatic significance are afforded by examining the structure of this 'slow movement'. The new theme is followed by the 'love' theme, in A major. The key then reverts to F♯, and the 'God' theme appears, initially in the lower register, but then extended by the addition of music full of almost operatic passion. Liszt constructs this out of the descending phrase that originally occurred at the end of the 'God' theme; this time, however, he makes it rise upwards a seventh before it descends, producing an effect of infinite yearning, a sort of striving upwards. The

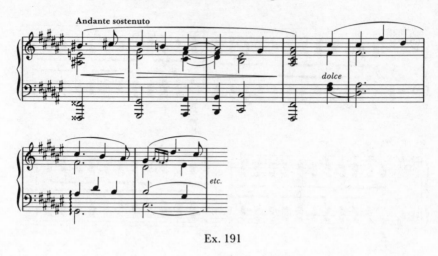

Ex. 191

Ex. 192

process is repeated in G minor, and at the climax the Cross motif from the 'Man' theme appears fortissimo in the bass, but played with the right hand, which returns to repeat the 'yearning upwards' phrase. This is repeated with mounting fervour, building up to an immense climax in which the new theme appears (marked 'fff'), again in F♯ major. This is the apex of the work, the emotional high-point, and the psychological turning-point. This, one feels, is what the Sonata is all about.

Given the ingredients identified so far, the 'slow movement' can represent only one thing: the redemption of Man after the Fall. If this is so, we would expect the 'Fall' episode to be omitted in the recapitulation. Examination of the music reveals this to be the case; the 'God' theme leads straight into the 'love' theme.

We are left with one unidentified theme, the very opening of the work (see Ex. 192). This music is hesitant, groping, mysterious, dark. The falling notes of the scale give the effect of motion coming out of stillness, diversity out of unity. Surely this is a portrayal of Creation? 'In the beginning of creation, when God made heaven and earth, the earth was without form and void, and darkness over the face of the abyss.'

We are now ready to consider the whole programme, presented here in the words of a lecture given at Cambridge in 1963 under the auspices of the Divinity Faculty, and described as 'what was known as the scheme of salvation':

It began with an alleged rebellion of Satan against God in which angels fell. By direct acts of God, Adam and Eve were created, apparently as adults, not only innocent but fully righteous. Their descendants were intended to restore the number of the angels depleted by the heavenly revolt. Moved by envy, Satan persuaded our first parents to disobey one absolute command of God, that they were not to obtain knowledge, and so brought about their fall from original righteousness, in consequence of which they transmitted to all their offspring, by natural generation, a corrupted nature wholly inclined to evil, an enfeebled will, and also the guilt of their sin. Thus all mankind lay under the curse of sin both original and actual, justly the object of Divine wrath and destined to damnation. In order to restore his thwarted purpose God sent his Son who, assuming human nature, was born on earth, whereon was wrought the drama of his death and resurrection. Jesus, pure from all defect of original and actual sin, alone fulfilled the conditions of a perfect sacrifice for human sin. By this God's legitimate anger with guilty mankind was appeased and his honour satisfied; he was graciously pleased to accept his Son's sacrifice, enabled to forgive sin, and man was potentially redeemed.[2]

The music of Liszt's Piano Sonata in B minor follows this in every detail. The Introduction presents, in order, Creation, Man and Satan. The first subject of the exposition presents Man in combat with Satan – we may take this to be the eternal element in human nature. The 'Man' theme then appears in duet with itself (bar 55), a clever way of suggesting Adam and Eve in Eden before the Fall. This is followed by the 'God' theme, which begins the second subject-group. The 'Fall' sequence has already been described. After the Fall, the music passes into the development section, built out of the 'Man' theme; the immense dash and verve lead to a climax, where Man appropriates to himself the 'Creation' theme – which calls forth an angry outburst (the 'God' theme in C♯ minor, 'fff pesante', bar 292). The passage that follows pits the 'Satan' theme against the 'Man' theme, the latter turning into a cry of desperation, the former becoming ever more insistent. A long-held discord resolves into F♯ major, and the new theme appears. This must represent Christ. Liszt's use of F♯ major as a 'mystical' key has been mentioned in the previous chapter. In *Christus* the only music in F♯ major occurs in the 'March of the Three Kings', where it represents Christ. The 'Christ' theme is followed by the 'love' theme, and the prominence of the Cross motif in the ensuing music, already described, points to the drama of the Crucifixion.

We can now see the significance of the fugue. Knowing that Liszt uses fugue to represent a movement towards God, it becomes clear why he constructed the fugue subject by joining the 'Man' theme with the 'Satan' theme, making a straight line in contrast to their opposition to each other elsewhere. At the end of the fugue the 'Satan' theme is dropped, and the 'Man' theme combines with itself in a dancing rhythm, leading to the recapitulation. Here the same first-subject material is presented, since Man's struggle with the Devil is eternal, but, after the coming of Christ, took place in a new context. Instead of the Eden passage, the 'Creation' theme combines with the repeated chords from the 'God' theme. The 'Creation' theme then alternates with the 'Man' theme, building up to a furious climax, at the end of which the 'Satan' theme is 'destroyed' (bar 590); Liszt introduces rests between statements of the theme exactly evoking Satan's dying convulsions. The 'God' theme follows, then the 'love' theme, recapitulated in B major. The coda of the work presents a triumphant version of the 'Man' theme in B major, together with a dancing accompaniment, leading to the most majestic statement in the work of the 'God' theme, also in B major. Originally the work ended at this point.[3] The final version ends with the 'Christ' theme in B major, followed by a passage of rising chords in the right hand, and the 'Satan' theme deep in the left-hand register marked 'p sotto voce', obviously a picture of the soul's passage to Heaven, leaving the Devil down below. The 'Man' theme finds quiescence, and the work ends, as it began, with the mysterious 'Creation' theme.

The above outline ignores details, all of which can fit into the scheme quite logically (the most obvious being the stretto version of the 'love' theme – indicating increased energy – which in the exposition follows the Fall – self-love – and leads to God's anger, but in the recapitulation follows the 'God' theme after Satan's destruction, and leads back to God at the end of the work). To accept the hypothesis, one must first accept the idea that Liszt not only *might* use a programme secretly, but that he *could* use one, and still produce a work of such stature. It is significant that the Piano Sonata is, of all Liszt's compositions, a virtuoso exercise in transformation technique; the suggested programme is itself about the transformation of Man brought about through Christ. Thus there occurs a perfect fusion of programme and technique. It is worth repeating that Liszt's other great works are programmatic – it is not impossible that the piano concertos are as well. Liszt viewed programme music as a 'legitimate genre of the art' – these words appear in English in a letter written in French (*L*, II, 329) – and it is quite irrelevant whether particular musicians and critics think 'absolute' music is superior to programme music. The greatness of the Piano Sonata is today acknowledged. Anything that might illuminate the mind of the man who composed it should be explored. If Liszt did use a programme, it is in keeping with his usual practice; furthermore, it is logical that for his single contribution to a form perfected by Beethoven[4] he should have chosen to tell in music the greatest story.

The final point to consider is the date of composition. The Piano Sonata is the first member of the trilogy completed by the *Faust Symphony* and *Christus*. The last of these was the first to be planned, Liszt's first mention of it occurring in 1853. But it is clear that he and the Princess had been discussing the idea for some time. In this case, the Piano Sonata represents a self-summing up, combining the piano with composition and Catholicism. It would be a logical step, having decided upon a musical treatment of Christ.

# 15

## LISZT'S PATH AS A COMPOSER

Any serious study of Liszt must search for the unity that underlies his varied output. Clearly this unity is not simply musical. It must either therefore not exist, or must lie in his approach to music itself. In other words, it must be psychological. In 1861 Liszt touched on the subject of his musical development in a letter describing his visits to the Comtesse d'Agoult while he was in Paris:

> The question of Wagner and the music of the future, and my own part in the modern musical movement had been touched upon several times since my first visit. I returned particularly to this subject – and told her quite firmly that I had no need of friends, or the support of a faction or the newspapers to continue on my path . . . She was struck by my voluntary isolation, and perhaps also by the strange development of my artistic life – which she had never suspected, but which now stood revealed before her eyes. Listening to me speak thus of myself, of my egoism and my ambition, of the part I give to the public and the part which is reserved for the artist himself, of the complete identity of my former efforts with my ideas of today . . . she felt I know not what emotion.    (*Br.* V, 198)

Later, in Rome, Liszt touched upon the subject of Wagner again:

> As for being miserable, I profess not to have any cause to be on my part. 'God loves a cheerful giver,' says St Paul. I leave it to Wagner to make himself miserable – I do not have his genius, and can therefore do without the things it entails! What folly to wish to fill the whole world with oneself – simply to bring upon oneself more and more misery and dissatisfaction!    (*Br.* VI, 182)

It is clear from these remarks that Liszt did not regard himself as in any sense a rival of Wagner's, if only because the two men occupied different ground. Yet during his lifetime Liszt was constantly derided as an inferior Wagner who followed feebly in the great man's footsteps, a view not extinct today. It is important to see that Liszt never trod Wagner's path; which is not to say that Wagner did not try to follow Liszt.

A third remark provides the clue to Liszt's whole musical life: 'My life has been nothing but a long quest for the path of love, singularly guided by music, the art at once both satanic and divine: more than any other, it leads us into temptation' (*HFL*, 287). Here we have in juxtaposition all the familiar elements of Liszt's art. When do they first appear, and what relationship do they bear to one another?

Let us take first the theme of love. Liszt's first songs, composed in Rome at the age of 27, were settings of three of Petrarch's sonnets. They are love poems, and though the piano solo versions are in various keys, the songs are all in A♭ major. They established the association in Liszt's music between A♭ major and the theme of love. It is found repeatedly. The three *Liebesträume*, originally songs, are in A♭, as is the 'Gretchen' movement of the *Faust Symphony*, the only orchestral piece by Liszt written in that key. The basic key of the symphony is C minor, but the 'Chorus mysticus' that closes the work is in C major. The key changes to A♭, however, for the entry of the voice with the words 'Das Ewig-Weibliche Zieht uns hinan' ('Eternal Womanhood leads us above'), sung to the main theme of the 'Gretchen' movement. In the *Faust Symphony* Liszt portrays love as the power that transforms Faust and overcomes Mephistopheles, in other words as the bringer of redemption. The idea of redemption through love is basic to both Liszt and Wagner. Liszt, however, treats love, human love, as stemming from God, and therefore sacred. In 1845, for example, in the text of *Le Forgeron* by Lamennais, these words occur:

> Oh, que la vie est rude!
> Mais l'amour l'adoucit.
> Que ses maux sont nombreux!
> Mais le courage les dompte.
> Courage donc, frères,
> Ne cédons pas, luttons, oui, luttons,
> Luttons en hommes, Dieu sera pour nous,
> Il nous regarde d'en haut.

> (Oh, how hard life is!
> But it is softened by love.
> How many are life's evils!
> But courage overcomes them.
> Courage then, brothers,
> Let us not give up, but struggle on,
> Struggle as men, and God will be with us,
> He watches us from on high.)

The key signature is one sharp, but at the words 'Mais l'amour l'adoucit' the music goes straight into A♭ major. Furthermore the text points a connection between love and courage. In Liszt's music the words 'Courage donc, frères' are set in the key of E major with a change of key signature to four sharps. E major is the key of much of Liszt's religious music, including *The Legend of St Elizabeth* and *Christus*. 'The Beatitudes', the first part of *Christus* to be composed, is in E major. In the *Faust Symphony* the 'zum Anfang' theme of the Faust movement is in E major, as is the 'amoroso' second-subject theme. This use of A♭ major and E major points the connection between love and divinity. But love is also a moral force in Liszt, and gives the courage to fight against evil. In *Christus* the 'Stabat mater dolorosa' has a key signature of four flats. Here, however, it signifies F minor, but the relationship to A♭ is surely intended, since Christ died as a symbol of God's love for mankind, and the piece describes the Crucifixion. Similarly, the only symphonic poem in F minor, *Héroïde funèbre*, is an elegy for those who died in the 1848–9 revolutions; the fragment of the Marseillaise that appears in the middle points to the cause for which they died, and links revolution and religion in Liszt's music via the common theme of martyrdom. The piano piece *Funérailles*, also in F minor, should be mentioned in this context.

'To love is to ascend into Heaven', wrote Liszt (*LOM*, 51). It should be stressed that, far from sentimentalizing the theme of love, Liszt made it the basis of his musical work, seeing in it the foundation of a religious view of human psychology. In this he drew upon experience, pointing the moral that love is a gift, and brings with it a new awareness. Like music, it links the human and the divine, and can be misused.

This leads us to a consideration of Liszt's statement that music is 'the art at once both satanic and divine'. The first thing we are likely to think of is the number of pieces by Liszt that describe Hell, death, Mephistopheles and the macabre. They are among his most celebrated works. Together they add up to a Lisztian portrait of evil. More importantly, in the *Faust Symphony* we are given a psychological portrait of Satan himself.

It may be argued that Goethe's Mephistopheles is not the same as the Biblical Satan. But here we are considering Liszt, not Goethe, and in the music are certain clues to what Liszt was thinking. Furthermore we have Liszt's own words as authority for assuming that he imposed his own interpretation upon the Faust legend. Writing from Rome in 1864 to the Comtesse d'Agoult he said:

I am restraining my impatience to know what is to follow your discussion on *Dante and Goethe* [published in 1864 in the *Revue Germanique et Française*] ... You know that these same poetic subjects have long held my attention, and that I too have applied myself to them in so far as they seemed to me to relate to music and to myself. (*LMA*, II, 410)

We should therefore assume both works, the *Faust* and *Dante* symphonies, to be autobiographical. It is relevant to note that both works were first planned as operas. Undoubtedly Liszt's reason for changing them into symphonies is not unrelated to his remarks quoted above.

In the 'Mephistopheles' movement of the *Faust Symphony* is the theme which occurs in another work of Liszt's, the *Malédiction Concerto*, discovered after his death. The title is not Liszt's own, but derives from the fact that in the manuscript the word appears over the opening theme. 'Malédiction', of course, means 'curse'. Over the theme that also appears in the 'Mephistopheles' movement is written 'orgueil' ('pride'). So clearly Liszt used the theme with a programmatic intention. The interesting point is that in the symphony there is nothing written in the score to inform us that the theme signifies 'pride'. The other themes in the movement are parodies of those in the Faust movement. Thus we have the clear idea that pride is the source of corruption. We could not know this is if the manuscript of the *Malédiction Concerto* had not been discovered.

The date of its composition is not known, and has to be deduced from the manuscript handwriting, which is not Liszt's. Humphrey Searle dates it as *c.* 1840, possibly earlier. However, parts of the work exist in separate manuscripts by Liszt, each with an earlier date. The opening 'Malédiction' theme occurs in a sketch book which dates from the early 1830s. More remarkably, 16 pages of a concerto for piano and strings exist which contain three themes later used in the *Malédiction Concerto*, which are presumed to be what remains of a work performed by Liszt in London in 1827, which Moscheles described as containing 'chaotic beauties'.

We have now arrived back at Liszt's adolescent years. Moscheles' remark is highly significant because all Liszt's youthful works are the opposite of chaotic. Searle calls them 'the products of a clever schoolboy who happened also to be a brilliant pianist' (*SML*, 2); earlier he remarks that the music written in Liszt's teens 'shows practically no individuality at all' (*SML*, 1). What does characterize these works is their symmetry and neat, sectional organization. Many of them are brilliant variations on some pleasant tune, often operatic, and in the Czernian mould. They show a complete mastery of a certain style. This is true of the opera *Don Sanche* written in 1824–5, which is remarkable for being unremarkable considering who composed it; yet it shows a melodic gift and a familiarity with the different types of aria fashionable at the time. Quite clearly opera was a natural medium for Liszt the young composer. But everything is correct and controlled, the Allegros are busy in the conventional way of Italian opera, while the slow melodies are gently sentimental and perfectly uninteresting. None of this is at all Lisztian. 'Chaotic beauties', on the other hand, most decidedly are. 1827, it seems, saw the birth of the real Liszt, the Liszt who used music to portray himself.

1827 was also the year Liszt first felt a desire to become a priest, a desire thwarted by his father, who died the same year. Twice subsequently Liszt wanted to enter the Church, and on each occasion his desire was thwarted. This period of Liszt's life discomfits most of the composer's biographers, but it is interesting to note Liszt's own remarks added to a copy, now in the Library of Congress, of Johann Wilhelm Christern's *Franz Liszt's Leben und Wirken* published in 1841, and considered to be the first Liszt biography.[1] Christern's style, which is romantic and flowery, calls forth much censure from Liszt, but a rare comment of praise occurs at the passage describing the conflicts in the soul of the young musician between duty to his art and his religious feelings: 'This page is very nicely written' ('Diese Seite ist sehr hübsch geschrieben'). Liszt cuts Christern's claim that he wrote Masses 'without the excitement, the irritation of his soul allowing him to concentrate', adding that it had been his wish 'to live in a monastery and to compose sacred music like another Beato Angelico'. All this refers to the period before 1830. Christern's attempts to deal with Liszt's love life call forth the following from Liszt: 'This whole *Love Paragraph* must out – another (short) connection must be found with what follows.' Regarding 1830 Liszt adds: 'The "Symphonie révolutionnaire", although completely sketched and partly worked out, must be left out of this biography.'

The interest of this lies in that the features familiar to us from Liszt's music here first coalesce in his life, and at exactly the same period, namely around 1830. Why should Liszt want to excise the reference to the *Revolutionary Symphony*? It is important to consider the date of his remarks – they were for a projected second edition in 1842, which did not in the event appear. Thus they represent his thoughts before the Weimar period, and before he started composing church music. We should note the ease with which Liszt accepts the religious element, and his reference to an Italian painter when imagining himself composing church music. Yet it is the religious element that biographers would have us believe Liszt suppressed, choosing instead the fleshpots and a career as a virtuoso. What Liszt himself chose to suppress is an account of his love affairs and any mention of his music for the revolution. They must be 'left out of this biography'. The implication seems to be that they may be included at a later date, on the assumption that by the end of his career, and his life, Liszt will have had the time to resolve these discordant features. Musically they coalesced to form the Cross motif, which symbolized all three – love, revolution and religion. Redemption through love was the clarion call of the Romantics, but Liszt had to live through its separate ingredients before he could weld them into a unity, at which point he produced his great choral and orchestral works. Liszt's desire to enter the Church first occurred when he was about 16, and is clearly connected with the awakening of the emotional life that occurs during adolescence. In so far as his childhood had been happy, and he was now experiencing a disturbance of that happiness, the Church symbolized this sense of loss, which, to the extent that it causes the desire to regain what is lost, lies at the root of Liszt's attitude to God. When Liszt composed the theme which he called 'Malédiction' he put this attitude into music. The primary definition of 'curse' is the wrath of God, the punishment for having disobeyed the divine law. To return to God, the curse must be lifted.

In the *Malédiction Concerto* the 'curse' theme is immediately followed by a piano cadenza based, rather startlingly, on the triads of F and B major, a tritone apart. In Liszt's later music, the tritone symbolizes the Devil. For example, the second *Mephisto Waltz* ends with the notes B and F alone. Other examples abound. Liszt, already in the 1830s, identified the Devil as the reason for the curse.

Here we have, psychologically speaking, the origin of Liszt's approach to programme music. If music is divine, then the purpose of men is to use it to return to God. The path to the divine is blocked by the Devil, who must be overcome. In Liszt the Devil is the explanation for man's seduction away from God, which in turn explains God's anger, and why men are cursed. The sense of being cursed derives from the desire for restoration to an imagined former estate. In biblical terms, redemption is preceded by the Fall of Man brought about by Satan.

In the *Malédiction Concerto* the tritone music is followed by the theme marked 'pride'. Here we find the same idea as that used in the *Faust Symphony*: Satan as pride. In the symphony, Mephistopheles is not an independent character; he is the dark side of Faust himself. This is a way of saying that pride, or selfishness, is what estranges Man from God, and it must be overcome in order to attain divine happiness. For Faust this is achieved through his love for Gretchen.

The histrionic character of the *Malédiction Concerto* suggests very strongly that Liszt was acting out a drama. The music starts in E minor and ends in E major, Liszt's 'religious' key. A theme marked 'teneramente amoroso' appears near the beginning, and at the end reappears marked 'ff delirando', while the 'pride' theme is 'transformed'. At the centre of the work a long unaccompanied passage for the piano, marked 'recitativo', has the words 'disperato' and 'Andante lacrimoso' over the music, which starts with the 'curse' theme. The following section progresses towards a climax where the 'curse' theme appears in the orchestra, after which the 'devil' tritone piano cadenza leads the music into a triumphant E major close. At this point the 'pride' theme is transformed and marked 'ffff avec enthousiasme', clearly the climax of the whole work, the 'curse' theme having left the scene. The subject of the work is therefore really the 'pride' theme rather than the 'curse' theme. The curse is lifted by a transformation of pride with the help of love. The same idea is described in the *Faust Symphony*, with the difference that 'pride' is personified as Mephistopheles. Liszt's real point here, symbolized by his parody of Faust's themes, is that Mephistopheles represents the element in Man's nature that estranges him from God. The music gives us Liszt's interpretation of the Faust legend, rather than Goethe's. In both the symphony and the concerto love dissolves pride. In the *Malédiction Concerto* Liszt clearly depicted the drama that later formed the basis of the Sonata and the *Faust Symphony* – the idea of redemption that lies behind the Cross motif, and led to the composition of *Christus*.

Here we must consider the rôle of thematic transformation in Liszt's serious works. It is nonsense to pretend that the *Malédiction Concerto* is absolute music, just as it is equally evident that Liszt's use of the 'pride' theme from it in the *Faust Symphony* is more than fortuitous. At the very least it shows that in 1854 Liszt remembered an unpublished work of his dating from 20 years earlier. The only reason for connecting the two could have been programmatic. Liszt's favoured musical form was throughout his life variation form, but in his serious works variation came to play a dramatic rôle, not just a formal one, and this rôle was entirely connected with Liszt's universal preoccupation with the theme of redemption. In the orchestral works redemption equals transformation, and this is clearly the function it has to fulfil, at a stroke explaining how Liszt could revolutionize form by giving primacy to the content. The content was never without meaning, and from this derived the programme. Hence the absence in Liszt of any true development process in the Beethovenian sense. In Liszt the music has a representative function, and is altered by a dramatic process. Writing in 1857 to his cousin Eduard about the E♭ Piano Concerto, after quoting the theme of the finale and then the slow movement, Liszt said:

It is only an urgent recapitulation of the earlier subject-matter with quickened, livelier rhythm, and contains no new motive, as will be clear to you by a glance through the score. This kind of *binding together* and rounding off a whole piece at its close is somewhat my own, but it is quite maintained and justified from the standpoint of musical form. (*L*, I, 330)

Earlier in the letter, he spoke of *Les Préludes*, 'which, by the way, are only the *prelude* to my path of composition'. In 1856, when Alexander Ritter asked for some of the symphonic poems, Liszt replied:

You desire *Orpheus*, *Tasso*, and *Festklänge* from me, dear friend! *But* have you considered that *Orpheus* has no proper *working out section*, and hovers quite simply between bliss and woe, breathing out reconciliation in Art? Pray do not forget that *Tasso* celebrates no *psychic* triumph, which an ingenious critic has already denounced (probably mindful of the 'inner camel', which Heine designates as an indispensable necessity of German aestheticism!). (*L*, I, 296)

Quite clearly Liszt was conscious of his own approach. The 'path' from *Les Préludes* led to, among others, *Christus*.

# Liszt's path as a composer

Not all the symphonic poems use thematic transformation; *Orpheus*, for example has none. It cannot be coincidence that this work represents the holy power of music. There are 12 symphonic poems (the later no. 13, *From the Cradle to the Grave*, being not part of the original set), but the last to be composed was no. 10, Hamlet, which uses transformation but contains no redemption: 'I am not dissatisfied with it,' wrote Liszt, 'He [Hamlet] remains just as he is, pale, fevered, suspended between heaven and earth, prisoner of his doubt and lack of resolve!' (*Br.* III, 111). This contradicts the remarks made about Liszt's attitude to Hamlet quoted by Searle (*SML*, 4). These remarks refer to Bogumil Dawison's interpretation of the rôle, of which Liszt says 'his conception of the rôle of Hamlet is quite new' (*Br.* III, 58). There is no reason, however, to assume that Liszt copied Dawison's interpretation in his own symphonic poem, for which he clearly had his own conception. Furthermore Searle is wrong when he says the work was written 'as an overture to Shakespeare's play', which it was not. Liszt himself gave his reason for writing it: 'As one was missing to make my symphonic poems a dozen . . . I have just thrown off a *Hamlet*. We tried it yesterday with the orchestra' (*Br.* III, 111). As with Faust, Liszt clearly chose the subject for his own musical and psychological reasons, its importance lying in the fact that it was the last of the set to be composed, and was composed precisely to make up the set. In that sense it represents the keystone, and is in contrast to all the others in that it describes failure, not success, in terms of the transformation of themes. (Ophelia is not a Gretchen figure, hence her original omission entirely from the music – her shadowy appearance was added later.) In this way, Liszt points the moral of the whole set.

It is significant that Liszt first began to put this to music in the 1830s, since those were the years when he was a follower of Lamennais and a supporter of movements towards social reform. His defence of Lamennais to the Comtesse d'Agoult showed that he did not regard the 'curse' as applying simply to the individual, private man, but by extension to society at large:

Don't you think that this indifference, this sacrilegious neglect of the fate of our unfortunate brothers which has withered our hearts may not also be a consequence of our corrupt nature to which violence must be done? . . . Don't you see the devouring, all-powerful flames of charity ceaselessly turning round and round within a circle of selfishness, 'Oh, if you knew what it is to love'?

(*LMA*, I, 91)

With these words Liszt nailed his colours to the mast, not only in life but also in music, for Liszt did not separate the two. The 'circle of selfishness' is the curse depicted in the *Malédiction Concerto*. Already in 1834 Liszt invoked love as the antidote. From this follows the connection in Liszt's music between revolution and religion, a connection he found

303

personified in the Abbé Lamennais, whose influence must ultimately be seen behind all Liszt's serious works.

By 1847, when he met the Princess Wittgenstein, Liszt had formed a clear picture of the character of Satan. After reading Milton's 'Paradise Lost' he wrote to her:

> Satan is restless and active, holds forth, struggles hard, argues, engages in diplomatic negotiations, etc. Now to my mind, Satan has no business to be doing all these things. Satan, made great and of infinite dimension, can only be Doubt, speechless Dejection, grasping Silence. Of course he emits – as the Sun–Spirit of Darkness – rays of Death and Negation – but deep within himself remains untouched by them. He does not negate, he does not die – he suffers in doubt. Truly a Satan of this calibre does not easily lend itself to portrayal in epic and rhyme – but if I am not mistaken, it seems to me that such a figure would lie more in accord with today's poetic sentiments.                    (*Br.* VI, 15)

Liszt here sees Satan not as a character, but as a state of mind, which explains why he turned away from Goethe's Mephistopheles, whose cynicism and wit make him almost attractive. To express doubt and negation Liszt resorted to musical parody for the very good reason that these things can only exist in relation to what is being doubted and negated. This corresponds to Liszt's preoccupation with the ideal first and foremost, from which his use of programmatic devices in music derives.

It is clear then that Liszt did not intend his 'diabolical' music to be Satanic in the literal sense. His portrayal is in fact remarkably true to the original meaning of the word 'diabolic', which derives from the Greek 'diabolos', meaning 'mud-slinger', just as Mephistopheles means 'not loving of light'. This is an important point, for presumably if the Devil really did play the violin as in Lenau's poem used by Liszt as the programme for the first *Mephisto Waltz*, then the music would be irresistible, whereas Liszt's is dark-hued and macabre. It is not meant to do the Devil's work and lead us into temptation.

At the end of the orchestral version of the first *Mephisto Waltz*, Faust and his girl 'sink in the ocean of their own lust'. What the music conjures up though is more like the gaping jaws of Hell, a subject treated in the *Dante Symphony*. Here the lovers Paola and Francesca have been consigned to Hell because of lust, but Liszt's use of the 'Nessun maggior dolor' theme in the fugue of the 'Purgatorio' section introduces a note of hope for the lost souls. Again, this is a Lisztian interpretation imposed upon Dante's poem, and expresses the idea that after the Fall there remains the hope of redemption. Once again the Lisztian conjunction of love, divinity and music forms the basis of the work. Lust is a sin because it turns Man away from God, or in Lisztian terms men are tempted to use love, which is divine, for selfish ends. It is Satan's crime to claim for himself what stems from God.

This ultimately leads back to the question of creativity itself, a subject treated in the Piano Sonata. The opening theme of the work, representing Creation, occurs repeatedly just before the 'angry God' section that precedes the slow movement. Here the idea of the Fall is clearly expressed. Just as in the Garden of Eden, Liszt's Satan tempts Adam and Eve in the guise of love, so the consequence is Man's usurping the rôle of Creation, for Liszt the ultimate crime against God. The connection here with Liszt the composer is obvious. Again we return to Lamennais, whose writings contain the idea that God creates through Man, and therefore art is a part of the divine creation. Because Liszt believed this to be true, he was virtually forced to come to terms with the fact that music, whose primary function is to express feeling, imposes a moral obligation upon the composer, since through music we can know beauty. This provides the link between religion and art in Liszt, and explains how the elements of love, beauty, religion and music dictated his approach to programme music, leading to the oratorio *Christus*. The relation between Liszt's works lies precisely in the fact that because *Christus* is programme music, it follows that his programme music must be religious for there to be a consistent approach. At this point we should recall Liszt's remark: 'Programme music is a *legitimate genre of the art*.'

Liszt's first use of thematic transformation in a programmatic composition was in the piano piece *Harmonies poétiques et religieuses* written in 1833. Half-way through the music appears a hymn-like theme in G major which is clearly the 'real' theme, of which the earlier transformations act as an anticipation. Thus the composing process is backwards, but the listener hears the G major theme as a revelation after so much gloomy restlessness. The end of the piece is in a mood of despair, however, which may be the reason why Liszt later rejected the piece, and recomposed it as *Pensée des morts* in the set *Harmonies poétiques et religieuses*.

In 1834 he composed his second piece using thematic transformation, the unpublished *De profundis* for piano and orchestra. Here the psalm theme, set to the words 'Out of the depths have I called to thee, O Lord; Lord, hear my cry', appears at the end as a triumphal march. The work was written for Lamennais.

The 'curse' theme of the *Malédiction Concerto* is thought to have been written at this time, and the whole work completed before Liszt embarked upon his career as a travelling virtuoso. The fact that he included music from the 1827 concerto may reflect his first desire to enter the Church. Certainly during the period between the death of his father and his return to Vienna in 1838, Liszt had fully formulated in music the idea of redemption through love, expressed through thematic transformation.

These works were preceded by the sketch for a *Revolutionary Symphony*. As it is unfinished, we cannot know whether the work would have used thematic transformation, but the fact that the later *Héroïde funèbre*, declared by Liszt to be a part of the original symphony, does not, points to the probability that the earlier work would not have done so either. This is strengthened by Liszt's use of the *Marseillaise* and his intended use of other themes not invented by himself. Obviously they were chosen for what they represented, and in that sense the symphony would have been programmatic, describing the successful revolution at a time when Liszt thought the revolution would succeed. To that extent, there was no call for thematic transformation. The development of the redemption idea took place after 1830, in the wake of the failed revolution. That this failure contributed to Liszt's outlook is confirmed by *Héroïde funèbre*, which is evidence of Liszt's preoccupation 20 years later with the same idea. But the inclusion of the 1827 music in the *Malédiction Concerto* puts all this into perspective. It is evidence that the subjective element in Liszt's music appeared first, before his involvement with external events. These events he viewed from the point of view of his own idealism, which led him to write music about them.[2] This is the Romantic attitude, which cannot divorce art from life, and therefore sees life in terms of art.

The values Liszt attached to life derived therefore from music, his whole career being the attempt to impose these upon the world, and to put his ideas into his compositions. Thus the programme works which do not contain thematic transformation are about Liszt's concrete ideals, such as the revolution, Man, nature and religion, love and beauty. The pieces which do use thematic transformation are about the process of change that is required to eliminate those things that stand in the way, such as pride, selfishness, doubt, despair, in other words those things Liszt identified with Satan. The result of this attitude is that Liszt objectified suffering in his music instead of expressing it, as Wagner did. This lies at the root of all Liszt's serious music, in which gloom gives way to jubilation. The journey is from the human to the divine, a progress requiring effort. Only in *Christus* do we find the Wagnerian chromaticism that directly portrays suffering, when Christ sings of his despair in the Agony in the Garden. Here Liszt makes his point; Christ was divine, but made human. In Liszt's other music the human rejects suffering through faith in the divine. This explains the unique character of his 'Tristis est anima mea' and relates to the ensuing 'Stabat mater dolorosa', in which Liszt deploys the fullness of his dramatic powers to describe the event of redemption – the Crucifixion. It is because Christ represents redemption that *Christus* is the quintessence of Liszt's art.

# Liszt's path as a composer

Liszt was able to apply to a religious subject the operatic approach others felt unable to, since they reserved a special style for religious music. All Liszt's music is ultimately operatic in style, but he never wrote an opera after his childhood. Instead he used the dramatic style natural to him in the service of the idea of redemption. It is clear, therefore, that Liszt was perfectly right to claim on the eve of his arrival in Rome 'the complete identity of my former efforts with my ideas of today'. Liszt's use of the Cross motif was more than just a musical symbol. It summarized his life and art. His achievement was to put into clear musical and dramatic terms a fully worked-out scheme of the drama of redemption.

This may account for the gradual estrangement of Wagner and Liszt during the Weimar years, when Liszt turned away from his original plans to compose operas, and instead produced programmatic and religious works. In doing this he may not have been conscious of what lay between them, since his admiration for Wagner was second to none. But certainly Wagner never really understood Liszt, as Cosima's diaries show: 'He is sorry that my father writes oratorios' (*CWD*, 18 January 1879); 'my father plays his "Dante" to us, R. has serious reservations with regard to the material' (*CWD*, 22 September 1880); 'R. talks about my father's latest compositions, which he finds completely meaningless' (*CWD*, 22 November 1882); 'At breakfast a letter from Herr Levi . . . brings us the extraordinary news that during a discussion of his *Christus* my father flew into a rage with the poor man . . . Long discussion . . . of this curious incident, reflections on the character and life of my father. Dismal conversations!' (*CWD*, 3 September 1879).

Other remarks by Wagner recorded by Cosima confirm the fundamental difference in attitude of the two men: 'R. says he would prefer to see [Liszt] writing symphonies than a *Via Crucis* or a *Seven Sacraments* ("He should give us Hell as the first sacrament")' (*CWD*, 20 November 1878). Speaking of *Tristan and Isolde*, Wagner says: 'To sin as a sinner, how wretched, how vulgar! Learn through sin to be a saint, a god!' (*CWD*, 23 November 1882). Liszt, on the other hand, called *Tristan and Isolde* 'l'amour terrestre', and *Parsifal* 'l'amour divin'. In Dante, Tristan and Isolde, along with Paolo and Francesca, have been consigned to Hell through lust. The picture of the lovers in Hell in the *Dante Symphony* is the composer's programmatic statement that corresponds to Wagner's whole opera (the exception being the love scene in the second act, presented by Wagner as a nocturnal idyll, a kind of 'Liebestraum'), together with his remark about 'Hell as the first sacrament'. In Wagner, the love element is released by a magic potion, takes place at night in secret, and is destroyed by the 'real' world. In Liszt the love element is treated alone: the human and the divine. The first exists in Hell, as love exists on earth; the second promises a world of beauty, the point being that it is part and parcel of the first. For Liszt the 'reality' is the divine vision; for Wagner the 'reality' is a cruel world.

The problem came for Wagner when in *Parsifal* he wanted to cross this divide. To do so, he stole Liszt's Cross motif. But Parsifal is an unreal figure; when a spear is thrown at him, it hovers in the air as if by magic. This is the equivalent in Liszt of staging 'The Miracle of the Roses' in *St Elizabeth*, which he would not allow. In Wagner, the most convincing character is Kundry, whose suffering and desire for redemption is expressed in the music. But, as has been pointed out,[3] in *Parsifal* redemption is really rescue. This corresponds to the rôle of Hercules in Liszt's choral version of *Prometheus*, a rôle he removed in the programmatic symphonic poem, adding an opening theme resembling closely the 'curse' music in the *Malédiction Concerto*, and a fugue towards the end. Liszt's Prometheus is redeemed, not rescued. Wagner, in not seeing redemption as a psychological affair, reduced it to the rôle of a *deus ex machina*. The missing ingredient lies precisely where Liszt succeeded most: his portrait of the Devil.

In *Lohengrin*, for example, there is divinity, love, temptation and loss. These are the ingredients of Eden, corresponding to the exposition of Liszt's Piano Sonata. In *Parsifal* there is suffering and redemption, but no real Devil figure, the equivalent in Liszt of the *Faust Symphony* without the 'Mephistopheles' movement – the essential point of the whole work. Liszt recognized this when he invented the 'curse' ('Malédiction') theme in the 1830s, and identified it with the Devil. This was the first and necessary step in the drama of redemption, conforming to the basic structure of the Old and New Testaments, each requiring the other to give it meaning. Liszt in this sense emerges therefore as a realist, and Wagner as a 'romantic', in that from the start Liszt involved his art in a total context, while Wagner used music as a form of wishful thinking. In effect he left the solution to God, then complained when God did not rescue him.

In Liszt, God is not external, but internal. Everything Liszt did is consistent with this attitude; his music enshrines what he called 'the great doctrines of humanity' – freedom, equality, brotherhood, love and peace. These Liszt associated with beauty, transferred from art to life. He therefore reversed the process by writing programme music that attempted to redeem life through art. This he regarded as the task of artists, since Man's ability to create belongs to God. Thus emerges the idea that God is the better part of man – which seems to lie behind the 'L'Homme–Dieu' letter written in August 1855, the year Liszt turned definitively towards the Church in his music: 'The deification of man becomes a nonsense if in the first place you get rid of the idea of God' (*Br.* IV, 243). Liszt is the only composer in history to describe in music 'the idea of God'. The pursuit of this idea lies behind the bewildering external variety of his output, and explains the uninhibited and innovative character of his compositional process. By inventing the device of thematic transformation and associating it in his mind with the redemption process, he was free to range far and wide in search of programmatic illustration. The lasting paradox about Liszt is that his appeal, in spite of appearances, is in the end intellectual. It is a measure of his stature that, faced with the crisis of his age, he used his art to portray uncompromisingly what he saw as psychological truth: the inevitability of struggle, the strength of faith and courage, and the inspiration of love.

Is this what is conventionally called 'Romanticism'? Or is it, as admirers of Liszt have always instinctively felt, intellectual honesty in pursuit of the truly human?

# APPENDIX: CHRONOLOGY OF LISZT'S YEARS AT WEIMAR

*Public*
(Works performed)

*Private*
(Works composed)

**1848**

Feb.: L. at Weimar + Conradi. Princess in Weimar June. Lives in Altenburg. L. at Erbprinz Hotel. Princess hopes Weimar Grand Duchess Maria Pavlovna will ask brother (Tsar Nicholas) for divorce. L. visits Wagner, Dresden. Aug.: W. visits L. who conducts *Tannhäuser*. *Ov.* 12 Nov. and says opera must be given.

Sketches exist for *Faust Sym.*, *Dante Sym.*, *Mazeppa*, *Hungaria* (cantata), *Héroïde funèbre*, *Les Préludes*, *Berg-Sym.*, 2 Piano Concertos, *Totentanz*, *Années de p.* I & II, *Transcendental Studies*, Mass commissioned 1846. *Harmonies poét. et rel.* begun 1847. *Male-Voice Mass* and *Les Préludes* composed 1848. Revolutionaries threaten Pius IX in Rome.

**1849**

16 Feb.: 1st perf. *Tannhäuser*. Schumann's *Faust* part II. May: Wagner is concealed by L. at Weimar after Dresden rev. Hears reh. of *Tannhaüser*. June: Bülow visits L. first time. Aug.: *Tasso* and *Goethe March* perf. Sept./Dec.: L. + Princess visit Heligoland.

Hungarian revolution. Tsar refuses divorce for Princess. L. moves into Altenburg. 17 Oct.: death of Chopin. János Scitovsky becomes Archbishop of Esztergom and Prince-Primate of Hungary (met L. 1846). L. composes *Tasso*, *Funérailles*, *Consolations*, *Berg-Sym.* 1st vers. Completes *Totentanz* and revises *Dante Sonata* and 2 Piano Concertos.

**1850**

Jan.: Raff visits Weimar. End of Feb.: *Berg-Sym.* April: Joachim visits L. 24 Aug.: 1st perf. *Prometheus*. 28 Aug.: 1st perf. *Lohengrin*. Operas perf. include Rossini, *Conte Ory*; Donizetti, *La Favorita*. Oct.: Joachim leader of Weimar orchestra.

Jan.: L.'s mother in Weimar. L. finishes *Héroïde funèbre*, *Berg-Sym.* 2nd vers., *Prometheus* (choruses and ov.), 'Ad nos' organ piece, *Pater noster IV*.

# Appendix

June: Bülow at Weimar as pupil of L. Dec.: Bülow's ov. *Julius Caesar* perf. under L. 14 Dec.: *Wanderer Fantasie* (L.'s arr. of Schubert for piano and orchestra) perf. Works perf. include Raff, *König Alfred*; Berlioz, *Harold in Italy*; Liszt, *Tasso* 2nd vers.; *Berg-Sym.* 2nd vers.; Schumann, *Bride of Messina* ov.

1851 — L. composes *Mazeppa* (orchestral) and *Transcendental Studies*. Transcribes Beethoven's 9th Symphony for 2 pianos.

20 March: Berlioz, *Benvenuto Cellini*, Weimar. Cornelius visits L. for fortnight, returns autumn. Nov.: 'Berlioz Week' at Weimar (B. attends). Dec.: Joachim resigns as orch. leader. Works perf. include Wagner, *Faust Ov.*; Byron/Schumann, *Manfred*; Liszt, *Male-Voice Mass*; Verdi, *Ernani*; various Berlioz works.

1852 — L.'s decision to 'se rejeter fortement dans le système catholique'. Composes Sonata in B minor (1852–3). *Ave Maria I* 2nd vers. 1852–3: Princess's husband in Weimar, makes property agreement, daughter to inherit.

June: Brahms visits L. for 2–3 weeks. July: L. visits Wagner, Zurich. 3–5 Oct.: Music Festival at Karlsruhe; L.'s conducting criticized by Hiller. Bülow, Cornelius, Joachim, Remenyi, Richard Pohl go to Basle to visit Wagner. L., the Princess, her daughter and W. go to Paris. L. sees children after 8 years' absence. W. sees Cosima. Agnes Street comes to Weimar. Laub becomes leader of orch. Works perf. include Wagner, *Flying Dutchman*; Liszt, *Berg-Sym.* (another version).

1853 — July: L. discusses *Christus* with Wagner, plays *Faust Symphony* (not yet written down), 'some' sym. poems, 'some' piano music. L. composes *Festklänge*, *Orpheus* (1853–4), *Domine salvum fac regem*, *Te Deum II*, *An die Künstler* (later *Die Ideale*), 2nd *ballade*. Death of Grand Duke Karl Friedrich (1828–53). Son Carl Alexander succeeds, prefers drama to opera (which was favoured by his mother, whose influence now wanes).

July: L. visits Holland, Belgium, North Germany. Summer: George Eliot and Lewes stay at Weimar; often at the Altenburg. Rubinstein visits Liszt. L. and Princess write musical journalism (12 articles). Works perf. include Berlioz, *Flight into Egypt*; Schubert, *Alfonso and Estrella*; Rubinstein, *Siberian Hunter*; Liszt, *Festklänge*, *Orpheus*, *Les Préludes*, *Mazeppa*.

1854 — Death of Lamennais. Final version of *Berg-Sym.*, *Hungaria* (sym. poem). Aug.–Oct.: *Faust Symphony*.

# Appendix

Feb.: 2nd 'Berlioz Week'. B. conducts L.'s E♭ Concerto, L. as soloist. July: Tausig becomes L.'s pupil. Aug.: L.'s 3 children spend summer at Weimar. Cosima and Blandine go to live in Berlin with Mme von Bülow. Works perf. include Schumann, *Genoveva*; Cornelius, *Mass*; Liszt, *Ave Maria*; 'Ad nos' organ fugue (in Merseburg), *Psalm 13* (in Berlin).

**1855** Princess's husband obtains civil divorce. Death of Tsar Nicholas I. Frescoes of life of St Elizabeth installed in Wartburg. Jan.: Baron Augusz writes from Hungary about the commission for the *Gran Mass*. 2 May: L. to Wagner that work is finished. *Psalm 13, Gran Mass, BACH Fantasy and Fugue, Dante Symphony* (1855–6). *Prometheus* reworked.

Jan.: L. conducts in Vienna at Mozart Centenary Festival. Feb./March: Berlioz conducts *Corsaire* ov. and *Damnation of Faust*. L. & B. quarrel about Wagner. April: Bülow asks for Cosima's hand in marriage. May: BACH fugue, Merseburg. Aug.: *Gran Mass* performed in Hungary, L. conducting. 8 Sept.: *Hungaria* performed in Budapest. Oct: L. and Princess with Wagner in Zurich. Act I *Walküre* perf. in private. L. meets Kaulbach in Munich.

**1856** April: L. receives first numbers of *St Elizabeth* from Roquette. June: Festetics objects to *Gran Mass*. Augusz intervenes. Oct.: L. discusses loud ending of *Dante Symphony* with Wagner. *Die Ideale* (1856–7). *Hunnenschlacht* begun. Summer: W. studies L.'s sym. poems; begins *Siegfried* Sept.

7 Jan.: A major Concerto. 22 Jan.: Bülow plays L.'s Sonata (Berlin). 26 Feb.: L. conducts his works at Leipzig – press opposition. 3 May– 2 June: L. conducts at Aachen Lower Rhine Music Festival – opposition from Hiller. 18 Aug.: Bülow and Cosima marry; L. present. 5 Sept.: *Faust Symphony, Die Ideale*. 22 Oct.: Blandine marries. 7 Nov.: *Dante Symphony* a failure (Prague). 10 Nov.: *Héroïde funèbre* Breslau. 29 Dec.: *Hunnenschlacht*. Dingelstedt Intendant at theatre.

**1857** Final chorus of *Faust Symphony*. Begins *St Elizabeth* – slow progress.

March: L. conducts his works in Prague and Budapest. 15 Dec.: Cornelius, *Barber of Bagdad* – hostile reception (L. conducting).

**1858** Princess's daughter's 21st birthday – inherits mother's estates (and income). Spring: L. reads new book on St Elizabeth by Danielik. Asks for musical material from Hungary. Resigns his post, but resignation refused. *Hamlet*.

# Appendix

| | 1859 | |
|---|---|---|
| Jan.: Wagner and L. become estranged. April: L. receives Order of the Iron Crown – raised to the Austrian nobility. Oct.: 'The Beatitudes' perf. at Weimar (during marriage of Princess's daughter and Constantine Hohenlohe). | 1859 | L. meets Hohenlohe, Papal Chamberlain (brother of Princess's daughter's new husband). Sends copy of *Gran Mass* to the Pope. Okraszevsky (steward from Russian estates of Princess) promises a Russian divorce from the bishops upon payment of large sum. May: L. composes 'The Beatitudes'. Sept.: Hohenlohe invites L. to the Vatican. 15 Oct.: Marriage of Princess's daughter at Weimar. Princess goes to Paris. 13 Dec.: L.'s son Daniel dies. Prelude *Weinen Klagen*, 'The Beatitudes', *Psalms 23, 137, Te Deum I, Mephisto Waltz* no. 1. Revises *Psalm 13*. |
| March: protest against New Music, signed Brahms, Joachim, Grimm, Scholz. 15 Aug.: L. made Officier de la Légion d'Honneur. | 1860 | Spring: Russian Catholics grant divorce, but Bishop of Fulda objects. L. meets Hohenlohe. Persuades Princess to go to Rome; she leaves in May. L. writes letters to her *re* church music. 14 Sept.: L. makes his Will. *Les Morts, Psalm 18, Responsorien, Pater noster (Christus), An den heiligen Franziskus von Paula, 2 Episodes from Lenau's Faust*. |
| 8 March: *Dance at the Village Inn (Mephisto Waltz* no. 1), Weimar. May: L. visits S. Germany. 25 June: *Psalm 18*, Weimar. Aug.: Conference at Weimar to found Allgemeine Deutsche Musikverein; Wagner attends. 17 Aug.: L. leaves Weimar. Goes to Berlin and Paris. Sees Comtesse d'Agoult, plays to Napoleon III. 21 Oct.: L. arrives in Rome. Wedding for 22 Oct. cancelled. Lives alone at 113 Via Felice. 23 Oct.: Princess writes a Will, referring to 'mon mari, Mr François Liszt', signing it 'Carolyne Liszt'. | 1861 | Work on *St Elizabeth* |

# NOTES

## 1. 1830: a revolutionary symphony

1 Taken from *Liszt Pédagogue* (a diary of Franz Liszt as teacher kept by Madame Auguste Boissier in 1831–2). The entry is for Tuesday 7 February 1832, Lesson 12. English translation by Elyse Mach as preface to *The Liszt Studies* (New York, 1973), pp. ix–xxxvi.

## 2. 1834: Lamennais and *Words of a Believer*

1 Quoted in Abbé F. de Lamennais: *The Words of a Believer. Translated from the French* (London, 1848), p. 21 (Memoir).
2 Roland N. Stromberg: *European Intellectual History since 1789* (New Jersey, 1975), p. 89.
3 Alec R. Vidler: *Prophecy and Papacy* (London, 1954), p. 257.
4 For an English version of most of this long letter see *PL*, 106. 'The minutely observed particulars are so untypical of Liszt,' says Perényi 'that they suggest an intense experience.'
5 From a letter of Liszt, dated 30 August 1874, to his biographer Lina Ramann. Quoted in Hedwig Weilguny: *Das Liszthaus in Weimar* (Weimar, 1977), p. 3.

## 3. 1848: revolutions and a Mass

1 John Farrow: *Pageant of the Popes* (London, 1943), p. 335.
2 See also *BruS*, 315, which gives details of the visit. The cathedral at Pécs was being restored. Scitovsky left Pécs in 1849, before the restoration was completed, and this is why the 1846 commission was not carried out at the time.
3 Quoted in Tamás Nádor: *Liszt Ferenc életének krónikája* [The Chronicle of Franz Liszt's Life] (Budapest, 1975), p. 167.
4 L. B. Namier: '1848: Seed Plot of History', and F. Fejtö: 'Conclusion', in *1848: a Turning Point?* (Lexington, Massachusetts, 1959), pp. 68 and 95.
5 Liszt's remarks addressed to Haslinger on the corrected proofs of the work in the Liszt Museum at Weimar. Quoted in Weilguny: *Das Liszthaus in Weimar*, p. 14.
6 Extract from Theodor von Bernhardi: *Aus dem Leben Theodor von Bernhardis* (Leipzig, 1893–6). Quoted by Ernest Newman in *The Man Liszt* (London, 1934), p. 179.

## 4. Weimar: Liszt, the Church and Wagner

1 Quoted in Vidler: *Prophecy and Papacy*, p. 147.

## 5. 1861: Rome, Cardinal Hohenlohe and Princess Wittgenstein

1 The following list of the Princess's books is taken from *SFL*, 100:

*Boudhisme et Christianisme*, 1 vol.

*De la prière par une femme du monde*, 1 vol.

*Entretiens pratiques à l'usage des femmes du monde*, 1 vol.

*Religion et monde*, 1 vol.

*L'Amitié des anges*, 1 vol.

*La Chapelle sixtine*, 1 vol.

*La Matière dans la dogmatique chrétienne*, 3 vols.

*L'Église attaquée par la médisance*, 1 vol.

*Petits entretiens pratiques à l'usage des femmes du grand monde pour la durée d'une retraite spirituelle*, 8 vols.

*Simplicité des colombes, prudence des serpents: quelques réflexions suggérées par les femmes et les temps actuels*, 1 vol.

*Souffrance et prudence*, 1 vol.

*Sur la perfection chrétienne et la vie intérieure*, 1 vol.

*Causes intérieures de la faiblesse extérieure de l'Église*, 24 vols.

After her death the Princess's library passed into the hands of the Hohenlohe family, and is at present located in the library of Prince Viktor Hohenlohe at Friedstein. There is a complete set of the *Causes intérieures* in the Washington Library of Congress. For more detailed information see *Émile Ollivier et Carolyne de Sayn-Wittgenstein: Correspondance (1858–1887)*, ed. Anne Troisier de Diaz (Paris, 1984), pp. 33–4.

2 Etienne Laubarède: *Henri Lasserre. L'Homme, l'écrivain, l'oeuvre* (Paris, 1901).

3 *Memoirs of Prince Chlodwig of Hohenlohe Schillingsfürst* (London, 1906), I, p. 141.

4 Princess Marie Hohenlohe's account is given in *An der Schwelle des Jenseits*, ed. La Mara (Leipzig, 1925), pp. 40–8.

5 *Ibid.*

6 Item 713 in the *Autographen-Katalog No. 577 of J. A. Stargardt* (Bibliothek Wolfenbüttel). The catalogue, printed for an auction in Marpurg in 1967, includes extracts from the manuscript 'Nachlass' of the Princess Wittgenstein.

7 August Göllerich: *Franz Liszt* (Berlin, 1908), p. 62.

8 From a letter written by Dr Vernon Harrison, founder and chairman of the British Liszt Society. The letter contains information given to Dr Harrison by Liszt's great-great-granddaughter, Mme Blandine Ollivier de Prévaux. Quoted by kind permission.

9 Daniel Ollivier: 'Lettres d'un père et de sa fille', in *Revue des Deux Mondes*, 1 January 1936.

10 See *WRC*, 24: 'The entire nation celebrated in 1873 his Jubilee, the fiftieth year of his artistic career. They played his magnificent oratorio "Christ", which he called his "musical will and testament", the words of which, drawn from the Bible and from the Catholic liturgy, were also composed by the master.'

## 7. Liszt and Palestrina

1 Liszt's own approach to the problem of church music finds expression in the advice he gave to Cornelius on the subject (*L*, I, 136; September 1852):

I congratulate you very sincerely in having put the fine season to so good a use by finishing the church compositions you had planned. That is an admirable field for you, and I strongly advise you not to give in till you have explored it with love and valour for several years. I think that, both by the elevation and the depth of your ideas, the tenderness of your feelings, and your deep studies, you are eminently fitted to excel in the religious style, and to accomplish its transformation so far as is nowadays required by our intelligence being more awake and our hearts more astir than at former periods. You have only to assimilate Palestrina and Bach – then let your heart speak, and you will be able to say with the prophet, 'I speak, for I believe; and I know that our God liveth eternally.'

2 Cosima's letter is quoted, in French, by Lina Ramann in *Franz Liszt als Künstler und Mensch* (Leipzig, 1880–1894) Part 2, vol. II, p. 458.

3 Arthur Hutchings: *Church Music in the Nineteenth Century* (London, 1967), p. 77.

4 *Memoirs of Hector Berlioz*, trans. Ernest Newman (London, 1932; repr. New York, 1966), p. 158.

5 *BruS*, 111, to Prince Friedrich of Hohenzollern-Hechingen, January 1862:

Le régime musical que je sais ici n'est pas à beaucoup près aussi abondant et substantiel que celui auquel j'étais habitué. Jusqu'à présent je n'ai rien entendu qui m'ait donné le désir de l'écouter plus attentivement – à l'exception pourtant des Messes de Palestrina et de son école dont le caractère de sublime permanence se manifeste dans son entier à la chapelle du Vatican. Le nombre des Chantres est assez restreint; mais les proportions accoustiques de la chapelle sont si excellentes et le Choeur si bien placé (vers le milieu de la nef, mais un peu plus rapproché de l'autel) que ces 24 ou 30 voix au plus produisent un effet très imposant. C'est un encens sonore qui porte la prière sur ses nuages d'or et d'azur! –

À d'autres églises on cultive un genre de musique dont je suis loin de contester les charmes et les avantages . . . seulement pour le goûter avec abandon il faut un degré de naïveté d'impression que je désespère d'atteindre. Les ouvertures de la *Gazza ladra* et du *Barbier* de Séville, les cavatines de Norma et d'Ernani qu'on entend parfois à des occasions où elles ont au moins le mérite de la surprise, ne m'offrent pas plus d'intérêt que les théâtres où l'on ne représente que des ouvrages qui ne gagnent pas à être trop connus.

6 Quoted in Hutchings, *Church Music*, p. 61.

7 The full title of this book is: *Nouvel eucologe en musique. Contenant les offices des dimanches et fêtes de l'année et de la semaine sainte recueillis et annotés par M. l'Abbé de Roquefeuil. Avec les plainchants en notation moderne et dans un diapason moyen par M. Félix Clément* (Paris, L. Hachette et Cie, 1851).

8 The same error occurs in the 'Motu Proprio' itself, although I have not seen this pointed out. The relevant passage says: 'Special efforts are to be made to restore the use of the Gregorian chant by the people, so that the faithful may again take a more active part in the ecclesiastical offices, as was the case in ancient times.' The chant was not used 'by the people', but by the clergy.

9 *Br.* VIII, p. 61, no. 62, to d'Ortigue, 24 April 1850. The 'work you mention concerning the liturgy' was probably *Dictionnaire liturgique, historique et pratique du plain-chant et de musique d'église au moyen âge et dans les temps modernes* (1854), compiled by d'Ortigue and Théodore Nisard.

10 See Göllerich: *Franz Liszt*, p. 310.

11 This theory of 'the tonality and modality of Gregorian chant' is referred to in Liszt's letter to d'Ortigue dated Rome, 28 November 1862 (*Br.* VIII, 156):

Permets-moi donc, cher d'ortigue, de rester persuadé qu'un peu plus tôt ou plus tard, quand l'heure en sera venue, je te rendrai un office analogue à celui dont tu as su bon gré à Niedermeyer, et que la démonstration de la tonalité et de la modalité de la Musique présente (tant bien que mal affublée provisoirement du sobriquet de Musique de l'avenir) ne sera pas moins évidente pour ton esprit et tes oreilles, que la démonstration de Niedermeyer de la tonalité et de la modalité du Chant Grégorien.

12 With the same harmony that appears on p. 819 of the *Nouvel eucologe en musique*.

13 The manuscript of this piece is in the National Széchényi Library, Budapest. It was published in 1978 in the New Liszt Edition, *Individual Character Pieces II*, p. 28.

14 The author was Franz Sales Kandler, who died before the book was completed. The title says: 'verfasst und mit historisch-kritischen Zusatzen begleitet von [Kandler]. Nachgelassenes Werk hrsg. mit einem Vorworte und mit gelegentlichen Anmerkungen von R[aphael] G[eorg] Kiesewetter'.

15 Liszt's letter to Witt (*L*, II, 246, written in (?) 1874) says: 'I have still the hope that you may yet at some future day be called upon to give your powerful assistance in connection with the teaching and practice of church music in Hungary.' A further letter (*L*, II, 282, written in (?)1875) repeats these sentiments, ending with the words: 'In a word: Come to us, and let us work together in Budapest!'

16 This letter is quoted by Émile Haraszti in 'Histoire de la Musique', in the encyclopaedia *La Pléiade* (Paris, 1963), II, p. 535.

## 8. The Masses

1 Ferenc Bónis: *Mosonyi* [in Hungarian] (Budapest, 1960), p. 64.

2 Karl Kirkenbuhl: *Federzeichnungen aus Rom*, quoted in J. Huneker, *Franz Liszt* (New York, 1911), p. 270.

3 Alfred Habets: *Borodin and Liszt*, trans. Rosa Newmarch (London, 1896), p. 170.

4 The full title is: *Graduale Romanum quod ad cantum attiret, ad gregorianam formam redactum ex veteribus MSS. undique collectis et duplici notatione donatum. Notae recentiores* (Paris, Adrianus Le Clere et Soc., 1857). It contains Liszt's markings, indicating use.

5 Alfred Habets: *Borodin and Liszt*, p. 175.

## 10. The oratorios *St Elizabeth* and *Christus*

1 Robert Collet on Liszt's choral and organ music in *Franz Liszt. The Man and his Music*, ed. Alan Walker (London, 1970), p. 320.

2 See *Source Readings in Music History*, selected and annotated by Oliver Strunk (New York, 1950), pp. 847–73.

3 English version taken from Ambrose Lisle Phillips, *The Chronicle of the Life of St Elizabeth of Hungary, Duchess of Thuringia* (London, 1839), p. 43. This is a translation of Montalembert's *Vie de Sainte Elizabeth* (Paris, 1836). The miracle of the roses does not figure in the account of St Elizabeth given in *Butler's Lives of the Saints* (4 vols., 1956).

4 Camille Saint-Saëns: *Musical Memories*, trans. Edwin Gile Rich (Boston, 1919), p. 123.
5 *Ibid.*, p. 127.

## 12. The late religious works and *Les Morts*

1 Letter to Gottschalg dated 11 March 1862, reproduced in his book *Franz Liszt in Weimar und seine letzten Lebenstage* (Berlin, 1910), p. 60.

## 13. Liszt's programmatic use of fugue

1 Peter Schwarz: *Studien zur Orgelmusik Franz Liszts* (Munich, 1973), p. 65.
2 Vladimir Vasilevich Stasov: *Selected Essays on Music*, trans. Florence Jonas (London, 1968), p. 179.
3 Béla Bartók: 'Liszt-Probleme' (an address delivered in 1936 to the Hungarian Academy of Sciences), in *Franz Liszt. Beiträge von ungarischen Autoren* (Budapest, 1978), pp. 122–32.

## 14. Liszt's Cross motif and the Piano Sonata in B minor

1 Wilhelm Jerger: *Franz Liszts Klavierunterricht von 1884–1886 (dargestellt an den Tagebuchaufzeichnungen von August Göllerich)* (Regensburg, 1975), p. 57, Monday 6 July 1884.
2 Printed in *Objections to Christian Belief* [essays by various authors] (Pelican Books, 1968), p. 70. The author, J. S. Bezzant, goes on to say: 'This outline has been so shattered that the bare recital of it has the aspect of a malicious travesty.' In 1963 maybe, but not in 1853 when Liszt was composing his Sonata. The 'scheme of salvation' accords with his view that 'music may be said to be . . . "Christian by nature" ' (*Br.* VIII, 170) and that programme music was 'a legitimate genre of the art'.
3 The original conclusion to the Sonata is reproduced in Sharon Winklhofer: *Liszt's Sonata in B minor. A Study of Autograph Sources and Documents* (Michigan, UMI Research Press, 1980), p. 237. The author traces the history of the work using Liszt's manuscript sketches. Her analysis uses the description 'Expressive Form', focussing upon Liszt's use of tonality, and resting upon the assumption that it is 'absolute' music. But Liszt asked 'to be allowed to decide upon the form by the contents', the Sonata showing, as much for example as the *Faust Symphony*, his genius for characterization in music.
4 At the time when Liszt was composing the *Sonata* he wrote a long letter to Wilhelm von Lenz (*L*, I, 147–53, 2 December 1852) in which he discussed von Lenz's book *Beethoven and his Three Styles* (St Petersburg, 1852). Liszt did not agree with the division into three styles, preferring instead two categories:

> Were it my place to categorise the different periods of the great master's thoughts, as manifested in his Sonatas, Symphonies, and Quartets, I should certainly not fix the division into *three styles*, which is now pretty generally adopted and which you have followed; but, simply recording the questions which have been raised hitherto, I should frankly weigh the *great* question which is the axis of criticism and of musical aestheticism at the point to which Beethoven has led us – namely, in how far is traditional or recognised form a necessary determinant for the organism of thought? –
> The solution of this question, evolved from the works of Beethoven him-

319

self, would lead me to divide this work, not into three styles or periods, – the words *style* and *period* being here only corollary subordinate terms, of a vague and equivocal meaning, – but quite logically into two categories: the first, that in which traditional and recognised form contains and governs the thought of the master; and the second, that in which the thought stretches, breaks, recreates, and fashions the form and style according to its needs and inspirations. Doubtless in proceeding thus we arrive in a direct line at those incessant problems of *authority* and *liberty*. But why should they alarm us? In the region of liberal arts they do not, happily, bring in any of the dangers and disasters which their oscillations occasion in the political and social world; for, in the domain of the Beautiful, Genius alone is the authority, and hence, Dualism disappearing, the notions of authority and liberty are brought back to their original identity. – Manzoni, in defining genius as 'a stronger imprint of Divinity', has eloquently expressed this very truth.

We see here the preoccupations that may have led to the Sonata. First the idea of genius as divine, secondly the authority of genius in the sphere of beauty, thirdly the problem of authority and liberty. By equating beauty with divinity, Liszt justified making music describe the drama of God in terms of the Old and New Testament, since the answer to authority versus liberty he found in Christ ('Christianity is liberty through love'; *Br.* IV, 146), the symbol of 'dualism disappearing'.

## 15. Liszt's path as a composer

1  See the article by Carl Engel in the *Musical Quarterly*, July 1936.
2  Late in life he wrote (*L*, II, 267, 8 December 1874): 'My friends are those who haunt the *Ideal*; there, dear friend, we "recognise" each other.'
3  See Robert L. Jacobs: *Wagner* (London, 1935), p. 175:

>   The culmination of *Parsifal* – the redemption of Amfortas, to effect which Parsifal resists the seductress, Kundry – did not, like that of the other great works, cause his motives to transcend themselves . . . It is as if the idea of redemption symbolized for Wagner an aspiration, not an event . . . The discords only resolve when, having spent their anguish, the solemn diatonic Grail music rescues – one can say redeems – them.

# INDEX

*Note:* Works/compositions are listed under names of authors/composers

# Index

# Index

# Index

# Index

277; *Requiem für die Orgel*, 139; *Trauerode*, 262; *Trois odes funèbres*, 199. **Piano**, 94, 112, 267; *Années de pèlerinage*, 22, 138, *Marche funèbre*, 138; *Bénédiction de Dieu dans la solitude*, 9, 27, 278; *Funérailles*, 30, 32, 298; *Grande fantaisie sur la clochette de Paganini*, 6; *Harmonies poétiques et religieuses*, 9, 21, 94, 148, 215, 237, 278, 305, *Pensées des Morts*, 20–1, 94, 305; *Il penseroso*, 199, 203; *L'Africaine*, 78; *Lyon*, 10, 21; Piano Sonata in B minor, ix–x, 148, 267, 281–2, 305, 308; *Recueillement*, 199; *Sposalizio*, 252, 259; *Unstern*, 170. **Piano and orchestra** *De profundis: psaume instrumental*, 20–2, 94, 305; *Grande fantaisie symphonique*, 22; *Malédiction Concerto*, 237, 274, 298–9, 301–3, 305–6, 308; Piano Concerto in E♭ major, 271, 302; *Totentanz*, 94, 267, 280; Schubert's *Wandererfantasie*, 113. **Psalms**, ix; Psalm 13, 145–9, 267–9, 271, 273; Psalm 18, 145, 149–51; Psalm 23, 145, 151–2; Psalm 116, 145, 152–4; Psalm 124, 145; Psalm 126, 154–5; Psalm 129, 145, 155–7; Psalm 137, 145, 157–60. **ARTICLES** 'Berlioz and his Harold Symphony', 162–5; 'De la musique religieuse', 17, 19, 221; 'De la situation des artistes et de leur condition dans la société', 19; 'La Sainte Cécile de Raphael', 240; 'On Future Church Music', 16, 19–21, 35, 87. **LETTER** 'L'Homme Dieu', vi, 308
Liszt Academy, Budapest, 89
Liszt Museum, 65, 158
London, 169, 299
Longfellow, Henry Wadsworth, 235–40
Loreto, 79
Louis Napoleon (Bonaparte), Prince, 30, 33; *The Extinction of Poverty*, 170
Louis Philippe, King of France, 4, 30
Löwenberg, 64, 73
Lucca, Mgr de, 62
Lucerne, 46
Ludwig II of Bavaria, 58, 168
Luther, 15
Lyon, 23
Lyons uprising, 10

Machiavelli, 37
Madonna del Rosario, 71, 73
Madonna della Stella, 79
Magne, *see* Wittgenstein, Marie
*Magnificat* plainsong, 94
Maistre de, 32, 36
*Maîtrise, La*, 10
Maltitz, M. de, 55, 59
Mara, La, 63, 138

Marcello, Don, 24, 76, 88
Marseilles, 65
*Marseillaise*, 3–4, 20, 32, 35, 73, 298, 306
Martini, 78
Mass, Sung, 88
Mastai-Ferretti, Cardinal, *see* Pope Pius IX
Maximilian of Mexico, 137–8
Mazzini, 36
'Medicean' Gradual (1614), 95, 98
Meluzzi, Salvatore, 69, 122–4
Mendelssohn, Felix, *Elijah*, 163; Psalms, 145; 'Reformation' Symphony, 287; *St Paul*, 163
Mennais, Abbé de la, *see* Lamennais, Abbé F. de
Mephisto music, 281, 288, 290, 298–9
Mérode, Monseigneur de, 40, 71
Metternich, 30
Metternich, Princess, 112
Mettenleiter, 89
Meyendorff, Baroness Olga von, 165, 194, 235
Meyerbeer, 3, 24; *La Prophète*, 277–9; *Les Huguenots*, 4, 23
Mickiewicz, *Dziady*, 163
Mihalovich, 99
Milan, 62
Milton, John, *Paradise Lost*, 304
Minette, *see* Wittgenstein, Princess Carolyne
*Missa Papae Marcelli*, 95
modal theory and harmony, 91
modes, harmony of, 91
Modena, Duke of, 73
Mohr, Father Joseph, 224
*Monde, Le*, 23, 24
Montalembert, Charles, 7, 9; *Vie de Sainte Elisabeth*, 166, 169–70
Montceau, 27
Monte Mario, 71, 75, 77–8
Moscheles, 299
Mosonyi, 167, 169
Mozart, Wolfgang Amadeus, 22, 88; *Requiem*, 140
Munich, 37, 58, 168
*Musica Sacra* (periodical), 98

Nádasd, 28
Namier, L. B., 31
Napoleon, Emperor Louis, 6; *The Extinction of Poverty*, 6
Nardi, Mgr, 71
National Workshops (Paris), 30, 32
*Neue Zeitschrift für Musik*, 70
New York, 49
Newman, Cardinal, 38
Nicholas, Tsar, 54–5

# Index

# Index

Rouvroy, Claude Henri de, *see* Saint-Simon, Comte de
Royalists, 4
Rubinstein, Anton, 184
Rückert, 183
Russia, 28–9, 31, 52, 54–6, 58–61, 66

*Sacerdos in aeternam* plainsong, 95, 269
St Francis of Assisi, 218
St Ignatius Loyola, 224
St Paul, 40, 184
St Peter, 186, 196
St Peter's, Rome, 60, 67, 69, 76, 89, 97, 197
St Petersburg, Archbishop of, 61;
    Metropolitan of, 57, 59
Saint Roch, 5
Saint-Saëns, 100, 191, 200
Saint-Simon, Comte de, 5
Saint-Simonists, 5, 6, 170
St Thomas, 74
St Tropez, 63, 64, 73
Sainte-Beuve, 11, 17
Salieri, Antonio, 221
*Salle Taitbout*, 5
Salua, Father, 74, 76, 78
Salvagni, Fortunato, 70, 73, 75–6
Salvagni, Peppina, 70
Sand, George, 8, 23–4
Santa Francesca Romana, 78, 235, 250
Santa Maria Maggiore, 229
Sayn-Wittgenstein, Carolyne, *see*
    Wittgenstein, Carolyne
Sayn-Wittgenstein, Louis, 58
Sayn-Wittgenstein, Prince Nicholas, 52,
    54–5, 61, 66–7
Schober, Franz von, 31
Schopenhauer, Arthur, 43
Schorn, Adelheid von, 39, 43, 48–9, 51, 66,
    79
Schubert, Franz, 22, 152
Schuberth (publisher), 129, 149, 152, 184,
    235
Schwarz, Peter, 279
Schwind, Moritz von, 165, 169
Scitovsky, Bishop János, 28, 30, 76, 109,
    127–8, 131
Searle, Humphrey, 3, 22, 131, 185, 212,
    252, 299, 303
Seville, 25
Sgambati, 99, 138
'Singulari nos' encyclical, 15
Sistine Chapel, 49, 69, 96–7, 121–3
Slavonic songs, 3
Smetana, Bedřich, 168
social reform, ix, 4, 303
Society of St Cecilia, *see* Cäcilien-Verein
Society of Jesus, 224

Solesmes monastery, 89
Solfanelli, Abbé, 75, 79
sonata form, 283–5
Spain, 26
Spontini, Gaspare, 24–5, 88–9
*Stabat mater dolorosa* plainsong, 94
Starnberger See, 73
Stasov, Vladimir, 280
Steinle, 247–8
Strasbourg, 30, 73
Street, Agnes, 45, 120
'système harmonique grégorien', 92
Switzerland, 21, 24, 41, 215

Táborszky and Parsch (publisher), 248
Talleyrand, Baron, 55
*Te Deum* plainsong, 94
ternary form, 152, 283
Teutonic songs, 3
Theiner, Father, 71
thematic transformation, 21, 112, 281–2,
    288, 301–6
thematic material, 140, 146, 148, 236–9,
    245, 249, 255–6, 269, 283–4, 299, 309
themes: Christ, 293–4; Creation, 293–4;
    Excelsior, 237; fall sequence, 289, 293;
    hammer-blows, 288; God, 291–4; love
    and redemption, x, 21, 205, 207–8, 239,
    246, 253, 256, 263, 288–92, 294, 296–8,
    300, 302–9; Malédiction, 299–302, 308;
    Man, 292–4; Martyrdom, 298; redemp-
    tion, *see* love; Satan, 289–91, 294, 298; Te
    Deum, 236, 238–9; Zum Anfang, 290, 297
Tivoli, 258
Tonkünstler-Versammlung, 46, 63, 71, 73
transcriptions, 22
Trefort, Minister, 98

*Ueber das Leben und die Werke des G. Pierluigi de
    Palestrina*, 95
ultramontanism, 36–8

Vatican, 48, 60, 66–7, 70–1, 74–6, 78–9, 87,
    99, 165
Vatican Council, 38–40, 50
Vatican Edition (plainsong), 89
Vaux, Baroness de, 17
Verdi, Giuseppe, 64; *Requiem*, 139–40
*Vexilla regis* plainsong, 94
Via Felice (Rome), 66, 70–1, 243
Via del Babuino (Rome), 70
Via dei Fiori (Rome), 65
Vicaire, Cardinal, 77
Victor Emmanuel II, 37
Vienna, 24, 28–30, 60, 62, 184, 214, 258
Villa d'Este, 68, 72, 73, 75, 77–8, 224, 227,
    230–1, 240, 250–1

# Index